## YOU HAVE RETURNED TO US, RASPAHLOH!"

"Returned?" said Bart Lasker, sitting on a cushion near the temple's central fire, which burned low. "I've never been here before."

"Look at the statue," whispered the old monk. "That is your master, the Lord of Darkness. For those who serve the Dark Lord, there is no death. And you do remember, Raspahloh, because you have been here *before* in another life. Now you must rejoin us." The old monk leaned closer. *"Who are you?"*

Adrenalin suddenly coursed through Lasker's veins. This was insane! And yet he did remember something of this place. He had seen it in dreams all his life, or so it seemed. He fought the words, fought the very idea, but found that his own personality was just a small, screaming protestor as his mouth formed and uttered the words:

"I am Raspahloh, champion of the Dark Cause, Warrior of the Hidden Realm, *Killer of Dalai Lamas!*"

# MYSTIC REBEL

Ryder Syvertsen

**PINNACLE BOOKS**
**WINDSOR PUBLISHING CORP.**

PINNACLE BOOKS

are published by

Windsor Publishing Corp.
475 Park Avenue South
New York, NY 10016

First printing: April, 1988

Printed in the United States of America

*To the memory of Franklin Bandy, a writer of great imagination and wit, and a true gentle-man.*

# Author's Note

Tibet is a nation twice the size of the United States, a plateau surrounded by the tallest mountains in the world, the Himalayas. It is strategically located between the Soviet Union, China, and India. The climate is dry, the sun strong in a cobalt blue sky during the day, the nights always bitterly cold, even in summer.

Awesome vistas of eternally snow capped mountains filled with bears and the blue maned snow lions, alternate with warm valleys where farmers cultivate barley and wheat. In the north is the completely unexplored area called the Thang, where it is purported the ancient shamanistic Bon religion of Death worshippers still exists to this day.

The people of Tibet are of a Mongolian stock more related to the native American Indian than to the Han race of China. Another distinguishing factor is the Tibetan language, which, unlike Chinese, uses an alphabet. The cultural tradition is highly developed and exists in an unbroken line since prehistoric times. Tibetans are a religious people, worshipping their Holy Lamas, called Rimpoches, as Bodhisattvas—holy teachers of the Buddhist *dharma* (law-truth).

Dharma revolves about two main ideas: 1) loving-kindness is a way to spiritual progress, and 2) reincarnation, controlled by a person's *karma,* the inescapable results of his moral actions. What you do in this life determines the nature of your next birth.

Perhaps because so many males enter the lamasaries that cling to the steep mountain slopes, Tibet is largely unpopulated. As of 1959 there were only seven million people in the entire Kingdom. Its empty land and vast resources beckoned to the Chinese Communist rulers, who realized that if the tenacious religious culture of Tibet could be destroyed, if Tibet's people could be subdued, China would have vast new resources of minerals and timber, plus a place to put its excess population.

If the Chinese could make the Dalai Lama, the God-King of Tibet a prisoner in his own palace, make him a figurehead to "rule" Tibet their way, the Chinese would succeed in their aims.

But Tibet resisted. That mysterious land of the walking dead, of hungry ghosts who preyed on human flesh, of the fierce Migyu (Abominable Snowman), land of dragons, demons, mysterious visions seen in crystal clear lakes, land of fierce nomads and bandit horsemen—Tibet—would not easily be subdued by the militarist nightmare visited upon it.

R.S.

# Prologue

*Was it not said by the great Padmasambhava twelve hundred years ago: When the iron bird flies and the wheeled horses come to Tibet, the nation will be no more? Surely there could never be such things, and thus Tibet shall last forever . . .*

# March 17, 1959

In the uppermost chamber of the palace called the Potala, on the red Mapoori Cliff at the center of the City of the Gods, Lhasa, Tibet, a shaven-headed young man in maroon robe sat in lotus position. Before him rose the golden twenty-foot-high thousand-armed statue of Chenresig, Lord of Compassion.

He was the God-King, the Precious Jewel, Ocean of Wisdom, Fourteenth Incarnation of the Dalai Lama, yet he was but nineteen years old. His eyes half closed, he was deep in *vipassana* meditation-trance. For the past five hours he had been in exactly the same position, back straight, palms folded in his lap, mind focused on the nothingness beyond all.

Time seemed to stand still. The smoke of incense

wafted lazily toward the ceiling. The deeply burnished statue draped with *khatag* scarves glistened in the flickering light of seven butter lamps set before it. Yet even here, in this lofty sanctuary, could be heard a cacophany of noise, of shouting voices.

The Dalai Lama's companion in meditation, seated in like posture to his left, was an aged lama named Lungpo Dawap. He lost concentration and opened his eyes. The incense sticks in the sand-filled vessel before the statue had not quite burned to the bottom. It wasn't quite time yet for Lungpo to disturb His Holiness from his meditation.

*What is going on?* Much agitated, Lungpo rose on arthritic legs, hobbled to pull back the curtains to the balcony, and stepped out into the early evening twilight. What he saw below was a huge crowd, tumultuous, surging, shouting, filling the entire square at the base of the Mapoori Sandcliffs. There were so many people moving about that it appeared from his vantage point like a stirred bowl of barley soup dotted with red berries. The red was the Tibetan women's silk top hats, the brown-like-barley was the fox fur and lambskin hats of the men.

And they were shouting, *"Your Holiness, we will protect you!"*

And, *"Death to the Chinese!"*

"Oh, no," Lungpo gasped. "No killing."

The crowd surged toward the twin staircases below, and was held in check by a line of black-clad men. The Dap Dops—the leather-togaed seven-foot-tall monk guardians of the palace.

Lungpo looked down at the scene with alarm. He was of the rank of *Gelong* and therefore supposed to be calm. Yet who could be calm in these times? Lungpo had recently traveled the length and breadth of the kingdom to appraise the situation, and report to His

10

Holiness. He had seen evidence of Chinese brutality. Crucified, disemboweled monks and burned monasteries left in the wake of the iron-wheeled horses that spat fire and thunder. And now the Chinese "Liberation" Army was at the gates of the city.

Suddenly three horsemen—fierce Khampa tribesmen wilder than anything since the hordes of Genghis Khan—rode into the square, sabers held high, their ancient bolt action English rifles slung across their backs. The crowd parted as they rode to the line of Dap Dops and dismounted.

An angry argument ensued. The old monk could guess what it was about: The leader of the Khampa was insisting his message to the Dalai Lama was urgent. The spokesman for the Dap Dops was insisting that His Holiness was not to be disturbed.

As if to punctuate the disagreement, there were two loud reports—like thunder—in the distance. The crowd suddenly fell silent. Lungpo looked west and saw smoke rising over the Norbulinga, His Holiness's summer palace. Then more shouts rose from below, louder, more vociferous. "War—war—war. We will fight, we will fight!"

Lungpo saw the Dap Dops part for the three Khampa horsemen. Clutching his maroon robe around him, he made haste to bring His Holiness out of the other world.

Lungpo picked up the oak stick and gently tapped the silver bowl sitting on the red-brocaded pillow next to His Holiness. The resonant *ping* wavered through the still dry air. The lines of gray incense smoke wafting up toward the jeweled ceiling wavered and then steadied again.

The young Dalai Lama looked up and smiled.

"Your Holiness," Lungpo stammered, "Chinese are

on the hills around the city, their cannons have fired on the summer palace."

"Ah, how pleasant the past few hours have been for me," said the young lama. "What is it you say?"

"Your Holiness," Lungpo gasped, bowing like a bobbing doll, "the Chinese are shelling the Norbu Linga—your summer palace. They must think you are there. Soon they will breach its walls and find you gone. Then—" His voice was drowned out by the metallic scream of a pair of Chinese jets slashing the sky over the Potala.

Lungpo quivered and fell to the feet of his superior, holding his hands over his ears.

The Dalai Lama pursed his lips and said, "They are just iron birds. Do not fear. All is as was foretold. This is just the sign of impermanence—as the great doctrine of Sangye, the Buddha states. You should not fear this change. It gives proof of our great path to liberation from the endless wheel of birth and suffering. A thousand years of isolation is ending, just as the Padma-sambhava predicted."

"Is it true, then, master?"

"Yes. The dark ages begin."

"What do we do?"

"What is the crowd chanting?"

Lungpo stood up with some difficulty. "Your holiness, the crowd is saying they will protect you. I beseech you, do not accept Brigadier Fu's demand that you go to the Chinese military base. The Dap Dops are letting up three Khampas—perhaps messengers—"

"Go and let them into the chamber then."

Upon seeing His Holiness, the three Khampa, tall heavily boned men with daggers at their belts, fell to the carpeted floor and prostrated themselves three times. The Dalai Lama asked them to rise.

"Your Holiness," said the muscular Khampa leader,

"the royal family is safe in Chenbu, thirty miles south. They await you. We vow we will see Your Holiness and attendants to the Indian border. The journey will be arduous by horseback, over little-marked trails through the Himalayas. Arrangements have been made for your reception in India. But we must go now. The others are waiting for your answer, oh Compassionate One."

The Highest Lama in Tibet, the fourteenth Dalai Lama, sighed. "We see now that the astrological predictions were more accurate that anyone had imagined. The years of tumult and oppression have now culminated in a choice—surrender to the Chinese military or flee."

"The people are ready for fighting," Lungpo said. "Perhaps we should—"

"Tell the people to fight against an overwhelming force?" The Dalai Lama shook his head. "It is hopeless."

"But Your Holiness, the people, led by the Khampa tribesmen, are already in revolt in six provinces. The fighting is spreading this way. The government *must* encourage them to fight."

A disturbance at the door again. Two young chelas—student monks—on His Holiness' staff were in hushed earnest discussion with more Khampas.

The young God-King sucked in his lips, took one long look around. It was this way and no other, he realized. Tibet would at least live in spirit, if he were not taken. If he were a captive, or killed, Tibet would die. He said, "These brave men who ask me to leave mean well. I will go with them."

"Thank Buddha," said the Khampa spokesman, "that His Holiness has agreed."

Bowing, he turned to Lungpo. "Please have His

13

Holiness put this on—'' He held up a khaki brown people's militia jacket.

The Dalai Lama smiled. "A simple private's uniform, that is good." He stood, allowed his monk attendants to put his arms into the coarse material, and said, "Let us go."

"And His Holiness should carry a rifle," added the Khampa, "so he will be like the others—so the Chinese soldiers will think he is real."

"No, I will never carry a firearm—even in disguise."

He looked about, as if for the last time. Then the young man who carried the destiny of his people said, "I will need my glasses." He picked them up from the bronze table, slipped them on. "I fear I will never in this incarnation see the palace again."

No one said anything. The God-King walked out with none of the haste of the others, and serenely descended the secret passage to the rear exit of the giant palace.

There was a white horse waiting, and a hundred Tibetan soldiers and tribesmen, the scene lit by orange torchlight.

Above, a meteor shot across the heavens. The Dalai Lama caught its motion, and stated, "It heads south—so do we."

He let himself be hoisted atop the horse.

# Chapter 1

## Spring 1989

Bart Lasker, a tall brown-haired American wearing an unbuttoned blue workshirt and rumpled khaki pants, made his way down a crowded New Delhi street. A three-day growth of stubble was prominent on his chin. Above firm-set lips, his dark brown eyes looked tired. Yet Lasker moved rapidly, his eyes picking a path through a plethora of carts, and throngs of sari-clad women shoppers. He fended off a beggar on crutches, and brushed away a street hawker insisting the "Englishman" buy the hand-made rug displayed on an extended arm.

Bart was in a hurry and in a bad mood. He also had a hangover and an unsettled stomach. The streets of New Delhi were humid and fetid, and getting more so every moment. Soon the full extent of the April heat would capture the capital city of India, and the stench that now teased Laskers nostrils would rise in intensity.

The city had been torn by Sikh-Hindu violence just hours earlier, following an assassination attempt on the Defense Minister. Troops had cordoned off the burned-out stores along nearby Chandi Chauk Street, where the worst trouble had occurred. And yet here, on the Street of Silver and Gold, just two blocks from the smoking ruins, hawkers plied their trade as usual. Commerce never stopped in India, not even for death!

Bart at last came out onto a broad tree-lined boulevard. Connaught Place. He passed the first sandbag barrier. The dusky Indian soldiers behind the barricade eyed him cautiously. They weren't interested in Europeans. They were looking for Sikh terrorists, or Sri Lanka terrorists, or any of a dozen other separatist, revolutionary, or religious terrorists plaguing the nation. Yet he felt their eyes lingering on him. It was uncommon to see a foreigner looking so disheveled.

Lasker had a peculiar sweatiness on his palms, the kind he always got when he needed money. His meeting with Donnely, the fixer, the agent for CIA jobs and other unseemly things, could provide enough cash to dry those palms. Malcolm Donnely always had jobs, but never easy or legal ones, for pilots such as Bart Lasker. Bart had first laid eyes on the ruddy-faced Donnely in Singapore. That was a long year ago, after Lasker declined to re-up in the U.S. Air Force because, owing to certain minor and major infractions, they wouldn't let him fly anymore. He had heard there were jobs in Singapore for pilots who didn't care what they carried. All one had to do, so the scuttlebutt went, was to hang around certain bars in Singapore's seamy section and wait.

After two weeks of waiting, and drinking, and getting broker and broker in one dingy gin mill after another, Donnely had spotted Lasker's wings on his bomber jacket—or rather the mark where he had torn the wings off. He had sidled up to Bart, and in the age-old fashion of a spider approaching a fly, asked: "Looking for some work?"

Lasker said, "Maybe," and that had been the beginning of it.

"First," Donnely said, "you have to sober up." He gave Lasker a hundred-pound note and the address of a good hotel. "See you there in two days."

Lasker soon was routinely flying sealed packages from the Burmese border to New Delhi in a chartered plane. After six months, he had made enough for a down payment on *Good Baby,* his twin-engine Vicker P3 Mail plane. She was being dumped by Singapore Mail service for a fraction of what she was worth. Still Lasker had to borrow heavily from Donnely because the seller wanted cash.

And he had been in hock to Donnely ever since.


Bart turned off Connaught Place into Westminster Way, a side street that wound sinuously into the notorious Chandra District. Soon he was standing in front of the brass door of the Excelsior Hotel. The burly doorman knew Lasker, opened the door. His scar-face and ominous look gave anyone an instant grasp of what went on inside: an illicit gambling place, or a bordello. Actually, it was both. Donnely, among a lot of other things, owned and ran this place.

Lasker walked across the marble-floored lobby, nodded to the Vietnamese madam with a long cigarette holder, and proceeded up the sweeping gold-railed stairs, pushing past three men in tuxedos descending with their rented young party women in evening dress. What was it—10A.M.? It looked like a nightclub going full blast at 2 A.M.

Bart entered through the purple swinging door, nodded at the door woman, a redhead—like all of Donnely's decorative door women. He showed her the note Bart had found in his box at the hotel, with Donnely's signature on the bottom. She smiled and said, "This way."

This was the Game Room. Roulette, blackjack, and

other tables doing a lusty business under subdued lights. It was the place you'd likely find Donnely any time of the day. He liked to keep an eye on the high rollers, in case they rolled too high. Then he would make a discreet gesture to the dealers and a magnetic device would reduce the high rollers' winnings. Very scientific, very crooked.

Beneath the smoke of cigars and the smell of expensive perfume of the professional ladies was a sweet smell of opium.

The redhead, not finding Donnely where she had expected, crooked a finger and led Lasker through the room and to the left. The lights were dimming. He brushed his way past waiters carrying trays of Mai Tais and Singapore Slings, received numerous smiles from very young Vietnamese girls lounging in cheong soms slit to their navels. The light in the room was growing weird—all blacklight-purple.

They found Donnely sitting like Trader Horn in a straw chair holding a Mimosa, or whatever the hell that pink drink was. Two young long-legged things wearing only rhinestone panties and high-heel shoes were at each of his thick legs. Donnely's white ascot tucked in his dark blue epauletted shirt cast Day-glo purple light into his face. He saw Lasker approaching, and smiled, his teeth a garish red-purple in the room's blacklight.

"Ah, Bart my friend, you are on time—most unlike you. So you got my note? Wish to do a job again?"

The girl on the left leg moved over to give Lasker standing room. "Tentatively," Bart admitted.

"Fine fine. Oh, wait a moment, here's the entertainment. We'll talk afterward."

The center of the large room suddenly burst into the brassy wail of an unrestrained, possibly stoned, orchestra. The lights dimmed even further. The idle talk

18

died. All eyes went to the red spotlight and to the performer coming into it.

In the dim redness was a tall slender woman, naked except for her rhinestone necklace, two similar ankle bracelets, and rhinestone-studded panties. She had several black snakes coiled around her waist and on each slender thigh. She began to undulate to the music, grabbed the head of one snake, started to use it to tease each of her large breasts. The crowd went wild.

"Isn't that something?" Donnely said.

"I don't like it," Bart replied.

"Nothing pleases you. You need to get more enjoyment out of life." He frowned. "I've just spoken to your new employer, and I told him all about your excellent piloting abilities. He is most impressed and anxious to hire you."

"I'm not sure yet whether I want the job. You have a habit of setting me up for jobs that no one in his right mind would take. I hope that this one doesn't involve drugs or—"

"I understand your concern. But sit down, Bart, and have a drink—and a girl, if you wish. I really don't need both of them."

Lasker sighed. "Donnely, aren't you getting a little old to indulge in all of this—"

"Decadence?" Donnely harumphed. "Not by a long shot, my boy. Do you know how many suffering people there are in the world who wish they were in my shoes? The least I can do for them is appreciate and indulge in what I have. Have some Dom Perignon—a very good year." He poured Lasker the champagne.

"Thanks." Lasker leaned back in the rattan chair. "How much does this job pay?"

"How much? Why, a lot, my boy. A lot." He leaned over so that his words would not be drowned by the music. "How does one hundred thousand sound to you?"

"Rupees?" Lasker asked, figuring about ten thousand dollars.

"English *pounds*. About one hundred twenty thousand dollars, U.S." He laughed. "Of course, you will have to impress on your prospective employer your eagerness to carry out his small task. And your ability to do so."

Lasker was stunned. "That's a lot of money. It must be a very dirty job."

Donnely laughed. "It's a piece of cake, Bart. A piece of cake. Just go see the man."

"Is this guy good for the money?"

"Nobody is reliable. You will get the cash, though, I assure you." He again leaned over. "In fact, I have it already. I will hold it for you—minus my usual twenty percent commission. You'll make a lot of easy money. Easy, indeed." A horselaugh.

The brunette on the floor was inching Lasker's zipper open with her teeth. "Stop," Bart said gently. "You don't have to do that."

"By now that's all she wants, Lasker. Sex. She's in love with you. Though you probably don't need it right now—I know you have a good thing in the rich bitch—Jenny is her name, right? You should marry her, milk her of all that dough."

"Don't mention Jenny. She's my private business."

"Lasker, grow up! It's all pussy, and money, and power. You could marry her, and live comfortably for the rest of your life—if you weren't so damned idealistic."

"Not many people call me idealistic. I don't like to use women. I like my women to like me."

Another short snorting laugh. "Greta here likes you—don't you, Greta?"

The pug-nosed brunette looked up and nodded.

"See? She likes you. She *adores* you Lasker. Enjoy. Life is for enjoyment."

"Save the philosophy."

"Seriously, when you return from this lucrative job, Bart, you should open a place like mine. Maybe not in India, you don't have the diplomatic connections to do it, but in, say, Kuala Lumpur—lots of dancing Thai beauties in a glass wall behind the bar. I have connections. If you would care to invest most of the profits of your flight, I believe I could—"

Lasker said, "No thanks. I want planes. I'll run my own air charter line. Not be a goddamned pimp."

"A pimp?" Again that horselaugh. "No, Bart. I am a man who is king in his own castle." He gestured around. "All this is what men dream of—women, power, wealth. And you call me a pimp."

Lasker said, "The address?"

Donnely sighed, pulled out a pad with his fat fingers, picked up a gold pen. He scribbled a name and address, tore it off, handed it to Bart. "I wish you the best of luck. And we shall have a drink on that charter service of yours when you return. Indeed we shall. Perhaps when you are well heeled, you will be fun again. Right now, you've become a real drag. People want a glimpse of paradise. And this place is as close to that as any man can get."

"It's as close to a *sewer* as any man can get." Lasker put the piece of paper in his shirt pocket. "I'll need cab fare."

"Broke, huh?" Donnely pulled a roll of rupees from his pants pocket, and counted out twelve one-hundred rupee notes. Lasker took them.

"If I take the job, the money better be here when I come back."

"My integrity is world renowned, my boy, you know that!"

Lasker left, Donnely's horselaugh ringing in his ears.

21

# Chapter 2

The minute he hit the street outside the club, an orange Hillman cab with blue smoke stuttering out its exhaust pipe careened expertly to the curb in front of Bart. The back door opened and discharged two elderly British types. Lasker didn't let the door shut, and he got in. He was relieved to be in the cab, uneasy about the big lump of money in his front pocket Donnely had given him. He said, "10 Chennings Circle," the address on the paper Donnely had passed to him.

The sweaty mustached driver turned around. "We will be there in good time, sahib. My name is Ahmed and I am much more than a driver. I am a guide, a protector, an advisor to many tourists. And I will, if you let me, show you the city, so that you will know—"

"I know New Delhi. I live here. Just drive."

Ahmed sounded disappointed, "Most certainly, sahib. I drive you quickly." He pulled out into traffic with a series of coughs and backfires and continued his banter. "I see now that you are a capable person, who knows the ways of the city and I am most anxious to get you to your destination or any other—" Bart didn't

22

listen to the rest. He was satisfied that the cab was wending its way through the streets toward his destination.

They had to detour around the Sikh quarter, then the smoking old Hillman turned off Connaught Boulevard onto a side street. "Shortcut," Ahmed the Driver said, gleefully. Lasker was dubious but soon they came out into broad Chennings Circle, with its tall palm trees and line of hotels and office buildings.

The cab pulled up at the address, a tall green-glass-fronted office tower. "I shall wait for you, sahib."

"Suit yourself, I don't know how long I'll be." He paid with a hundred-rupee note and didn't ask for change. A new look crossed Ahmed face. "Most generous, sahib, I will wait."

Bart smiled. Twelve bucks American. Maybe money was important.

He entered the lobby and paused at the directory next to the elevator bank. There it was. Ferrari Import-Export Corp.—thirteenth floor.

He rode the elevator up to thirteen. The door slid open. Right in front of the elevator was an oak door with the letters FIEC on a logo—a white lion jumping across a blue globe. He tried the doorknob. Locked. He rang the buzzer. There was a movement inside, a shadow at the peephole. The lock clicked open.

A delicately beautiful Indian woman—aquiline nose, gracious white-toothed smile, dressed in a red sari with gold threads running through it—opened the door. There was a red caste mark between her eyebrows.

She quickly glanced up and down at him, frowned deprecatingly. "Yes?"

"I'm Lasker," he said, "I'm here to see Mr."—he looked at the piece of paper—"Losang."

"Do you have an appointment?"

"Yes."

23

*"Really?"* Lasker could see the pupils of her dark eyes contract. "Perhaps you have the wrong office?"

Lasker understood. He brushed his chin with forefinger and thumb and whispered, "These clothes are a disguise."

"Oh . . . well—" The door opened more fully. Lasker stepped in, tucked his shirt into his waistband as she led him across the gray carpet to the door of an inner office.

"Mr. Losang, there's a man here that says he is a Mr. Lasker. And that he has appointment."

A hoarse lispy voice replied, "Yes, good—send him in."

The dark-eyed woman left, shutting the door behind her. Lasker found himself not facing anyone at all, but staring across an empty desk at the back of a black leather chair. He thought the chair might be vacant, for nothing happened for a long moment. Then Bart saw smoke curling over the top, and a fat hand with many thick silver rings on its fingers on the chair arm.

The chair swung slowly around. Its occupant was a rotund man in a dark pinstripe suit with a small multicolored rectangular pin in the left lapel buttonhole. He was sucking on an ivory cigarette holder containing a long pink cigarette. His moon-shaped face was of a faintly coffee color, his eyes a bit slanted and dark. He was smiling broadly. He had a lot of teeth.

"Ah, Mr. Lasker, I'm so glad that you have come."

Lasker figured the man to be Burmese by the way he held and carefully articulated the *th* sound. But he was big-boned, and Burmese usually aren't. And under that odd accent was educated English. Oxford? Donnely hadn't told him a thing about Losang except that he had a piloting job. Now he wished he knew more.

"Please have a seat," the man said, motioning with

a large hand at a Morris chair to the side of the desk. "You come highly recommended by Mr. Donnely."

"He knows my abilities."

"He says you're the number one adverse-weather high-altitude pilot in the world."

"One of the best . . ." Lasker sensed something. He could feel money in this office, smell it. Was it the polish on the silver samovar and serving set over on the sideboard? Or the probably-genuine Gauguin hanging on the wall?

"Did Mr. Donnely tell you I will pay one hundred thousand pounds for the job? Is that satisfactory?"

"Well," Bart said, slumping down a bit in the chair. "That could be a lot—or a little. It depends on how dangerous this flight is. Where am I supposed to be going, and what will I be carrying?"

"Mr. Lasker, can you see the little pin in my buttonhole? It is a flag of my country. Lean closer, take a good look."

Lasker did. It was a sunrise, the yellow sun over a white peak with blue and red beams coming up. It didn't look familiar. Losang asked "Do you know what country this represents?"

"Not sure."

"This is the flag of Khawachen—known to the outside world as Tibet."

"Part of Communist China?" Lasker was disappointed. He said, "No dice. If you think I'm going to fly into China without permission, you're crazy."

Losang waved his ringed fingers dismissively. "The flight in and out will be ignored by the Chinese. The only thing that should concern you is your plane and your flying skills. No interceptors will challenge you. No anti-aircraft rockets will be fired. We will see to that. And the landing area is secure and prearranged. You will be flying to a landing strip just a few miles

25

on the other side of the mountains. At this time of year the weather should be most favorable, also.''

Lasker said, ''How can you arrange to have the Chinese ignore me?''

''You will be mistaken for one of their regular patrol flights. Your plane, I am told, is an old Vickers twin-engine—very similar to their patrol craft. Painted the right way, it will slip by unnoticed. And their craft, the one you will replace, will not be in the air. We will arrange that. You will replace it, fly unchallenged over the mountains and to your destination, unload, and quickly be back in India, one hundred thousand pounds richer. You will receive further details if you wish to take the job . . . Well, what do you say?''

Bart shook his head. ''No dice, sorry. Even if all that can be arranged, the *mountains* you lightly brush over are the Himalayas, the highest mountains in the world. The few passes you can snake a prop aircraft through are swept by winds that make a hurricane look like a gentle breeze—any time of year. Besides, I would be trusting people I don't know to arrange that I don't get shot down. I could easily lose my plane, my life. The Chinese have these things they call MIG Jets, you know. Each has a twin cannon on its nose. And rockets. All just for shooting down unwelcome guests in their airspace. Good-bye, Mr. Losang, nice talking to you.''

Bart stood up.

''Sit down, Mr. Lasker. Perhaps . . . I could do better on the pay. We can discuss that. But first let me explain a little. Tibet is *not* China, it is an independent nation *occupied* by the so called 'People's Liberation Army' of China, against the will of Tibet's inhabitants. One day Tibet shall be free again, and your flight will speed that day.''

Lasker said, ''That's nice, but it's your problem, not

mine. But just for curiosity's sake, what is it you want me to fly into this free country occupied by the Chinese? Guns?"

"You wouldn't be carrying arms, nor passengers. Merely medical supplies. And bundles of Chinese money."

"Money?" Lasker sat down, intrigued.

"Yes. Chinese renminbao. We want you to land in a well-defined field just beyond the mountains, and deposit urgently needed supplies of medicine and food, plus the money. The money is to bribe the border-area Chinese officials to let a high *lama*—that's one of our holy men, sometimes called Rimpoches—enter India. The bribe includes a hundred refugees with him. It has been all set up, but we need to fly in the money."

Bart thought a minute. "You have people that will make sure that my plane is mistaken for one of theirs? That I won't get shot down?"

"Yes. And you will be doing a service to the world and to—"

"Skip the humanitarian stuff. How much better on the money can you do?"

Losang stared at him a long time, his eyes flickering as if he was adding something up in his head. Finally he lisped out, "Twenty thousand more pounds. That's the limit. It's a lot of money," he emphasized.

"I might do it, then. Maybe."

"Good. I assure you, there will not be as great a danger as you suggest. We will supply charts, weather reports from within Tibet, everything will be smoothed for your flight. You will receive further instructions and your plane will be painted with Chinese markings at Phiyang, our forward field, near the border. Do we have a deal?"

Lasker thought for a long minute then said, "How

about my deciding once I will reach your forward field—Phiyang?''

The man folded his many-ringed hands on the glossy desktop. ''You drive a hard bargain. Fly there, talk to my friends, the cousins Namgyal and Wangyal. They will convince you that all I say is true. You will see.''

''Well then,'' Lasker said, accepting a cigarette from the turquoise-encrusted silver case Losang leaned over to offer him, ''I propose this: When I get to Phiyang, and see the supplies are as you say, and I see the charts and other things you mention, and am assured as to exactly how the Chinese will *not* shoot me down, then I will go to Tibet. Agreed?''

''Agreed,'' the big Tibetan said. He lit Lasker's cigarette with a silver lighter.

Lasker took a long drag. ''One more thing—I need start-up money, for fueling the plane, and so on. Twenty thousand rupees?''

''Done.'' Losang then pushed a button on the intercom set. ''Padmina will show you out, and give you the details. You must be there at Phiyang by noon tomorrow, New Delhi time. It's three hours more or less by air. All right?''

''Right. The sooner the better.''

The Indian woman came in and stood by the door. ''Padmina, all has been arranged. Mr. Lasker is working for the cause.'' He turned to Lasker. ''Good luck. I assume you will be calling Malcolm Donnely back to tell him you have accepted the job, with said conditions. Please give him my regards.''

They shook hands. The Tibetan's shake was fleshy but strong.

The receptionist gave Lasker a folder and a ''Good luck.'' Her smile seemed to have a hint of irony in it.

\* \* \*

Once the American had entered the elevator, Padmina hurried to the window and watched until she saw Lasker enter the orange cab and saw the black sedan pull out behind him as he pulled away.

She went to the inner office, stuck her head in, and said, "Your Eminence, is it all right if I go down to the shop and get some sweetmeats for eating with my tea?"

"Certainly," Losang replied. "Please get me some of those—what do you call them—jelly rolls with chocolate on top and some coffee. I am visiting America next week, and I want to practice Coffee Break." Padmina left the office and went downstairs, but before she entered the shop, she found a public phone. She dialed a local number.

After three rings the phone was picked up, but no one spoke a word. Padmina said, "The American has accepted the job. . . . Yes, he's leaving from the Delhi airport. Yes . . . he is to take off at around nine . . . to be in Phiyang at noon. Yes, I saw the black sedan pull out after his car. . . . Good."

She hung up, pleased with herself. Still she felt a pang of guilt. Her employer, Mr. Losang, was good to her. She didn't like to betray him. But a girl had to watch out for her future. And that meant money.

Padmina was almost back to the building when she turned suddenly. She had forgotten to get the coffee and jelly rolls.

# Chapter 3

Bart had found Ahmed's cab waiting. Why wouldn't he be? Lasker was a good tipper. He gave him Jenny's address, told Ahmed to make it fast. He had to get to Jenny's, tell her the date for tomorrow to go to the races was off. She wouldn't like that. But telling her on the phone was worse.

The cab started jerking as if the gears were going out. Bart leaned forward and asked, "Are we going to make it?"

Ahmed smiled. "Oh, yes. Minor problem. I don't know much about transmissions, and I installed it."

"*You* installed it?"

"Yes. I and my two brothers made the whole cab. Out of parts we found in the junkyard, and even on the side of the road, you see."

"Made it?"

"Yes," the drive said proudly. "I call it 'Twenty-one.' A lucky number, is it not? It is made from twenty-one other cars."

"Don't drive too fast." Lasker sat back. He wondered if he—or the cab—would make it in one piece.

"Little rattle, that is all." Ahmed proved it by whizzing in and out of traffic and rattling on at a good clip.

Donnely said he should marry Jenny. Jenny was rich, long-legged, curvacious, and madly in love, or at lease obsessed with having sex with Bart. Maybe the bastard was right—maybe Bart should just cut himself into the family business, and be lovingly cared for, given what he wanted. *No.*

He remembered when they first met. The very first time he flew Good Baby into New Delhi for Donnely. Bart had a week to kill and a big roll of bills. He had toured the expensive places—sober yet. He went to the tennis matches and sat next to the beautiful blonde—Jenny. She smiled, and he thought, *This is the one.*

Jenny Sedgwick. She was everything a man could want—jovial, beautiful, sensual. But her world was high above his. He realized that when he went to her house. They were leagues apart. Oh, she didn't care, but the first time Bart met her father, Mr. Sedgwick of Sedgwick Industries, he knew it wouldn't work. Mr. Sedgwick asked him a few sharp questions and then told Bart he disapproved of Jenny going outside "the social circle" to meet men. He said that he had done a credit and background check on Lasker and come up with disturbing things in both areas. He suggested he would pay Lasker off to "beat it."

Bart had stormed out of the cocktail party. That had been the first storming out. There were many after.

He then went on a lucrative job for Donnely. Moving some people without papers from Nepal to New Delhi. And someone tipped off the cops. They impounded his plane. Then the trial, the dank cell. Donnely got him out, but absorbed all the money Bart had.

Bart got the plane back with a big note attached to it—Square One. He was back to nearly-broke. He started drinking, and didn't stop. And one day Jenny found him. She pulled him out of it. She'd bankrolled him since then, but he couldn't live off Jenny forever. Just until a break. This job was it, Bart hoped. He considered all the money he borrowed from Jenny exactly that way. It was a loan, to be paid back.

Ahmed screeched over in front of the Sedgwick residence. "Such a beautiful house, sir, is it yours?"

He didn't answer.

"I shall wait for you, sahib."

"Might be a while," he said, getting out and paying. "A hundred ought to hold you."

Ahmed was right—it was a beautiful house, a mansion as a matter of fact. A relic of the Colonial Era, the days when England pulled all the strings in India. And it was Jenny's home. Or rather one of many homes owned by her family. There were also several "cottages" suitable for the rich to rough it in, in the Indian countryside. And of course, back in Britain, the really big place.

Lasker took a deep breath. He had a hunch this would take some time. He proceeded through the open gate, up the drive to the front stairs of the mansion. The white nehru-jacketed servant he encountered was Akmar Singh, who knew him well, and was always happy to see him. Probably because Jenny paid well for him *not* to tell her father Bart had come. Akmar saluted smartly, and immediately opened the big glass door with brass trim.

Bart stepped into the cool three-story-high lobby filled with rose marble and potted palms. It would have looked all right as the entranceway to the Louvre. There were twin staircases, one on the right, and one on the left. High above the lobby floor, a stained glass skylight let in the bright Indian sun, in a long smoky shaft.

He had been awestruck the first time he'd come here, to "Palms House," but now he scarcely looked at it.

32

James, the head butler, all decked out in a white tuxedo, approached and asked, "Shall I tell Miss Sedgwick that Mr. Lasker has arrived?"

"Yes, that's right," Bart said, and he sat down, like a petitioner of old, in the plush Victorian chair by the potted palms.

"Very well, sir." James trotted off to the downstairs intercom, he supposed. Bart didn't wait long before Jenny appeared on the left staircase, wearing her sinuous white thing from Galerie Lafayette. "Bart, what a surprise."

He stood up. "You could come a little closer—the echo is interfering in what I'm hearing. It sounded like you're glad to see me."

"Oh but I am. Father is away, you know." She swept excitedly down the staircase on her silver pumps. Her long blond hair was up in a bun, held in place by jeweled pins. She was beautiful like this, of course, but Bart would rather have seen her in the tennis shorts and tank top he'd met her in.

Jenny threw her arms about Bart and kissed his cheek, then suddenly pulled away. "Why, you need a shave. I've been positively speared. And you're all sweaty—but I'm glad you've come by. It will make my little surprise for you all the better. Come." She started leading him down an oaken gallery lined with oil paintings of muttonchopped ancestor types. Then she threw open the door of a large, tiled bathroom. "There, inside," she said proudly. "Go in—look in the wardrobe. Your surprises are there."

Bart did as she asked, and she trailed behind. He pulled the louvered wardrobe door open and saw a light blue sport jacket, some shirts, and a pair of slacks hanging inside.

"For you, from me—and France. I picked them out

last month, when I was there, and had them sent on. They just arrived. Are the sizes right?"

Bart, saying, "You shouldn't have," took one of the shirts out, stripped his blue workshirt off, and started to put it on.

"No, darling, first a shower. Right? And a shave—"

"You're saying I smell—"

"Well—" She sniffed.

"Okay, guess I do." Bart put the blue shirt down and pushed her out the door. In a second he was stripped and in the shower. He made it quick. He found an electric battery shaver in the cabinet. New. Never been used.

On the shelf in the wardrobe was a gold watch. The kind that says Rolex, and has twenty-one jewels. Then he looked it over, sighed, and left it there on the shelf. He came out dressed in the new shirt and trousers, but sans jacket.

"Scrumptious."

"Thanks. Now can we talk? I came over—"

"Yes, come on, into the conservatory." Jenny giggled.

A pair of Indian menservants in turbans jeweled enough for a maharajah bowed and opened the conservatory's oak door. The couple came out on a sunny terrace. There an obsequious small woman in a powder blue sari bowed, or rather curtsied in the English way.

"Tamara, would you pour me some diet Coke—what would you like, Bart?"

"Diet scotch."

"Always the joker. Tamara, pour Mr. Lasker a tonic water."

"You might let me pour it," Bart objected.

"Bart," she whispered, "Stop this and tell me—where are we going tonight? Oh, I know tomorrow we'll go to the track, but tonight—"

34

He took a sip of the tonic. "That's what I came to discuss—" He glanced at Tamara, and she caught the hint and retired from them. As the servant woman skitted off to, he supposed, the maids' quarters, Jenny noticed he hadn't put on the watch.

"Don't you like the watch? It's gold, and twenty-one jewels. I thought—"

"It's fine, but I don't want it. I told you, I don't want you buying me things."

"Nonsense, I can afford it—and—"

"And I can't? Goddamn it, Jenny, I don't want to live like this. I'm going to start my own business."

"Nonsense. Daddy will come around and put you in a good position in the company."

"No, I won't let him. I can support myself. Just had a run of bad luck."

"But Daddy wants to help, he honestly likes you."

"He *dis*likes me. I have no breeding. Besides I'm an American. Just a boy from Cincinnati." Bart took another sip of the tonic, made a face, and put it down. "Is there anything like scotch to put in this tonic?"

"Bart, you shouldn't."

"Yeah. . . . Listen Jenny, about tonight—"

"Bart," Jenny interrupted, putting down her glass and staring at him with her big blues, "I'm horny. It's been two weeks—how long has it been for you?" She leaned forward, showing her stunning cleavage.

"Come on—it's been the same time for me."

"Then"—she smiled—"Let's go. I've redecorated the bedroom that faces the garden. We haven't done it in there—"

Lasker's eyes rolled up, but he felt his desire rising. He was as anxious as she was. He took her slender hand and they went down the hall together and into the room. It did look nice; the sunlight was streaming

35

through the trees beyond the casement windows onto the wide white cover of the bed.

Jenny shut and bolted the oak door behind them. "There. The garden is locked off, too. No one will see us. We can leave the windows open to the light."

It seemed that her gown could be opened by the pull of a single zipper—the one between her breasts. This she did, and it dropped away. There wasn't a thing underneath, except a pair of pink panties that said Tuesday. Today was Tuesday. Jenny approached him, slowly, first stepping out of her silver high-heeled shoes. She had him now. He let her open his shirt. Soon her lips were sliding across his chest, kissing his curly brown hairs.

She pulled him to the wide bed. They fell onto its soft surface. The sun was brilliant on her alabaster legs, the curve of her arms, the well-formed upturned breasts.

Bart lay back. He felt his zipper being opened. He'd wanted to tell Jenny now that he'd be going on a trip. But—he'd wait.

Afterward Lasker found his package of Benson & Hedges, opened it, took a cigarette, and handed one to Jenny. She sat up against the headboard, and put the cigarette in her mouth. He lit both.

Not saying anything, they sat blowing smoke rings up at the ornate ceiling. He crushed his out, and put on his clothes. Obviously she had spent the silent time thinking, for Jenny said, "Daddy will have to be resigned to the fact of us two. I'll make him understand and accept it. Then, we can get married."

"I told you—after I have my own money," Bart said, standing up and adjusting his wildly toussled dark brown hair in the big dresser mirror.

"Oh, Bart don't start that again. Daddy has a position for you, I can arrange it with him. Then—"

"I told *you*. After I get my own money, I'm setting up the air charter business."

She sat bolt upright. "And just how is that money to be made?"

"I'm a pilot—I can make money."

"Working for Donnely? You work for Donnely and he gives with one hand and takes back with the other—and he gets you into trouble—Where are you going?"

"Look," Bart said, more softly, "let's not spoil it. I'll be away for a while—a few days. That's what I came over today to say. I'm going on a small job and it will earn me enough to make the down payment on the planes."

*"No!"* she exclaimed, half sobbing, "Not again."

He went to her, took her in his arms. "We *will* be married—if you want to live with me in a house a lot smaller than this one. And if you'll let me run my own affairs. Like an air charter business. You can help me run it, if you want. Bookkeeping or something."

She laughed. "One little trip for Donnely and you'll have enough money for that? What are you going to fly? Guns? Drugs? Spirit away some criminal?"

Lasker said, "Listen, I'm sorry, Jenny. I just can't live on handouts. This job won't give me a fortune, but I've been saving. It will be enough for a down payment."

"Oh Bart, it's always dangerous working for Donnely. Please don't go." Then her Irish temper—her grandmother on her mother's side—took over. "I won't be here waiting like a lap dog!"

"It's only three days, tops."

"I won't marry a sucker—a *dreamer*—"

Lasker tore open the latch lock and stormed the considerable distance to the grand entrance doors, beating the junior maharajahs to opening it. He flashed past the startled Akmar and rushed into the street.

# Chapter 4

Ahmed's orange cab wasn't at the curb, and he wouldn't have taken it even if it was. Bart had to walk. Walk a lot.

Women shoppers rushed past him, some in flaming colored saris, and bare brown midriffs. Most had nose rings. Meaning married—hands off. Would he marry Jenny? He wondered if he would even see her again. Lasker walked on, past stately houses and then down side streets, into the real city of slums and utter desperation. Only after some blocks did he realize he'd left his other shirt and pants in the tiled bathroom where he'd taken a shower. He felt his pocket—fortunately, he had put his wallet in it. In the wallet was the information about the meeting at Phiyang, taken from inside the folder cover. The cover was in her bathroom too. *Damn*—still he wasn't going back. He'd made his exit. He'd send someone to retrieve the stuff, maybe not bother. Let her keep the damned shirt and pants—have one of the servants pick it up with brass tongs and send it to be de-fleaed and decontaminated. Or whatever the hell Jenny wanted.

The streets were teaming, and hot. The new shirt's collar cut into his neck. He opened some buttons. He tried to walk in the shade. And there he almost stumbled over a man sitting in the roadway.

A coffee-colored man, shaven-headed, about sixty years of age. He had a small wispy black beard. The man was seated upon a dusty multicolor quilt. He looked up inquiringly. "Fortune, sir? I will tell the future. Will you marry? Will you travel? Thirty rupees."

Lasker thought it quite a coincidence. Both questions were the very ones on his mind.

"Please sit down," the man said, rolling out a small rug on the pavement. He moved an empty carton box that partially prevented people from trampling him, so that Lasker, too, was shielded. What the hell, Bart thought, and sat down on it.

The man looked Chinese rather than Indian. But though his dark dispassionate eyes were slanted, as the Chinese, he had a deep brown complexion like some of the locals. The seer smiled, "You need a prediction. I speak English. I have a special prediction for you."

"Like what?"

"Please," the man said, pointing to the sign: FUTURE REVEALED, 30 RUPEES. Lasker anted up. The man continued, more softly, and in an odd accent. "If you want the predictions that my ancient science is capable of bringing, you must clear your mind; you are unsettled."

Lasker had to agree. He tried to sit calmly, and in a few moments, the man continued, "That is better." Then, solemnly the seer uncovered what looked like a large breadboard, from under a cloth with gold weave in it. He then fished out several small tins from under his maroon garment, opened them. Each held colored sands: red, black, blue. He started sprinkling the colored sands on the breadboard, humming and making swirling patterns with the sand. "This is the sacred sod from under the tomb of Tri Rigpa Chen," the seer said. Lasker almost laughed aloud. Really now, he thought much amused, why not the sacred bones of King Tut?

The man finished the swirling pattern. He produced a cookie tin that said ENGLISH BREAKFAST BISCUITS on it. The battered blue tin was full of cooked white rice. Evidently he had been eating it, for there were chopsticks in the tin with the rice.

"This rice represents the twelve basic elements of creation." He looked very serious, so Lasker nodded. "I now will pile it into the five skandas of human consciousness." He made one pile, then four others, on the same breadboard, over the colored sand.

There goes his lunch, Bart thought. Then the seer sprinkled more sand on the rice piles, a different color for each one. He mumbled and the sand—amazingly—started smoking. The rice shifted, and fell to the side. The seer studied their angles and so on, and then asked, "Please—I need your head."

Lasker leaned forward. The seer began feeling the bumps on his head—phrenology. The old prediction method Lasker had had done once before, years ago in Hong Kong. The man said, "Okay, I know now. Very interesting."

Lasker asked, "Well? Will I marry?"

"You won't want to," the seer replied enigmatically. Then he looked up, "You are going on a long journey. But first you will lose a friend to death—very soon."

That got Lasker's attention. Could this man actually see the future? With bated breath he asked, "Where am I going? Which friend will die?"

"As for where you are going—I cannot say. Another world, perhaps. Not death—much worse."

Lasker frowned. He didn't need this kind of talk right now.

"Which friend is going to die?"

40

"A new one."

Bart didn't have any new friends. Or friends at all. Strike two. What made him think this man could really read the future? Silly idea. Waste of money. Nevertheless he asked, "If you can't say where I will go, can you tell me when?"

"Tomorrow. I see your karmic path leading to an immense world-change. Very unusual, and for you there is much much danger." He looked up at Bart with smoldering fire in his eyes, unblinking.

"What sort of danger?" Lasker found his throat was a bit dry. Tomorrow he *was* leaving—for Tibet.

"Danger to your mind and soul."

Suddenly the sound of bullock carts, pedicab bicycle bells, grunts and shouts, car horns, and Sitar music that had been their companion for the whole discussion died. Lasker felt the skin crawl on the back of his neck. But the pause in the noise was a fluke. Not magic. It resumed immediately. Perhaps he just had something in his ear.

"Can you be specific?"

"That depends . . ." The man's eyes drifted to a smaller sign. DEEP READINGS, TEN RUPEES ADDITIONAL.

Lasker bought.

The man chanted again, lit some incense, and stuck it in the central pile of rice. "This is the mandala of the Kaliyantra Tantra, ruled by the lord of future actions." The seer watched the smoke of the incense for a long time, watching how the wind acted upon it and the incense ash. It eventually broke and fell to the left, the orange rice heap side of the "mandala." The seer wet his cracked lips. "You will be . . . possessed by evil. The outcome is uncertain after this."

He looked up at Lasker. "Your future is bound up with the Eastern world, not the West." He wiped the

41

sand and rice off the board with a quick brush of a wisp broom. "Thank you for your money."

"That's all?"

"That's all? This could not be done by anyone else in New Delhi. In all of Asia perhaps." The seer was angry. "You will see." He looked darkly at Lasker. "Guard well your soul, American."

"Jeez—" Bart stood up too fast; he saw stars. Unsteady on his feet, he walked away. The seer started calling out, "Predictions. Will you marry? Will there be a child in your future? What will Dame Fortune bestow on you—"

What the hell was he doing giving such dour forecasts—trying to kill his business? It was no big prediction, Lasker reasoned, to say that he would take a journey. After all, he didn't belong here. He was a foreigner. And yet . . . the other stuff. Why didn't the seer just give some happy talk, some pap that would please, like they all do? Why the hell had he listened? He was nervous enough.

Bart was really hungry now. He passed a corner puppet show, all done in black silhouettes—a shadow play. The princess had to marry the evil lord; the good prince had to stop it from happening. He had seen this one before. It was delighting the gathered kids, as always. The good prince always won. That was more like it.

He walked on to Praneth Street, where there was an excellent little café, the Surma. Only problem with the place was it served no liquor. Soon he was stepping into its open doorway. Bart had eaten there on and off for a year, and the place never changed. Fans turned languidly on the ceiling; moths vied to get at the lights behind the red paper shades along the wall. The deep red wallpaper printed with black elephants was peeling a little more than the last time he'd come.

He took what he knew to be the coolest seat—the one at a small table next to the open window. There were only a few scattered customers.

Hamdi, one of three Tamil brothers who had come from the south of India a few years back and set up the Surma, came over. He smiled, and handed Lasker a well-worn paper menu. He set down a battered metal pot of hot tea and a cracked cup.

"So good to see you again, sir. Please try the okra special, sir. The cook has a way with okra. I will be back shortly."

Lasker perused the menu. He was very hungry—perhaps that was part of the reason for his continuing foul mood. Let's see, he thought, what'll it be? Poori or kurma, or the bhriyani? Kurma sounded better. Cool creamy sauce, and chunks of lamb. But the okra might be the freshest thing. He poured himself several cups of the darjeeling while waiting. It was cool enough to swallow. By the time he decided on his choice of food, the oily-haired waiter-proprietor came back.

Hamdi pulled a pencil from behind his ear and wrote down Lasker's order on a small yellow pad. Lasker, figuring better safe than sorry, said "I would like the okra special."

"Most wise," Hamdi smiled, and went off toward the kitchen.

While Bart waited, he stared out at the tumult of the street—a riot of noise and color that was India personified. It was near sunset. The Moslem cryers on the minarets in the south part of the city started wailing away, calling the faithful to prayer. As the few passing Moslems threw down their rugs right where they were in the street and bowed to Mecca, the Hindus went right on buying and selling and moving.

He had finished the tea. Hamdi would bring a fresh pot.

Bart fished in his breast pocket for a cigarette. He found the pack, and matches, but he didn't have an ashtray. He looked around to the nearby tables and spotted one and reached to snag it. That was when he noticed the short Sikh wearing the faded orange turban sitting in the corner seat. The little man was looking down at his plate, but still Lasker got the distinct impression that, an instant before, he had been looking his way. Nerves? Maybe not. Lasker couldn't recall ever seeing a short Sikh. They just didn't *come* short, as far as he knew.

It seemed only a moment later that the steaming okra and peas, held in a mass over the rice by congealing goat cheese, arrived—with light puffy poori bread on a paper plate beside it. "Enjoy."

The okra was fresh, spiced just right, but he finished only half of it before pushing it away. He felt eyes upon him. That man—the Sikh. Was he staring at again? Bart casually reached to tie his shoelace, and turned his head in the process.

The orange-turbaned man was gone. His money fluttered on the table, held by a salt shaker. So he hadn't been watching Bart. Just jumpy nerves. Still, he didn't remember orange turbans on Sikhs either. Weren't they tan, or white? And Sikhs had beards. Maybe some did wear orange turbans—rank or something. Maybe he wasn't a Sikh at all, but from some other sect that wore turbans.

Lasker sat for a while thinking about the day: Donnely, Jenny, the seer. He was tired. He stared out for a while at the twilight-covered scene. Then he stood up, signaled Hamdi for the check. He paid, got the change, and left the customary ten percent, exiting into the darkening turmoil, into the heavy smells of spices and incense.

# Chapter 5

Bart wandered for hours, then headed back to his hotel before the last shops closed. The Dil Pranath was a small Hindu-run place, a hotel generally not frequented by Europeans—or Americans. It had air conditioning, and was clean, but the only phone was downstairs.

Lasker entered the lobby and went over to Jamal, the young desk clerk, who was reading a comic book called *The Avenger* at the desk. He picked up his room key. "Jamal," he asked, handing over a hundred rupee note, "be sure to wake me at six A.M. Pound like mad. I have to get up."

"Sure thing." the kid said, pocketing the cash and going back to his comic.

Upstairs, Bart turned the key in the door and entered. The air was cooler inside. He had left the air conditioning on all day. Bart hit the cool sheets and lit a cigarette. He thought about where he was going, and where he was, and where he had been. A year ago Jenny had lived for a week with him here. That was something. They had spent days without going out, sending Jamal to the Surma for meals, sleeping and screwing and talking till they were almost merged, it seemed. And then they fought, as usual; she left. Jenny had put some money on the dresser and he didn't give it back; instead he drank it up. With the thought of that drunken rampage in his mind, he crushed out the cigarette and fell asleep.

A sharp series of raps on the door shook Bart from a dreamless sleep. He jerked bolt upright, and found he had been sleeping in his clothes. He called out, "I'm up, thanks, Jamal." He went to the sink, splashed water in his face, combed his hair. God, he'd better shave. He looked like a terrorist, blood red eyes and wrinkled clothes and all.

He found another shirt, and the pants were permanent press and looked all right. He walked to the window, to see what kind of day it was, pulled the curtain back. Hot, sunny, steamy. What else was new? He glanced at the clock. Six-thirty. Damn, he'd better get going. Got an appointment in Phiyang. And then Tibet. He let the curtain fall back into position. The big Tibetan—Losang—knew that Bart was just talking when he said he hadn't decided to make the flight. Lasker needed the money, and he knew it. That's why Donnely had sent *him* and not some other sky jockey. He had sent the most desperate. A man with a dream is the most desperate.

If it looked at all possible, he was going to Tibet. Probably the most dangerous thing he would ever do in his whole life.

Bart went to the dresser, pulled open the top drawer. The Whalther PPK automatic was there, oily and cold to the touch as he lifted it up. He pulled the magazine out and checked it, slapped it back in. Making sure the safety was on, Bart pointed it at his image in the dresser mirror. "Donnely," he said, "if the money isn't there when I get back, this is for—you."

He thought about bringing the gun along. But airport security would probably pick it up—and besides, he had never used the thing. Still, it was with reluctance that he replaced it in the drawer and headed downstairs.

He tossed the key to Jamal, and Jamal handed him the Dil Praneth's "continental breakfast"—a styrofoam cup of black coffee and a sweet bun. He took it. Bart sipped the coffee as he stepped out into the blinding morning light.

He had set his old watch, and put it on. It said six forty-five. Had to move it, get a cab and—

He smiled. For there was the Hillman cab at the curb. Ahmed was snoozing, his head on the sill of the driver's window. Lasker went over and shook him awake. "Ahmed, it's me, your benefactor. I want a ride."

"Sahib?" Ahmed said, wiping his eyes, "Is it really you? A fortuitous coincidence. Get in, my friend." Lasker did. "Where are you going? Perhaps back to the pretty house?"

Bart told him, "No, take me to the airport. Fast."

"Airport, sahib? You're not leaving New Delhi, not leaving your private most excellent driver that you only just hired?"

"No, I'm not leaving, I'm just just taking a short business trip. I have a job that will take several days. When I return, Ahmed you can be my chauffeur—how'd you like to drive me and my lady around, be a real private chauffeur?"

"Oh most excellent, sahib! Today is my lucky day! You have found a true friend in Ahmed, you must be sure. I will continue to show your woman and your kind self all the beautiful things in New Delhi, as your personal driver. I will come to Hotel Dil Praneth."

"If I make it back," Bart mumbled to himself. The little man drove him out into Willingdon Crescent. "This is the seat of the British Raj in India until 1949," he said, pointing at the Parliament building. "The building was designed . . ."

47

Lasker made appropriate pleased noises as Ahmed rattled on. He finished the coffee and the bun. They passed a stretch along the Government Row that was fortified with sandbag pillboxes and concrete barriers. The strife continued. The cab cut into Upper Ridge Road, past the monotonous whitewashed hospital, which got a full tour guide rundown—including statistics on how many people it housed and how many injuries it treated. Bart thought he must be making it up, but it *sounded* good. He remembered an ethnic joke about the English and told Ahmed.

Ahmed laughed. They were clattering along in a stream of limos and other taxis on the airport access road in just minutes. Lasker wouldn't be late.

"I am so glad you are not leaving, friend. Oh, and what is your name?"

"Bart Lasker."

"A good name. Most dignified."

That was pouring it on a bit thick. It was a name. Lasker now noticed a car—black Mercedes limo, tinted windows—pull out behind them when they had turned onto the airport road. He thought he saw an orange-turbaned man next to the driver. But then it dropped behind.

He had the window open, and watched the newly planted palm trees along the road zip by. They were about a quarter-mile from the big glass terminal when the limo appeared again, weaving out of a lane behind them to keep pace with the taxi.

Following?

The traffic slowed. Some sort of clog. Ahmed inched along. After a few minutes, Bart saw why. A patrol car blocked the way. A set of Indian patrolmen steered the traffic into one lane, doing a security check, he supposed.

Ahmed beeped the horn. The bigger of the cops walked along the stretch of cars ahead of them and came over to the cab, saluted Lasker. "Sorry, sir, for

48

the delay. There is a small demonstration at the Gandhi memorial statue—"

Ahmed snapped, "I have a most important foreign gentleman in my cab—I have to hurry."

"Sorry," the cop repeated. "It will clear up shortly. No problem."

"Maybe I can get out and walk?"

"Not wise, sir. It will be only a few moments. Things are in hand."

Lasker thanked him for the information and the cop headed back to the barrier. He could hear the chanting, growing louder and louder, as they inched forward. There were perhaps thirty cars in front of them now, and ahead of them, on the right, the twenty-foot-high statue of the greenish bronze statue of the Sadhu, Mahatma Gandhi, founder of the nation. Evidently some people thought little of him, for they were yelling epithets to his memory, and another group were guarding the statue and showering it with garlands. It looked like a budding confrontation.

Bart figured the officer didn't want to admit it, but maybe things were a bit *out* of hand ahead.

Ahmed, complaining for his benefit, was moving the orange Hillman forward in anxious jerks. There were a few hundred people milling about the statue, in two groups. Both groups were shouting and waving signs. They were held in check by a thin line of khaki-clad police. They were two cars from the barrier.

Then there was a scream and a shot. The mob protecting the statue from the others burst the police lines and stormed at the—apparently Moslem—opposition. "Death to the murderers," they shouted.

The policemen at the barrier seemed surprised when the shot rang out and the mob stampeded at them. They turned and raised their batons, but the mass of red-clad rioters surged forward. More screams and another shot. A woman fell, blood oozing from her forehead.

The cops grabbed their pistols and began firing over the heads of both mobs, which had met in bloody confrontation over the bleeding woman.

A rock impacted on a Bentley's windshield ahead of them. Ahmed put the little cab in reverse, tried to jump the curb and back off, saying over and over, "I don't like this, sahib, I don't like this." Lasker didn't either. Backing up was a good idea, but there was no where to go. Cars had tangled, horns blaring, all over the place. Lasker was wondering if they should get out instead, make a run for it.

And now, from a blue bus some feet behind them, a horde of screaming men carrying swords poured forth, to join the melee. All were screaming something nasty in Hindi.

The Hillman's motor stalled. "Oh sahib, I think we're in for it now!" Lasker could only agree. All of a sudden the bus mob was behind the Hillman, in front of it, on top of it. They beat on the Hillman's hood and roof, as Lasker and the driver swung at them from the windows.

They smashed some glass, slashed the tires, and moved on, like a wave, joining the fracas ahead.

"Let's go—" Lasker shouted, and started to open his door.

Then he saw the man with the orange turban kneeling on the grass about thirty yards away, a metallic tube held on his left shoulder. And the tube was pointing their way. The man behind the turbaned guy slid an object into the back of the tube and patted him on the head.

Lasker had a sudden recognition of the metal tube. A *bazooka*. He yelled, "Get out, Ahmed; run for it." Bart jumped from the cab just as the bazooka fired.

The high-explosive shell hit the taxi, in the backseat right where Bart had just been. The cab's frame bent out and erupted into flames. Lasker rolled behind another car just in time. Then, while the Hillman burned, he scrambled away, dodging red-eyed fanatics and burning cars until until he was at the statue's base. Bart rolled to Gandhi's metal feet. There he huddled against the pedestal in a sea of rose petals and placards.

The mob was dispersing, panicked. Its rapid fadeaway was enhanced when a burst of automatic fire swept the line of now-abandoned cars. They dropped their placards and weapons and ran for their lives in the face of the awesome firepower. Lasker scrambled over a dead body lying with its eyes open staring up at the metal Mahatma. One fellow that wasn't afraid anymore. Bart felt as if he'd throw up, and did, right on Gandhi's metal-sandaled toes. Then he pulled himself together.

*Ahmed. Where was Ahmed?*

Bart looked around. The men with the bazooka were nowhere to be seen. Possibly they had gotten in the car that now careened away, doors half-open, across the grass lawn.

A single policeman, head bloodied, stood over a fallen comrade, and emptied his pistol wildly at one of the fleeing cars. Bart crawled back along the line of abandoned cars, to one fallen figure after another, calling out, "Ahmed?"

Aside from the cop, the only people still around were the ones that were either dead or flopping about neardead. Bart turned over body after bloody body. "Ahmed?"

No, *this* man wasn't Ahmed. Even without a face, you could tell by his big muscular build. Lasker kept searching.

He went to the burning Hillman—as close as the flames would allow. And there he saw the charred arm hanging out of the driver's door. Ahmed hadn't gotten out.

Sadly, he moved away. At first he crawled along the cars, then he ran. He had to get to the air terminal, get to Good Baby. Whatever had happened, he had an appointment in Phiyang.

He ran the last hundred yards, along with a few other people who came out of hiding in the shrubs and wanted to get to safety. Gasping in short breaths, he reached the barred glass door. Bart showed his papers to the soldier looking out. The door opened a crack—for him alone. A lot of others didn't get through.

Lasker started breathing more controlled breaths, getting a hold on himself, as he walked across the air-conditioned building's inlaid linoleum squares. He heard a jet taking off. Good, the airport wasn't shut down. If you shut an airport in India every time there was a riot, there would be no air traffic, he realized.

Some official was holding debarking passengers behind a rope barrier, thanking them for their understanding of the inconvenience of waiting before they left the building. "Damn bother," muttered one Britisher to his lady friend.

Lasker headed toward the access ramp to Hanger C, where he kept Good Baby. Had he just imagined that the man with the bazooka, the man that had killed Ahmed, was the same short Sikh from the restaurant?

As the ramp guard again checked his papers, Bart suddenly remembered the seer's words: "A new friend will die—very soon."

Ahmed.


Good Baby, all 33,000 pounds of silver-skinned twin-propellered spunky metallic streamlined bulk of her, was standing there, ready for flight. Lasker ran to her, immediately started kicking the blocks from under her big Michelins.

Then the brown-coveralled man with grease-streaked

blond hair and a menacing lug wrench clutched in his hand was coming toward him.

"And where do you think you going, deadbeat?" the man asked through clenched teeth. He beat the wrench against his palm.

"Hans, I have the money."

The menace turned to crinkled-eyed smile; the lug wrench relaxed from its upward angle. "You do? All twelve thousand rupees? Cash?"

"Sure," Lasker slipped his hand in his left pants pocket and extracted the roll of thousand-rupee notes Losang had given him as "start-up" money. He peeled off twelve bills and Hans took them. He recounted, smiled again. "Well, she's all ready to go, Lasker. But you'll need *this* for the port engine." He unzipped a coverall pocket, took a black ignition wire from it, handed the wire to Bart. "Nice plane, but it won't run without this."

Lasker said nothing. As the mechanic walked away, he climbed a ladder to the port engine, opened the housing, and replaced the wire. Then he put the ladder back along the wall and climbed up into Good Baby's open door. He lifted the door, spun the valve shut, and went through the cabin to the familiar cracked-leather pilot's seat. He sat down, picked up the headset, and called the tower for clearance. Then, as he waited, for the reply, he picked up the clipboard, went through the minimum flight-check—basic instruments, oil pressure, fuel—and started priming up the big engines. The hanger doors had been opened by Hans. And after the props came to life and steadied, he taxied out onto the line.

He wanted to get airborne. In the sky maybe he could calm down. He wondered if the mechanic had noticed how much he was trembling, or the sheer terror in his eyes.

# Chapter 6

Two hours and forty-five minutes later, Lasker was over Phiyang. He pushed the plane's stick forward and Good Baby's nose angled down toward the landing strip. From five thousand feet up, it was just a brown line next to a set of gray-white structures set inside a ring—Phiyang was an ancient walled town in the Indian state of Ladahk. Right next to Tibet.

The plane's tires squealed in anger upon hitting the hard-packed dirt. Good Baby bumped along, shaking him and everything that could be shaken. He cursed as he roared the engines in reverse, and managed to stop before the clearing gave way to dry brush.

Bart turned the plane and bounced back toward the single concrete-block building with the radio antenna on its top. A gray-haired man with field glasses hung on his chest came out. Lasker slid opened the window and yelled, "I'm Lasker."

"Well, I'm Joe," the man said. Then he demanded landing money.

"Where do I put my plane?"

"Right there's fine. We don't get much trade."

Lasker cut the engines and debarked. The old guy relieved Bart of a thousand rupees and invited him inside. It was hot and dusty, and the air smelled like ripe cow shit.

"Where are the cousins?" Lasker asked. He had gone over the instructions from Losang on the plane, and expected to be greeted by two guys called Namgyal and Wangyal.

"They're coming. You're a bit early."

As the man opened the door, two pint-sized boys rushed out with cans labeled RED DEVIL. They went to the plane, broke open the paint cans with sticks, and one placed a stencil against the bottom of the port wing.

"Hey—"

"It's okay," Joe said. "They've been hired to re-decorate your plane, Chinese-style." Lasker watched a red-and-yellow Chinese flag being painted on the port wing's underside.

"They're brothers—twice as much money that way." Joe laughed. The wind and sand slapped at Bart's flight jacket.

They went inside the block building.

Lasker gave him a dirty look and said, "I hope they're careful." The question "What the hell am I doing here?" went through his mind, alternating with a picture of Ahmed's blackened arm sticking out of the burning cab.

Lasker looked around at the room: a table, some battered chairs, antiquated radio equipment, and on the walls, yellowed Indian government posters—regulations, probably ignored.

"Want a Kingfisher? That's Indian Beer."

"I know," Lasker said, seating himself. "Thanks, I will have one."

Joe reached under the radio receiver console and opened a small refrigerator, pulled out a pair of dusty bottles that claimed to contain beer, and twisted off the caps. He handed one to Lasker.

55

"How much?"

"Nothing—for you. Us white guys gotta stick together."

Joe leaned his pockmarked face over the table, after Lasker took a half-bottle swig of beer. "I must warn you," Joe said in a conspiratorial tone, "Most of Phiyang's newer inhabitants are from the north—low creatures with bad habits, including cannibalism. They come over the mountains, at night, carrying the statues of their demon-gods on their shoulders. There are many murders here. You just transact your business quickly and leave. Foreigners don't do well here—except for Old Joe, that is. Why, they found a German tourist just last week, down a well, his head all eaten away—"

The door opened, interrupting Joe's tale, and a tawny high-cheekboned man wearing boots, a plaid shirt, jeans, and lots of turquoise and silver jewelry came in. "I'm Namgyal," he stated. He was carrying a big roll of paper under his shoulder. Namgyal, Bart decided, looked like a Navaho he had once met in the Air Force. Though the Navaho wasn't forty years old, as Namgyal appeared to be.

They shook hands, taking measure of each other. "Are you from Mister . . ."

"Losang, of Ferrari Import-Export," said Lasker, as prearranged.

Namgyal smiled and said, "The weather is nice for flying." They sat down at the one big table.

Namgyal eyed Joe, who finished his beer, nodded, and left. After he'd shut the door, Namgyal said, "I have here the chart's Mr. Losang promised you." He spread them out. "You have fuel enough?"

"I could fly all the way back to New Delhi if I had to."

"Good."

56

Bart examined the top chart. He had to whistle. They were marked, "Property of the Indian Government, Ladahk Computerized Weather Center, Military Commmand, Frontier 1."

"Where'd you get these? They're just—let's see—"

"They are weather isobar charts just three hours old. We have friends in high places. Sympathizers. We asked for the latest charts—"

"And got them. Very good. It will help a lot." Lasker saw some trouble spots on the isobar readings around some of the mountains to the east, but none straight north. Namgyal spoke. "You are to take the flight path marked by the red dotted line. You note it is lower than the mountains in many places—and goes through several twisting passes. But the weather is good there. You will land on the other side of the high mountains, in the foothills near the village of Gattok, on a"—Namgyal paused—"on a dry riverbed."

"A riverbed?"

"Yes. At this time of year, it's hard and smooth. There you will be greeted by Lama Youngden or a representative. They will ask you who sent you. And you will say Mr. Losang sent you. You will immediately unload, and take off again. That's it."

"What about my getting shot down? Go over that one again."

Namgyal explained that Bart was to fly the exact route—known to them—of the regular Chinese spotter aircraft that patrolled the area near the border—only the Chinese plane wouldn't be there. It had been arranged that the Chinese would miss that one flight, owing to "engine trouble."

"A lot depends on that," Lasker commented. "Like my life."

"We have a lot to lose too," Namgyal reasoned. "Don't worry, it's arranged."

Namgyal explained the route further, drawing his finger across the maps—elevations, barometric pressure lines. It was all there.

Lasker glanced anxiously out the small window at Good Baby rocking in the dusty wind. She looked like a stranger now, with the red Chinese flag with five yellow stars painted on the cockpit door and the wings. There was Chinese writing on the tail instead of his NC number.

Namgyal finished his spiel and asked, "Well, what do you think? Do you think you can fly that route and back? I understand that you are an extremely good pilot. And Losang was very impressed by your responses in your interview with him. He says we can place our full trust in you."

"Nice of him. He's right, I'm the best of pilots. The plane is reliable. You get what you pay for. The route is okay, I have oxygen gear, and the plane is capable of high altitudes, and can maneuver through the passes."

"Then we load the cargo and you leave"—Namgyal looked at his watch—"in a half hour. You won't have much daylight time getting back."

"Nor much fuel," Bart added, using a small protractor on the map to calculate distances and fuel consumption. "Not much at all in the way of spare fuel, but enough. I'd rather travel light. The cargo is one ton. That's enough. How about we get this show on the road? The sand and wind aren't doing my plane any good. Is the load here at the field?"

"Wangyal is on the way here now with the truck containing the supplies. We kept it outside of town. That is safer from prying eyes. The Chinese have spies in Phiyang, since we are only a hundred miles from the border."

Lasker said, "I want to inspect the cargo as it's loaded."

"Fine. You will see it is as stated."

Further discussion was halted by the noisy arrival of the supply truck. The driver was a look-alike to Namgyal except for his hair, which was long and in a ponytail, pulled back the tarps—revealing three crates. They hefted them out next to the plane's door ramp.

Bart pried opened each of the cartons to see what was really inside. He figured that if they didn't contain anything nasty, the Chinese, *if* he had to make a forced landing, might not shoot him.

He was surprised that there really were no arms in the crates. Just medical supplies—splints, antibiotics, syringes, and bandages in the first two crates. All with Indian writing on the labels. His eyes widened when he saw the third crate not only contained the rather worthless-outside-of-China renminbao dollars, but also several plastic ziplock bags full of gold coins.

"How do you know," Lasker asked Namgyal, as he resealed the lids, "that I won't just head south with the money? There must be five hundred thousand dollars' worth of gold alone. More than I'm getting paid for this flight."

"Rimpoche says you are a man that can be trusted."

"Rimpoche? Is that Losang's last name?"

"No, his title," Namgyal said, smiling strangely. "Don't you know?"

The cousins were strong as workhorses, and worked like horses too, and together the three of them loaded the crates on Good Baby in a few minutes. Lasker lashed them down.

That done, he got behind the stick, and the cousins turned her wings into the wind, which was fortunately blowing right from the south, along the short runway. Bart started up the engines.

God, he hoped the weather held. In poor visibility,

since the engines kicked up swirls of dust, he started Good Baby moving.

He pushed the throttles forward, revved the engines to maximum, and rolled bouncing toward the bushes. The plane lifted, wobbled up into the sky.

He thought about continuing to head directly south, and fought with his conscience for a few moments. There sure was a *lot* of money aboard. But people desperate for freedom were depending on him. A thousand feet above the dust, when he broke into clear deep blue sky, he banked the plane to a north heading. Duty had won.

Good Baby was headed toward the glistening ice-clad peaks of the Himalayas.

# Chapter 7

He was coming up on the border between Ladahk and Tibet at twelve thousand feet, as arranged. Bart checked the gauges. Fuel consumption okay, oil pressure 160, both engines.

He put Good Baby on a gradual ascent. At fourteen thousand he snapped the rubber oxygen mask out of its holder. He adjusted it to his chin and nose and turned the valve on. He breathed in cold rubber-smelling oxygen. He hated the hiss of the airflow, the feel of the cracked and pitted rubber of the mask on his face. But it would only be for an hour.

Lasker's plan was to get five miles from the border and immediately turn east-northeast eighty degrees, as the patrol plane he was replacing would have taken that route. They frequently overflew the border a few miles, and no one cared.

The mountains were there on the horizon, already beyond impressive. The plane entered a wide cloud bank. He decided to stay in it, rather than climb higher. It was good cover against curious eyes. Of course, he couldn't avoid Chinese radar.

There was nothing but the whiteness outside—a uniform tapioca. He sat and stared at it for ten minutes, projecting before him pictures that made him happy: a set of planes sitting on a runway—his air charter line. Jenny's face. The pile of British pounds being pushed into a suitcase he would pick up at Donnely's office at the Excelsior.

Suddenly the whiteness evaporated. Ahead, blotting out half the deep blue sky, were the majestic snow-capped peaks of the Karakoram range. Lasker felt a sense of foreboding. It was one thing to see altitude marks and contour lines on a map, another thing to be staring at the real thing! He again checked all the instruments, to make sure Good Baby was up to par. She was.

Off to his right was massive Karakoram itself, the twin summits surrounded by plumes of white wind-blown snow catching the sun. As he watched the slow dance of the white mist above it, a rainbow appeared. Blinding to look at. Good luck?

Thirty degrees to Karakoram's left was Dahligiri, a single vertical escarpment of jade green, beneath a heavy cumulus cloud, whose shadow gave it that color.

Lasker looked down. Beneath him, the Ladahk barley fields were tan squares. And green cultivated terraces on sculpted hillsides neatly delineated cultivation from the gray-brown arid terrain. There were also twisting white lines in the gray-brown. Military roads.

He was fifty nautical miles from the demarkation line between Chinese-held Tibet and India—the UN cease-fire line enforced since 1969—when Good Baby began to take some clear air chop. He'd been in much worse, but it was sure to increase as he tried to slip between the mountains.

Still it looked as if the weather forecasts were right. No black thunderheads as far as he could see. And that was plenty far.

Bart was now five miles from the cease-fire line,

turned to the bearing that the Chinese spotter plane would have been flying. God—what if it *was* up here? Which one would they shoot down?

He looked down through the side window. There were circular scars on the earth below now. Concave artillery craters. And ugly black lines—fields of barbed wire.

The border. He winced. He slid the ruler along the line drawn in red on the map spread on the co-pilot seat. He was exactly on the course that he had been told to take, and his timing was exactly right, according to Good Baby's reliable chronometer. It was 2:46 P.M.

The markings on the plane should fool anyone taking him in with a telescope. Now, if the PLA Air Force didn't decide to send up a jet to look him over, he should be okay.

After five tense minutes more of flight, he descended to ten thousand and took off the stinking cold mask. He was flying over a concrete runway that had tiny white swept-wing objects parked along its side. MIG interceptors. Bart again checked his course, the instruments, the altitude. He'd be there in an hour more. Quit worrying, he told himself, wiping his sweaty palms on his flight jacket and putting them back on the trembling stick. If they were going to challenge him, they would have already.

Karakoram and Dhaligiri were to his starboard now, and coming up were the peaks marked K-2 and K-3 on the charts. K-2 was Everest's principal challenger for the tallest-mountain-in-the-world designation, and looked it. The two peaks slowly separated as he approached. These were the babies he had to fly between. A piece of cake. He gritted his teeth. In another seven minutes he was between them, a few hundred feet off rolling glacial fields, feeling the full force of winds.

Good Baby's wings quivered. The nose wanted to wander. Every bolt and nut strained to release. Wind speed 340 knots. Jesus, he thought, this better not keep up!

This was the most difficult part of the whole flight. But if the Chinese could do it, so could he. Bart gripped the stick so tightly his knuckles were white. Ten minutes of terror and he finally left the narrow pass and its glacial walls behind. He turned the nose down and descended through a layer of haze toward a series of round-top hills. He hoped the *right* hills. On the map they looked distinctive; here they didn't.

The turbulence got worse again. Good Baby yawned and shook. The tree-dotted slopes swept by a frightening speed. Tail winds. Airspeed 440 knots, altitude 12,340. "Everything okay," he heard himself saying. "Just a few more minutes and you'll see the hook-shaped lake . . ."

There was a grayness ahead—rain clouds. Right where he had to fly to get to Gattok.

Altitude 12,900, just high enough. Plane rocking, barometer dropping rapidly. First spatter of rain on the windscreen. Just hang in there Good Baby . . .

The monsoon-like rain started smashing against the windscreen like a set of jackhammers. He had lots of room now, though, rose to 13,400, and pulled above the worst. He changed headings to WNW. Back on course. The cloud below passed. Rain stopped slapping the window. There were hundreds of smaller, tree-covered hills now, as far as he could see. The Tibetan Badlands.

Check chronometer. Ten minutes ahead of schedule. Throttle down a bit . . . okay.

Where the hell was the hook-shaped lake? He scanned the misty horizon. Something . . . blue—yes. There is was. Among a set of smaller round lakes—the landmark lake. Just west of it would be the dry riverbed. Maybe five minutes more. That's all. They'd be there waiting for him, outlining the dry riverbed with torches. A piece of cake!

The nomad yak herder, clad in the bearskin he had personally ripped from said bear, looked up from the cooking fire he was tending. His black pupils scanned the deep blue heavens. There it was, the annoying buzzer. A metallic speck, glistening in the evening sun. A flying machine. He had heard of them, but never seen one. The filthy Chinese were up to their tricks even around here. Evil business, flying around in the sky where only dragons and funeral birds are supposed to be!

His herd of yaks and dromos chewing on the sparse short grass of the mountain valley noticed the intruder also. The big bull yak looked up, snorted a note of defiance. Its hairy tail switched. The buzz became louder. It sounded like an angry bee.

The nomad decided to do something about this evil thing before the yaks got all bothered, and started running every which way. He put his palm over his eyes to shield it from the bright sun reflecting off Three Demon Mountain's glacier.

The noisy metal bee was heading his way. He started chanting a protective mantra, the one a pilgrim on his way to Lhasa, the City of the Gods, once taught him. He manipulated his fingers into the appropriate sky-protector *mudra* hand positions. *This* potent spell should ward off the evil metal thing!

The bee of metal passed over Three Demon Mountain and dropped out of his sight. The nomad listened to the sound move away. He was pleased with the efficacy of his mantra. He pulled on his left earlobe and went back and squatted down at the fire again. Good spell.

Then he uttered an expletive. The business of removing the sky-thing had caused him to forget the cooking pot of *tsampa* in the earthern pot. The fire had made it a black mess. Also the boiling pot of tea and yak milk was now curdling. Quickly he removed the pots from the flames, and poured out the burned-smelling contents of *tsampa* into his wooden bowl. He tasted it. Ruined. Tasted like charcoal, instead of barley and butter.

Cursed be the Chinese and their metal sky demons.


Lasker was finally untensing. The blue lake was just fifty or sixty miles ahead—he was feeling better about the trip, deciding that it was going to be all right after all. Then an orange flower blossomed on one of those green hills. Something shot up trailing a crooked line of black smoke behind it. It turned in his direction and kept climbing, gathering speed.

An air defense missile. "Shit!" he yelled, and pulled the stick back and turned sharply to starboard, climbing away at right angles to the object with the fiery tail that kept approaching.

Bart didn't make it. There was a whoosh right off the port wing—a white painted SILK-5 missile shot by, and then there was a flash. Blinding red. And then the concussion. A set of golfball-sized holes appeared in the port wing, black oil, and then flames started coming from that engine. Bart frantically pumped the CO-2 button, cursing at his stupidity for thinking he could fly into Tibet. The damaged engine's propeller stopped spinning.

Pieces of the missile hit the windscreen, shattering it and coating him with glass fragments.

The plane was stalling. He banked her, hoping the damaged wing wouldn't snap off, and plunged spinning and afire, out of control. The other engine was sputtering, the oil pressure in the far red.

Lasker fished around for his parachute, which hung on the back of the seat, pulled it over his shoulder as Good Baby plunged at a forty-five-degree angle heading for a brilliantly sunlit glacier.

*She was going down.* Bart had maybe two minutes. He snapped the chute pack's cinches on and tightened the harness. He heard the second engine scream and throw its propeller.

Suddenly it was eerily silent, except for the rush of wind. Only then, in the silence, did he realize—I'm alive. A missile near-missed, and I'm alive. A feeling of cheating death, an exhilarating feeling—

*But you're not alive for long, stupid. Get the damned door open and jump.*

The plane rolled over on its back. The white glacier filled his whole view. Bart saw a small shadow jerking across its white face—the shadow of his little plane, hurtling downward.

# Chapter 8

*Time to bail out.* Bart reached over and grabbed the door handle with his left hand and pushed and turned.

*Nothing.* It wouldn't turn. The temperature—damned door was covered with a thin layer of slippery ice. Frozen shut.

*Panic.* He smashed his shoulder against the door futilely, then stopped. He reached behind the seat and snagged the tool kit, pulled it onto his lap, not looking out the window—the scream of rushing air, like a Stuka dive bomber, told the story.

He took out the ball head hammer and smashed at the ice, and then tried the handle again. Nothing. He smashed out the Plexiglas and crawled up and forced himself through it, cutting his hands, shredding his flight suit. He didn't care. For an instant his left foot was stuck, then he fell free, in a shower of sparks and smoke from the burning plane. He tumbled away.

*Now, open the chute.*

Lasker pulled the cord. Instantly there was a pop and then a terrible jerk. His body had been in a foetal position, so it was as if someone had hit him across the midsection when he snapped out. Good Baby, fully ablaze, whizzed past him trailing smoke. He felt the searing heat, breathed in the awful black fumes, thinking for a second he would be fried alive before she passed onward.

Then Bart sucked in icy fresh air, hanging, rocking back and forth in gusts of wind.

With eyes streaming tears, he watched Good Baby smash into the middle of a set of three barren hills beyond the glacier. The orange ball erupted briefly skyward, and then a smoldering black cloud reached up from the smudge. That was all that was left of his dreams.

The funny thing was, as he rocked back and forth, heading down toward an unknown land, his plane destroyed, his future nebulous, he kept thinking of how beautiful the landscape was. The sky above was clear and cobalt blue, the ice caps on the mountains glistened. A magnificent peaceful scene of endless mountains and—

There were jagged granite rock outcroppings spotted with snow below. Rugged terrain, and approaching at a good clip. Lasker was heading in sideways, sure to be a rough landing.

*This is it.* He saw a bounder field coming up, and pulled the chute lines to make himself drift left, toward a clear snowy slope.

*A hundred feet up, fifty—*

He hit hard, did a somersault off his stinging legs. Hit again, on his head.

Then blackness.


Lasker found himself sitting on the icy ground with one leg under him, the other stretched out. His back was up against a boulder. He felt as if he were coming out of a dream, waking up in the morning. His head hurt, though, and it was cold—too cold. Where was his blanket? Why was the air conditioner up so high?

He looked around. He was in a rock-strewn field, patches of snow, shadow from the left—he turned his neck, winced. It hurt, so he turned more slowly. Through bleary vision he saw mountains, ice-clad, in the distance. One was partially blocking the sun, whose red beams shot up over and around it, into a cobalt blue sky.

What? Where was he? Slowly, he remembered: the flight, the missile, the door that wouldn't open—the parachute drop. He was in *Tibet*. And amazed he was alive. How long had be been unconscious? The sun was low—it must have been hours. God, what condition was he in?

Cautiously he moved his extended left leg. It didn't respond at first, stiff and numb. He hoped it wasn't shattered. Slowly, ever so slowly, he rubbed it and then he straightened it out, continuing to rub. His hands were almost unfeeling. Frozen. But slowly they started tingling. And hurting—awfully. They were swollen and more blue than fleshy.

Lasker gradually felt the pin pricks of sensation returning in both his legs as the blood cautiously and then throbbingly rushed in. He tried to rise, couldn't. His *back*.

No, it was okay. Another try, he managed to stand, leaning on the boulder. He stomped his feet on the ground, breathing heavily with the exertion. His head pounded. His eyes were clearer now. The terrain all around him was caught in the slanting rays of the sun. It was all lunar-like—desolate. Six or seven inches of windblown snow on the stony ground, not a blade of grass, or shrub, or tree. Sheer white rock face of an immense cliff a hundred yards to the west. A yawning crevasse, ice patches. His breath sent out mist. He'd freeze here tonight—had to find shelter. He tried to move—something was holding him in place. He felt down to his chute harness—still attached to him were the life-saving lines.

Lasker unhitched his chute harness clumsily. The parachute lines were stuck between some rocks, making it more difficult. He managed to extricate himself from the tangle. Then a sudden stabbing pain between his eyes drove him down to his knees gasping. He held his head in his hands waiting for the pain to subside. When he drew away his hands, he saw blood.

He touched his head all over gingerly. A little more dried blood. Cuts, he hoped, not a crack. He started forward, toward what, he didn't know. Bart had to get moving—or freeze.

There were marks, huge crooked footprints in the snow. Whose?

Then he laughed. The marks in the snow were his own. He must have landed on his feet, rolled, and then slammed against the boulder. He glanced at his wristwatch. The crystal was shattered, the hands stopped at four thirty-five.

The sun reached a space in the sawtooth mountains, reflecting off a glacier. He winced, squinted his eyes. Now that pain had begun to inch up his senses, he could better assess his injuries: A slammed shoulder, a gash on his forehead, trickling half-coagulated blood. His fingernails torn on his left hand. His whole body ached from the impact but no broken bones.

Situation? Bart was on a barren slope, miles short of his destination, without food or anything like survival gear—and he was hurt. But he was alive. For now. He'd have to find water. And warmth.

And avoid troops. The Chinese had shot him down, and they would be looking for him. Blast Donnely and

Losang and the damned cousins and their promises. Someone had let him down. Or all of them.

He had lost Good Baby and was in the middle of the Tibetan wilderness, without so much as a pack of matches—

A thought occurred—perhaps some of the supplies on the plane had survived the impact—if he could find the wreckage—but even if he did. . . . It was 260 mountainous miles back to Ladahk. He was only maybe 50 or 60 miles from his intended destination. He had no choice but to head NNW and try to find the landing field. The Blue Hook-lake. He had good boots; his legs were bruised but okay. He felt a lump in the lining of his leather flight jacket. He reached in—God, he had his compass! He checked his bearings. NNW was roughly parallel to that white cliff. There was nothing for it but to walk, to put one foot ahead of the other.

A constant wind made a howling noise in his ears. His mouth was dry. He walked and walked. Pain was a constant companion. And numbness. His feet and legs were aching. His left hand alternately burned and froze. Fire and ice. He had to find some shelter, since it was getting dark. Even in Nepal in May, the temperature could drop to 40 below zero in the mountains. Who knew what it could get down to in Tibet? The warmth of the day waned as the sun gradually descended behind the mountains in the west. He walked on. One foot ahead of the other.

Awesome vistas unfolded before him—jagged ice-capped peaks, quartz and mica escarpments dazzling like starfields, rosy pink afterglow on cliffs. But he spent little time admiring the landscape. Its barren beauty taunted him. It only meant death.

\* \* \*

*Gurgling sound.* Where? There—he staggered over a slaggy rise. He had found water—a roaring stream frothing icy fresh water. He bent and cupped his hands to drink, until he was satisfied. Bart realized he had nothing to carry any water in. He dried his hands as best he could against his jacket and stuck them into his pockets. His hand touched something hard, rectangular. Then he remembered—his candy bar. No. Not now. Something to look forward to. Such a little thing really, a candy bar. How unimportant the money seemed now, with his life in the balance. How much money had he thrown away in his life? How many feasts had he taken for granted? True wealth was shelter, enough food to fill your belly and people to share it with. He clutched his jacket tightly to his body and shivered with the cold. And walked on, under a sky rapidly filling with myriad stars.

*Shelter, water, food, step, step, step.* . . . He repeated the phrase over and over. But it didn't make him any stronger. Then he thought: *Kill Donnely, kill Losang, kill the cousins.* That did it—he was moving with a new resolve. *Revenge, revenge, revenge, revenge.* He now felt remarkably uncold—warm, as a matter of fact—especially his forehead, which seemed to radiate heat. Funny pictures filled his mind. Donnely laughing. Bart swung his fist at him. "Think I'm funny? Huh?" He swung again. But Donnely seemed to be able to dodge his blows, keep laughing.

Jenny appeared, said, "There's a trail ahead, a hut—keep going . . . keep going."

Lasker did. Every so often he stopped to check the bearing of his compass. He found he couldn't read the numbers, or the needle was missing—was it missing? He saw nothing but endless snow-patched boulder fields ahead, agate and mica. No trail. No hut. Nothing but the snow and gathering night. Were there any people

73

in this frozen waste? "Hey, anybody here?" he shouted.

The echo came back to him in a hundred falling voices. *No one.* The last rays of the setting sun lit the few cirrus clouds with red and pink light. A sudden chill seemed to come into the air, and the blue sky became black.

The wind howled and blew the snow about like sand. The snow stung his cold face and clung to his eyebrows and lashes. He pulled up his flight jacket around his nose and mouth and made sure his collar was up. His nostrils kept sticking together and his sinuses were stinging with pain. His breathing grew labored with the exertion of walking through snow up to his ankles. He fell. He got up and fell again. He struggled to his feet and with grim determination chanted "North-north-west, north-north-west, north-north-west," with every step. He could see now only by the blue light of a crescent moon.

Lasker stumbled, injuring his knee, reopening the gash in his forehead. He blacked out but came to on impact. He lay there for a moment, the breath knocked out of him. Dimly in the moonlight, he made out what seemed to be a low stone building at the top of a hillock. He picked himself up stiffly. Desperately he walked toward that object. What was it? A hut? A dim hope welled up inside him. Or was it an illusion?

Bart walked faster. Whatever it was was on top of a hillock. He put everything he had left in it and staggered up the 300-meter slope and fell to his knees and wept. For it was not a house at all—just a pile of irregularly shaped slate. Each slab of slate had some cryptic inscriptions on it. People had made this sometime—maybe centuries ago.

Lasker sat there numb. How far had he walked out

of the fifty miles to the landing strip? Ten, fifteen? All for this? It was cold, so damned cold.

He couldn't go on. It was over. Might as well eat his candy bar. No use saving it now. He pulled it out and chewed on it. It snapped off in sharp slivers. It was frozen. And he found something else in is pocket. *Matches.*

New hope. But his glee was short-lived. There wasn't a scrap to burn anywhere—not a tree, not a twig, not a blade of grass. It was as if he were on the moon. He crumpled up his candy wrapper and wedged it under some pieces of slate. His fingers were so stiff he could barely handle the matches. He lit five matches before it caught. It burned brilliantly for a few moments before turning into a dull glow. In that brief flash of light his eyes chanced upon the nature of the slate writing. It was a mani pile. He remembered now. He'd seen such piles in India. Pilgrims left them in lofty places of religious significance. This was a Pilgrims' route. They would come again.

But no one might be here again for months. The Tibetan inscriptions, in the moonlight, looked magical. What god were they written to—or what demon? The light of the crescent moon made the pile of rocks loom up like a demon and the writing curled up like snakes. Bart understood dimly that he was suffering from hypothermia—exposure. And that he had very little time left. He closed up in fetal position and tried to save whatever warmth he had left, deep inside. He knew he would die here, alone.

The stars above him seemed to blossom open, like flowers of the night.

# Chapter 9

Lights moved on the mountains. Torches. Silently they danced along, like drunken fireflies. Eighteen torches and the shadowy figures barely discernable beneath them. They walked a trail so faint that only their familiarity with the route enabled them to follow it. Occasionally the torches, flared by the night wind, cast orange light upon the faces of those who held them: tawny high-cheekboned faces, men with long matted hair and glinting copper bracelets, and silver rings dotted with green turquoises. They carried weapons—rifles, swords, daggers, and bows made of catalpa wood, quivers of iron-tipped arrows.

There were eight women among them, in long dress-like garments with aprons of bright rainbow colors, now dark and sooty from travel. Those in the rear led the horses and odd yak-like animals with black-and-white pelts on tethers. There was rustle of silk and leather, but little other sound to denote their coming.

The trail they followed led them to where the man from the sky lay. The forward man, Rinchen, spotted Lasker first. He put up his big hand and the caravan stopped in its tracks. Slowly, silently, the man called Rinchen advanced closer to the prone figure. He nudged it over with his soft-booted foot. The stranger moaned. Half crouching now, the forward man brought his torch close to the man's face. Four others of the band came forward. The stranger stirred and then, startled, sat up.

Lasker was staring straight into the barrel of an Enfield bolt-action rifle. The man glaring balefully down that barrel had a long "lantern" jaw and wore a carved bone necklace. He looked like a savage Genghis Khan. Bart was suddenly being frisked by another man of like Mongolian stock who had a coin in place of one eye. It glinted in the yellow torchlight. A glance told Bart he was surrounded by eight or ten men, all of a savage appearance. The tawny men were dressed in pelts and leather, their faces covered with smears of greasy soot. They were tall and broad, had rifles slung over their shoulders, swords sheathed in scabbards, daggers stuck in their wide sash belts. Lasker's worst fears had been the Chinese soldiers, but these men must be *bandits!* Lasker felt his compass being lifted and studied, then remarkably, it was put back in his jacket. Not good enough? Aside from that, he had nothing to give them. They would kill him, he was sure. But he was cold . . . so cold. What did it matter now?

The man with the coin eye came forward, saying something in a gutteral tongue. The tall "Genghis Khan" type glared hard at Lasker. He didn't dare move or speak. In the awful silence that ensued, the seconds seemed to stretch to eternity. Genghis Khan drew back his rifle and reached for his belt. Lasker's heart stopped beating. His throat constricted, his mouth was dry. This is it, Bart thought. He's not going to waste a bullet on me; he's going for his dagger.

But what the big man held in his hand was not a

dagger, but a canteen. An old beaten copper canteen. Bart gratefully reached forward and took the offering. "Thank you," he gasped. He placed the canteen to his mouth, tilted it. The warmish invigorating brew wasn't water. It tasted something like beer. No, *Chang,* the barley-and-malt beverage of Nepal. He'd tasted it once before. Thoughts raced through his mind. Maybe they're not bandits. Maybe they were just checking to see if he was armed. Who were they?

He took his lips from the canteen and asked, "Anyone speak English?"

No reply.

"I'm a pilot. Airplane—*pilot.*" He moved his free hand in a motion like a plane and made a buzzing sound.

Looks of consternation. They thought him mad perhaps.

"I want—help."

Again, bewildered silence.

Bart attempted to hand the canteen back. The long-jawed rifleman made some sort of unpleasant exclamation, and with his eyes wide in anger, he stepped back. He reached for the dagger in his belt, and drew it. And he wasn't the only one. Several men rushed forward with glinting daggers drawn. Lasker got up on his haunches in alarm. "Friend. Friend." No one seemed to understand what he said. They let him drink, and now they were going to kill him. What had he done wrong?

Suddenly an old man with a shaven head, dressed in a loose fitting coarse maroon robe, rushed from the darkness behind the torches. He raised a hand just in time to stay a dagger. Lasker heard him repeat the word "friend" and then say, *"Thokpo, thokpo."* Lasker nodded his head. *"Thokpo—friend, Thokpo."*

The eyes of the man with the poised dagger flared,

78

but he slowly lowered it. Bart had spoken his first word in Tibetan, it seemed. And not a second too soon.

The robed old man's eyes crinkled, and he smiled. *"Thokpo,"* he said softly again, and turned to the mad one. He made some sort of elaborate statement that Bart hoped was in his behalf. It seemed to mollify the giant and he put his dagger back in the sash and turned away.

With a look of gentle concern, the old man bent down and lightly touched Lasker's forehead wound. Lasker winced. The old man quickly withdrew his hand and then examined first Lasker's right wrist and then his left. He seemed to be taking Lasker's pulse.

Then the monk, or whatever he was, very gently placed both of Lasker's hands on the canteen and then took it from him again. The monk had handed it back with both hands. Lasker was confused. Why was he handing it back? The monk again repeated the procedure, placed both of Bart's hands firmly on the canteen, then took it back with both hands. The light began to dawn in Lasker's mind. Oh, use *both* hands? Maybe it was some sort of taboo. The Muslims never use their left hand, he knew that. These people seemed to insist on using both hands. Was that it?

Lasker took the canteen again, handed the canteen back to the monk with both hands. He was rewarded with a smile and a nod. The monk patted him on the head as if he had been a good boy. Lasker realized he had learned his first lesson in Tibetan etiquette.

Suddenly Bart could sit up no more. His eyes rolled back and he slumped to the ground. He heard the monk shout something. Then several rough hands bore him up and carried him to a horse. Bart was flung unceremoniously over the steed's saddle and tied on. After this it was all a blur; he fell in and out of consciousness. He was aware of nothing more than the sway of the horse and the sound of its hooves. They were moving.

He must have passed out for a while, for the next thing Bart was aware of was pounding. He thought it was the sound of his heart pounding in his ears. But the sound grew steadily louder and more insistent. Lasker's heart seemed to be beating in rhythm to the shaking of the universe. His face was burning hot. Visions of an exploding plane, blinding snowfields, and faces in torchlight passed before his eyes. Then he saw a dancing red light. He had opened his eyes to a campfire, saw seated figures. They were pounding on large skin-headed drums with long sticks. It wasn't his heartbeat, it was drumming that he heard.

Warmer. He was under some blankets. Too warm. Bart struggled to push off their encumbering weight, to move his legs, his arms, but couldn't. He moaned.

No sooner had he stirred than a wrinkled, gray-haired woman knelt down beside him. She had a huge chunk of amber as a pendant on a silver bead necklace. Her hair was parted in the middle, and had small turquoises held in it somehow. The woman pulled the pelts and blankets up to his neck, and lifted his head. She put a steaming bowl to his lips. It smelled like stew. Thick soup with small chunks of meat in it. It was hot and burned his tongue but it felt so wonderful to eat. He was so hungry. When Bart had finished, the old woman wiped off his mouth and gently lowered his head. She walked off with the empty bowl.

As he turned his head to follow her movements, Bart realized he was wearing a heavy fur hat on his head, and that its flaps were over his ears. His ears tingled and burned—they were warming up.

Lasker waited awhile, then again tried to prop him-

80

self up on one elbow. He succeeded with some difficulty. His head seemed to weigh a ton. His fever-blurred eyes went slowly into focus. As his vision cleared, he was able to make out that, some distance from the fire he was lying near, faintly outlined by the campfire's glow, there were several circular tents. Bart could see a little fire within one, through the weave. There were yaks nibbling at some short brown grass, and some small black-and-white longhorn cattle too. Or maybe they were goats? Lasker let his head fall back on the pillow of fur.

The men who were drumming began chanting now, strange chants, sonorous, slow. Who were these people that he was among? Simple shepherds wouldn't be so heavily armed, would they? Bart still couldn't dismiss the possibility that they might be bandits. But if they were, why hadn't they taken what they could and left him to die? In the cold night air, even thinking proved to be too much for Lasker. One thought passed though his mind as he snuggled down under the heavy blankets. He was *warm*.

While the stranger slept, Cheojey, the doctor-monk, prepared medicines. Sitting by the campfire, as the others watched him work, he opened several bags, and from one took some sediment of wormwood, and from another some precious lama bone. He put them in a small pan of water and set it to boil over the edge of the fire. The men who were gathered round made comments, asked questions, and one in particular—Rinchen Sondup—grew impatient. Rinchen said, "You are wasting expensive medicines that we ourselves need on this stranger, Lama Cheojey." Rinchen began stirring the fire with a stick, causing sparks to fly up.

81

"No, keep the fire low," the monk asked. "The medicine must not become too hot."

"Why make medicine for the foreign devil? Bah—" He spat in the fire.

"Rinchen," Cheojey replied, stirring the brew. "It is the Buddhist way—to treat strangers with compassion."

"We are at war, there is no time for mercy," snapped Rinchen. "I say, kill him now." Sparks flew as he again jabbed his stick in the fire for emphasis. He viewed this with satisfaction, then standing abruptly, he asked, "What say you, Tsering?"

Lama Cheojey looked at the leader of the rebel band known as the Snow Lions.

Tsering Gangshar stared with his one good eye into the campfire coals for a long time. Finally he sighed and said, "We will determine if the stranger is a friend as soon as he is well enough to be questioned. If he doesn't recover, we won't have to kill him, which saves a stain on our karma. If he does recover, it will not take long to find out whether he is truly friend. We are now less than twenty li from Chaar-lum, where resides someone that speaks this south-of-the-mountains tongue the stranger uses. And the all-wise *Rimpoche* there will know if the stranger speaks true."

Tsering's word was final. Rinchen grunted acknowledgment of this. Lama Cheojey smiled in secret triumph. Tsering was a compassionate man. Given the circumstances of great hardship and war, he followed the way of compassion as much as possible.

Cheojey continued preparing the elixir of restoring life. He poured out the small amount of boiled sediment of wormwood and lama bone and added it to the contents of his third pouch—cured snake venom and grinds of pomegranite. He rolled the resulting mixture into little black pills. After a poultice was applied, to draw off the pain of the injuries, and some mantras of purification were chanted, *maybe* the stranger would recover.

He would start treatment when next the stranger awoke. But he'd need his wooden sorcerer's scepter. Cheojey rose and went to the shrine tent to fetch it.

Bart was awake once more. He watched a figure come out of one of the tents and walked purposefully toward him. As the shape approached near the fire, Lasker could see the maroon of his robe. The monk.

The old man took Lasker's pulses again. He pulled Lasker's eyelids down and stared searchingly into his eyes. The monk stuck out his tongue as he pressed down on the corners of Lasker's mouth. Lasker got the message, and stuck out his tongue, which the monk perused carefully. The monk then took something out of a small intricately carved silver box. It was a stick of some sort. Lasker couldn't quite make it out. The monk walked around him shaking the thing and uttering strange sounds in rhythm to the drums. Well, Bart thought, what did he expect—aspirin?

The old woman reappeared carrying a mortar and pestle. She sat nearby and began to grind up some meal to which the monk, who had stopped his gyrations, added some dried twigs and herbs. To this he added some liquid from a heated pot fetched from the fire. More grinding with the pestle. Then the results formed a paste. The old woman proudly showed Lasker this. The monk wrapped the paste in a cloth and applied it to Lasker's forehead gash. It was soothingly cool at first, and then caused his forehead to tingle with a pleasing sensation.

Exhausted from the trek, and weak with fever, Bart drifted off. He was vaguely aware of being lifted onto a pelt and being carried stretcher-style into a tent. Once Lasker was placed inside, he was covered with more wool blankets and pelts. The darkness of the tent, the satisfying warmth in his belly, the sound of the drums, lulled Lasker. But he struggled to stay awake.

Lasker took a good look around him while he was left alone. The floor of the tent was covered with woven mats. A brick-and-stone shrine of some sort was in the center of the tent, a shrine with a bronze statue of a bull-horned, many armed demon on it. A carved cup sat in front of it. The candlelight—or rather light from some sort of flame floating in a votive bowl—illuminated it eerily. There was something about that carved cup . . .

Lasker gasped. It was a skull, a skull with its top chopped clean off—not a cup at all. It was a *human* skull. Cannibals! He nearly gagged. A sickening nausea went through him.

Lasker remembered Joe, the airport attendant at Phiyang telling him, ". . . *they come at night over the mountains, carrying the statues of their demon gods on their backs. They make human sacrifice . . .*"

Were they saving him for sacrifice? Was that why they didn't kill him right away? He had to get up, get out of here—

A dark shadow fell over the tent. The tent flap opened. In came the old woman followed by the monk. He was carrying a wooden bowl filled with something liquid. He put it close to Lasker's face, and he caught the smell—rancid, horrible. Was it a drug to put him in a stupor before he was disemboweled, sacrificed to their demon, *eaten?*

Lasker turned his head violently to the side when he felt the bowl at his lips, spilling some of the contents on his neck. "No," he shouted. "No, I won't drink."

The bowl was withdrawn. Words passed between the robed old man and the woman.

Lasker's heart pounded. If he could only get—up. He struggled, fell back.

The monk set the cup of brew down on the mat beside him and once again took Lasker's pulse on both wrists. Then the monk pulled back the heavy pelts and blankets and examined his wounds. Lasker tried to get a hold of himself. Maybe the foul brew was medicine—but what of that demon? His eyes went to the bronze figure caught in the flickering light.

Apparently his wide-eyed, frightened stare at the statue caught the robed man's attention, for he shook his head and said, *"Thokpo—Sangye—Buddha."* He smiled benevolently down at Lasker.

"Buddha?" Lasker asked. Did he mean he was a Buddhist? "Buddha? Are you Buddhists?" Lasker knew Buddhists don't kill or sacrifice people—or animals.

*"Buddha,"* the robed old man said again loudly, and raised his hand and gestured with it, pointing to a small shelf high up over the demon image. There Lasker saw a seated-Buddha statue. How had he missed it before?

*"Buddha—thokpo,"* the monk said, and stood up and moved his hand between the demon image and the Buddha. Did he mean the demon was a "friend" of the Buddha?

The monk came back and again raised the vicious black brew in the bowl to Lasker's lips. *"Buddha, thokpo,"* he said. The monk put the brew to his own lips and swallowed some.

Lasker understood the demonstration. And figured the man must be saying he was a Buddhist, and the liquid was not poison.

Oh well, Bart thought. I'm in his hands, have to trust someone sometime. He let the monk place the brew to his lips and drank some. Then the monk put a misshapen black pill on Bart's tongue. Lasker closed his eyes and swallowed, chased it down with a generous slug of the noxious brew. The monk patted Lasker's head as if he'd been a good boy. He picked up the empty bowl, adjusted the blankets, said something to the old woman who squatted herself down on a blanket nearby Lasker. Then the monk left him.

Lasker couldn't stay awake any longer.


*Down, down he fell through a black void. Visions of green, rustling curtains of green, smothering cloth over his face . . . the smothering cloth was pulled away—he was seated on something loathesome, something alive that squirmed under him. He dared not look down at it. He was in a dimly lit huge marble building. The towering green fire before him flared through a hole in the marble floor. Cowled figures in green marched before him, bearing pieces of human bodies—arms, legs, heads. Then Lasker was staring into one of those cowls, at the glowing red eyes in the blackness within. A cup was pressed to his lips. A skull-cap cup. It contained a green puss, green puss that he must drink for some reason, or die. Lasker tried not to drink, but a hand with an iron grip grasped and held Lasker's chin. The green-robed figure lifted the cup to Lasker's mouth, forcing him to drink a horrible-tasting liquid. He grew insensible after the first sip, consuming the rest of the liquid. He wanted more, he growled out a request. It was not his voice—it was a demon animal's cry. The assemblage of cowled figures laughed at the sound. The one who had made him drink now pulled down the cowl. He was Donnely, and he was laughing too.*

*"You want more, Lasker?" Donnely taunted. Lasker growled, whined, begged piteously. "Then have more," Donnely smirked. The green-robed figures came at him, forcing more of the noxious liquid—liquid that would make him a monster—down his throat.*

*Lasker had to have it, he drank it thirstily, slobbering on himself, wimpering.*

*When he had drunk out of the last cup, the robed figures massed together. They moved forward, against him. They were on three sides of him, crowding him. Bart got up, and limped on clawed slimy feet, his own feet, toward the fire, toward the yawning bottomless pit of green flame. The flames began to lick at his naked cold monster's body. Donnely stepped forward, and with a tremendous shove, sent Lasker over the precipice. He was falling, falling . . .*

Lasker shouted, "No, no, Donnely, please don't— don't push me in."

Dolma Nima, the old woman who was seated nearby the stranger and was keeping an eye on him, looked up when he shouted in his barbarian tongue. She put down her *mala* beads, the 108-bead rosary that she had been reciting *Om Mani Padme Hum* with, one mantra for each bead. Was it the fever breaking? If so, he would need liquid—some tea.

The man stopped shouting and his eyes opened. He was breathing heavily. Perhaps he was having a nightmare. That often preceded a break in fever.

Dolma, saying soothing words, went to the stones with a small yak-chip fire in them, and lifted the kettle, poured him some tea.

Lasker knew it had just been a dream—he was still here, in the tent. The old woman came to him, with a cup. He was startled, then smelled the hot tea. He nodded and sipped some.

She felt his head. Her hand didn't feel cold to him now. Bart felt more clear-headed too. His fever must have gone. He felt a *lot* better, as a matter of fact, he decided. Maybe it was because of the black pills and other medicine.

"Thanks," he said. She put the teacup back on the rock stove and left him, after uttering something softly.

Lama Cheojey came back with Dolma and took the man's pulse again, and gave him some more of the life-restoring brew. The patient drank without resistance, smiled, and lay back. Dolma was right—he was much less feverish—but his pulses indicated he still was a long way from being fully recovered.

Cheojey was pleased the stranger had made progress, for he had added some unfamiliar herbs he'd picked the previous day to the medicinal brew, and was unsure of the outcome. After all, the metabolism of outlanders is not the same as that of a Tibetan. Who knew if they responded in the same way to treatment as *normal* people?

A good doctor, Cheojey was well versed in the three-body theory of disease and had been trained to tell the medicinal properties of various plants by touch, smell, and taste, and to gather them for making preparations. But he was not used to working in such primitive conditions. In the Lud-po monastery he had had a complete pharmacy with everything he needed—but the Communists had burned it down. He sighed. It was best not to think of such things now.

The stranger who fell from the sky was not used to this good climate, having come from the fetid too-heavy air of the lowlands. The special medicine ought to stimulate the channels of his central nerves, help fight the shock, and help him adjust to the thin Tibetan air and the rapid temperature change from day to night. The stranger's energy channels of bile and air would open up, hopefully, and let him live. But that was up to Sangye, the Buddha.

Their band of rebels, the Snow Lions, had to move on, regardless of whether or not the stranger was well, in a few days. If the patient could ride, the hot sun of this time of year, being out in the fresh air, could only help his health. But if he wasn't much improved by then, Rinchen might persuade Tsering that the Sky-man was too much of a nuisance. Then, despite all of Cheojey's efforts, he might be killed.

# Chapter 10

After a more restful, dreamless sleep, Bart awoke to the sun streaming in the open tent flap. The old woman who attended him came over and said something cheery. He felt the heavy pelt blankets sliding off his body. He sat up, tried to get on his feet, but was too weak.

The woman called out and the monk came in shortly. Together she and the monk managed to lift Lasker under his armpits to a standing position. It took all the wind out of Bart to stand, but it was worth it. Bart didn't feel feverish anymore, and the numb sensations in his extremities were gone.

Using the two helpers as human crutches, he limped out the open tent flap into the sunlight.

Several men sat by the burned-out campfire. A few faces turned to Lasker and his companions as they moved out of the tent and came towards them. He sat down knee-high on a flat stone.

Lasker was getting his first clear, daytime look at the men and women he was with. All were dressed much the same—sewn pelt jackets, turquoise jewelry. But one man, whom he heard called Tsering, had an additional distinction: His right eye had been replaced by a burnished copper coin, and a huge scar ran from that injury down his cheek and into the curls of fur of his lambskin jacket. He had two dirk handles sticking from his wide coral-encrusted belt, not one. He gesticulated and shouted out what Lasker interpreted as orders, and the men moved to take down the tents. Tsering's raven-feather headdress shook and the wings flopped open, as if the hat wanted to take flight, as he barked command. Apparently he was the leader.

The women were sturdy types, and possibly well built and comely under their smears of resin and their bulky garments. They wore woven dark blue or brown sleeveless dresses, down to their boots. They had necklaces that were composed of large chunks of coral and amber beads, and pink and silver beads strung through their tied-back hair. Two women had their hair woven up into huge coxcombs of multiple braids supporting headdresses of large blue-green stones.

It was a very well armed group, in a primitive way. By the burned-out fire were stacked some well-oiled but ancient single-bolt rifles, their wooden stocks carved with designs. The handles of pistols jutted from several of the men's belts. Axes and spears, and short daggers with uncut semiprecious stone handles were abundant.

The biggest fellow, the one that had wanted to run him through with the dagger the night before, came over and sat near Lasker. Bart tried not to look in his direction. The man took out a brown bag, opened it, shook out some powder and shoved it up his nostrils, then inhaled. Snuff? Lasker took a glance as he snorted—and caught the big menacing dark eyes. He kind of sneered at Lasker, then turned his head and sniffed some more of the powder.

Lasker was glad the brute had something to do to occupy himself. The monk dipped a ladle into a pot brewing on some still-hot coals and brought its contents to Lasker's lips, indicating that he should take some. It tasted like cereal with butter in it. Thick, hot, a bit rancid, but it also felt as if it were putting hair on his chest. He'd had worse.

He begged off more. He had an idea. Bart put his palm to his chest and said, "Lasker." He slapped his chest. The monk seemed to understand, and he touched his chest and said "Ch-e-ojey."

Bart smiled and repeated the name, "Cheojey."

The monk then gestured at the mean snuff-sniffing guy and said, "Rinchen."

Lasker was excited about the prospects of communication, but as the monk pointed out various objects—rocks, the fire—and pronounced words, his attention wavered. Cheojey pointed to a horse. "Ta," he said. "Ta," Lasker repeated. The horses were close by, not tied. They wandered and chewed on some scrubby weeds. Bart was a pretty good rider—of the riding academy variety. If he could run to the closest horse, the sorrel that looked so sturdy . . . then what? Where would he go even if he had the strength? Bart dismissed the thought. He had, after all, been treated well. He tried to relax.

The monk kept teaching him the names of things, until he was losing the first words. Then the monk waved his hand at the entire group, and made clawing motions in the air. Cheojey said a long sentence that Bart couldn't pronounce. He was mystified by what Cheojey meant. Then there were guttural snarls from Rinchen. Probably meant, "Don't bother with the bastard," or something like that.

The one pointed out as Tsering came over and squatted next to Lasker and talked to the monk. Lasker somehow got an impression of calm and reason from the groups leader—he wasn't sure quite how. Tsering turned his black bead single eye to Lasker and asked

92

something. He made gestures of flying with his hand, and Tsering's wide lips created a sort of buzz.

"Yes, I'm from an airplane," Bart said. He made a flying gesture.

Then Tsering pointed several different ways. Bart got the idea—he wanted to know where Good Baby went down. Bart took his best guess and pointed toward the triple-humped mountain on the western horizon. Maybe if they found all that gold—if it wasn't dribbled out across half of Tibet—it would make them appreciate him a bit more. Maybe not. One problem was the Chinese markings on the plane. If the painted-on flags were still visible, if and when they found Good Baby, what would they make of them?

Tsering stood up and called out several names. "Thubten! Khumbun! Jamyang!" Three strapping young men came over. Tsering gestured in the direction Lasker had indicated, giving instructions. The young men got their sturdy mule-like horses and set off in that direction.

Lasker spent a long time on that flat rock by the fire. The warmth of the sun—surprisingly hot when you consider the night temperature—seemed to energize him. Cheojey put a few more clumps of—looked like yak dung—on the coals. The old woman put a pot on the coals and Lasker and the others had a porridgy meal. The Tibetan men then retired to groom their horses and roll up the tents. Evidently they were getting ready to move on.

Shortly after the sun reached its zenith, the monk doctor again drew Lasker's attention. Another language lesson. Cheojey started holding things up—cup, bowl, and so on, and reciting words. Lasker was a poor student. Nevertheless, they spent the next few hours doing this.

Later in the afternoon, while this show-and-tell was

still going on, Rinchen gave a loud shout. The big man pointed at some dots on the far defile. The young men that had ridden off that morning were returning, and all three of their horses were tied with bundles.

Tsering stood up and rushed toward the riders. They came galloping in, excited. And Lasker knew why. Their sacks must have been filled with money.

When the riders dismounted, they cut loose the sacks. One was opened. Tsering stuck his hand in and lifted a handful of gold coins and seared renminbao notes, to the awed voices of those gathered around him. All eyes turned to the American. Then one of the other sacks were open—a piece of the door of the plane, and on it, the Chinese red flag with five yellow stars.

He could tell by the looks he was getting that they didn't like the flag one bit.

"No," Lasker shouted, "I am not with the Chinese. It was a trick—to get into Tibet." Of course they didn't understand him.

Tsering snapped out something. His indecipherable words were soon translated into action. Two stalwart smelly lads came over with rope and tightly pulled Lasker's hands behind his back. Rinchen shouted and made a gesture of cutting a throat. He pulled his short blade out—and made for Bart. But Tsering grabbed him, and told him something. The monk joined the argument, aiming gestures toward Lasker, and smiling a lot. Lasker heard the word *Sangye,* the local word for Buddha, he had gathered. Rinchen walked disgustedly away, muttering. The lad let Lasker go.

Rinchen stormed over to the sorrel-colored horse and started saddling it. Evidently the broad squat beast was his. It had silver-looking stirrups and bridle. Rinchen was the goddamned Lone Ranger of Tibet, it seemed. All the other bridles were plain.

The sacks were tied to the youth's horses again, except one sack, which Tsering spilled out. It contained some pieces of half-burned papers. Tsering went through the charred remnants with a stick. He lifted something, a dark half-burned green piece of paper.

*Please God,* Lasker thought, let it be—yes it was—his international driver's license. It had been jammed under the seat, in the leather folder. The license had his picture on it.

Tsering examined the printing, exclaimed, "Englisher," and smiled.

"Yes," Bart exclaimed, "it's English, I'm an American, *American,* that's right. I'm a friend, *thokpo,* like your monk buddy said." On an inspiration, remembering Losang's name for Tibet, he said, "*Thokpo—Khawachen,* friend of Tibet."

Lasker sensed again the great intelligence behind Tsering's coarse mutilated features, in the depths of that single dark eye over the high resin-smeared cheekbones. He repeated the words, tried a smile.

Tsering half smiled back, handing Lasker the burned license. Damn, that was some improvement. Bart really was just guessing at their loyalties. But *Englisher* had seemed to bring a smile, seemed to have some weight in a positive direction. These rugged men must be rebels, anti-Chinese, after all.

The big black hair tents were rolled up and packed onto the yaks. Lasker was tied, hands behind his back, to his great dismay, and rode on one of the young women's horses. She held the reins. The several sacks of gold got a yak to themselves, ridden by the old woman, Dolma. Tsering rode his horse to Lasker's left, Rinchen to his right. An honor guard.

Where the hell were they going? Lasker noted that everyone took turns riding the horses, and no one except Dolma, the oldest, rode any of the yaks or odd long-horned black-and-white cows Cheojey called *dzo-*

*mos*. The animals kind of moved along by themselves, but occasionally a rider directed them, if they tarried, with a sticks and sharp commands.

Lasker had seen what some of their other loads were—sacks of barley and blocks of—was it butter?—and he smelled cheese, lots of rancid squares of cheese. There were burlap bags that smelled of pungent tea bricks too. This was a fully loaded small caravan, on their way to some market. And market probably meant Chinese.

His heart sank. But then he noticed something. They seemed intent on not making a lot of noise. Anytime a pot or pan started clinking, it was tied down more securely.

He was sore all over, sore as he had never been in his life, and his back ached at each bump of the big-shouldered animal along the trail. He tried to concentrate on the awesome scenery. There was nothing else to do.

Were they taking him to the Chinese? What would he say when some English-speaking interrogator asked what the hell he was doing here? "Sorry, my plane got lost"? That wouldn't be so hot. Damn, what could he say? "I want to talk to the U.S. Counsel." There, that was better. "I *demand* to be released to the custody of the U.S. Ambassador."

Better yet. In any case, these people weren't toting the Red Chinese line. There were no pictures of Mao, no little red books of Mao's sayings. And there was a Buddha statue. Lasker had a dim memory of reading that the Chinese forbade the worship of Buddha in Tibet after they took over, that the Chinese persecuted the Buddhist religion. He must be with people who were, if not actively opposing the Chinese, at least not sympathetic to them.

The caravan proceeded onward, heading west, down

a dry canyon. Lasker watched the walls of layered multicolor sedimentary rock move by. This fantastic winding terrain reminded him of Utah, but high above was a line of sky so deep blue that it looked closer to black. The Mica-impregnated cliffs that caught the white sun high above glistened like diamonds.

After an hour, they left the winding canyon, and ascended on a twisting precipitous trail along the side of a mountain. It was the equal to, if not higher than, the peaks he had smashed the plane into.

Damn, were they going to the top? It got steeper and he could see the trail narrowed. The sure-footed animals didn't flinch, though occasionally the hooves of one would dislodge small rocks that would tumble away into the abyss. Bart never heard them hit bottom. Where the hell were they headed? He stared intently ahead, hoping they would soon be over the top. It was cold again, bitterly cold. His head ached, and so did his chest. He felt as if he had lead weights on his legs—

The altitude. They must be way over fifteen thousand. How did they take it?

Amber and alabaster cliffs glowed in the low sun to the east and contrasted to the white frost on the sunlit peak ahead of them. Finally, the caravan reached the top. Mist shrouded the path of the descent ahead. The other side of the mountain, Bart found, was not granite, but black basalt in appearance. It proved even more slippery and slower-going. They descended through the clouds, and he breathed easier. Also, there was a warm mist.

The source of the mists and heat soon became visible. A hot spring bubbling into a tree-filled valley. It was almost worth being a captive of these rough men to see such beauty. Above the steamy verdant valley, in perfect impossible contrast, a blue-white glistening wall of glacial ice hung precariously from the other slope. The melting glacial ice created a thousand-foot-high waterfall that plunged into the hot bubbling stream below it.

Tsering came up alongside Lasker when the trail leveled off. He seemed amused at Bart's awed expression. His black eye winked, as if to indicate, "Yes, I know, it's beautiful."

They rode onto the floor of the lush valley, past clumps of monstrous red rhododendrons and violet wildflowers and pink crysanthemum-type blooms, a man's height easily.

The monk was exclaiming here and there, slowing his horse, leaning out and snipping various blooms and buds and stuffing them into his saddlebags. Occasionally he would taste one twig or another, or one flower, and then either spit it out or stuff it in his bag. Once or twice he called out and stopped the whole group. He dismounted and picked some sample of plant or dug up the root of some odd flower—again as always shoving it into various colored sacks, and the sacks into the saddlebags. Herbal remedies perhaps.

The sun was creating a rainbow in the mists rising from the interaction of the icy waterfall and the hot springs ahead. The group went down the mile-long length of the valley, riding along the stream of warm water. Then they began once again climbing, though not as steeply.

The sky started to boil with black clouds, and a cold wind whipped at their clothing. Then the sky suddenly was rent by lightning; hailstones started to pummel down. The scene was turned nearly totally dark, on the turn of a few seconds.

Evidently Lasker wasn't the only one alarmed. The leader of the group, shouting, pointed toward the cliffside to the left of their ascent. The pace quickly picked up as the storm's darkness intensified. Lasker's body

98

was pelted with golf-ball-sized ice balls, grit, and pebbles whipped up by the cyclonic winds.

What sort of shelter was Tsering heading for? He saw nothing. Perhaps a hidden cave? Lasker's horse was pulled along so fast he dug his heels into his mount to stay on. They were halfway up the slippery shale toward the indicated spot when the full fury of the storm hit.

Titanic peals of thunder, multiple flashes of lightning rent the heavens. The hailstones slacked off and a titanic downpour took its place. Tsering's horse entered a rock overhang behind some brambles that couldn't have been more than a few feet deep. But it was something. Lasker heard a grinding, scraping noise. *Loud.*

To the left, heading their way, was a wall of mud, a mass of rumbling certain death, perhaps eight feet high!

# Chapter 11

Rinchen was the next to disappear under the rock overhang. Bart was surprised that this rider, too, was immediately swallowed up by the shadows. Evidently the overhang was deeper than it appeared. The rumbling mass of primordial ooze was now fifty feet closer—a few more seconds and it would swallow up all of them.

The yaks and dromos knew the danger, and strived to reach the sanctuary first. A wild scramble up to the brambles began, Lasker kicking the sides of his horse, the unmounted men and women making a surprisingly rapid sprint toward hoped-for safety.

Lasker's mount plunged into the stygian darkness after the others, just as the ooze slopped at the horse's hooves. He was in total darkness, yet the animal somehow sensed where it was going, for it kept moving forward, and upward.

Shouts and animal cries filled the blindness. Tsering—Lasker had gotten to recognize his rough voice—shouted out commands. The wall of mud could be heard grinding by where they had just been.

Then the fearsome clamor slowly died. All that was heard was the downpour. Someone had dismounted, found a bit of tinder in his bag, and sparked away. A torch ignited. Bart could see, not that there was much to see except uneven rock walls. A cavern. The animals had reached its end and, perhaps aware that the danger had passed, quieted down.

The gangly youth called Yarang was bent down, intent on producing a fire with the torch. Soon the flame caught in the tinder he had extracted from a bag. Yarang blew on it. As the smoky flames grew, larger sticks came out from packs and were placed in the small fire on the cave floor.

Bart was coughing from the dust raised by the animals, and from the smoke, which filled the air. The Polyphemus-like Tibetan leader, taking pity, helped Bart from his saddle and even untied his hands. Torches moved forward, the caravaners evidently anxious to explore their sanctuary. He followed along, mostly to escape the smoke.

There was an eeriness about being in here, with the echoes of every whisper amplified a hundredfold. They entered a wider area, and there was—Bart gasped.

They were in a circular smooth chamber carved out of the living rock of the mountain. A completely man-made area. Under their feet were stone tiles, neatly fitted together, irregular in size. The smooth walls had shadowy niches in them from floor to ceiling, which arched some thirty feet above them. Tsering brought his torch forward to reveal that each three-foot circular niche contained a statue of an extremely thin man. There were dozens of such niches, and each one held a statue, carved directly from the rock.

Lasker was not alone in his surprise and wonderment. Indeed, the reaction was widespread and immediate. Tsering and the monk and most of the others—but not Rinchen—fell to the stone floor and prostrated themselves three times before the images.

Then the caravan leader picked up a torch and proceeded further into the shadows at the far end of the chamber. His flame soon illuminated a much larger statue, a six- or seven-foot-high thin figure. A man with a stone crown much like that of a European king. The elongated figure was smiling, sitting like the smaller versions, cross-legged on a stylized lotus blossom foundation. This statue, however, had one additional point of interest: it had a single glowing rough-cut diamond in the middle of its forehead. Bart thought, If it's really a diamond, it could fetch over a million dollars. Suddenly he was much more interested in exactly where they were in Tibet, and wondering if he could find this place again.

Immediately, several of the women rushed to join the discoverer, clutching joss sticks. They set them up in the sand before the statue and lit them, bowing and saying hurried prayers—probably of thanksgiving.

There was now noticeable a small sound. The trickle of a stream of water along one wall, which investigation proved the case. There was also a pile of dusty firewood. All the comforts of home.

The animals were left in the natural cave, and the Tibetans set up a clean-burning fire in the center of the circular cave. They started wringing out their sopping clothes, and Lasker started doing much the same. He must have looked miserable, dripping wet and coughing.

He sat as close to the flames as possible, nearly singeing his boot fronts, shivering despite a blanket over him.

Soon the buttered tea was prepared—water from the stream and chunks of brick tea put in a pot on the fire. When it was brewed, one of the younger women, called Tenpa, who, Lasker had deduced, was married to Tsering, leaned over and dropped in chunks of burned barley. Bart noticed, when she threw back her long wet hair, that Tenpa was quite comely—aquiline nose, smooth light-coffee complexion. The downpour had washed all concealing resin off her face.

Soon the hearty mixture was passed around in a communal earthen bowl. Bart, raw to the bone, drank heartily. He surreptitiously watched the young Tibetan woman, now shorn of her outer garments of coarse wool. He could see her figure clearly, lithe and graceful. Her features were smooth and regular, high cheekbones, mysterious gentle dark eyes. She turned her face away when she noticed he was staring.

The monk leaned over to address Dolma, the old woman, and they both giggled, gesturing at Lasker. Evidently they had observed *him* observing Tenpa.

Lasker's eyes, once they were off the Tibetan woman, were again drawn to the far end of the cavern, where the big statue was invisible, the giant diamond glinting in the orange light cast by the fire. Avarice was no doubt written for all to see upon his face. Bart tried not to look at the large stone image too much. But he vowed to remember every detail about the cave's location when they left this place. If the circumstances permitted, he would pry that gem of all gems loose and hide it in his clothing before they left. And thus make his fortune in one fell swoop.

Very shortly, they were all bone dry. At this extreme altitude moisture evaporated almost immediately. The furs and blankets were put down and they lay down and rested. Lasker couldn't close his eyes. The eye of the idol filled them. He listened to the wind howl outside. The warmth of the fire eventually made him very sleepy though. His sore body cried out for his mind to let it rest.

And then it happened: From out of the far depths of the cavern came an eerie high-pitched noise—a voice, singing something. Lasker bolted upright and looked over at the shadows by the stone idol. The wild song ceased. Footsteps. Rinchen, and a second behind him two other men, pulled out their swords. All waited breathlessly.

The footfalls continued, the unseen intruder coming closer. They were soft steps, like a barefoot child's. Lasker saw a figure come into the torchlight, dimly. It was gray and wraithlike and had three legs.

Several women screamed—and the men all jumped up—holding their swords at the ready. The wraith stepped closer, became a human, a very diminutive human that rushed closer into view. It was a bedraggled scrawny old man. He began shouting and gesticulating with a knobby walking stick—the third leg.

Rinchen laughed, put back his sword into the scabbard. The ancient, shriveled, rag-clad man spat out indignations. He lifted the knotty cane and swung it forward, swooshing it at the assembled refugees from the storm. Evidently he didn't like company. His rotted teeth and near nakedness, beneath a long gray beard and masses of filthy hair, were startling. He looked quite awful. But unself-consciously and apparently unafraid, the little man kept moving forward, continuing his tirade.

Tsering stepped forward to block him, grabbed the cane. He seemed surprised that the old man was able to hold on to it. He must have had great strength. He began pushing Tsering toward the crevice entrance, shouting "Get out, I was here first," or something of that nature, Bart supposed.

Surprisingly, the leader of the caravan let go of the cane, and spoke back quietly, respectfully. He allowed the ragman to tug him by one sleeve to the entrance crevice as Lasker and several others tagged along. Tsering was pushed between the animals and almost ejected. Tsering, in the wind of the entrance, made motions to the sky, evidently saying the weather was too bad to leave.

The hermit—or whatever he was—shouted some angry expletives and again pushed Tsering. They were close enough to the outside that the cold wind fluttered the ragman's long tangled hair. Why did Tsering let himself be treated this way?

The caravan leader continued to speak to the hermit apologetically, with broad gestures. The hermit seemed to ask a question, pointed to the rest of them. Tsering answered, held out his hands with the palms together gesture of pleading, and actually got down on his knees before the hermit.

The hermit stepped half into the crevice, his wild hair flying in the icy wind. He started humming loudly, remarkably loudly, it seemed to Lasker, for an old man. But perhaps the acoustics amplified his voice. In any case the old man's gnarled filthy fingers started making the oddest motions, interlocking and bending as he hummed. He held them up above him, jabbing at the sodden patch of sky visible in the entranceway. His fingers worked in more elaborate patterns—mudras—while he sang. Every one of them stared silently at his actions. Tsering kept his position at the man's knees. In a few minutes the storm winds died down, and his hair stopped flying about. In another few minutes, sunlight actually streamed in the crack.

The hermit put down his hands, and cackled in a satisfied way. Gesturing for Tsering to rise, which he did, the hermit then turned and walked past the astonished onlookers, back into the dark recesses of the cave. Lasker saw him slip behind the idol with the diamond in its forehead, and disappear.

Bart's mind was blown—was the change in the weather a coincidence? The storm had come up as quickly as it had died down. Had the mad, naked man actually stopped it? Whatever the case, to Tsering's sharp commands, the tired group quickly packed up its gear and left. They didn't bind Lasker, but they never let him out of their sight.

The caravan, skirting the caking mud via a high trail, again headed west. They traveled for hours, until the white pearl sun was already half below the distant peaks, barely illuminating the ice tops with red. Then he saw the place that must be their goal.

It was a sight to behold. There on the precipitously steep escarpment of the mountain facing them, like some sort of a medieval vision, some sort of fairy structure, was a Lamist monastery. It consisted of a dozen multistoried, terraced buildings, whitewashed with red-and-brown beaming, clinging to the very rock of its mountain, an integral part of it. Its many cantilevered roofs, each with a dozen points of gold catching the setting sun, beckoned to him. *Civilization.* A seat of learning, of religion. Safety, shelter. A way home.

The caravan wended its way along the twisting narrow path among upthrust spires of rock. The sound of raging rapids grew louder as they approached and Bart soon saw the red sandstone chasm that gaped between them and their destination.

How were they ever to get across? It wasn't long before he found the solution, albeit a disturbing one: like a spindly coarse set of spider threads, there was a bridge. It was four fist-thick woven ropes, loosely strung across the 300-foot-wide abyss, so that the ropes hung down some thirty or so meters closer to the raging waters. Lasker felt a sinking feeling in his gut—surely they didn't intend that they walk across on the ropes— how could you keep your footing? How about the animals? And yet there was no other avenues of progress to the monastery.

# Chapter 12

Suddenly, two shaven-headed young boys material-
ized out of thin air, on the cliff's edge. They were
dressed in robes of coarse maroon similar to Cheojey's
outfit. They shouted, *"Tashi Delek,"* and came forward. Tsering talked to them, gesturing at the pack
animals and horses. Each boy nodded and they lifted
conch shells tied at their waists to their lips. They
started blowing them. A long high vibration surprisingly loud. In a moment, from across the abyss, somewhere in the monastery, a conch horn responded
wailfully.

The boys took charge of the animals, and herded
them some distance down along the cliff. Lasker could
discern several other yaks grazing there—each animal
had several colored ribbons tied to its horns.

Rinchen came over to Bart and shoved him toward
the ropes—making sounds suggesting he wanted him
to start across. Bart said, "No way, *you* go," and gestured accordingly.

There was much laughter as Dolma and Tsering's
wife, Tempa, brushed past both men. Dolma first put
her feet upon the lower rope, her hands holding onto
both top ropes. She and Tempa, who followed her,

107

made rapid progress and were soon well out above the foaming rapids.

Bart was amazed. The "bridge" as they came close to its midpoint, dropped a good twenty feet closer to the rapids. The thick ropes, attached to some pines on either side of the abyss, creaked ominously. Still Dolma and Tempa continued on undaunted, like a pair of practiced tightrope walkers. Only once did the younger of the two wobble so much that her body bounced on the taut side rope. They were, in a few moments, on the other side. They started shouting and waving, encouraging the next person to come across.

Lasker plunged ahead—"If you can make it, so can I." He rushed out about ten feet with abandon, and then made the mistake of looking down. He froze then started backing off. But his rear end was met by Rinchen's sword tip. With much laughter, they both managed to cross, the ropes stabilized by Rinchen as Lasker wobbled this way and that.

All the way across, Lasker was yelling, "Donnely, I'm going to live through this! I'm coming to get you, you hear me, Donnely? You did it to me again, and I'm gonna get you!"

The process of crossing was repeated behind Lasker, until all were across.

The entourage continued the journey. It was a good thousand-foot climb on the winding narrow cobbled path to the monastery's huge wooden gate, which was shut tight. A sonorous conch shell blew again inside. And then Lasker heard drums, the accompaniment of many chimes and cymbals and gongs. A welcoming serenade?

The lamasary looming ahead was really a remarkable sight. On the white walls he could now see long pennants furling in the wind, and occasionally, as they approached, he spied a lone shaven-headed saffron-robed monk standing at the top of the battlement to the right of the massive wooden door, watching them. Then the watcher monk disappeared. Shortly after he departed from his perch, the huge wooden gate slowly opened. Some maroon-robed boys came out and waved.

Lasker, as they got closer, began to hear voices, hundreds of low throaty utterances in cadence, amid the wild drumbeats and cymbals. The caravaners increased their pace. They soon entered through the gateway and Lasker found himself in a wide, sandy courtyard.

A red-pillared temple of squarish 150-by-150-foot dimensions, perhaps two stories high, three at its center, faced them. Many shaven-headed young boys in coarse maroon robes, gathered silently around them. No girls.

Tsering came over to Lasker and gestured him forward. They walked up the steps of the temple. The temple was basically a roof held by many closely packed columns. Bart saw flickering candlelight in the dark interior, and hundreds of seated monks, half lost in thick clouds of incense seated on the floor.

Apparently their quiet entrance caused no disturbance to the ceremony.

One of the hundred or so monks seated facing the three statues at the temple's far end turned his head. He took quiet note of them, gathered his robe, and stood up, heading their way. Tsering, when the monk reached his side, leaned to his ear and spoke. The monk moved off, disappearing among the pillars.

The one-eyed caravan leader and Lasker stood there, in that other-wordly temple, waiting for what seemed like ten minutes. Finally, a thin young monk-boy, wearing the first western gear Lasker had seen since his fall from the sky—a red nylon down vest—came to them. He looked at Bart intently and smiled. *"Sprechen Sie Deutsch?"*

Bart shrugged, dug into his minute knowledge of the German language, and said, *"Nein. Verstais*—English?"

The boy smiled, "Yessir, I do understand English."

"Thank God," Bart said. "Tell these people I am an American, that I must get back to India as soon as possible."

The boy spoke in Tibetan to Tsering. Then he said, "Tsering wants us to walk—so that we don't disturb the puja when we discuss further."

They went back down the stairs and into the courtyard, a dozen boys solemnly following at a distance. Lasker poured out a succinct version of all that had happened to him.

"Tsering will tell the others," the boy promised. "Do not fear, the Rimpoche will verify your story and all will be well. We are Buddists, sworn to help all sentient beings in whatever way we can. My name is Tinley Norbu, what is your name, American?"

Lasker told the boy his name. "How come you speak English?"

"I am of the Sherpa. My father was guide to many expeditions on Chomolongma—you call it Mt. Everest. He was killed last year in a fall, and I was sent here by my mother, to become a monk. I will do so and pray for my father. You will be made comfortable, you can stay here tonight. Then perhaps tomorrow, when the puja is over, you can speak to Shemer Rimpoche."

"Shemer Rimpoche is the head lama?"

"Yes."

"Can't I speak to him now?"

"Tomorrow. The ceremony will go on all night," the boy said. "It is the festival of Marpa, who is very

110

important. It is very auspicious that you come at this time."

"Are there—Chinese here?"

"No. Don't worry. We will hide you from the Chinese. Do you need to eat or drink?"

"No, I'm fine."

"Then it would be beneficial for you to sit with us for a while and listen to the puja—it will be a blessing to you."

"What is a puja?"

"It is a ceremony, to benefit all beings. This particular one calls the hungry ghosts from their terrible rounds in the afterlife, so that they might come learn the dharma, and be in the presence of the Rimpoche and receive his blessings."

"Oh."

Lasker and the boy had walked a long circle around the perimeter of the courtyard, and now climbed the steps again. Tinley spoke to Cheojey, who came to join them.

Lasker tapped Tinley on the shoulder. "Tell Cheojey that I am grateful for his medicine and for his help."

The boy spoke to the monk, who nodded and smiled. He said something to Lasker, which Tinley translated as, "Cheojey-la says you are most welcome. And he adds that he is sure you are to be pleased with your interview with Shemar Rimpoche. He will know how to help you get home. His Buddhist lineage—the Purple Hats—are very clairvoyant."

Lasker was told to remove his boots. They sure looked strange there, those two hiking boots in the pile of strange multicolored Tibetan monks boots on the portico of the immense smoke-filled lamasery temple. Evidently he had to accept their offer to sit in on the goings-on, whatever they were. At least it would be a

111

bit warmer among all those closely packed bodies, out of the wind. The temperature, Bart had found, dropped like a meteor at dusk.

They entered and Lasker's eyes had a tough time adjusting to the dark. Tinley walked alongside, tapped him on the arm, and pointed to some small red cushions that were piled near a red wooden pillar. Tinley whispered, "Take one." Lasker did. Lasker and the others took a place on the stone flooring at the back of the crowd of monks sitting in rigid lotus position. Tinley put his pillow down, leaving room on his right for Lasker. Lasker sat on his cushion American Indian style, cross-legged. No way was he going to try the ankle-busting double lotus position. He noted that Tinley and Tsering took half-lotus positions, and Cheojey slipped into the steadying full lotus.

Tsering sat to his left and Cheojey just beyond that. They faced in the same direction as the monks, squared off to the front of the temple.

When the fog of incense parted for a while, Bart could get a look at the three gilded statues at the front—in the flickering butterlamps were also many smaller statues of diverse deities, some quite sexually explicit, locked in embrace. All had some manner of dress as if they were real people—hats and robes and garlands—all had scarves, dozens of them, draped over their shoulders. The two side statues were apparently figures representing some man of ancient times, not remarkable except for their exquisite detail. But the biggest statue, in the middle, was a three-headed god with the clinging female consort impaled upon its golden penis. The three-headed one had golden necklaces and bangles of silver skulls. It had dozens of arms—all holding something—cleavers, swords, pickaxes.

These people were definitely *not* Midwestern protestants, Bart thought.

To the left side of the statues was a high platform, and a man in a brocaded robe sat there so unmovingly that Lasker had thought he, too, was one of the statues. But now he moved, shook some sort of scepter. On his head was a peaked purple hat like a cloth version of a Roman centurion's metal helmet. That must be Shemer Rimpoche, Lasker realized.

The man in the gold brocade robe put the scepter or whatever it was down and picked up and started manipulating a drum rattle like a child's toy in one hand, rolling it back and forth to make its little hammers hit the tightly drawn skin. In the other hand he grasped a bell of a very high pitch, which he rung seemingly at random intervals.

Bart looked around at the assemblage. These monks were a cool unaffected lot, he thought. His appearance must be way out of the ordinary around these parts but few had even cast a glance his way. Perhaps they were in some sort of trance. This music could get to you. He was falling asleep already.

The Rimpoche's noisy little demonstration suddenly ceased. And so did the drumming and gongs. All was silent, for a long time. No one moved. He was just about to ask Tinley what was happening when the boy leaned over and said, "You will like this next part— the chantmaster and his monks are well known throughout the province. They are from the Gyutok monastery—they sing quite beautifully."

True to the boy's words, there entered a set of six saffron-robed, bare-headed monks, all holding what looked like octagonal hat boxes. They all sat down to the side, at right angles to the guy on the throne. The new arrivals adjusted their robes, then opened their boxes on their little lacquer tables and took out some flat objects. These they unfolded into red-and-blue stiff octagonal hats with brass ornaments on top, in the shape of flames. They put them on. Lasker was reminded of the mortar boards college graduates wear.

The oldest monk took an ordinary hen's egg from his robe and leaned over and placed it in front of him. The Gyutok chanters spent a good deal of time settling themselves, adjusting their robes in more comfortable positions, and then finally, cymbals crashed. They started chanting, the oldest monk of the new arrivals starting first, singing in such a low tone that Lasker's ears hurt. Then somehow, the old monk joined his first note with a second tone that harmonized on some weird frequency. The other monks cut in one at a time, adding their voices. Bart had never heard two-tone singing.

After a while, he whispered to Tinley, "What's the egg for? Do they worship it?"

Tinley smiled, cupped his hand to Lasker's ear, and whispered, "No, it's for concentrating upon. They cannot sing without the egg."

The low, drawn-out chanting died down after a while and the Rimpoche rattled his rattle drum again, and rang his extremely high-pitched little bell. Then there was utter silence. It didn't end. In a half hour Lasker imagined that he could actually hear the candles flames fluttering. He guessed they were all in silent meditation. He was bored. And after a while, it got colder, much colder. And a chill wind rose. He was feeling distinctly uncomfortable. Plus the incense seemed to grow more pungent, fanned by the damned icy wind. He sat coughing, a tickle in his throat, his feet and hands numb from the cold.

Then the chanting started up again, to the beat of a set of drums that the chanting monks had taken up. The show was on the road again. To take his mind off the chill, he got into listening to the new more strident dirge the monks were singing.

114

The chantmaster would recite something loudly in a sotto-basso voice, and then the whole hundred plus members of the all-male congregation responded in lengthy throaty mumbles.

Just when Bart couldn't take sitting in the increasing cold, and had decided to stand and leave, a burly monk came around among the sitters, and put blankets over selected individuals. Lasker wondered if the monk could tell who was cold and who wasn't. In any case, Lasker was on of the recipients of this kindness, and glad of it. All the comforts of home. Except rest. He sat and listened, but was falling asleep now. So from time to time he was jabbed by Tinley on the shoulder. "Sit up straight, Mr. Lasker, and you will be less tired," the boy whispered. "You will receive the blessing energy."

Lasker frowned. The only blessing he wanted was a feathered bed. In India—or better yet, in the U.S. with a private stopover on the way—of course—to pry that mega-diamond from the idol in the cave.

Bart closed his eyes. Soon he, too, was finally as still as the others. Lulled, lost in the incense and dimness of the temple, absorbed in the slow rhythm of the proceedings. But not asleep. He saw Jenny in his mind, and then Donnely. Then the thoughts stopped. Lasker just sat. No mind. No thought. Just being. Just relaxed, totally relaxed.

It was becoming light—the dawn—all of a sudden. How had he managed to sit here all this time? The eastern sky glowed like a red flame and beams of all colors illuminated the mountain peaks. A bird sang. A solitary bird, and that seemed to signal the ceremony's end. The Rimpoche took something from a small pot to his side and a monk, bowing first, came and took the invisible thing handed to him. It was passed back through the sitters, from hand to hand. Lasker couldn't imagine what the hell the microscopic thing was. But when he was handed it, he found it to be half a grain of rice. Somehow, when a monk passed him the tiny rice fragment and he took it in his fingers, it was a powerful emotional experience. Bart felt like sobbing, though he didn't have the slightest idea why. Perhaps he had fallen victim to some sort of spell.

The monks began to get up slowly, and shuffle out into the glorious red dawn. They filed out one row at a time, past the Rimpoche, who tapped the head of each monk with what looked like a long rubber-tipped stamper.

"Get in line with us for the blessing," Tinley whispered. Lasker stood up, his bones aching, his legs feeling totally numb. He could barely walk. Slowly, as Bart rubbed at his legs, he felt the circulation returning and started hobbling along with the others, last in line.

Tsering and then Cheojey walked up and got tapped softly by the man leaning down with the stamper. Then it was Lasker's turn. Feeling foolish, Bart looked up at the man with the long stamper. And he gasped. For pouring out of the crown of the Rimpoche's hat was a bowl of shimmering colors, like a rainbow.

A smile appeared below the rainbow, in the wrinkled dark face. Shemer Rimpoche shook a little wand at Lasker. The room spun and collapsed into itself.

Lasker awoke lying on a rug on the temple floor. Cheojey was holding his right eye open with his thumb and forefinger. He sat up, and looked around. Except for Cheojey and Tinley, they were alone.

"W-what happened?" he asked.

Tinley said, "Rimpoche will see you now."

# Chapter 13

Lasker looked toward the throne. It was empty. And then he felt someone tapping him on the shoulder, and turned. There was prune-faced Shemer Rimpoche, down on his level. Shemer didn't have the rainbow coming out of his head now. He was, however, grinning from ear to ear, like the Cheshire cat, and said something.

His voice, Lasker recalled much later, had seemed to come from deep down below his throat, not from his vocal chords. The voice had a resonance as if Shemer Rimpoche were speaking from a long distance away.

Lasker stared at the little prune-faced man in the gold brocade robe. Tinley said, "Rimpoche asks did you have a nice sleep?"

"H-how long was I out?"

"Just minutes. He asks did something startle you?"

Lasker explained.

Shemer Rempoche spoke, not waiting for a translation. Tinley said, "The Rimpoche tells you that you are quite unique to see such an aura around a person. Rimpoche also asks if you will sit with him over at the chantmaster's bench. He wants to hear about your problem—I explained about it while you were indisposed.''

"I see."

Tinley excused himself and went over to a pile of white cloth materials to the side of the throne and lifted one thin cotton bolt about a yard long. He brought it to Lasker. "Here, place this *Khatag* over the Rimpoche's shoulders. It is our way of showing greetings.''

Lasker took the scarf, leaned over to the Rimpoche, and laid it over the man's shoulders. The Rimpoche said something that must have been thanks, then he took the scarf off and put the scarf over Lasker's head. The hairs on the American's scalp seemed to stand on end with electricity when he heard the cotton rustle over his neck.

Shemer Rimpoche inquired as to the health of Lasker, who replied that he was "well, thanks to Cheojey.''

"Good good.'' The Rimpoche asked if Bart would enjoy some tea and fruit. Lasker said, "Yes,'' when Tinley gave him the eye. The Rimpoche invited him over to the little lacquer tables and they sat down. He had the sense to let Rimpoche sit down first. The Rimpoche chose the cushion behind the table that had a small flower vase with several mountain flowers in it. Without any summons, a young monk appeared quite quickly with plates of some sliced oranges and pears and a fantastically decorated ceramic pot of tea with cups.

The young boy-monk poured the tea and disappeared. Lasker hoped that he wasn't getting into trouble by saying yes to the repast. He remembered the canteen-etiquette experience he had when he first met Tsering and the others. But evidently he now made another etiquette mistake: Tinley had to lean over and say, under his breath, with urgency, "Mr. Lasker, please do not place your feet so they face the Rimpoche." Lasker shifted slightly. Tinley was just what he needed if he was to survive in these locales.

Shemer Rimpoche sipped his tea, his face lit up now by the orange rays of the rising sun streaming off the glacier in the distance. Time seemed to stand still while they just sat and sucked on the fruit and drank tea. The Rimpoche, before he spoke again, spent some time arranging the vase of flowers to his right.

Finally, the Rimpoche spoke, and Tinley translated: "There, the flowers are better. Now you may begin your account."

"Believe me," Lasker said, "I did not expect to be in Tibet very long . . ." Lasker related his story, accurately as possible, from the moment he stepped into Mr. Losang's office to the time he arrived at the monastery. Lasker ended with, "And I wish only to return by the quickest means to India—"

Once that was done, the "Precious Jewel" said something to Tinley, who smiled. Tinley said, "Rimpoche verifies your story."

They must think the holy guy is a walking lie detector, Bart thought. In any case he exhaled a sigh of relief. Now he would be okay. Just had to get them to help get him back across the border. That was what he asked for next, together with a map. He wanted to fix the location of the cave with the idol in it. The idol with the big-ticket diamond in its forehead!

The Rimpoche said, through Tinley, that taking Bart to the border would be arranged. Then he told Lasker that it was too bad he couldn't visit longer. That Tibet had many interesting sights. Rimpoche said he enjoyed the company of Westerners, and that it had been a long time since the last visit of someone from over the mountains. "We at the lamasary have been visited, perhaps twice in the past—once in the pig-wood year—

119

the turn of the century—by a British explorer. Then a German came and stayed with us for some time. That was in 1938. Both of them were charming gentlemen. I enjoyed hearing about your world over the mountains."

Lasker did a bit of mental calculating. 1899–1900? The Rimpoche must have been even older than his face full of wrinkles implied . . . considerably older. Bart had heard somewhere that these holy priests of Tibet were put in office as tiny children, but even so, a little calculation put him at around ninety years old *plus*.

Rimpoche said, "I am sorry that I could not speak to you earlier—you caught us in the midst of our puja, our ceremony honoring the saint who translated the *dharma* teachings into Tibetan so long ago. You are familiar with our religion, Mr. Lasker?"

"Not much. I understand Buddha came to earth to help mankind, sort of like Christ," he offered.

"Yes. Very good. An excellent understanding. Buddha taught that mankind is on an endless chain of suffering, birth, death, and rebirth. In our many lifetimes there is much suffering caused by the karma—the accumulation of wrong actions on our part toward others."

Lasker almost frowned—was this to be a sermon? What about the business at hand? Getting him out of Tibet before the Chinese strung him up.

The Rimpoche seemed to sense his mood of impatience. "Well, perhaps we shall save that discussion for another time." Taking another sip of the thick green tea mixed with butter, he then said, "You, as an American without papers, are in danger here in Tibet. You should certainly return as quickly as possible to India. We are in a remote monastery, but even this area is frequently visited by the Chinese. We are, as you know, an occupied nation, we are allowed our religious practices again only recently. And at the indulgence of the Chinese authorities. And though it appears to be the policy of Beijing to allow some relaxation of their strict reign, there are those Chinese that flaunt this attitude, and still repress religion. Our province of Gyadong is ruled by Major Tse Ling, who is one of these repressors. You are profoundly lucky to have fallen down out of the sky into the arms of Tsering and his Snow Lion rebels. They are a bit wild and crude, but they are loyal to His Holiness. If you hadn't met up with them, you perhaps would have fallen into the clutches of Tse Ling's patrols."

Bart asked, "Snow Lion rebels?"

Tinley laughed. "Yes, Tsering-la calls his group that. Snow lions are actually Himalayan leopards that are very rare nowadays. They are fierce cats of great power, with blue-colored manes. They will claw you if you come too close. Tsering's Snow Lions claw at the Chinese, when they can. In any case, Tsering wishes you to bring what remains of the gold to Youngden Rimpoche, as you originally intended. Younden Rimpoche's party are making for the border. You can go with them. Will that be a satisfactory arrangement? It is the only way Rimpoche knows to return to India."

"That would be fine. Thank you all very much."

The Rimpoche clapped his hands together. Tsering came in, bowed his head to the floor three times, and sat down on a cushion. The Rimpoche spoke to him. Each time he finished a sentence, Tsering nodded and exhaled some air, a gasped *ah* at the end of every sentence of the Rimpoche, as if he took it to heart.

Tinley leaned over and said, "Tsering now has been told that you are a fine friend, and should be trusted as a friend. See, I told you he knows everyone's heart." Tinley winked.

Shemer Rimpoche motioned in the air, and two

monks came over with a carved stained wood chest about the size of a toy box. The holy man opened it and extracted a beaten-silver object with ornate designs perhaps six inches square, held on a leather thong. He said something to Tinley, Tinley leaned over, and translated as usual, "The Rimpoche wishes you to raise your left arm."

Lasker did, and felt the thong go over his neck and under his shoulder. Then his arm was lowered and he was bid to slide back to his cushion. Tinley whispered, "It is a beautiful *gau* you have received, Lasker. Please, you should really thank the Rimpoche."

"Thank you very much," Lasker said, fingering the strange and a bit heavy silver box. It popped open and he saw that it held a little Buddha statue with some red string on it.

They all smiled, and the Rimpoche giggled a bit.

Tinley translated his remarks: "You are quite welcome. The gau has a relic in it which will protect you." The Rimpoche spoke again, at some length, to Tinley, who smiled and nodded profusely.

Tinley turned to Lasker excitedly, squirming like any child offered something good. "Shemer Rimpoche says I am to accompany you, Lasker. He says that it is best that we both join Youngden Rimpoche's party, and cross the border into India with them. Rimpoche says that the generous bribe money you bring should easily handle two more people—a disguised American and a young boy. Rimpoche wants me to train as a monk in Dhramsala, India, the seat of His Holiness' government in exile."

"Fine by me," Lasker smiled, thinking, This is great. I will finish my job, get the money to Youngden, and cross the border. When I get back, I'll collect 120,000 pounds. It will all come out okay after all. *But—the diamond in the idol!*

"Tinley," Lasker said, "Thank the Rimpoche for me. But ask him if he has a map."

Tinley did, and the Rimpoche looked cross and said something.

"No map, Lasker," the boy translated. "Sorry." Shemer started to gather up his robe. The attendant monk moved quickly to help the old man stand up.

Tinley said, "Rimpoche says you must be very tired, and perhaps we should all have some rest—and breakfast!"

The interview was over. And he was right, Lasker was tired. As they stood, Lasker added, "Tinley, I'm very happy to have you come along with me. It's been like having no mouth or ears, these past few days. Don't worry, I'll show you the ropes in India."


After some mo-mos—heavy dumplings with chopped and spiced vegetables and yak meat inside—and some noodles floating in a beef broth and hunks of delicious bread, eaten at a table with many monks, Lasker caught a few hours' sound sleep.

Bart was given some Tibetan clothes for his rather smelly and soiled Western gear. He put them on. Tinley said, "It would be best if you looked as Tibetan as possible. There is one thing—" He got Lasker one of the floppy fur hats. *"There,"* he said, as Bart placed it on his head, a bit askew. "But something else is wrong."

"What?"

"You need a shave. You must keep clean-shaven. Tibetans don't have facial hair—except the oldest men—and not many of them." Lasker was given a small sharp knife, a steel mirror, and some gritty soap, and then directed to a basin of water. He shaved as best he could.

"How's this?" Bart said, once back with Tinley in the courtyard.

"Better. Now smear some resin on your face—" Tinley handed him some.

When that was done, Tinley was satisfied.

Bart was just crossing the entranceway out of the courtyard with the others when he heard someone call. He turned and there was Shemer Rimpoche, standing at the top of the temple stairs. He called out, "Goodbye, my friend, see you again next lifetime. Good fortune on your travels."

Lasker smiled, and started to say, "Goodbye, and th—" Suddenly his tongue caught in his mouth. Had Rimpoche spoken in English? Or *had he spoken at all?* The distance to the stairs was about seventy feet, and the man spoke in an even low voice. No, he hadn't spoken. It was *telepathy.*

As if catching Lasker's amazed thought, Shemer Rimpoche doubled over in laughter, and the assistant monk had all he could do to keep him from tumbling down the three steps.

Lasker turned and, with a weak-kneed stride, continued along with the others, none of who apparently had heard anything at all.

As they descended the cobble path, Bart ruminated: First the hermit's weather magic, then the rainbow above Shemer Rimpoche's head, then telepathy . . .

No, it couldn't be—it was all hallucinations brought on by exhaustion, strange food, the incredible altitude. Perhaps he was still sick, still had a fever . . .

As Lasker walked with the others down toward the rope bridge, he wondered though, if it all could really be true. If it was all *really* happening.

# Chapter 14

Saleem Chun, the fur-edged hood of his blue nylon ski parka drawn up over his orange turban, stood on the desolate Tibetan hillside. He carefully observed every movement of his five assistants, who sifted through the airplane debris scattered for a hundred yards.

By the dark cast of Chun's features, he was Indian, but his eyes slanted, his eyebrows arched. Chinese features. In fact, his full name, Saleem Tse-Chun, told the story: Chun was of mixed Chinese-Indian extraction. He favored the wearing of a turban for its exotic appeal, and because his hair was thinning. Chun was forty, and for the last ten of his forty years he had been the top assassin of a certain powerful man in Hong Kong. Chun's employer had important interests in this restricted border province of Tibet. Interests that had brought Chun by helicopter to this remote hill.

Saleem Chun kept shifting his weight from one cold foot to the other, waiting for his Chinese crew searching the scattered wreckage to turn up something that would solve this mystery.

It was Lasker's plane, it had to be.

It had, unfortunately, taken three days for the air search to find the wreck, and another day to arrange for his flight from Hong Kong to Kathmandu and then to here. Still, he had expected a body, and there wasn't one. He had also expected the wreckage to contain rifles and small arms, destined for the rebels. Yet there were none.

The plane had been hit by a SILK-5 missile—but obviously not a direct hit. This site was twenty-one miles from where it took the hit. Lasker had managed to parachute out. Did he dump the cargo of arms out too? Unlikely. Then where was it?

One of the Chinese soldiers came scrambling up to Chun, his hands extended. "Mr. Chun, I found this gold coin—and some burned pieces of paper money, Chinese money."

Chun took the coin in his slender dark hand and turned it over and over. "Indian gold coin? That's all? No guns, rifles, ammunition?"

"No sir."

"Not even *pieces* of guns, one cartridge?"

"No sir."

Chun couldn't understand it.

The dull thud-thud-thud brought Chun's deeply set dark eyes up to the blazing sunlit sky. He didn't like squinting, extracted his French white-framed Polaroid sunglasses from his jacket, put them on. Ah . . . yes, there was the small fast Bell high-altitude chopper. Chun had sent it off to search the whole area, the minute that he had discovered there was no body. For the past hour, as the men worked, the chopper had searched for the parachute, or any sign of the missing airman.

Saleem smiled. Not many people from the West could blithely fly across the Tibetan border. Yet, there had been no trouble for Chun, of course. The local Chinese leader, Major Tse Ling, had cleared them through Air Defense. And there would be no trouble flying back to Kathmandu. Tse Ling arranged the air clearance and the Chinese soldiers' assistance, because Chun and she worked for the same person. Tse Ling's extracurricular employment, of course, was unknown to the Beijing authorities.

While the chopper wheeled in from the south, Chun let his shaded eyes drift to the closest snow-topped Himalayan peak. K-2, the second tallest mountain in the world. The sun was reflecting off K-2's icecap. Made it seem like the mountain was silver afire.

The black chopper settled down in a storm of dust and pebbles on the flat area a hundred yards away. Chun ordered an end to the search, the five men followed him to the black helicopter, got in the rear door. Chun took the seat next to the pilot.

"Any sign of Lasker's chute?" asked Chun.

"No sir," replied the pilot. "I've flown a search pattern from here back to the Air Defense missile base, and twelve miles further. I've been all around this place. It's rugged country, though, he *could* be down there in some gulley. Even the cargo could be."

"Right. Let's go. Quickly, return to base."

As the chopper took off and wheeled toward the south, Chun pulled off his parka. He sat watching the ground sweep by below. It was a big slagheap, he thought. Not a tree in sight. Chun reviewed his situation: Working as an assassin had taken him many remote places in the world. South America, the Middle East. . . . And when his employer had found out that a Tibetan exile group had hired the American pilot to fly into Tibet, most likely bringing arms to the guerrillas fighting against Tse Ling, Chun had been dispatched to New Delhi. For nothing must upset Tse Ling's "special project." Chun had personally fired the bazooka at Lasker, but the American was fast and lucky. Chun had only succeeded in killing a cab driver. And Lasker had managed to get into Tibet and disappear. Damn it! Now he'd have to find the man and complete the job. Failure was *unacceptable* to his employer.

Chun stared at the approaching peaks and their summits of ice, golden in the sun. Tibet. No longer an isolated place, not by air. But still a place where one could do something so secret that anyplace else in the world it would be impossible. Something was happening here in this remote land that would be world-shaking in its consequences. And more important, immensely profitable for Chun's employer.

Was this American somebody special? Perhaps a CIA agent? Why were no weapons found in the wreckage? And what of the gold coin in his pocket? Could it be that Lasker had brought money, not arms, into Tibet? Why? Who was it for? The rebels couldn't use it—you couldn't buy arms in Tibet—or could you? Perhaps it was possible that some profiteering Chinese officer was diverting shipments of arms. . . . One thing was certain: Lasker had to be found and interrogated.

Tse Ling's troops would keep looking for Lasker. He'd be found. And just in case he wasn't—Chun would arrange for a watch on this man Donnely, who it appeared was the intermediary between the Tibetan exile group and Lasker. If Lasker made it out of Tibet and contacted Donnely, two of Chun's assassins, armed with machine pistols, would grab him right in the Excelsior.

The American would be tortured by Chun himself, to find out what the hell he was up to, what he knew of the Green Salt Project.

Chun prided himself on being an efficient, careful, and when it amused him, sadistic questioner. Getting the truth from this American flyer was just what Chun wanted to do, after all the trouble he had caused him.

Chun smiled, thinking about Lasker's flesh being torn, peeled from his chest as he screamed, of the electric wires that would be attached to his testicles. Lasker would talk. And then, when he had told all, the flyer would still be tortured, *just for fun*.

# Chapter 15

Bart caught the tail-end of many hours of heated barter between monks and caravaners in the courtyard. Then, transactions over, the party again descended the long cobbled path from the monastery and crossed the rope bridge in much the same paranoia-inducing manner as they had the day previous. Lasker was glad for the few hours of sleep he had snatched before leaving. Still, he was so tired that he had little fear upon the recrossing over the gorge.

They gathered their animals from the boy shepherds and were well along the trail on the other side of the divide. He was in control of a horse now, and the slow measured steps of the well-trained animal lolled him. He was nearly dozing when the cutting sound of some sort of horrible horn—much like a truck's highway horn—echoed though the mountains. His hair stood on end.

"Tinley, what is that?"

Tinley rode alongside him and said, "That is just the song of farewell—pretty, isn't it?"

"Jeez."

Later, Lasker asked, "Who is this dreaded Tse Ling?"

Tinley replied, "The people in this province are un-der a terrible regional governor, Major Tse Ling. Her troops demand tribute from all the monasteries, even loot them."

"Tse Ling is a *woman?*"

"Yes, she is a witch really, not a woman. She is a butcher. Her troops visit every remote village and monastery and demand payment for not doing dam-age. She is called the Virgin Dragon."

"Tinley, I'm confused. Are we among caravaners—traveling traders—or rebel fighters?"

Tinley laughed. "Every Tibetan is a resister. But some will do it with a knife or a gun. Tsering and these caravaners are what you would call *secret* freedom fight-ers. Rinchen, for one, cannot count the Chinese he has killed."

"And what is Cheojey Lama doing traveling with them?"

"Cheojey is a medical monk, of the Panya order—or was. The practice of religious medicine is prohibited now. But the Chinese leave us to our superstitions, and it is not uncommon to see a monk, who has lost his monastery to fires set by the Chinese soldiers, traveling with a caravan."

"Why do you continue to resist? The Chinese have won the war, haven't they?"

"True, not much can be done to drive them out of Tibet, but we harass them. Tsering and his men have, in the past, prevented some of the more blatant acts against the people. Tse Ling's soldiers know that if they behave too badly, they might awaken with their throats being slit. We have little hope, for now, of ex-pelling the Chinese from Khawachen, our Land of Pre-cious Snows, but all Tibetans can at least resist those acts Beijing does *not* condone. But killing is not good; it is against our Dharma."

130

"Dharma?"

"Dharma is the teaching of the Buddha—teachings that lead to enlightenment."

"I see . . ." Actually Bart *didn't* see. But he wanted to ask something else. "Tinley, could you fill me in a bit on some other things? I don't know much about Tibet. I've been in the dark for days."

"Certainly. But in exchange, please tell me some things about your country. I have heard many strange things about the West. And I am fearful of what I will find beyond the mountains. What is *America* like? Are there horses, or just trucks and cars?"

"Well, there are horse riders, what they call cowboys in America. But most people own a car, and there are roads of—stones—everywhere, for thousands of miles."

"It must be very smoky, from the traffic."

"In some cities, yes."

"These cities—do they have big houses?"

"Yes. Some big buildings are just offices too, for business, you understand?"

Tinley nodded. "Big offices?"

"Well, some have sixty, or seventy stories—"

"Stories?"

"Levels. There are hundreds of these buildings, made of colored glass, in our cities. And our cities have millions of people in them."

Tinley laughed, and translated for the others, who joined in the mirth.

"No, seriously," Lasker said.

"Oh, you are great storytellers in America, just like us Tibetans." Tinley laughed. "Seriously, I want to *know* about America. No more jokes."

"I'm telling the truth. There are millions of people in Western cities, and they work in glass towers fifty stories high."

131

Tinley just smiled. Then he tried another tack:

"If America is so crowded, how do you squeeze by each other?"

"It's very big—bigger then Tibet."

"It must take many weeks for even automobiles to get from one place to another."

"People fly from city to city, in airplanes. Some of our airplanes hold four hundred people at a time."

Tinley turned and told what Lasker had said, and everyone cracked up. Old Dolma actually fell off her horse from laughing.

"You are a great storyteller, Lasker, truly funny. No airplane can hold so many people, it would not fly." Tinley said.


Tinley continued to ask about America and, in return for Bart's "tall tales," taught him some Tibetan words. During the long ride, Tsering came alongside and, with Tinley translating, told Lasker what he wanted to know of the situation in Tibet.

"China has progressively increased oppression and levied more and more taxes since they took over our country. They bring modern things but none of the fruits of modernization help the Tibetan people. Now our language even is considered a second language to Chinese. In the 1980s, they started to ease up on us, allowing us to rebuild some of the twenty-five hundred monasteries and temples the Red Guard destroyed in the so-called Cultural Revolution. They let us wear our native dress again, and move about more. But it is surface reform. They still hold us in an iron grip. And against their 'liberalization' stands the old guard—the inheritors of the insane Cultural Revolution of Mao's China. Major Tse Ling is the most monstrous of those who oppress us. She has been in charge of this province

132

for two years. She has done many awful things already. She doubles taxes, and sends falsely accused people to Smoke Mountain—a vast prison camp that none return from.''

"What is she like—personally?"

"She is called the Virgin Dragon. She hates men, has never had one. Her base is in Chamdo, the regional capital. She has instituted a new policy: If the people do not increase their tribute to the government, her troops loot our religious shrines for gold and precious stones to make up the difference. So we hide many precious religious objects in the hills. She has sent out scores of troops to search for them, but the Chinese are picked off there. Small bands of rebels like the Snow Lions control the mountains. Chinese soldiers don't climb well, and they can't even breathe the high air—without tanks on their backs.''

Bart let that information digest for a while. The path became narrow so they had to go single file. Tinley had to ride behind him. He enjoyed the surreally beautiful terrain, took off his shirt to the noonday sun.

When Tinley next rode alongside Lasker, the subject of their conversation changed. "Tinley, what would have happened," Bart asked, "if Rimpoche had said that I was lying?"

"You would have not been hurt as long as we were at the monastery. But the Snow Lions take no prisoners. Out of respect to the Rimpoche, they would have taken you out of earshot of the monastery, and killed you. Since Shemer Rimpoche confirmed that you are a friend, bringing supplies to Youngden Tulku Rimpoche, as you said, you are one of us.''

"Do you think we'll come across more Chinese before we reach Youngden's party?"

"Once we pass through the next village, there is little chance of meeting any. They stick to the lower trails, as they are afraid of the rebels—and the migyu.''

"Migyu?"

"Ape people. I think the English call them the Abominable Snowmen. They are pointy-headed white-furred creatures like us, but eight feet tall. They like to mate with humans—"

"They really exist?"

"Most assuredly, they do. I saw one myself once when I was eight. They throw big rocks and are very dangerous.''

Now it was Lasker's turn to laugh in disbelief.

"I understand in India that they worship many gods, and not the Buddha. What is your belief in America? Do you study the dharma?" Tinley asked.

"No, we are—mostly—Christians."

"What is that?"

"We follow Jesus, of Nazareth. I don't suppose you've heard of him."

"Oh yes, I have—he taught kindness and forgiveness to a brutal race. Cheojey Lama knows more about this man, he has studied out ancient records in Lhasa, where this Jesus studied.''

"Studied—in Lhasa?"

"Yes. Would you like me to ask Cheojey to tell you about what we know of your Jesus?''

"Sure.''

They camped for the night. After they ate Cheojey came over on Tinley's request, and under the myriad stars, related the story through Tinley. *His* version of Jesus's life: "Jesus, who we know as Yasu, was a living Buddha, a great lama that had achieved enlightenment and lived in Western Heaven—Dewachen—beyond all suffering, some six hundred years after the Buddha taught at Bodhidharma, in India.

"Yasu, taking pity on mankind, wished to reincarnate and continue his work to benefit all beings as a Bodhisattva, a fully enlightened being who incarnates as human out of compassion for others. But the great prayers of a distant race in the faraway desert—a place called Judea—brought his rebirth *there*. Such was his compassion—Yasu gave up Dewachen for them.

"Of course, our astrologers foresaw the place of his birth and three of them, bearing gifts, followed the great celestial directions to him. The three astrologers presented gifts and helped his early survival. Then when Yasu was fourteen, he journeyed with the three to our city of the gods, Lhasa, to be installed as a great Rimpoche. He stayed in Lhasa for some years, performing many miracles and driving out many demons. But he wished to return and help his desert people. So at the age of thirty, he began the journey back to Judea. We knew little of his life after that, distances being what they are, until the modern era, when your missionaries came and gave us more information. I understand that much like many of our present Rimpoches, after giving many great teachings, Yasu was martyred by the occupation troops of a foreign nation that had seized his country."

Lasker just sat back against a rock stunned by the fantastic story, and asked, "This is all in the Lhasa archives?"

"Still to this day, if the Chinese haven't destroyed it," Cheojey concluded sadly. "They like to burn books."

Lasker had been constantly thrown by what he saw, heard, and experienced in Tibet in the past week, and this tale of the lost years of Jesus was just one more bewilderment to ponder.

The trek wasn't all beautiful scenery and teachings by

135

Cheojey. The men had been brewing their estimable barley beer *chang* and they proceeded to drink it in volume every night, laughing and shouting out wild tales. Lasker was dragged over to taste the stuff, which he found smelled like cereal and tasted a lot like a vanilla milk shake. But it got you drunk. He, too, was soon enebriated and acting out, staggering around trying to describe flying Good Baby with hand gestures and buzzing noises plus rudimentary Tibetan. This they found most amusing and Bart received many slaps on the back and joined in many a drunken chorus of songs he couldn't understand. He taught them "Row Row Row Your boat" and "Home on the Range," which they parodied with him and then sang in a fair way.

He wondered what any hermits and solitary herdsmen out there would think hearing the English songs echoing through the mountains in the starry night.

One drunken night of revel, the third since leaving the monastery, was particularly wild. That night, thoroughly smashed on the barley beer, Lasker introduced arm wrestling to the group, which they took to like hogs take to mud. Lasker bested some of them, and lost after putting up a decent showing with the others. But Rinchen slammed him down on the rock table as if he wasn't pushing at all. That made Rinchen soften up to him. A sort of truce, it seemed, brought on not by liking Lasker but by the fact that Lasker lost well, and would soon be leaving them—and good riddance, according to Rinchen.

It was that night that Tsering decided Lasker needed a Tibetan name. As is the custom, the lama named him. He became Tharpa Bardum.

"Whats it mean?" Lasker asked.

"Joy of Death."

"Great. Joy of Death. Appropriate. Real appropriate," Lasker muttered.

# Chapter 16

It was the fourth day since they'd left the monastery. Around noon everyone suddenly grew very silent.

Lasker turned on his mount and saw Tinley moving up toward him. "Tinley, what is it?" he asked as the boy came alongside him.

"Cheojey says that there are Chinese near—he has a sense for this."

"Great," Lasker said, "what do I do?"

"The floppy hat and nomad clothes you put on at the monastery will be enough disguise. You have dark brown eyes, that is good. You will look like us with just a bit more preparation."

They stopped and Lasker dismounted. Dolma, who had assisted Cheojey in treating him, smeared resinous material on Bart's face. Tinley slapped his pants with some trail dirt. He added more incense—rubbing it into Lasker's blackened, sooty hair.

Tinley said, "Now get back on the horse. The best course is to say nothing, even if they ask you questions. We are notoriously close-mouthed as a people, when confronted by Chinese. They won't think it unusual." Tinley looked him over. "You look very much like us—don't worry."

Lasker *did* worry, especially when he heard the motors of approaching vehicles. Three jeeps and two trucks, and a column of a dozen soldiers carrying automatic weapons. His heart made a lump in his throat. The caravan and the Chinese passed each other at a level and wide place on the trail. The Chinese were a desultory-looking bunch. Their uniforms were unkempt and soiled, their manner that of drunkards. There were old Tibetan storage boxes and big lumpy bags—dzomo-skin bags like the Tibetan carried—in the backs of the jeeps and hanging on the sides of the trucks—loot?

When the caravan and the Chinese troops were alongside each other, some of the Chinese soldiers made rude gestures at the women caravaners, and laughed.

They were obviously in a dangerous mood, but still, for a while, they kept moving past. Lasker thought there would be no trouble, and they would be allowed to pass unmolested, except for comments. But there was one among the Chinese who didn't smile and joke: the rigidly erect, buttoned-collar young man who stood up in the last jeep. Just as his vehicle came alongside the first rider, Tsering, the sullen officer barked out a challenge.


Lieutenant Wong had decided to ask a few questions of the caravan. Wong had received a message that an American flyer, downed by the Air Defense Unit, was somewhere in the province. He didn't see anything but primitive Tibetans in this ragged group, but perhaps they had seen something.

There was also the matter of the cargo the American plane carried. Gold coins. The bags attached to those yaks looked bulging and heavy . . .

Wong decided to ask for their papers and check them out.

"Stop," he insisted, holding up his hand. The one-eyed man in the lead of the caravan translated into Tibetan; they slowly complied. The stinking bastards *better* comply, Wong thought, for his men liked nothing better than exercising their marksmanship on human targets.

Tsering responded to the man with the lieutenant's marking on his sleeve. In *Chinese*—all Tibetans were expected to know Chinese. The one-eyed rebel leader leaned down from his mount. He took some soiled travel permit papers from a leather saddle bag. The Chinese officer inspected them carefully. He handed the papers back to Tsering and asked whether they had seen any foreigners.

"Just Chinese," Tsering said.

"Don't be smart!" the Lieutenant snapped. He stepped down from the jeep. The Chinese soldiers had their weapons up to firing position on their hips, and watched the lieutenant as he walked slowly down the line past each rider and yak, kicking this bag then that one, eyeing each man and woman purposefully. He stuck a knife into each sack, spilling barley and some butter. It was outrageous conduct but no one stopped him. Lasker almost fainted every time the knife ripped a bag. When the last bag was pierced and no gold coins fell out, he was relieved and much perplexed. Where had Tsering hidden the gold?

The sullen Chinese officer then went toward Rinchen. The big Tibetan on the sorrel edged his hand ever so slightly toward his dirk handle. The meanest arched-eyebrow expression and half-snarl appeared on the big man's oily face.

The Chinese officer, for all his youthful arrogance, and despite his SMG backup, seemed a bit afraid to approach Rinchen. And no wonder. Rinchen was a truly frightening fellow.

The officer moved on, closer and closer to Bart. Every artery in his body pounded. Bart kept his eyes down. The officer, when he reached Bart, scrutinized him as he did the others, started to step onward, then stopped, asked him something.

Tinley came up and said something to the officer, gesturing toward Lasker.

The officer's face contorted in a smirk, then he burst out laughing.

The officer went back to his jeep, got in. He and the jeep pulled out in front of the column of sloppy men. The soldiers continued their march.

Once the Chinese were out of sight, Lasker said, "I thought I was a goner, Tinley. What did you tell him?"

"I told the officer you were afraid of all Chinese, that you thought the Chinese were gods from another planet, and you considered yourself unworthy to speak to a god. You were fortunate that he found it amusing, they are the worst bunch we have seen in a long time. I doubt they would have arrested us. They would have killed us all if they found the gold, and probably taken it for themselves."

"Where IS the gold?"

"In sacks *inside* the sacks of grain."

Tsok, the village that was the Snow Lions' first stop-over, was still two days away. Lasker, therefore, was getting a good workout in spoken Tibetan, mostly vocabulary, from Tinley in exchange for his continued "preposterous" tall tales about the Western world.

Lasker had done some backpacking in the mountains of Colorado, and thought he had seen the night sky about as clearly as any man alive. But now, "spectacular" seemed too simple a word to describe the Tibetan sky—awesome was more like it. The curtains of the Northern Lights flickered like a red and blue and green crown over the mountains after each sunset. Tinley noticed Lasker staring up while they made camp.

"We call it Amida's robe," said Tinley. "Yes, it is beautiful. Is the sky in America like our sky?"

"The American sky is almost always blotted out at night by scattered light from the buildings and streetlights—and pollution, I'm sorry to say."

"Pollution?"

"Smoke from chimneys and cars and so on. Here you have virtually no pollution. Your sky is filled with stars, as numerous as grains of sand on the beach."

"What's a beach?"

"The sand along the shore of an ocean."

"Oh, yes, the ocean—a giant salt lake," Tinley said. "I have heard of it."

Lasker started pointing out the constellations and naming them for Tinley. He had a tough time picking out even the most familiar ones, because their primary stars were lost in the myriad others easily visible to the naked eye in these sublime elevations.

The women were preparing hot *chapatis*—flat Indian-style pancakes with vegetables and onions mixed in. The smell wafting his way in the darkness was enticing. He and Tinley raced to the campfire, and were dished out generous helpings by Dolma. Tinley called her Ani-la.

As they ate, Lasker asked what that "Ani-la" meant.

"Mother. All the older women are called Ani-la."

141

The hot chapati and lots of buttered tea devoured, Lasker walked away from the campfire to lie down and look at the stars again. Maybe everything would work out—they'd catch up to Youngden Tulku Rimpoche and give him the money, get Tinley to point out the hermit's cave on a good map. The caravan had not gone back through the mudslide valley where the diamond in the idol was secreted, so Bart had reluctantly given up hope of getting it—for now. But if he just could know where it was . . .

After a while, he heard footfalls. The monk. The old man sat silently staring up, finally remarking that it was a beautiful night—something like that. Lasker said "Yes, beautiful," in halting Tibetan.

He slept in the open, as the other did, even though it was icy cold. Lasker was snuggled down in some heavy pelts with his head on a saddle. The womenfolk camped a bit off—Tibetans seemed to favor their own sex as company. But later he heard the women—at least some of them—slip into the beds of their male friends—or husbands—and there were somewhat restrained noises of lovemaking. No such visit by a comely young thing for Lasker. He had begun to notice the women were exactly that—comely. The younger ones had pretty light-coffee skin and almond eyes and good complexions. And though not slender, they had a grace to their sturdy bodies. Bart lay thinking about Jenny, her blond hair, her eyebrows, the nape of her neck, her breasts. Oh yes, her big upturned breasts.

Soon he was drifting off to sleep. Then all hell broke loose. The horses whinnied, men shouted. There were growls, loud catlike growls. Flame-tipped sticks were carried into the darkness, thrown into the rocks near the horses.

"Tinley," Lasker said, "what is it?"

142

"Snow lions," whispered Tinley, in awe. "A rare thing nowadays—good omen."

At dawn Lasker's nose, the only part of his anatomy exposed, was icy and numb. But with the rising sun, the temperature was rising too. They had some tea and tsampa and were on the trail again, pleasantly warm internally. Lasker remembered to shave to keep looking Tibetan.

They traveled through rolling hills and colored rock formations. There were chortens, waist-high monuments containing wrapped prayers, and mani piles along the trail. No sign of the modern world. It could have been a hundred, a thousand, years ago.

For lunch, Dolma and some of her female helpers cooked up a stew of yak meat and noodles, and either they were abnormally delicious or the fresh air made them taste that way to Lasker.

Dolma asked Tinley something. Tinley turned to Lasker and said, "She wonder if you like Tibetan food."

"I don't know about Tibetan food in general, but she's a good cook, that's for sure."

Tinley translated and Dolma's chest swelled and she put extra food on Lasker's plate.

Vistas that would have made the Grand Canyon second on your list slid past them. The hot sun baked Bart's skin—despite the resins on his face. He stripped to the waist by noon. His once blue-white skin was now getting damned brown. The women giggled when they looked at him.

Lasker felt curiously elated. Perhaps it was the joy of knowing he was heading home. Perhaps the altitude made him giddy. In any case he rode along feeling quite serene.

They left the well-defined trail and cut diagonally away from it and headed over rolling barren hills.

Lasker told Tinley, "This area looks a lot like a place in America called Bryce Canyon, in Utah—beautiful."

They topped a slaggy rise and before them was an immense blue glacier, blinding in the sun. Plumes of mist rose from its mass. It hung over a valley and that valley appeared to hold the same trail that they were now using.

"Tinley, are we going to continue this way? It's pretty, well, steep. . ."

"I think we have to go under the ice in order to reach Tsok by the short route. Don't worry."

They progressed toward the valley on a steep trail. Pebbles fell at every footfall of the animals. They reached the valley floor of rolling knee-high grass, coming closer and closer to the glacial overhang. The group was to pass directly under the perilous mass of icy death. He could feel the cold wind coming off the glacier, battling the warmth of the sun. They were soon crossing frigid little streams at the base of the glistening blue ice above.

Lasker was worried a lot less about the Chinese than this giant ice flow.

"Surely, Tinley, there's got to be some way around the thing, we can't go *under* it!"

"That's the shortest way."

The trail led into the shadow of the glacier, along an icy stream.

The clatter of the hooves started to sound like the pounding of wet hammers. Tsering called out and the group stopped. The men began tying cloth over the animals hooves.

That done, they continued in single file underneath the ice. Bart's almost forgotten feeling of fear on the bridge was multiplied threefold. The fall of a shard of ice sent a tree down fifty paces behind the last horse.

"Hey, you can't be serious," Lasker whispered, as they continued to ride along under the giant icy overhang.

"Be quiet," Tinley implored.

Finally all were out of the shadow of death and onto a grassy slope. The cloth was removed from the animals' hooves, and they stopped for a tea break. Lasker thought, "Wait till I tell Jenny about this."

It was during that tea break that Lasker heard the tremendous crack. He turned to see the mass of the blue glacier slide down and crush the whole damned trail that they had just traversed. He looked at Tsering, who shrugged and smiled. Lasker lost himself in drinking the warm tea. These people were crazy, he decided. Very crazy.

They were again on the beaten track. There were tire tracks in the dust. Chinese had come this way.

"Tsok is just over the ridge," Tinley announced. It was about four in the afternoon, at a guess, when Bart noticed wheeling birds high above. He said, "They're really *big*. Are they Asian Condors?"

"No, they are funeral birds—I think Westerners call them vultures."

They came upon a large cracked chorten garlanded with wilted necklaces of red flowers. "It is," said Tinley, "the landmark that designates the approach to Tsok. But the flowers are usually replaced every day. It is a bad omen that they are wilted. Surely something is wrong for the town of Tsok to neglect its religious duty."

Tsering left the group and rode up the rise to have a look ahead. He came galloping back shouting.

\* \* \*

The Snow Lions made the crest of the basalt hill and Lasker saw for himself what remained of Tsok: it was a burned out shell of a town, some fires still smoldering.

As they rode down closer, following Tsering's urgings, cartridges were placed in the ancient rifles. Everyone was alert. A snarling black mastiff headed their way, but when he got close, his bravery evaporated and he ran away, tail between his legs.

The horsemen clip-clopped into the dusty main street. Lasker's heart sank. The signs of massacre were evident. They passed several naked bodies swinging on ropes hung out of second- and third-floor windows. There were no signs of life aside from the dog. It smelled of decaying bodies. The town hummed with flies.

They came to the town square—a cobble-paved area around a single water faucet. The square was filled with bloody, torn bodies—men, women, children. Some had no heads attached. Many of the dead had their legs and hands tied behind them. The smell was now appalling and Lasker and the others covered their noses and mouths with pieces of cloth to continue.

"Tsok," said Tinley, "was butchered; they did not resist. There are no Chinese bodies, and you see they were tied and then murdered. The smell indicates that it happened several days ago."

The riders started chanting now, *"Om Mani Padme Hum, Om Mani Padme Hum."*

Lasker asked what it meant.

"Hail to the Jewel in the Lotus," said Tinley. "It is untranslatable, really—it is the most powerful protective mantra." Lasker started mouthing the strange words to himself. He was sickened. He had never seen such carnage! It was like the scenes he'd watched on TV of airline crash sites. Who had done this? *Why?*

146

They rode on past that square of utter madness. The rebels dismounted and, with their few old guns and their knives at the ready, spread out. They climbed atop the roof of each house—Tibetan houses had their doors on the roof—which were interconnected. The rebels searched through each building one by one.

Lasker felt he had to join in the search. Climbing on a roof to enter a building, he went into a room, saw a hand sticking out from under some overturned boxes, which Bart moved. It was the body of a man—and with him a young child. The child's hands were hacked off, and the man's penis was stuffed in the little boy's mouth.

Bart leaned against a wall, and threw up. Tinley had climbed down the ladder after him, and tugged at his sleeve. "There is nothing to do in here—Chinese have killed everyone. Please, come outside."

Lasker nodded, and went to climb up the ladder. "Why? Why did they do this?"

"Who knows?" said the boy. "Come up. We will go to the temple at the end of town—maybe they have left the monk there alive. . ."

Just as he and Tinley were about to enter the temple's portal, Tsering came out of its shadowy interior. His arm placed across the way, he blocked them. But Tinley said something and they were let in. Lasker heard a creaking sound, stopped in his tracks.

Once Lasker's eyes got adjusted to the dimness, he beheld the most gruesome sight he had ever seen. The creaking sound was the monk hung by his feet from a rafter of wood, swaying back and forth in the wind. But it wasn't just a hanging.

There were sticks driven straight through his abdomen and out his back. His eyes had been burned out—

the pokers that had done the job were lying on the ground below him, what was left of his eyes adhering to them. He had no sex organs.

The bronze Buddha, its face smeared with excrement, sat behind a pile of human body parts. Bloody piles of sex organs, hands, and feet. They were stacked bloody bit upon bloody bit before the statue.

Lasker went out and retched again on the side of the building. When he got back to India, if he got back—he would tell—tell the world. Then he realized: The Tibetan exiles had been telling the world—for thirty years! And no one did anything!

Tsering and several men went in and began carrying out the torn and trampled *thankas*—religious paintings on silk scrolls—that had been thrown to the floor. They carefully rolled them up and put them into bundles, tied them to their saddles.

"What can I do to help?" asked Lasker. He and Tinley were set to collecting the scattered pages of Tibetan books—long, loose pages—placing them back into their laquered board covers, and tying them shut.

The vultures were dropping lower, whirling around, sometimes throwing their shadows across the pale sun above.

One of the biggest vultures alighted just atop the peaked roof of the temple. Lasker noted that the Tibetans didn't shoot the crooked-necked flesh eaters, but were even *calling* to them, asking them to come.

"What's going on, Tinley?" Lasker asked, as he piled the books he had reassembled up in a mound.

The boy replied, "The funeral birds are here to eat the bodies—it is their duty. And it is our duty to dismember the bodies and give the dead of Tsok the sky burial."

"You mean you feed your dead to the vultures?"

"It is our way. The bodies can feed the hungry birds.

148

This is compassion. The dead will be happy that their bodies could be of use as food to these creatures of the sky. All kindness is repaid.''

Lasker watched incredulously as, handkerchiefs over their faces, the Tibetans, including the women, dragged the bodies out into the street. They started to hack pieces off the bodies and fed them to the big birds, who dove and alighted among the humans, tearing at the flesh.

He watched body after body being consumed, the birds flying off with body parts, disappearing into the distance. The birds were unafraid, and efficient. They made quick work of whatever was offered. The human parts already hacked up in the temple were brought out last and fed to the smaller birds. *Gather and hack;* talking low to each other as they worked, the Tibetans recited mantras as the birds devoured their meals. Lasker was curiously unemotional now. He even helped drag bodies. Perhaps, he reflected later, he had been in shock. The little medical lama went to every body's ear before the bodies were hacked, and he whispered something—Tinley said it was the traditional instruction to the dead, reminding them of the guidance they had received in life from their lamas for their journey into the beyond.

By nightfall, they had dragged all the bodies from their places in and around the town—over a hundred. And the birds—all except the big ''King'' vulture, who sat holding a meaty arm in its beak up on the temple roof—had flown off.

When they had tied some salvaged books on the yaks, Tsering came over the Lasker and took him by the shoulder and said something Tinley translated. ''Cheojey Lama says thank you for helping out.''

149

Lasker was exhausted—physically, mentally, and it seemed, spiritually. The crescent moon lit their way as they rode out of town, past the chess-pawn-like white chortens lining both sides of the road.

Laster idly let his eyes roam over the chortens as they passed.

He somehow noticed that one of the chortens, which were made of cemented sections of rock, had a fresh coat of mortar in one crack. His mind *fixated* upon the crack. There was something telling him—that there was a person inside!

There was someone sealed inside, gasping for air.

He yelled out, "Stop."

# Chapter 17

Tinley was the first to turn and notice that Lasker, who had been trailing the others, had dismounted and was scrambling across the disordered piles of stones at the road's edge, toward the chorten. He yelled, "What is it? What do you see?"

Bart's fingernails dug into the white mortar of one of the stupas. "Help me, somebody," he yelled. He knew there was somebody trapped inside the stones, just as surely as he knew his own name. "I think some-one's trapped in here. Tinley, come here, help me take this stone out."

Lasker broke several fingernails clawing at the mortar between the ancient rocks.

Tinley rushed to Lasker's side and pulled at his sleeve. "Stop it, these monuments should not be des-ecrated."

"I tell you someone is trapped inside. Tinley, do you have a knife?"

"Yes, I do, but—"

"Give it to me," Bart snapped, wild-eyed. Tinley gave him the knife and Bart began to dig it into the mortar. "Get more knives—and sticks. We have to pry this big stone loose."

The others dismounted and gathered around. At Tinley's urging, Tsering's knife came out and dug at the mortar in the crack. Then another and another knife dug at the mortar.

It was just a matter of minutes before the block of stone was pried loose.

"Good! Come on now, *shove!*" Lasker implored, knowing nobody except Tinley knew what the hell he was saying. With Rinchen's mighty assistance, the big stone was rocked out of place. It tumbled free and broke in two.

There was a wail, a weak, subdued human cry— from inside the monument. A woman's wimper.

"It's true," Tinley shouted. "Someone *is* in there."

Bart reached inside, his hand closed around a thin cold arm, and with a feeling of great connectedness, he tugged.

Slowly Bart edged a young woman out of her tomb. The prisoner-of-the-stones gazed upon her savior with almond-shaped eyes streaked with tears. Her tangled mass of long black hair was encrusted with filth, but you could see she was beautiful. She was immediately taken from his arms. The women took over, pushed the men away, except for Cheojey. They lay the rescued girl on a pelt, started rubbing her legs. A canteen of water was put to her parched lips.

Cheojey Lama bent down to the woman curled on the pelt, saying, "There, there, it's all right. You're safe. What is your name?"

Cheojey felt so sorry for the young woman. She must have been near madness entombed there in the small space.

How had the American found her? Superior telepathic ability? Although most Tibetans had some such

152

ability, Cheojey had heard that Westerners had not the slightest psychic ability. That must be wrong.

Cheojey lifted her right wrist and rolled his fingers over her pulse centers. He was greatly relieved when he did not pick up the irregular, flat death pulse on the third nerve. But there was plenty enough wrong; she needed some Fa leaf tea and the Dommo black pills he had in his little cloth bag attached to his belt.

He called for some water to be boiled. That was already being done on a small fire started in anticipation of such need. Tempa, Tsering's wife, fetched his bag, and he took out six of the precious lama pills, saying, "Please open your mouth . . ."

The entombment victim managed to do so. He put the spicy black pills on her tongue, and she swallowed them with some water from the canteen. She stopped shivering in a few minutes, and Cheojey was much pleased. The patient had no fever, and as Cheojey lifted each closed eyelid, he saw her pupils react to the nearby flames. No shock.

He probed here and there, to see if she had any wounds. When his finger touched her right leg, she shouted out in pain. His gentle rubbing, sending his *chi* energy down the central channels with a mantra to electrically stimulate the leg, worked in a few minutes. The pain, the stiffness he could feel sparking up into his fingertips, and he frequently shook his fingers into the cool air to dispel the numb feelings.

Her eyes slowly opened, her grimace relaxed. She was breathing more regularly, though too deeply.

"What is your name, young woman?" he asked again.

"D—Dorjee Nima," she said. Her eyes were fluttering.

Cheojey gave her white bark to bite on and started putting acupressure on the ten main nexus points of lower circulation, which are located in the throat and back as well as the legs. Her color was returning. He could feel it, he didn't need bright lights to see it.

"She will be well," Cheojey whispered to Tempa, and Tempa rushed off to tell the others.

Lasker, on hearing the news, gasped out, "Thank God." He sank to the ground. Tsering gave him some Chang from a canteen.

Leaving Lasker, Tsering went over to Cheojey, who looked up and anticipated the question. "She will be capable of moving soon. She cannot ride a horse, so have them prepare a litter."

"Does she know what happened to Tsok? How did she get in the chorten?"

"Later," the monk doctor said. "Don't ask her questions now."

After a litter—two sticks and webbing laden with pelts—was prepared and attached to Rinchen's sturdy mount, Dorjee was placed on it. Tsering drew Cheojey aside, away from the others. "Cheojey," he said, "is this American some sort of devil to have found her? Or is he merely psychic?"

"I can definitely say he is not a ghost. There are no signs of possession. I treated him, remember, after he fell from the sky machine. He has none of the major or minor signs of possession. His pulses indicate nothing like that."

"Then how did he know that she was—"

Cheojey drew his hands across his chin. "I suspect he has some past-life connection with the entombed girl. It could have enabled him to sense her danger, feel her terror. A karmic link of extraordinary power with Dorjee Nima."

154

"Dorjee Nima? The daughter of the main land-owner around here? Ah, is that who she is? I remember her. A beautiful girl. A wonderful family. I saw the father among the—bodies . . ." he trailed off. "I suppose she knows."

They mounted up and moved on, both because Tsering was anxious to reach Youngden Rimpoche, and because he was fearful the Chinese slaughterers would return.

They made camp some hours later between a tumble of boulders on a moonlit hillside, and a fire was lit. The rescued girl was placed in one tent they erected for the night.

Tsering questioned her as she lay on pelts warmed by rocks from the fire, as Cheojey had instructed. "Dorjee, it is Tsering. You and your father knew me."

"Yes," she replied with a wan smile.

"What happened? Tell us."

"They—they came, Tse Ling's troops, fifty or more. They demanded that we tell them where Youngden Rimpoche was. T-they called Youngden an arch traitor escaping retribution of the people. We said we had not seen him—even though Youngden's party had just left the village the day before. Finally after they shot some of the children—in the square—we told them a lie. My father first made it up and everyone stuck to it. We lied that Rimpoche had gone southeast—actually he headed for Crystal Pass. Southwest.

"When they shot at me, I ran to the *stupa,*" she said, using another name for *chorten.* "I knew of the loose rock, I hid. But the Chinese soldiers saw me go in, and they—they laughed as they walled me in." She sobbed softly.

So, thought Tsering, scratching on the long scar un-

155

der his missing eye, it was as he had reasoned. The soldiers of Tse Ling's garrison in Chamdo had killed the villagers.

When the dawn came, Lasker's first sight was the woman he had rescued, stepping from the tent into the sun. The women had sponged her off, combed her hair, and dressed her in their extra outfit—chuba, boots, a worn blouse. Her hair was long, to her mid-back, and it blew in the cold wind. She was radiant.

She caught his eye and, as he scrambled to his feet, brushed her hair back self-consciously. She came to him.

Dorjee was tall, perhaps five eight, and beautiful, in the elegant strong Tibetan way. And she was familiar. Bart could *feel* her approach like a magnet; his eyes met hers. She smiled and hugged him.

"Thank you, my giver of light," she said, and Bart found out a kiss was not unknown to the Tibetans.

There was much teasing from afar, and laughter. Cheojey tried to quiet the raucous caravan men, and their lewd suggestions to "the new couple," as they called them, saying, "Stop this—you embarrass their privacy." But they were all a crude lot and continued to shout, "Hey, American, you must sleep with her." Or, "I think you've got something good there, ho ho."

Tsering watched amazed. The stranger didn't seem to know what to do. Surely he knew females . . . and their ways—or did he? Such public display by a woman of her affection meant that the man should immediately go off and should *prove* how much a man he was. Instead, the American just held her hand!

Rinchen harrumphed. With a desultory glance, he mounted up and the others did likewise, disappointed that Lasker didn't make for the rocks to make love.

156

"This American is stupid, like all Westerners," Rinchen commented to the rebel leader.

Dorjee was given one of the horses they had found wandering outside Tsok to ride. It was the gentlest of animals, as befit such a beauty. Dorjee wore a frown, disappointed no doubt, thought Tsering, that the stranger had repelled her advances. Perhaps he doesn't know our ways, Tsering thought. I'd better tell him what he is likely to miss unless he grabs Dorjee and takes her off alone.

As they rode alongside one another, Tinley said to Lasker, "Thanks to Dorjee Nima we know where Youngden is. Her heroic people misdirected the Chinese. We go now to deliver our gold to Youngden Rimpoche, and to bring you to him. But we must take the high shortcut. It is rather high altitude—and probably in disrepair . . ."

"Shortcut?" queried Lasker. "Is it dangerous?"

Tinley just looked at him. Finally the boy said, "Just a bit. It is not *quite* as easy as the route we have so far traveled."

They stopped at noon for the main Tibetan meal of the day—lunch. When they gathered at the campfire, Cheojey told the Snow Lions that it was an act of compassion, a gift of insight by the Buddha, that drew Lasker to the stupa. But some of the men said the American was a demon, to be left behind.

"I tell you," said Rinchen, "he is possessed with some creature from that hot stream we passed, or the unquiet spirit of one of the murdered townspeople." He inhaled some snuff and sneezed. Then he said, "See, there *is* something wrong. I never sneeze when taking snuff."

"It is your nerves," said Cheojey. "The man from

America"—he used the Chinese *Meiguoren,* meaning the Beautiful Country's man—"is not an evil or possessed being. Shemer Rimpoche likes him. We must do as Shemer Rimpoche said, deliver the money and Lasker to Youngden Tulku Rimpoche. So they will be able to cross the border to India."

Rinchen said, "It will be well to be rid of him—no human could know Dorjee Nima was in the stupa. He is a foreign devil. I do not like Westerners in general. Their light skin is unappealing, like sickly fish, and their eyes are like children's marbles—I have even seen blue eyes on some of the Westerners—can you imagine? Blue eyes? And they cannot take care of themselves, either, can't make a fire from flint, can't do a thing to survive without their machines. They are ignorant of the dharma, and have no god but money—like the Chinese."

Cheojay said, "Nonsense. The Buddha taught that all sentient beings are equal, and all aspire to enlightenment, once they are exposed to the idea. It is the dark ages in the West, that is all. And as for their looks, not everyone can be pretty like you, Rinchen."

There was much laughter.

But Rinchen kept to his point, telling that he distrusted the foreign "ghost." "Logically," he said, "Lasker could only have known Dorjee Nima was in there if he had been told so by the Chinese officer that spoke to him on the road. And why would the Chinese officer tell him this? Because the American is working with them. If he is not a bad spirit, then it is all a plot to lead the Snow Lions to destruction."

Rinchen vowed that he would keep an eye on Lasker, watch him carefully, until they dumped him with Youngden. He would kill this Lasker if he made the slightest suspicious move.

# Chapter 18

The Snow Lions left the well-trodden level caravan trail, and started up a precipitous ill-defined track. Bart was disapointed that Dorjee rode far to his rear. The sky became darker blue, almost black, and Lasker's ears started to throb, his breaths coming in uneasy gasps. The Tibetans were unaffected and walking besides their horses to save them the climb. Lasker needed very little encouragement to stay on his horse. It was still late afternoon but the air was icy cold as well as very thin. He grew irritable. Why did they always head so high?

"Is this a trail?" Lasker complained. "All I see is sliding gravel."

"Yes, it is a trail," Tinley, who was walking alongside the horse, said. "It is the highest in the whole province, the Chinese have trouble breathing here. It saves a day off the regular route to Crystal Pass. We can hope that Youngden Rimpoche's group is still in the long valley leading from the Crystal pass."

Lasker started developing a splitting headache, probably, he thought because of the altitude.

"Here, if you eat some of these sweetmeats," Tinley said, "your headache will diminish." Lasker took them and said, "Thanks." They were little balls of dough with sugar powder on them.

Lasker chewed on the sugary balls, which tasted vaguely of dried plum, and wondered how Tinley knew of his headache. Perhaps he had seen some sort of pained expression on his face. The sweets did help a bit, but Bart could hear his heart pumping wildly and irregularly. He was gasping for breath by the time they reached the top and started winding down the other side. The sun set, and they were still up on a trail a mere yard wide, overhanging a sickening ten-or twelve-thousand-foot drop. The area below had clouds in it that seemed to be rolling in from the east. They were grayish.

"Is there a fire, Tinley?"

"No, that is smoke from the prison called Smoke Mountain. There, Tibetan prisoners serve life sentences at hard labor for political crimes or patriotic acts."

"What do they do at Smoke Mountain—to make that smoke?"

"The smoke is from a factory there. They also use big shovels on trucks to bury something, a very dangerous thing sent from China. They send it here for burial because they don't want it near China! It's in big lead cartons. It's called n—nucalar—nuclar—"

"*Nuclear waste?*" Laskar asked.

"Yes, that's it." Tinley said. "I don't know what that is, but it is supposed to be bad. Is it?"

"Yes, it's very bad."

"The Chinese have an endless supply of it. A dozen trucks a month come from China via the Chungking-Gandong Road and the prisoners unload it and put it way down in the ground. The smoke is from digging too, and big shovels that move the dirt as big as houses around. Some of us have spied on them and seen these things. We wish we could rescue the poor people sent there, but there are a thousand of Tse Ling's troops there, and fences and all such things. It is impossible.''

"Where is this Smoke Mountain?''

"Three hours east of here, by fast horse. It is in a hidden valley, accessible only by a guarded road that comes off the Chinese highway. Conditions for the slave workers are horrible. Rumor is that prisoners that get sent there never leave.''

Lasker chewed that information over silently. He wondered if the outside world knew about Smoke Mountain. Probably waste from China's nuclear power plants, or decayed ICBM missile warheads, was sent there for disposal.

They descended rapidly down into a snowy valley and Bart got a burst of adrenalin. There was a terrible roar. Tinley pointed. Bart beheld two shaggy, gigantic horned animals of immense proportions. Their horns were down and they were preparing to engage, scraping the ground with their front hooves.

They rushed at each other and collided. The meeting of horns sounded like thunder. It echoed through the valley.

"What are they?'' Lasker asked.

"Wild yaks—and they are fighting.''

Tsering hustled the caravan into a copse of pine trees. Their animals were in a panic. Then Lasker and the others went to the edge of the trees to watch the awesome battle. These horned monsters were as shaggy as their yaks, and *looked* like yaks, but were three times the size. The huge beasts hung with heavy tangles of hair bellowed, pawed the ground, lowered their heads again, and ran toward each other. The shock of horn hitting horn was heard like a cannon shot again. The cause for the battle appeared to be a herd of five or six smaller but still formidable females off to the contestants' right.

Tinley said, "Giant yaks are sacred animals to Tibetan

Buddhists, yet some desperate villagers now kill then—one yak can feed an entire village all winter. So there are few left. This is most unusual to see! They block our path anyway."

The awesome encounter went on for an hour. The pair were like ramming Sherman tanks. The caravaners began picking their favorites. Wagers were made—turquoise-laden belts for silver stirrups, or blankets for woven chubas. And no one, least of all the American, wanted to go on until they could ascertain the winner. Lasker picked the slightly smaller, faster one, betting Tsering his compass against Tsering's knife. But a natural conclusion to the encounter was not to be.

Six Delta-wing Chinese jet fighters came screaming over the valley. Their hurtling intrusion shattered the nerves of both prehistoric contenders. The giant yaks bolted in opposite directions as the females scattered every which way.

Lasker along with the others spontaneously shouted invective and waved his fists at the jets, to his great surprise. The caravaners had their troubles keeping their animals under control.

Lasker and his rugged companions were obligated to head onward, all bets off. It was a steep track that led directly to their destination: Crystal Pass. It was a long green valley that shimmered like a mirage.

There were signs that a number of animals and humans had passed the same way. "Just a day or so earlier, slow-moving too," according to Rinchen. How he knew by sniffing at the stones and feeling the gritty soil was beyond Bart. "There are no vehicle tracks, or cigarettes of the Chinese," Rinchen concluded. "It must be Youngden Tulku Rimpoche's party."

Bart was exhausted and so were the others. Before continuing on down the long verdant pass, they stopped for a repast of butter tea, and pieces of dried yak meat.

162

"Tinley," Lasker asked, "you call yourselves Buddhists, yet you eat meat—I thought Buddhists ate no flesh."

"Buddha allowed the eating of meat if vegetables are not plentiful, or if a particular person's health is in jeopardy if he does not eat meat. Because life is hard enough. The Buddha was not strict to suffering people. We do not kill animals, but we eat the animals non-Buddhists sell us. We only eat *large* animals, because many people can share one animal, lessening the sacrifice of life. Therefore we eat no fish. And we don't eat birds, they eat us."

"As I've seen . . ." Lasker said.

"If a yak should fall and die, we will, of course, cut it up and eat it." Tinley smiled, and tore a piece of dried yak meat with his perfect teeth. "Many Buddhists buy clumsy yaks."

"But if you don't kill, how can you fight the Chinese? Is it okay to kill *people*?"

"No, it is wrong. Because of this, most Tibetans did not violently resist the Chinese. But the many nomads and the rugged mountain tribesmen had long been fighters, and were eager to kill the invaders. They believe that it must be done."

"How about you, Tinley? Would you kill the Chinese—for what they did to Tsok?"

"No, because on the ultimate level, everyone is alike, just more or less deluded. The Chinese will suffer for their delusions. As a dharma practitioner, I know this."

Lasker said, "I would kill the ones that slaughtered the villagers . . ." His mind went to the naked dismembered children he had seen in Tsok, and then to Dorjee, who had been entombed alive.

After a bit, they moved along the warm, verdant pass. The trees gave way to twisted pillows of frozen green lava. Petrified rock flows from the time the Tibetan plateau was thrust up into the sky by the collision of Continental India into Asia. He wished he could share his amazement with Dorjee, but she kept away. The lava flow was a fantastic convoluted formation with its layers nearly perpendicular to the terrain. A geologist's heaven, an artist's challenge.

Farther along the pass, olive green stones about the size of eggs lay everywhere, causing their animals some slippery going. Lasker recognized them as the semiprecious stones called olivine. There were also strange electric-blue flowering bushes buzzing with black flies, jutting from the piles of green stones. Flies—huge buzzing black mosquito-like things that tortured Lasker. He was bitten a dozen times. The stings brought huge welts. The others weren't touched by the flies. Finally they relented.

Lasker was constantly turning around and looking at Dorjee, who rode poker-faced far behind him, ignoring his smiles. Had he performed some offense? He hoped not.

She had the most intriguing almond eyes, he thought, quite smitten. And her aquiline nose set between high cheekbones, her perfect light-mocha complexion, made Bart *yearn* for the slightest acknowledgment that he existed.

He wished he could postpone leaving Tibet. He wanted to court Dorjee, to be with her. He felt there was a link of some sort between them. Plus Bart was getting used to the rugged people and terrain, and liking both. The choked freeways and shopping malls of America—and even the twisting fetid alleys of New Delhi—seemed like a distant dream. Only Tibet seemed real.

As they traversed this spectacular valley, his reasons for wanting to return to India seemed ludicrous. Did he really want airplanes? Was that his goal in life? Planes scare yaks, make terrible noises that disturb people. They took people places, but did they really want to go? Laughable. And the money . . . what was it for? Cars? And

164

fine restaurants? He imagined bribing tuxedoed maître d's for the best tables in the choicest restaurants, envisioned those discos that scrutinized their lineup to see if those waiting were "hip" enough to enter. Ridiculous.

Here in Tibet, everyone was up against terrible hardships—brutal unforgiving nature, and the hated Chinese occupiers. Yet they had joy, their real life. Did he have a life back in India? Was it life to be obsessed with Jenny and with money, and solitary drinking, cars, fine clothes? What *were* fine clothes?

Could those people imagine the Tibetans, living day to day, with only the shirts on their back, only wanting to be left alone? Were they as confident in their religion, their way of life? What did the world know or care of what was going on here to Tibetans who just wanted to be left alone? Lasker vowed that when he reached India, he would tell the world of the Chinese slaughter at Tsok. He would do at least that. The world would hear.

But there was more to Tibet for him than hardship and slaughter. There was beauty, and *spirit* here. Life was more real, deeper, the people more generous and open than anything he could have imagined. So many people had helped him. Even Rinchen had his virtues. And if he were Rinchen, Lasker thought, he would probably feel the same way about Lasker. I'd want to get rid of Lasker too.

He would go back, but only because the Chinese were after him. Because he didn't belong here. But he'd never forget this place. And Bart would never forget Dorjee, the girl he rescued through the bizarre premonition.

Lasker knew in India he would endeavor to study more about Tibet's Lamist Buddhism, a belief system that with its reincarnation and karma and so on seemed to sustain these people, hold them up, make them strong. Indeed, it made them the most purposeful, open, and forgiving people Bart had ever met.

He had no more time for rumination, for the late sun glinted off metal in the distance. Perhaps the flash of swords raised high, far down the valley. Then as he rode with the Tibetans down the slope, Lasker heard a drumming, and saw splotches of color beneath the metallic reflections. He was soon able to make out the figures waving swords. Half-animal, half-human creatures, they danced in a circle. Demons of the mountains?

The semihuman dancers were making slow swirling motions in a circle about a hundred feet in diameter. They tossed the long brightly colored silken sleeves of their robes as they jumped about, then they would freeze in place, then jump and freeze again. The drum beats didn't seem to match, merely inspire their movements. Some of these silent bow-legged apparitions, Lasker noted as they rode closer, had fierce bull heads. Others had immense deerlike heads. But the oversized heads were blue or red in color and the mouths contained teeth like those of wolves. The ''deer'' were topped with antlers like the most gigantic bucks. Other dancers had phantasmagoric heads of horses or water buffalo.

The fantasy dancers were trailing streams of ribbon behind them.

Lasker could see the drummers now, orange-clothed monks with shaven heads sitting to the side, banging different-shaped drums with long twisted bows. There were a dozen or so.

The dancers, in their slow dipping and swirling motions, would occasionally charge the drummers, in false attack.

About a hundred yards farther away, he could make out black tents, their roofs bristling with sticks holding fluttering white pennants, some with symbols on them— prayer flags. There were brush-encircled corrals for many horses, including a magnificent white steed. There were also yaks that saffron-robed monks were pitching hay to. The Snow Lion rebels had at long last found Youngden Tulku's party.

Lasker asked Tinley, "Aren't they afraid of airplanes spotting them?"

"I don't understand either," Tinley said. "But Tulkus—living ghosts, like Youngden Rimpoche—always do the right thing."

The rebels rode down shouting and holding aloft their rifles.

The dancers in the valley, though far away, were crystal clear. It was like being in the top row of a well-designed theater—you could see everything.

The dancers stopped their performances and took off their big papier mâché mask heads and cheered their arrival. Tsering took the reins of the yak that carried the sacks of gold. He trotted forward toward the biggest tent with the most prayer flags—evidently Youngden Tulku Rimpoche's tent.

Bart watched as Tsering got off his mount and protrated three times to a man who came out. "It is not the Tulku," said Tinley. "It is his regent that has come out."

Tsering spoke to the old monk-regent, then came back to the group, still leading the yak,

"The Tulku is up the hill," Tsering said. Lasker couldn't make it all out, but got the gist.

"What is the Tulku doing up on the hill?" he asked Tinley.

"Talking to rocks."

"Yup," said Lasker, "why not?"

They all went up the slope, toward several figures among the boulders there. There was a big young man in the middle of the group, chipping away at a stone with a small pickax. He wore a silken pea-pod hat like Shemar Rimpoche had, only blue. Several attendant monks buzzed around him, untangling his robe from snags, helping him move by grasping his elbow. The young man with the silk hat seemed intent on killing himself on that precipitous rock ledge. He moved recklessly. He would have fallen a dozen times without his helpers securing him.

Lasker, Rinchen, and Tinley followed Tsering to his meeting with Youngden Tulku Rimpoche. Tsering again prostrated three times. The Tulku stopped his mad digging and shouted out *"Tashi Delek,"* came slipping recklessly down to Tsering. Again, his helpers supported his wild and clumsy movements. Lasker took a good look at his face. God, Youngden Rimpoche was just a teenager, a tall fat pimply-faced teenager with a shock of black hair hanging down across his high forehead. The youth stood still and heard Tsering's tale, which was told with much gesturing back at Lasker, and punctuated with lots of airplane noises and so on. Then Tsering, his voice boastful, went to get one of the sacks from the yak. He spilled its contents of gold coins out at the feet of the Tulku.

Youngden appeared to be unmoved as he said something softly.

Lasker asked his translator what was said.

"The Tulku said he has to dig in the rocks some more before examining the gold."

Lasker watched the Tulku pick up an elongated dull gray rock he had been inspecting and begin speaking rapidly to it, turning it around in his hands as he spoke.

"What's he doing Tinley?"

"I'm not sure."

As they watched, the Tulku cracked the oval rock open and extracted a perfect quartz crystal. He threw the outer covering of the marvelous thing down, and held the crystal up to the sunlight.

Then the Tulku sat down on his haunches and started speaking to the crystal, brushing it clean with the sleeve

168

of his robe. He listened, his neck crooked to the side. Finally he said, "Ah," and then put the crystal down and walked over to Lasker.

The Tulku shook Lasker's hand firmly and asked, "How do you do?"

Lasker felt foolish. "Fine, thank you,"

"I am practicing English, I have a set of Berlitz cassettes, and I play them constantly. Do I sound all right?"

"Perfect," Lasker said. He did.

"Good! and how about these?" The Tulku raised his robe and Lasker saw that underneath them he was wearing Levis. "Is that *hip?*"

"Very hip, Your Holiness." Lasker made bold to ask, "Er, what were you doing with the crystal?"

"Getting instructions. It has been here a long time in this pass and knows many things."

Lasker let that drop. "Rimpoche, aren't you afraid that if you stay here in the open you might be seen by Chinese planes?"

"There are many groups of traveling musicians and dancers in these mountains at this time of year, since it is the time of the paranirvana—the ascension of the Buddha. An airplane would be looking for a group of travelers that is trying to *hide.*"

"I see." Lasker was reminded of Ellery Queen's statement about "hiding in plain sight." It made some sort of sense.

The young Tulku thanked Lasker for the gold and for his concern. He blessed him by bonking his high forehead against Lasker's. It was quite a bonk, and unexpected.


Later, as the Snow Lions sat at the campfire drinking hot tea, Tinley said, "Lasker, it was a great honor to have the Tulku speak directly to you. What do you think of him?"

169

"Somehow I expected him to different. Older. He's just a kid, and a very clumsy one at that."

"His combined lifetimes give him a total age of three hundred and four years. And since Tulkus reincarnate as the same person, they *remember* their past lives. His carelessness on the hillside gives his assistants the opportunity to help him. Their karma is immeasurably improved by helping His Eminence."

"You don't say."

"Are all Americans irreverent—is that the word?"

"That's us. Besides, this Tulku of yours didn't seem upset when Tsering told him about all those dead people back there in Tsok. Is he coldhearted?"

"On the contrary. He is doing the Bardo Puja for all of them tonight. He is very concerned that they have died."

"He doesn't act it."

"Lasker, all of us die. It is how we lived our lives that counts—when we must be reborn, that alone determines whether our rebirth is favorable or not. All of us are in the grips of karma. For instance, it is your karma that you came to this place. And it was your good karma to do so."

"Good karma? Losing my plane? Practically getting killed? I was supposed to fly in and out a few hours."

"I was told that the dry riverbed you were to land your airplane on is not dry, Lasker. You would not have been able to land. A glacier shifted last month, and the river is replenished. They were waiting for you for several days, they believed that your airplane could land on water also. They don't know much about such things, never seeing an airplane land. It is all karma—you are here and the gold is here—and all is as destiny would have it."

"No such thing as coincidence? Accidents?"

Tinley said, "Oh yes, many. But most of what we see as haphazard is the fulfillment of karma we have ourselves created in our life this time around and in previous lives.''

Lasker nodded. The same superstition about past lives was endemic in all of Asia. And yet . . . it did explain a lot. Why live and learn and then lose it all at death? If life did go on, it would make more sense. Building your destiny from life to life—toward something higher. What?

''Tell me about this Tulku. Why is he so important?''

''He is the head of the Dempa lineage—the Blue-hat sect. He died in India sixteen years ago, and his reincarnation was recognized twelve years ago, when he was four years old, in northern Tibet. He is spiritual leader to ten thousand refugees in India, who have been too many years without their leader.''

''I thought only the Dalai Lama was reincarnated.''

''Not true, Lasker-la.''

Lasker smiled. This was the first time he'd been called ''la,'' a term of friendship.

''How come the Tulku couldn't reincarnate in India, where he died?''

''I don't know. He chose to do it this way. In any case, he was reborn in the remote north, and thus was overlooked, survived. Now he leaves Tibet. He has traveled twelve hundred miles so far. The Chinese cannot stop his destiny if it is to be with his people.''

''What did the crystal say to him?''

''I am told His Eminence was informed that he should move slower. Stay in this pass another two days.''

''That's ridiculous.''

Tinley shrugged. ''Advice from the mountain. All things move slowly in Tibet—nothing is done without much meditation to show the way. Besides, the Tulku has eluded the Chinese for twelve hundred miles. Could you do that?''

Lasker admitted he couldn't.

Tinley smiled. "You will understand the Dharma yet, Lasker-la."

Bart practiced Tibetan again with Tinley for awhile. He wanted to use these last few hours in Tibet as an immersion in conversational Tibetan. He wanted to continue to study the language back in India, and read some of their 133,000 books. It was becoming easy for him to repeat the most frequently used words. And he always thought he was *bad* at languages!

Someone approached them.

He looked up. Dorjee. She had slipped up to Bart and now she smiled. He smiled back.

She crouched next to him, handed him a blue ribbon, and left.

"What's this, Tinley?"

"I don't know how you say it in English. It is saying to you to come to her tomorrow—for the—male-female act?"

Lasker whistled. "When?"

"You'll see. I told her earlier that you didn't understand our customs. And she realized you didn't dislike her, that you just didn't understand her kiss."

"She thinks I rejected her? No way! When do I go to her?"

"Just relax, Lasker-la." Tinley laughed. "She will come to you tomorrow. See, the crystal did you a favor. We will stay here for a while. You will go for a long walk with Dorjee. And don't disappoint Dorjee this time."

# Chapter 19

About two hours after dark had fallen, Lasker was approached by the Tulku's regent, who led him to the big tent.

Bart entered the tent, and figuring "what the hell," he made the customary three prostrations to the Tulku. After all, this was the guy he was depending on to take him safely across the border!

His forehead was dusty from the rugs on the floor when he went up to Youngden Tulku Rimpoche and placed the khatag—found on a pile by the tent flap—over his shoulders, and received the scarf back.

The Tulku said, "I hope that Darshan Rimpoche is well?"

"Darshan Rimpoche? I don't—"

"You know him as Mr. Losang."

"Losang? He's a Rimpoche too?"

The Tulku laughed a tight little giggle. "Hoh! You do not need robes to be a Rimpoche. We are human like anyone, subject to the sufferings of the flesh. Darshan is on a path that is necessary in order to accomplish the spread of the Blue-hat dharma to the West.

"Now tell me of your journey here, Laska-la."

Bart explained about the flight in, the money, the

bazooka shell hitting his taxi in New Delhi, and about meeting the Snow Lion rebels and meeting Shemer Rimpoche.

"That is a terrible journey! I did not realize you had such difficulty. Tse Ling wishes no one to come into this province of Tibet. It is one of the few areas that no tourists are allowed to traverse. That is, I suppose, because of the goings-on at Smoke Mountain. Something is going on there that Beijing is unaware of—I have heard, through my people, that Tse Ling is working for certain elements of international scope, and they are even more ruthless then Beijing!"

"International elements? Who?"

"Someone who can mount a riot in New Delhi to cover an attempt on your life, someone that can support her meteoric rise through the ranks of the People's Liberation Army. Tse Ling is just thirty years of age, Lasker-la. Yet her political power is phenomenal, especially for a woman. Anything you want to ask me, Lasker-la, while you're here with me, alone?"

Lasker smiled. "Well, I *might* as well ask. . . . People are always talking about climbing into Tibet to ask this of a holy man: *What is the purpose of life?*"

"Ah yes. That one . . . *again.*" The Tulku ran his tongue around under his lips before replying. "We must be more than animals. Life is *not* just to be like animals. Most humans are acting as if they were just animals of the lower orders. Think for a moment—an animal makes a home for itself, so do humans. No difference. The animal provides for his sustenance and warmth, and so do humans. Again, no difference. Animals consume and consume and then they die. Many humans do just this. No difference. But we must take this chance of precious human birth to do something good for ourselves and other sentient beings. We must

174

help improve things. Bringing the supplies and the gold is your way of helping Tibet. And that is a good act."

Lasker half frowned.

"Oh, I know you might have been doing it for other motives, but it is your karma. Something you set out to do in this lifetime not planned by you in this life, but in your previous life. Life is running out on all of us—every moment is precious. Because of our ignorant actions, we are like children playing in a burning house. We should not stay in the burning house. The wise take refuge in the dharma, which tells the way out of the burning house. The Buddha, who is the emanation of Dorje Chang, the ultimate spirit, shows the way out of the burning house. He asks that we put down our toys—conceptions such as clinging to this and that—and leave the fire. Actions without thinking, such as hatred and jealousy, are the fire. They lead to bad karma and more suffering. Karma ties us to the endless wheel of rebirth, and endless ignorant suffering by our own hands.

"The path of the Buddha, the path of loving kindness and knowledge, leads out of the burning house. Leads into equanimity, the peace and happiness of enlightenment. People use their *minds* to try to get out of suffering—but it is useless.

"They come up with ingenious things—technology, politics—democracy, or communism—but they are wholly unsuccessful—due to the obscurations of their minds. One can't *think* a way out of the karmic trap. Only by realization of the true nature of things, only by enlightenment, can one apply the skillful means to the real solutions. Peace comes not from systems of thought, or from technology, but from the mind. Each person's mind must be clear. That is the way of the Buddha. Self-realization—achievement of the Buddha mind. That is enlightenment, awakening, the *purpose* of life.''

Enlightenment—there's that word again, thought Lasker, then he asked, ''What the hell is enlightenment—dissolving into the oneness?''

''Enlightenment is not dissolving. It is awakening. Buddha said, 'Wake up,' that is all. Be aware of your life. That is the first step. Do not follow your tainted thoughts without ceaseless reflection. Practice meditation. Meditation stops the ceaseless flow of stimulus-response, stops our patterns. Meditation is stopping all of the thoughts that hide the truth. Meditation is how the Buddha saw the pure, unborn truth. And that is the way each of us can see it, and develop.''

''And what is the truth?''

''That all is Buddha mind.''

''And Buddha mind is—what?''

The Tulku said, ''Lasker-la, there are many steps on the path. And many things to learn. But the truth, ultimately, is emptiness. You have perhaps heard us chant the heart sutra—the most sublime teaching of the Buddha. It says, 'No tongue, no taste, no hand, no touch,' and so on. All is emptiness. Reality is a fantasy of the mind.''

*''Whose* mind?''

*''No one's* mind. All is without attributes. Emptiness is emptiness. Emptiness is form, form is emptiness. Not to recognize that emptiness is the nature of all things, we are always accumulating karma, and thus suffering in this life and the following. If you wish to see what you have done in past lives, take note of your present situation. If you want to see what you will become in your future lives, you can look into the content of your mind. We create our illusions. Forever, endlessly lost in time-space.

''Perhaps you wish to meditate upon this . . . for a

while. We will sit then, on our cushion, for a few moments. And with your eyes closed, Lasker-la, dwell on nonthought, think of emptiness. . . . Just breathe in and breathe out—naturally.''

"Is that meditation?"

''More or less. You'll catch on. Any thought that arises, just let it drop, exhale it.''

Lasker closed his eyes, sat silent for a long while after the Tulku said this. It was hard to understand, but it sort of made sense. Oops—*thinking!*

He dropped the thought. But thousands of others crowded into his mind. He dropped each one, but they kept arising. Lasker inwardly groaned. Here he was forced into meditation—how the hell long would it be?

He was listening to his own mind—caught it raging, rambling—and each time Bart caught the fact that he was thinking, he dropped it, as the Tulku had instructed.

After what seemed like twenty minutes or so—but could have been five minutes—he started to feel his muscles relax. Bart became aware of small noises, the wind outside, and the scent of the flowers and incense seemed to grow. Bart dropped that observation also.

Were Tulku's eyes open? He took a peak. No, his were closed too, but he was holding one hand out as if he were grasping something—an invisible cloth. And the other hand was as if it were holding a needle. Making stitches in that invisible cloth. He wore an expression of perfect bliss which made the Tulku's lips slightly curled at the edges, like the Mona Lisa. What on earth was he doing? Lasker watched for a moment. He was supposed to have his eyes closed. Bart was viewing something private, he knew. Something he was not supposed to see. Bart felt embarrassed.

He sat more upright and closed his eyes again. Eyes

closed—just breathe in breathe out . . . that's all . . .
that's all . . .

*No. I can't do it anymore. I want to get up. This proves
nothing—this meditation thing is like waiting in the dentist's
office.*

*Anger.*

He dropped it.

Bart suddenly was in a state he never had been in
before—ultimate quiet, relaxed, at peace. He was lost
in a reverie he could not explain, try as he might, later.

The little gong on the red pillow sounded. Lasker
looked up, saw the Tulku holding the striker next to
the gong, and smiled.

"That was about one hour. Very good, Lasker-la."

"Hour? It seemed like—"

"Moments. Yes, I know. That is emptiness."

The Tulku recited a brief chant dedicating the merit
they had accumulated to all the sentient beings. They
had some dried Chinese fruits and some tea, and then
he left the teenage holy man alone.


The caravaners sat by the campfire and roasted strips
of yak meat. Lasker went over and sat down by them.
He stared into the fire. Life is a burning house? He
remembered Donnely sitting there with the two bare-
breasted junkie women at his feet, remembered the
stoned look on the girl that had tugged at his zipper.
He looked up at the moon, which sat atop a blue-white
mountain peak.

*Life is more than being an animal. And Karma is always
being accumulated . . . always.*

Donnely's mind was a sewer. Lasker's had been in
danger of becoming the same way. Would he become
a sewer rat in his next life? And what of the things

178

Lasker had done—had he contributed to that sewer of the future?

He tore off a piece of yak meat offered to him and chewed. Was there only fleeting happiness in life, then impermanence—and suffering? Crippled beggars in the streets of New Delhi, the tortured dead of Tsok. He sighed deeply. Mankind was without any idea of what it was doing. Without the dharma.

Fine, if everyone thought like the Tulku, all would be well. But mankind could never do that . . . *could* they?

He spat the half-chewed meat into the fire. It sizzled. He went to bed under the stars. The last thing he saw before he closed his eyes was the green meteor that shot by in the constellation Scorpio overhead.

In the middle of the night, Bart felt the brush of cool lips on his cheek. He opened his eyes and beheld Dorjee. She smiled, and motioned silently. Bart sat up, and she whispered something in Tibetan in his ear.

He understood she meant, ''Let's go someplace—alone.''

Looking around the camp, he saw no one stir. He was sleeping in his clothes, because of the cold night air, so he slipped off the blankets and pelts, put on his boots, and followed her. She led him by the hand—eager to be off quickly, and he was greatly aware that this was only the third time they had touched one another.

They were soon out of sight of the camp, walking all alone under the blazing stars, and an aurora borealis that lit their bodies with flickering irridescence. They were like neon fish in a black velvet frame. All alone in the whole world, with her, with this sprite, this *passion* of his.

''Where are we going?'' he said in his rudimentary Tibetan.

179

"Follow," she said, giggling softly like a child and running ahead in the aurora-lit flower-covered slope. He followed. Bart admired the way she moved, admired her confident stride, graceful and yet strong. The smell of a world perfectly pure and wild all about them, the supernatural colors of their presence below the flickering curtains of he celestial realm—it was like a beautiful dream.

She stumbled and Bart was afraid she was hurt. He rushed to her. As he grasped her, she gasped out short breaths of intense passion, like a caged cat. He held her little body tightly against his own and kissed her. Dorjee's breath was sweet, her body firm and yielding, playful yet concentrated in desire, all at one and the same instant.

She drew away again. She shook out her long black hair, tossed it back over her shoulders, and giggling, was off like a deer, while Bart tried to keep up.

He wanted her as he had never wanted another woman. Bart wanted this Tibetan she-cat with smoldering lips and lithe tight hard body. Wanted Dorjee's mystery, her erotic powers, her magical properties in his arms. She was not a woman, she was *all* women, all Lasker wanted, all he had ever striven to understand and possess.

It seemed as if they knew each other—her skin was soft, familiar, her lips moist, ready.

And he realized that what he had with Jenny was passion. This was warmth, feeling, tenderness. He felt himself opening up, letting go, with Dorjee in his arms.

She found a pile of rocks, dug around with her hands, bending to look for something—and as he reached her and wrapped his arms about her thighs, her slender waist, she lifted up a golden lantern. How did she know it was there?

There was tinder and a flint to spark also, and much

quicker then he could ever have done, Dorjee ignited the lantern wick.

They had less trouble making progress across the nightscape then. But several times he tried to stop their movements, to draw Dorjee to him, kiss her passionately, and *have* her there, in the open.

But she persisted in slipping out of his grasp, admonishing him to wait—and gesturing toward the shadow of a cliffside some distance away.

The world was just the circumference of the glow of the lantern, shifting, changing, always filled with flowers.

Lasker knew from Dorjee's responses to his yearnings that there was no question as to whether *it* would happen or not. She just wanted a particular place to lie down and make love. A place of concealment, perhaps, though from what or whom, Bart couldn't fathom.

He worried that they could get lost. But she was his guide—she had found the lantern and she took him steadily onward toward the black cliff, through huge tumbled rocks.

This was night. Not a night as usual, but one of wildness and freedom. Bart didn't *care,* he decided, if they got lost. With Dorjee it seemed possible to shake off the mundane shackles of ordinary life and soar on a dream, on the gossamer wind of fantasy and perfection.

She knew the path, steep but sure, and when they climbed for a while along the cliff, Dorjee stopped him, motioned with a wave of her arms. He looked up, saw nothing. She extinguished the lantern. He stood still, blind momentarily. Then there was just the faintest thread of blue-gray on the eastern horizon. One snow-capped peak glowed dimly of pearl snow. Above, atop the cliff, was a golden glow. In moments the sun would come up the way it always does in Tibet—suddenly, spectacularly, sending rays in all directions. As there was enough light now to pick their way, she left the lantern.

He could see something high on the top of the cliff. A glimmer of dull gold, perhaps a building's roof.

"You want to go up there?" Lasker pointed.

She said something that he took to mean, "It's not so hard," and she pulled him onward up a steep path through fallen rocks.

His heart was pounding wildly from the altitude, the sheer fact of her presence, and the feeling that something awesome was about to happen that would make his previous relationships with other women insignificant.

They ascended higher, the path a mere two or three feet from the cliff wall. The sun was now brilliant on the horizon. The dull gold object above now reflected its rising splendor. A gold roof, for sure.

The narrow path disappeared entirely a few feet farther on. She took his hands and pressed them onto the obsidian cliff face, and Bart felt indentations. Hand holds? She smiled, and like a mountain goat, Dorjee dug her soft Tibetan boot fronts into the niches and began to ascend rapidly.

Surely he would die before he reached the top of the cliff, Lasker thought. But wildly, perhaps from loss of oxygen, or from some spell she cast, he laughed and climbed after Dorjee like a goat kid as if he couldn't fall.

Bart was a rock climber of a sort, but this was too much—hanging a hundred and fifty feet off the jagged rock moraine below. Lasker was so exhilarated to be with her, to follow, that his climbing was magical, he seemed to flow into her rhythm and not even think of falling. Sooner than he could have imagined, they had surmounted the cliff.

Lasker held Dorjee, and they turned and looked back out over a world of ice and snow streaked in the distance with red shafts of rising sunlight. Closer by, the rolling green hills and even the encampment looked like some miniature diorama, unreal. The world was a bowl, and they were looking down into it.

She turned now, took his hand again, and led him up a path. The view of the building had been blocked by a rock outcropping, which they now rounded via crumbling ancient slate steps.

Lasker beheld before him a small, partially ruined, yet exquisite temple. It was beautiful, in the simple way of the architecture of old.

Like the ruined temples of Greece, this temple was surrounded by a veritable field of broken lintels and roof parts, but somehow looked as if it was meant to be that way. And with the sun glinting off its roof's many golden points and the rose reflection off the distant glaciers illuminating its alabaster columns, it looked like the most heavenly place on earth, sure to be inhabited by pleasant spirits.

Dorjee led him into the darkened interior. They passed into coolness like the night they just left—and the smell of stone and of a place perpetually clean, pure, and abandoned overwhelmed Bart. It was as if the temple was crackling with energy, a focus of life and sensuality.

They came out of the brief bare entrance hall and into a room illuminated by a slit in the lintels above. There was a shrine at its end, and a stone statue. Buddha, in the meditative position, a quiet half-smile on his pink granite face.

Half hidden in the darkness were two other statues to the right and left, out of the beam of light. One had many arms. Lasker recognized it as Chenresig, Lord of Compassion, the same figure he wore in the amulet on his neck.

Dorjee prostrated herself on the cold flagstones, which Lasker noted were appointed with many swirling patterns of inlaid mosaic tiles, pastel from centuries of weathering. Then she went to the statue Lasker was unfamiliar with to the left and repeated the process, and then to the Chenresig statue.

There was little, if any, damage here, he realized, that could not be attributed to wind and climate: a few cracks in the mosaics that might be shifts of the terrain over centuries, recorded for all time. On the walls were faded and peeling frescos depicting the various stages in the life of Buddha, from his pleasant early life as a prince of the Sakya Clan, to his ultimate realization under the bodhi tree, to the teachings of the Dharma in eighty years of wanderings, and finally his death from eating spoiled food that Buddha was too polite to refuse. There were clusters of tatters on the floors near the marble pillars—perhaps once thanka paintings, turned to dust by the years. There were seven bowls of silver for offerings of water before each statue.

Lasker was amazed at this place, but even more anxious to explore Dorjee's mysteries. After her prostration before the gods, he took her in his arms and this time Dorjee did not pull away. She seemed to squirm a bit and then her chuba slid off her shoulders. He helped it along. The garment dropped away and suddenly she was utterly naked. She took his hand and pressed it to her firm coppery pear-shaped breast. The couple slipped down on their knees and then reclined on the cold mosaics before the Buddha statue. She kissed his lips again and again, searching for his essence, it seemed, drawing him into an oblivion of passion and love, intertwined and complimentary. He felt Dorjee's hard breasts, and kissed and suckled on them.

184

Then his hands roved down to her triangle of smooth black hair, and the opening, like a wet rose petal beyond it, in her open thighs. Dorjee moaned and allowed his hands to search for her wetness, encouraging it. She tugged at his waist rope. In an instant his garments, too, were in a pile on the stone floor.

Bart's desire was feverish, stronger and tenderer at the same time than anything he could have imagined. He felt he had never known a moment like this before, that this was it—all the other times, were—sexual. Just sexual. Lasker couldn't wait. "Now, Dorjee, now," he gasped.

She didn't understand the words but she understood as he pressed into her silken thighs. Utterly desiring him, moaning with that desire, she whispered something that Lasker knew meant, "Take me."

He pressed into her with his lips to hers. She gasped a little and he let up the pressure, slowing but not stopping his penetration. He was in the portals of her femininity.

He lifted his lips from hers, and he looked in her eyes. Her features seemed lost in gentle confusion. She sighed and seemed smaller and weaker than before. No more the she-goddess with powerful climbing legs, but a gentle flower of the Himalayas. He braced his hands on the cold mosaics and she shuddered as he moved himself with an undeniable pressure and determination all the way forward.

A tear formed on her right cheek, and he made to pull away. But Dorjee grabbed him, held him tight, and pressed her hips up, and he understood, and pushed forward. Finally he felt a giving away, and at the same time heard a sharp intake of air through her nostrils. She cried out softly. He was suddenly in Dorjee all the way, completely merged.

They were slow and uncertain at first, despite his

throbbing desire to continue. But her hips rose again and again to meet his thrusts, to keep him in her whenever he drew back. And they began their dance. It was tentative at first, but soon they felt the coordination, the rhythm that was the confirmation of their love for one another. They became as musical instruments in perfect tuning, pouring out a rising wail of heavenly music. They became a symphony of motion, a wave of perfectly timed rhythm, as if they had known each other's body for a thousand years.

As he moved in and out of her, shivering in the power of the rising tide of ecstasy, as she rocked her head and moaned, muttered the names of a thousand diverse gods, they came together. She shuddered uncontrollably in multiple orgasms.

Bart's head swam. His legs quivered. It was as if he were having a thousand orgasms, not one. He envisioned the whole world going up and down and came again . . . perfectly synchronous. He was the multi-armed god and she the clinging consort and they were in the bliss-heaven he had only heard of.

With a sigh of promise fulfilled, she subsided, limp in his arms, and they lay there for a long time, sated. Then she stirred. And gently pushed from under him. He rolled on his back, tried to take her in his arms, but she shifted, saying gentle things and he knew she was going to do something else. Her lips slid down his body, kissing his chest, his navel, and then moved lower. As he shuddered and closed his eyes, Dorjee's lips encompassed his again fully engorged member in her almond-shaped lips. Slowly she moved her tongue over it. There in the half light, the sun's beams playing over the amazing vistas outside the deserted temple, he came again.

* * *

It was almost totally dark when they reached the lowest foothold and jumped down on the steep moraine at the foot of the cliff. As Lasker crushed his love in his arms once more, there was a cry—a familiar voice. Tinley came riding up, leading two horses. "Chinese soldiers have been spotted heading this way. The Tulku must move on, right now. This is to be the time of our parting from Tsering and our other friends. We must now leave for India with the Tulku."

Lasker got on one horse, and Dorjee took the other's leads and mounted. They were quickly galloping across the sun-streaked terrain with barely a look back at the cliff.

Lasker had just experienced as close to paradise as one gets on God's earth. Now this mad ride. *Impermanence*—the nature of life. The Tulku said it, it was true. Bliss is short, and pain long. Bart was having a taste of the bittersweet contrast of the two.


Youngden Rimpoche was dressed up as an old Nomad in a dirty black bearskin parka. Everyone of his entourage was mounted and ready to move out.

"Well, my American friend," said Tsering, pulling his horse alongside Lasker's, "this is good-bye." He leaned over and took Lasker's index finger with his own, pulling it. "This means we are brothers. May we meet again in another life, if not this one."

Tsering waved good-bye and rode off with the rebel band.

Lasker rode over to Dorjee, leaned over to kiss her. "Tinley, tell her she has to come to India with us, she *can't* stay here."

Tinley said as much and Dorjee shed a tear, looked pleadingly at Lasker. She said her soft words to Tinley, who translated, "Dorjee says no, this is good-bye. She must stay with her people, do what can be done for her country, however small what she does may be. Her country needs her. Perhaps, she says, someday you will be together, if karma allows—"

The rebels were calling out to her. Dorjee turned her horse with a violent jerk and rode madly off in their direction.

Lasker was thunderstruck. Did he mean nothing to her? He felt the pain of impermanence in his heart right now. Why couldn't she go with him? What is a lost cause against love? He was angry and confused. He had assumed, somewhere deep inside, that Dorjee would, of course, travel to India with him. But *she* had just as much right, if not more, to ask *him* to stay here, didn't she? And yet she hadn't.

Lasker sadly turned his horse and followed the Tulku's India-bound riders. He and Tinley rode at the end of the column heading south. The rebels rode off. They shouted, *"Lha Gyal Lo"*—Victory to the Buddha—to them from the ridge.

Lasker waved, then rode on. He felt as if he shouldn't be moving this way; every atom, every cell, of his body was tugging the *other* way. Yet he rode on south for a mile with the Tulku.

India—no more freezing, no more hardship. But . . . somehow it didn't seem that he was heading back to anything, only *away* from here. He began sinking into a profound depression.

Then a strange thing happened. The first of several strange occurrences. The horse stopped. He shouted, kicked, but it wouldn't move. The Tulku's entourage continued onward.

He was falling behind. Then Bart was struck senseless, couldn't shout out. *What was going on?* Some sort of cosmic flypaper held him. Fate? Karma? He was stuck on the vast green bowl of the valley floor. There was a roaring in his ears, the sound of thunder in a clear sky. Oscillating high-pitched sounds drowned out the sounds of the world. It was as if he were under water. Then Bart knew what this immovable force arresting his progress was. *Memories.* He had been here before. That mountain range, the procession south, the monks herding the yaks, the bells on their horns tinkling. Not a year ago, not ten years ago—but a long long time ago. He had been at this spot in Tibet. Suddenly the roar in his ears turned to a hum, as if he had surfaced. His ears popped. He could hear everything again. Just like that.

*What the hell* . . . Lasker turned the horse and rode back after the rebels, shouting and waving his arm for them to stop. Tsering was right on his heels, to Lasker's great surprise.

When he at long last caught up to them, everyone was surprised. Tinley asked, "Why did you come back to us?"

Lasker said, "Why was I going?" His eyes met Dorjee's then. And Dorjee rode over to him and leaned over and kissed Bart. The rebels roared their approval and shouted the name they had given him, "Bardum Tharpa," over and over again. They poured chang over his head.

Bart Lasker was now a "Snow Lion rebel"!

Later, Bart asked the boy why he had returned with him. Tinley replied, "Just obeying Shemer Rimpoche. He said I should go with you, to India. Since I'm not splittable, I follow his *first* thought."

# Chapter 20

The Snow Lions started a trek eastward, intending to trade their wares among several remote settlements. And who could blame them if, on the way, they ran across a Chinese mountain patrol, took them by surprise, and did a little mayhem to pay them back for the Tsok massacre?

Lasker jubilantly rode alongside Dorjee all day. When she was away from him, working on the meals or tending the animals, he continued his language study with Tinley. He bribed the boy with his "fantasies" about life in the West.

And each evening, under the shadow of the white-capped twin peaks of Dhalighiri pluming with mist, Cheojey taught the dharma, the precious doctrine. The medical lama had been *empowered* by the Tulku. The first night away from the Tulku, with all gathered around the campfire, the gentle monk expounded upon the esoteric meaning of the oft-recited protective mantra: *Om Mani Padme Hum.*

Lasker was surprised that it had to do with the teaching of the doctrine of emptiness. Each syllable of this mantra was for purifying a particular defilement of the human consciousness. "*Om* is to alleviate conflicting emotions tearing one apart," Cheojey began. *"Om* is offering impure body speech and mind to change.

"The path to purification is *Mani*—meaning jewel. The jewel represents pure intention, a desire to attain enlightenment, shining and pure. Just as the possession of a great jewel," said Cheojey, "is capable of eliminating poverty for its possessor, so the mind bent on enlightenment is capable of making the wish for enlightenment to come true.

*"Padme* means lotus, symbolizing wisdom, rising out of the mud of the river bottom and opening its blossoms in the pure air. Wisdom in its ultimate form is the realization of emptiness," Cheojey said. The aged monk spoke so slowly and clearly that Lasker found that he was able to pick out many words and phrases on his own.

*"Hum,* the last syllable, means immovability, a very resolute method," the monk continued.

"Thus, *Om Mani Padme Hum* means practicing the path of method and wisdom to transform one's imperfect body, speech, and mind to enlightened body, speech, and mind," Cheojey finished.

Each night thereafter, the surprisingly learned old man, without the use of notes, without losing his train of thought, logically expounded on one aspect of the doctrine.

Lasker spent a lot of time before sleep and also during the long rides in the daytime digesting these weighty teachings.

And each night he shared his bedroll with Dorjee, off from the others, their love again and again expressed. They shared their own private *dewachen*—heaven.

On the fifth night of their journey east, the lone lookout posted on a rocky crag came rushing down shouting, "A rider is coming—a Tibetan, I think, but I'm not sure. He is small, he could be a Chinese dressed in our manner."

Tsering, with Lasker along by his own initiative, crawled to the top of the rise. They took turns with Tsering's battered Chinese binoculars. The rider moving through the moonlight in the plain below was hell-bent-for-leather and was heading their way. Suddenly his horse dropped exhausted, throwing him.

They ran down the hundred yards to where the horse was screaming and the silent body lay. Lasker rushed to the fallen rider as Tsering looked to the horse—which was beyond help.

Then Tsering came over to Lasker, who had lifted up the rider's head, rubbed his face with snow. His eyes fluttered open. He seemed puzzled seeing Lasker, but when he turned to Tsering, he smiled. "I made it, *Lha Gyal Lo.*

Tsering said, "Akong! It is you!"

The rider was basically unhurt, just exhausted. They walked him back to camp, as he told his urgent message. The rider spoke too rapidly for Lasker to catch more than "the Chinese" and "great destruction." Later at camp after Akong—who turned out to be a distant cousin of Tsering—was seated and given hot tea and tsampa, Tinley translated as the rider repeated his story for the benefit of the others:

"It seems that Tse Ling, the Virgin Dragon, has posted a proclamation stating that the Tara fountain at the village of Chamdo is to be destroyed by right-thinking 'volunteers' from the populace. This is to be done at noon tomorrow. She personally will lead the 'attack on superstition.' "

Dorjee sat next to Lasker, occasionally asking Tinley to make sure Lasker understood. Lasker asked, "What is the Tara fountain? Why is it so important? Why should Tse Ling want to destroy it?''

Tinley explained. ''The fountain is a 150-foot-high rock frieze on a cliff, depicting Tara, the patron saint of Tibet. From her cupped hands flows a spring of water plentiful enough to provide for the whole town. The Tara was carved by the great Saint Milarepa in the thirteenth century of the Christian era. Legend has it that back then the town of Chamdo had a great drought and the people were dying of thirst, and then a miracle happened. The minute Milarepa completed the image of Tara, water poured out of it, and fresh water has issued from the cliff ever since.

''The people of Chamdo believe that if the statue is ever destroyed the water will cease. They also believe that vengeful demons will attack the town and drink blood from the defilers.

''Tse Ling claims that this is all mumbo jumbo. She wishes to liberate the town from Tibetan superstition. She wishes to prove to the town that the font of water will still flow when the frieze is destroyed, and that no demons will attack the town.

''She has now called for town volunteers to hammer away the figure, which exists to the south of Chamdo in a narrow winding canyon.''

Tsering's cousin wept. ''The town will die without the water and the demons *will* come—Tse Ling must be stopped. Please, I've come to ask you Snow Lions for help—to protect the people.''

''But we can't do anything,'' Tsering said. ''There are too many Chinese soldiers in Chamdo. Tse Ling's whole garrison is there!''

Can't anyone think of any way to help?'' asked Akong.

Lasker caught the urgency of the rider's appeal. In

the silence that ensued an idea came to him. *No,* he thought, it's too crazy.

Suddenly Dorjee's voice broke the silence. "Bardum Tharpa has an idea."

Lasker looked at Dorjee strangely. It was as if she'd read his mind. All eyes were upon him. He cleared his throat. It was now or never. "Dorjee is right. I do have an idea—but it's farfetched, dangerous—but maybe we can discuss it . . ."

As he spoke and Tinley translated, Dorjee shook out her long silken black hair. Her beautiful young features broke into a smile, the aquiline nose crinkled. She exclaimed "Ah," each time Tinley translated a few sentences. Later, Bart found out wives do that when their husbands expound.

When Bart was done, they all turned to Tsering, who said, "Yes I think it might work—and if it doesn't we can withdraw with little or no casualties. I believe it is worth a try. We can do more to damage Tse Ling with this plan—if it works—than all the armed combat we have engaged in so far."

Cheojey and Tinley—over his great objections—and all the women, including Dorjee, would stay behind and break camp. They would be ready to travel as soon as the men returned. Dorjee and the others would have fresh horses ready, and their rifles ready to help repel any pursuers behind the returning raiding party.

They rode like the wind; they seemed to be in a race. Tsering was yelling challenges, the horses were frothing at the mouth. Lasker was trailing the others, though he was riding faster than he ever had! Surely, he thought, I've flipped. I'm no Snow Lion rebel! I'm *insane!* Here he was risking his life fighting *for* Tibet, instead of *leaving.* Was he mentally ill? Had the thin air killed some brain cells of his that had to do with common sense?

Was he just doing this to impress Dorjee? Here he was riding toward what must be the biggest concentration of Communist armed might in the area—with a bunch of old rifles and eight men. He had relinquishing his safety, his fortune, and now he was on the way to relinquishing his life!

Fool . . . fool. He could hear Donnely's voice saying, as if he were there in the clattering hoofbeats of the Tibetan horses, as if he rode alongside Lasker and laughed out loud: *You gave up your fortune, your charter airline, for this—you fool, you fool, you fool . . .*

To counteract Donnely's voice, he started mumbling *Om mani padme hum.* "Hail to the jewel in the lotus. Hail to the jewel in the lotus." As the countryside full of stupas, twisted trees, and slag rolled by, he lost the macabre specter of Donneley in the dust.

They rode over a hill past startled peasants pushing a cart full of yak-dung toward a field where many Tibetans labored planting wheat. Wheat for the Chinese army of occupation's bread.

Chamdo lay just ahead—you could see the smudge of smoke from its many small cooking fires. They turned to climb the wheat field hill and go around the town. They would come at the Tara fountain from up above.


The Snow Lions spread out in the dense pine trees and bushes high above the roaring gusher of Tara. Lasker situated himself above the crown of Tara's head.

The plan Lasker had evolved depended upon surprise. And on the ancient legend that demons would protect the fountain. They had all put on the weird lamdro dance costumes—the long silk robes, the huge heads of fanged animals, and now would wait until the right moment. Lasker was dressed as a horned bat-demon.

Lasker, peering through the undergrowth, spotted the rebel leader on the other side of the canyon. He was dressed as the bull-headed demon. He waved. Next to him was Rinchen dressed as the antlered buck-god, Wammak. Both had positioned themselves near the upraised hands of the statue, near the roaring exiting water. What a torrent it was! Like a dam unleashed. It *did* seem to issue from the dry rock like magic. Perhaps it was an artesian well, sent out by underground pressure. Or perhaps it truly was Milarepa's miracle.

The others were all huddled in position in the high thick foliage at the top of the sheer cliff. The spray from the gushing water crashed down the hundred feet below, obscuring them.

God, this was a beautiful place! The head of Tara had a depression in its crown. Lasker crouched there like a flea in her hair. He sat in the moss-filled hole, his left arm wrapped about a small twisted pine tree.

He could hear the shouts of soldiers, the roar of a mob—they approached up the canyon. In the occasionally parting mists Lasker soon saw hundreds of villagers, and the Chinese soldiers with their AK-47 submachine guns.

They shouted, *"Death to the past. Down with superstition!"*

And then Lasker saw a small Chinese in uniform surrounded by a phalanx of hefty soldiers—a woman! She wore a brown cap with stars on it. She came to just ninety feet directly below and walked up the steps of a platform, carrying a megaphone. *She's so small,* Lasker thought. But there was no doubt when she started shouting orders stridently. She *was* Tse Ling!

* * *

Tse Ling looked around from her platform at the colorfully dressed Tibetan and Chinese school children with their Red Pioneer scarves on their necks. They all carried Chinese flags, their mothers and fathers with them, carrying rakes, hoes, knives—all to deface the fountain frieze. Some of these villagers looked greatly disturbed. Many of the women wept openly. They were terrified. So terrified that to save themselves they would take a chunk out of the sacred statue. Tse Ling clicked on the bullhorn and spoke:

"The more militant, the more correct and educated of you will step forward—who will strike the first blow?" She watched a soldier bring up a big hammer with a red handle to the platform. "Come on, who will be the forward-looking Tibetan to strike the first blow?"

No one moved.

"Come on! Who wishes to show that they are not superstitious? Who wishes to impress me—and our comrades with his forward-looking attitude? I assure you, you will be *rewarded!* A good attitude means advancement. . . . Perhaps a managerial post would not be too much for the first person . . ."

No one. You could hear a pin drop. The Chinese soldier with the hammer stopped smiling. Tse Ling barked orders. Rifles were unslung. Clicks of the safeties being taken off could be heard. The crowd started whimpering. One man, a desperately thin man with a ragged shivering wife and five children, stepped forward. It was obvious he needed some sort of advancement—or he would die. He smiled nervously. "I will . . . do it."

Tse Ling ordered that he be let through by the soldiers. He walked hesitatingly up the steps toward Tse Ling.

"Good. Come!" She smiled. "What is this forward-thinking man's name? Write it down!" Her lieutenant took up a pen and put it to his pad.

"Sonam Gyalsap," the thin Tibetan man said weakly. He glanced quickly and nervously up at the statue. "I will do it." He hit on his chest hollowly. "I am brave, forward-thinking." He looked for approval from his wife. She stared uncomprehendingly, then understood. "For the children," his eyes told her. "For food."

"Traitor!" somebody shouted, and the shout went up like a wave. "Traitor! Traitor!" It swelled.

At Tse Ling's motion, the lieutenant fired a salvo into the air. It rent the canyon. Ten thousand fruitbats, shocked by the shots, took to the air, and filled the sky with a flutter and screeching for a few minutes.

Tse Ling, now that she had gotten their attention, picked up her bullhorn and spoke to the multitudes. "Sonam Gyalsap, a forward-looking citizen of the Tibetan Autonomous Region, will be the first to take up the hammer against superstition. The water will not cease to flow. Neither will the demons of the mountains appear!"

Nervously Sonam Gyalsap took the red hammer and climbed the wooden steps erected the night before, leading to the right arm of the statue. He leaned out and lifted the hammer high over his head. He hesitated, looking up at the gusher issuing from Tara's hand.

"Strike the first blow!" Tse Ling commanded through her bullhorn. Sonam Gyalsap gasped, closed his eyes, and swung wildly at the elbow of the glorious statue.

"Caw! Caw! Caw!" came the raven's call—Tsering's signal! The rumbling horns of the Snow Lions' secret chorus cut in—and then the rebels stood up, Lasker included. They shouted out insane demonic screams as they stepped out of the mists in their bizarre outfits. The horned red bat-demon—Bart—appeared in Tara's crown. The antlered buck-god Wammok and several other fierce, fanged monsters appeared on either side of Tara, waving their arms in a fierce threatening manner.

As the villagers saw them, they shouted "Demons! The curse is fulfilled! Flee for your lives—or have the blood drained from your bodies!" They ran every which way, knocking over the Chinese soldiers, who, instead of firing, stood with their mouths wide open, staring up in shock!

The "demons" continued screaming. The soldiers on the wooden scaffold panicked and ran down the steps. One of these knocked into Tse Ling, pitching her forward off her feet, smashing her into the railing of the platform. She clung to the railing for dear life, her feet dangling over the edge, and watched as soldiers fell off the precipices in the mad scramble.

Tse Ling hauled herself back up on the platform, where she found she still held the bullhorn. "Fools!" she yelled through the instrument. "They are not demons. After them! Go after them!" Some of the soldiers began clumsily climbing the rocks alongside the falling water. Others commenced firing uselessly up into the tangled trees above, bringing a rain of chipped rock down upon themselves.

The Snow Lion rebels, in their fantastic costumes, moved down from purchase to purchase in the rocks, waving their wraith-like gossamer silk arms, some blowing on conch horns.

The mad stampede continued. Tse Ling's platform started shaking wildly. Beams were cracking as the crowd surged around the platform's legs, smashing their bodies against it.

"Stop!" Tse Ling yelled. "You are going to make it collapse!"

Suddenly, with a mighty creaking noise, the main beams snapped. Tse Ling felt herself falling. Several of the soldiers were trying to hold up the platform, but were crushed as the heavy structure fell.

Throughout it all, the fountain's face stared on sernly, impassively.


Later in the three-story office of the former land-owner mayor, Tse Ling, a bandage wrapped around her head, her sprained left arm in a cast, sat at her desk awaiting the arrival of two of her officers. She stood up and smirked evilly as they were brought in, handcuffed behind their backs. She glared at Lieutenant Wang and Corporal Tang. Both were sweating despite the coolness.

"Well? What do you have to say for yourselves?" said Tse Ling, her eyes tightening into small dots as she walked toward them. "Why were your soldiers so unprepared for rebel attack?"

"It was not my fault," blurted out the young lieutenant. "We were surprised—they had many men, you saw yourself—and the people pushed us—we—"

"Yes? You failed to catch the masqueraders—and for this"—she came around the desk and, with her good arm, ripped off his epaulets—"you become a regular soldier again." She turned to Tang. "And you? Have you nothing to say in your defense?"

The corporal didn't dare meet Tse Ling's eyes, but looked past her at the poster of Mao Tse-tung exhorting a crowd.

Tse Ling said, "So? Nothing to say?" She walked

back to her desk, reached into a drawer and lifted out a silver Tokarev pistol. She held it straight out, pointing at Corporal Tang. "I should shoot you right now. You've disgraced me and set us back ten years here. The people will think we are weak—cowards!" Her voice crescendoed into a shriek of rage.

The corporal winced, expecting a bullet.

"But . . ." She put the gun down. "Instead, I'll give you both one more chance to redeem yourselves. Track down these 'demons.' Take the helicopters—they can't be far away." She told the guards, "Release them."

They were uncuffed. "Remember," she admonished, "I want results! Don't you dare return without results!" The officers and guards saluted smartly and left the room.

Tse Ling was alone. The silence of the office hummed with her anger. Things were not going according to plan. Someone had to be blamed. And he couldn't be Chinese. Then an idea occurred to her that brought a smile to her lips. She called her aide-de-camp, Lo-Fun, into the office.

"Arrest the carpenters who built the platform. They will have a quick trial and be sent to Smoke Mountain for their crime."

"Yes, Major."

"And *execute* Sonam Gyalsap—the thin Tibetan man whose signal started the whole rebel deception!" The aide left.

Chun will like this, Tse Ling thought. More prisoners to work at the Green Salt factory at Smoke Mountain prison camp. Things hadn't turned out so badly after all.

She went to the window and watched the Tibetan scapegoat she had selected for punishment—Sonam Gyalsap—being dragged tied hand and foot to the whitewashed wall of the temple. She watched as the screaming man was secured to a post there and dispatched by the firing squad. Pieces of his head flew against the white wall. He slumped, blood oozing from his mouth. She smiled with satisfaction. Tse Ling had found a scapegoat, and gotten ten prisoners to boot. She was quite pleased with herself.

She closed the shutters and went back to her desk and took out the little bank-records book. She looked over the numbers. Two hundred and twenty-two thousand pounds in her Hong Kong account—and more, much more, soon. A *million* pounds. She would leave Tibet with a million. When Smoke Mountain delivered the final Green Salt shipment. That could happen by the year's end. She would retire, still young and beautiful, and also very *rich,* in the opulent, decadent, pleasure-filled West!

# Chapter 21

Lasker and the victorious mischief makers disappeared into the foliage above the gushing waters of the Tara Fountain. They stripped off their lama dance outfits as they moved, stuffing them back into their sacks. They threw the sacks over their horses, and then rode wildly back toward their camp. Lasker couldn't get over it. They had succeeded in routing a well-armed platoon of Chinese soldiers, and, at least for now, saved the statue.

At the rendezvous point, they were greeted by Cheojey and the cheering women. Rapid explanations of what happened were given while the rebels put the costumes in a trunk and slid it under the rocks. There was no sign that any of the stones had ever been disturbed. The costumes were valuable, but would be safe there.

Tsering kept glancing back toward Chamdo, expecting pursuers. He gave orders for the group to make for the high country, to a little-trodden road that winded its way toward Gyarung Pass. They set off, again looking like a small poor unexceptional caravan of traders. There was nothing to distinguish them from any other travelers in the mountains.

"Gyarung pass is rocky and gives good cover," Tinley said. "Anyone deciding to follow us cannot use vehicles. We will continue along to a small town—Yarang—where Rinchen's uncle is a minor official. We will do some business there."

Lasker was glad that Tsering was handling the little details of escape. He was embarrassed that he had never given it a thought.

He was lucky that he hadn't gotten them all killed. What the hell did he think he was doing, playing with people's lives? Bart had never been in combat. He must have been mad to lead them on the Fountain.

But he *liked* the excitement, the joy of doing something against the Chinese occupiers. And Dorjee was full of praise for his act. She said, "We have found a champion of the Tibetan cause in the brave American."

As they headed their caravan toward the high pass, one of the young men, Thutben, dropped back to watch for any followers.

In another hour, they were halfway up the rocky pass. The exhaustion of the attack and the ride back was now telling. The exhilaration having worn off, and Bart was altitude-sick again, feeling nauseous, with a splitting headache. As they climbed and climbed farther up through the clouds and the chill air, he felt his heart fluttering and his fingers were so cold he couldn't feel them.

"It is the cold shadow of the mountain," explained Tinley. "Once we are out in the sun again, all will be well."

They were almost at the highest spot in the pass—about sixteen thousand feet—when they had a problem.

Lasker heard a familiar sound. The thuck-thuck of a helicopter rotor beating the air.

Ordinarily the pursuit of groups of Tibetan rebels

didn't warrant air search. The Chinese were quite nig-gardly in their use of air power against "bandits."

But there was no denying the sound. And soon Bart could see the black speck—down below them, circling over the barley fields. Tsering passed Lasker the bin-oculars. Lasker focused in on the craft—a combat hel-icopter armed with rockets hung in racks under its fusilage. The helicopter was buzzing low over a line of ten or more Tibetans walking along a dirt road. The Tibetans must be farmers, he thought, for they had hoes and rakes and one wheeled a barrow.

"I have seen these metal dragonflies before, Las-ker," Tinley stated dryly. "They observe, but that is all. We must continue on with our weapons out of sight. It will be all right."

Lasker wasn't so sure.

Those in the chopper evidently decided the farmers were okay, for it veered away from them and headed up the rolling hills toward the rebels.

The chopper was quickly overhead. A black painted military-type machine, with red stars on the sides. It cast a rapidly moving rippling shadow along the icy slopes and over their path.

A loudspeaker cut in, "What are you doing down there? What is your destination? Stop where you are. We are landing. Prepare to identify yourselves."

Tsering raised his hand. The animals were being difficult, and Lasker's horse almost threw him. Lasker watched the chopper move off to the west, then wheel around. He didn't see a place for it to land. What were they doing? It was coming back, fast and low. And then he heard the clicks. He remembered those clicks from his time in the service. It was the sound of weap-ons systems being armed. Bart yelled, "They're going to fire—spread out." As Tinley translated, the group

205

broke for cover. Then the helicopter began burping smoke. Rockets were being fired at them.

Two rockets roared by them, too high, and smashed into the slope about a hundred yards beyond the caravaners, making a blossoming cloud of orange and black. At the concussion, horses stood on their hind legs, throwing some riders. The yaks brayed and tore at their ropes.

The chopper whooshed overhead, its landing skids almost taking the head off Rinchen, who pulled his ancient pistol, and, sitting in the open on his horse, fired at it.

By the time the death-dealing chopper came back their way, Lasker and many of the Tibetans had taken shelter in the big boulders.

This pass proved more deadly, for Dolma and her yak were cut down by the bullets. Bart's heart sunk. Several of the young men, who were out in the open firing their pitiful rifles at the craft, were also mowed down.

The helicopter fired the rest of its rockets and cut down two riders, Thubten and Yeshe, who were making for the rocks. The explosions seemed louder than before. And resounded.

There suddenly appeared a swirling white mist, and the ground under their feet trembled. The explosive report was replaced by a gathering rumble, as if they were standing next to a speeding freight train. The rebels looked up, and saw the entire snow crest above the pass giving way.

Fear of the chopper above changed to fear of being buried alive. For the whole mountain was moving as if in slow motion, gathering speed.

An *avalanche*.

* * *

*Nightmare* . . . Donnely's face, distorted, red, leering, coming closer, his breath on Lasker's face. "What's the matter, Bart, have a little fall? *Ha ha ha.*"

"Donnely? No . . . no you can't be here—what are you doing here? Where's Dorjee? I remember—the avalanche! Dorjee . . . is she . . ."

*More laughter,* the leering face, close again. "Dorjee? She's *dead,* Bart. Here, do you want proof?" And Donnely stepped back, opened a sack, and lifted out a beating human heart. "She sends you her love, *ha ha.* Here—take her heart, put it in your hand . . . ha ha."

Bart stared at the beating heart in the meaty extended hand. Dorjee's heart? He tried to take it, but Donnely pulled it away. "She's dead, so it's mine," Donnely grimaced, "cause I found it . . ."

"No . . . she's not dead . . . I—I'll get you, Donnely. You're a liar. Give me that heart . . ."

Lasker tried to stand but he couldn't. He looked down at his body and saw he was a corpse, a rotted corpse with worms coming out of it, crawling up at his face, from his cracked open chest.

*"No.* I'm not dead, I can't be . . . dead." Lasker wept.

"Sure you are . . . sure you are . . . sure you are . . ." Donnely slid away, far away, down an icy green tunnel. Then came Jenny, just her head, rolling at him, like a bowling ball. Her mouth was moving. "Bart, Bart, come to me, we can make love—love—love."

"But you—you have no body . . ."

"Come to me—come . . ." said the bodyless head. Then the head vanished.

Lasker searched around but saw just snow, blood on the snow. There was nothing but snow—and blood. As far as he could see, a uniform whiteness with trails of blood, and the wind was like laughter. And again he tried to sit up, to avoid looking at his rotted body and sit up, tried to move his arms. They weren't there. He heard crunching footsteps in the snow, and he twisted his head, all the way around, and heard a snap. And his head broke off its rotted stem while the ground and sky was rolling over and over. His head rolled, over and over, in the snow.

*"No body* here . . . nobody here. No body, *nobody* here . . . just a head . . . ha ha ha." Donnely's laugh again . . .

*"No. Please . . . no . . .* Put me back together—let me be, whole . . ."

*Blackness.*

Pain. All light collapsing into itself, a dull roar, becoming a thunderous rolling thunderclap. Flashing speeding lights, coming from all directions, falling . . . falling . . .

Good Baby burst into flames, the aircraft spinning heading toward the ice mountain—the door is stuck— got to get out . . . so cold so cold . . . the door is stuck . . .

He opened his eyes, just a crack. And they focused in the near total darkness on the blur in the corner. Flickering butter lamps—and three monks, sitting— floating—in the air! Monks on cushions, but sitting five feet above the temple floor, motionless, the incense smoke wafting around them.

Bart closed his eyes again. Hot . . . sick, he was sick. Raging fever . . . dreams.

"Dorjee . . . *Dorjee!"* he gasped, "have to find Dorjee!"

An icy hand touched his forehead, his closed eyes. And then words. Human words. Bart felt his head being lifted by a hand, felt the edge of a cup on his dry cold lips. He tasted. Some sort of thin broth. He took a sip, coughed, half choking . . . the cup withdrew. "No . . . more . . ." he whispered. Again the cup touched his lips. Bart drank a little more this time. "Bitter," he said.

He tried to open his eyes, couldn't. They hurt. Bart lifted his right hand an inch, but it fell back. He was exhausted from the effort. He had the sense that he was lying on his back, on something soft and giving. He expended another burst of energy, succeeded in shifting a bit. Again, Bart tried to open his eyes. This time he succeeded. But all was a blur.

Was it really so dark, or was something wrong with his eyes? He could discern some shapes—something tall and shaped like a man. No, it was a statue—multi-armed, golden. And before it, many flickering candles.

"Where . . . am I?"

Instead of an answer, a soft question—in English. The voice next to him, the shadow that appeared over him, blocking the candle light, asked, "Are you all right?"

Bart made to reply, and a cracked version of his voice came out. "Yes . . ." His throat felt so dry—his voice was just a rasp. The air came only with difficulty into his aching lungs, cool bracing mountain air.

"Where . . . how long?"

"Rest. You are safe. You are in a monastery called Shekar Dzong. You have been here six days. Now rest."

"Yes. I need rest . . . so tired . . . so heavy . . ."

The next time he stirred, Bart felt much better. He sat up slowly, looked around. He was on a pile of animal pelts, a blanket of green wool over his body. He had no clothes on under the blankets. He coughed out some fluid. He remembered the voice saying he was in a monastery. He was alone, alone in a huge cathedral-sized temple. No, not alone—an approaching figure, walking slightly, shadows on the face. Lasker strained his eyes to see.

A thin, small man in a draping green monk's robe, the cowl of the robe drawn up so his features were hidden in shadow, slid toward him silently.

"I am Zompahlok," the man said in a soft voice, coming closer, leaning down. Lasker tried to see the man's eyes in the cowl of the robe. He searched the darkness within that hood, to see his benefactor's face. And gasped.

Two green-jade cat's eyes flickered in that dry leather-like face. A man a century in age, at least. Cracks and gulleys for wrinkles, sunken in cheeks. And eyes like a cat.

"You have been very ill, high fever, ever since we dug you out from the avalanche. But now, your fever is broken, and you will be all right."

Lasker tried to fathom those eyes. But the monk stood up, turned and went to the statue, and started lighting several butter lamps arrayed before the statue. "You speak English," Lasker stated.

"Yes, I have a facility for languages, but it has been a long time since I spoke your language. I hope it is satisfactory?"

"Yes, very—" Lasker stopped in midsentence. The *avalanche*. They had been in the pass and— "Dorjee—the others—my friends . . ."

"I am afraid they perished. Only you survived," the monk said, turning to him.

Lasker sobbed, "Dead, all dead . . ."

"I am sorry . . ." The monk stopped ministering to

210

the candles and went away, as silently as he had arrived. For a long time, until he fell asleep, Lasker wept.

Despite his ominous look, the aged green-robed monk ministered tenderly to Lasker. Taking turns with younger monks, who had that same dry-desiccated look, those same green eyes, the old monk gave him first tea and juices, then when Bart could eat, baked buns and pieces of meat. They helped him to a toilet which was little more than a hole in the floor in a corner of the temple. He was strong enough to stand on his own in a few days.

During all the time Lasker lay there, recovering, he had observed the coming and going of daylight through the opening—an oculum—of about six feet in width at the zenith of the domed ceiling above him. In the night, when it was bitter cold, the green-robed monks came, and they piled firewood in the center of the temple floor in a circular depression and lit it, for warmth. The smoke exited through the oculum above.

He sometimes observed clouds in the deep blue sky. The moon started to shine through the circular oculum on the third night.

Questions had come to his mind—especially about the hideous multi-armed statue that the butter lamps illuminated. The ancient monk responded that it was their special temple lord, Yamantalai, a very powerful god whose attributes were hard to fathom for the uninitiated.

Lasker dropped the subject. Who was he to say it looked hideous? They had saved him, and helped him recover. Still, he wished to be away from the image.

He asked if he could be moved away but the old monk said, "Yamantalai will make you well." He wasn't forthcoming on the matter after that, and why should he be? He had done much for Lasker, saved his life.

Lasker didn't sleep well. All the nights since his first awakening had been filled with unpleasant dreams. Not as bad as that first feverish nightmare, but bad enough. Dreams of Dorjee, reaching out for him, just before the avalanche hit . . . and dreams of her calling to him, saying he was in danger. But the Dorjee dreams, however distressing, made Lasker hope that *somehow* she could still be alive.

It was morning. He opened his eyes to see the sun streaming down through the oculum high above, a welcome shaft of light and life in this temple of dark shadows. The huge central fire was just ashes now. There was the distant cry of birds.

The old monk Zompahlok came again, bringing a tray of food. Green tea, a lumpy stew of meat and tsampa, some rolls.

Lasker ate heartily. He said, between bites, "Thanks for helping me . . . but I must go now. I am well."

No response, except the monk poured more tea for him.

There was enough light in the chamber to clearly see the statue of Yamantalai clearly.

He rose and walked toward the three-story job. He couldn't say he liked the figure one bit. It was many-armed and had a bull's head with eight horns. The leering six-eyed face had a mouth of triple rows of razor-sharp silver teeth. Yamantalai's lips were set in a snarl, dripping shiny metal saliva. The statue was standing on a golden depiction of several human corpses—no, they were depictions of living beings crying out in pain as they were crushed by the taloned feet of the hideous demon god.

Each of the statue's dozen six-fingered hands held representations of torn human body parts—heads, arms, penises, breasts, all dripping silver blood. There were two smaller figures clinging to the statue, their slender arms around the giant demigod's neck. They were consorts, female sexual partners, their ringed hairdos crowned with real bones. And each had their metal vaginas open, penetrated by not one but a *pair* of the graphically depicted demon god's steel penises. The whole affair was monstrous beyond belief.

Streams of incense smoke arose from a hundred flaming sticks before Yamantalai like a curtain. There. were offerings before the statue. They were not typical Buddhist offerings of little butter cakes, called *torma,* or flowers. But stacks of large bones with meat on them—perhaps goat legs? There were many piled on silver trays before the hideous statue beyond the incense smoke. Lasker noticed that there was some sort of pit about a yard across before the statue's base. He moved forward to see better. He caught a flash of red and green prisms of light. Were they rubies and emeralds? If so, there were so many . . .

"Stop! Don't go any closer," Bart was warned. He obeyed the aged monk. Withdrew. Still, what was in that pit, was it a horde of jewels that they hid down there? He'd find out. But not now.

Lasker was allowed to survey the rest of the temple and told that only the votive monks could approach the base of the statue.

He finally asked the question he had long on his mind. "Is this a Buddhist monastery?"

The monk smiled for the first time, and Lasker saw that he had pointed teeth. He said, "No, not Buddhist. This is the place of the Bonpo, the Hidden Realm, known as Shekar Dzong."

Bonpo? Lasker knew little about the ancient sect ex-

213

cept that Cheojey had told him that it had practices that were indecent, and that the Bonpo religion was thought to be nearly eradicated. Yet he had been rescued, brought back to health by these monks. Maybe the stories of blood sacrifices, of evil rites, were just nonsense. Even the Tibetan Buddhists had some images that looked fearsome and ominous to Western eyes, but were actually some sort of aspect of truth and goodness, symbolic in some mystical way he couldn't fathom.

Zompahlok showed him that the temple wasn't one building, but a series of dozens of interlocking structures, all at different levels. Shekar Dzong was a bewildering world of masonry and ancient images linked by staircases, lit by torches.

Lasker asked for directions back to Gyarong Pass, or at least Chamdo near where the avalanche occurred.

"Why go there? All your friends are dead, I know this. Stay here."

"No, I can't. How far is it? We must be near the pass, right?"

Zompahlok's reply was, "We carried you a long way. It is summer, the slopes are very loose and ready to slide—as you are well aware. You must wait until the weather is colder before trying to get down the mountain."

He asked, "Am I a prisoner?"

The reply was, "It is just not safe to try to leave."

Bart asked to go outside, to see where they were.

"The single great door is being repaired, and it is the only way outside. You may go out tomorrow, once the hinges have been mended."

He led Lasker through the temple to an antechamber. There was a twenty-foot-high door, where monks on scaffolds were working. There was a huge dragon embossed on the bronze door and it was sealed shut by a long wooden bar. It would take several people to move its bar aside and open it.

"*Tomorrow* you may go onto the terrace."

Lasker tried to bide his time, tried to relax. That night the old monk led him to a small windowless room alongside the shrine. "You may stay here, as you are uncomfortable before Yamantalai."

He left Lasker. There was a bed, some Tibetan books, and a butter lamp. He tried the door once the monk left, found with great relief that it opened easily to his touch. Bart looked at the illustrations in the loose pages of the ancient books for a while. Then he dozed.

He was awakened by a younger monk and summoned to the temple. The green-robed monks—he didn't realize there were this many before—perhaps a hundred—had gathered before the image of the demon thing.

Zompahlok bade that Lasker sit on a cushion near the central fire, which burned very low.

Then a queer thing happened. They all arranged themselves so that they faced Lasker.

They started chanting; the cadence was unpleasantly slow. He looked around at all the faces, because for the first time their cowls were down. These Bonpo sure were an unhealthy-looking crowd. He'd seen better complexions on corpses.

They had pale faces—like cave fish, without color. Their jade eyes were sunken in, like orbs of corpses.

"Why are you staring at me? Why are you turned toward me?" Lasker asked. Zompahlok, who was standing to the left side, near a pillar, said, "They stare and sing praises because they are happy you are back . . . that you have returned to us . . . Raspahloh."

"Returned?"

"Doesn't the chanting make you remember? It was very long ago when you were last here . . . think . . ."

"I've never been here before!"

"Listen. Remember. Remember, Raspahloh, remember . . ."

"I tell you—" Then Lasker gasped. The old monk hadn't been speaking at all. His lips never moved. He hadn't been speaking English all this time at all. Lasker realized it was—

"Telepathy! Correct," said Zompahlok. "We have been conversing telepathically. Now think, Raspahloh, and remember."

Adrenalin was coursing through Lasker's veins. This was insane! And yet . . . he *did* remember something of this place. It *was* familiar. He had seen this place in dreams all his life, or so it seemed. Was this the place? He sensed an evil—awesome evil.

"Look at the statue, Raspahloh, and remember. You belong here. This is your *master*, Yamantalai. We worship him, we worship *Death*. We bring him sacrifices, remember?" Again the sharp-toothed smile. "It is easy to raid the villages near here, spirit away their unwary populations, to feed Yamantalai."

"Yamantalai," Lasker muttered, "God of the Death Realm, the Shekar Dzong is—*no*—I'm *not* part of this!"

"Yes. He is our Lord, *your* Lord of Darkness. Yamantalai requires sacrifices, and he repays us. He gives us powers—powers to live and to remember, forever. For we who serve the Dark Lord, there is no death! And you *do* remember, Raspahloh, because you are one of us. You have been here, in another life. And you must now rejoin us."

Despite the confusion generated in Bart's mind by the sonorous utterings of the monk, and the shock concerning the nature of the Bonpo temple, Lasker managed to stand up. He shouted, "No, I am not one of you. I do not belong here."

"Oh no?" Zompahlok said. "You think not? Well, then come with me. There are things I will show you that will persuade you to stay. If I am wrong, if you are not suitably impressed, the bronze door will be flung open and you will be free to leave."

Lasker went with him, on that promise.

Zampahlok walked silently along the stone pavement of the temple. They entered a rear stairway, descended the torch-lit stairs. Zompahlok led Bart down several flights, then through one dimly lit chamber after another. Some were filled with dusty oaken chests with the same dragon motifs as the bronze door. At last they came to a subterranean chamber that was circular and about fifty feet wide. It was filled with many life-sized seated statues that were dressed in ancient faded silk robes. The statues wore peaked green hats on their heads. Incense and lamps were arrayed before each.

"We pray to all of the children of Yamantalai also—one each month of the 360-day cycle."

"Great," Lasker muttered. "Now show me what we came to see and then I can leave."

"If you *want* to leave after you see it."

"Right."

Lasker was more angry than fearful. These monks were parchment thin and had no weapons he could see. He would be able to overpower them and get out anyhow, but he might as well see if he could get out without resorting to violence. Evidently they mistook him for someone else. Well, he'd soon rectify that false impression!

"Come, Raspaloh, to the other end of this chamber, and behold the secret that will change your mind about leaving."

I must be going truly mad, Lasker thought, to cooperate in any way with this dried-up corpse of a man. But he followed. They entered through an arch to another chamber, much smaller. There was just one statue at its far end.

"Come, and see. . . . This will be a shock, Raspaloh, a shock that is necessary. I believe that it will make you remember who you are at last."

A fluorescent sort of green-blue light shot out in beams like small searchlights through tiny holes in the stone wall at the edge of the ceiling.

"The light—" Lasker muttered.

"Is derived from underground incandescent gasses. Eternal light for the Chamber of Raspaloh."

The icy grip of the monk's hand on Lasker's sleeve drew him near the figure. It had a peaked green hat coated with the dust of centuries. It was a seated figure that wore ornate green cloth garments, dully reminiscent of silk. Lasker failed to see what distinguished this statue from the others in the chamber outside. He studied it, touched the green robe. It disintegrated at his touch.

"Very old," said Zompahlok. "Look carefully now, and you will know why you are here with us now."

Lasker studied the statue's face. It was a depiction of an old man. He was tall and had a slender aquiline nose and dark green marble-like eyes. The cheeks were wrinkled, very life-like—and those eyes—it was as if it was not a statue, but a dry desiccated corpse.

"It *is* a corpse, Raspahloh! It is *your* corpse!"

Lasker gasped, *"No!"* He fell to his knees before the figure. He denied the monk's utterance, but knew the monk spoke the truth.

"Yes, Raspahloh. It is *you.*"

"How—" Lasker's senses were reeling. He felt sick to his stomach. Yet he couldn't draw his eyes away from the cold green orbs of the preserved corpse.

218

The corpse's stare, those unblinking green orbs, seemed to draw him in. And then they *blinked*.

It was alive! As much as he tried to break away then, Bart couldn't. He felt an energy—a horrible, ancient, malevolent energy leap forth from the spot between those green eyes. The energy spiraled out toward Lasker, expanding and coalescing, and hit him like a ton of bricks. He collapsed to the floor, overwhelmed with past life memories, a million incidents sealed in the eternal *akashic* records, now unleashed, overpowering his present-day mind, weakening that essence within him that was Bart Lasker.

"It is time to begin the Ceremony of the Awakening. Come, we return to the temple, Raspahloh. *Come.*"

Lasker got to his feet, and with his mind swirling, he obeyed, stumbling after Zompahlok.

# Chapter 22

The monks, who had waited for them to return, began chanting. Low, ominous intonations in a cadence befitting worshipers of dark forces. Bart was led to a cushion and sat as before, with all the monks facing him. Their jade green cat's eyes bore into his soul. He was frozen in place, held as if by a giant unseen hand, his heart pounding wildly in his chest. A mist formed in the air before him, coalesced. Five figures. They were ghost-like figures of hideous red-eyed animals, jet black leopards—saber-tooth prehistoric creatures. They circled him. Their yellow eyes glowered at him, their huge dripping mouths issued snarls of hunger. And try as Bart might, he could not move, could not lift a finger. Only his eyes moved, tracking these menaces from another world.

The awesome cats seemed to be inhibited in their movements. They raged, they paced back and forth, desperate to get at him, but were held off by some invisible force. Bart saw the red circle drawn in blood outlined on the stone floor. It acted as some sort of psychic barrier between him and the monstrous saber-toothed cats. The black leopards paid no heed to the monks beyond them. The creatures wanted only Lasker.

The pacing of the cats back and forth beyond the blood line went on for what seemed hours. Then they turned and leapt away. As if they had been called by some unearthly master. Into the darkness.

But there was no relief for Lasker in this, for the cats were immediately replaced by the shimmering appearance of new menaces. Seven counterclockwise-circling demons. Two-legged, charcoal-gray-skinned creatures, vaguely human but with long hairy arms, immense slavering jaws, pointed fur-matted heads. They were completely naked but wore much jewelry: necklaces of bones, pendants of small human skulls—children's skulls—strung between the bones.

Lasker managed to shake his head back and forth, denying what he saw. "Must . . . be . . . dream . . ." he gasped out. But Bart knew it wasn't a dream. He tried to shake it off anyway, even tried to laugh at it. But then one of the demons, the one with the head of a bull, and fierce red eyes, suddenly stepped across the red blood stream-barrier and loomed over Lasker. His demon face came close to Bart, his hot sulfurous breath singed Lasker's cheeks. And then the demon lifted a gnarled clawed hand, touched Bart's bare chest with one of his long talons, and scratched a long deep gash through his robe, down into the meat of his flesh. And Bart screamed out in pain, but still could not move. Pulling its talon from the bleeding gash, the demon uttered something immensely low and grating—a sound like death itself.

It said, "You . . . are . . . Raspahloh . . ."

Lasker stuttered out, "I . . . am . . . Raspahloh!" And he felt the dissolving of his being, an emptiness sucking him, spinning him down, far away. Lasker was still there, but faint, a screaming voice lost in the tide of a more powerful personality. Not gone yet, not gone . . . but no longer in power of his body, no longer in control. The demon and its entourage vanished.

"Do you want to leave Shekar Dzong *now?*" Zompahlok smiled.

"No . . ." Lasker said, "I want to stay." Why did he say that? His voice was not his own. It was deeper, throatier, it said he didn't want to leave . . . but he *did.* Oh God, he wanted to leave this place, this horror. But Lasker was imprisoned within his own body!

He tried to scream, but Lasker had no lips to scream. The lips were Raspahloh's to control now. It was, for Lasker, the time of ultimate fear. A fear that only someone who was living, yet dead, could ever know!

And now visions flooded him in the semidarkness, visions of riding a black steed through the mountains, flashing scenes of rape and pillage, of burning temples. He, Raspahloh, had been the champion of the Bonpo, and the Bonpo were in a deadly war with the new religion, at war with the Tantric Buddhists. It was a war fought with sword and with club, but also with black magic and psychic powers. It had raged for a hundred years. And Raspahloh's side was bound up in Tantric spells, vanquished by Buddhist Dap Dop fighting monks and the hundred thousand riders of Kublai Khan's assisting army. What was left of the Bonpo force retreated, withdrew—to the Hidden Realm, Shekar Dzong.

Zompahlok leaned over him. "Who are you?"

Lasker fought the words, fought the very idea, but he found his own personality just a tiny screaming protestor as his mouth formed the words and uttered, "I am Raspahloh, the champion of the Dark Cause, Warrior of the Hidden Realm, *Killer* of Dalai Lamas."

Zompahlok was pleased—he knew from his mind link that the subjugation of the present personality had begun. Raspahloh must train in the secret martial art of Bonpo *E Kung* once again, become their Mystic Assassin once more. Raspahloh would lead the Bonpo counterattack, long delayed, against the alien religion. Against the Lamas that had *stolen* the secrets of Bonpo for their religion of peace and humility, for a religion of weakness.

Raspahloh was more gifted in the psychic warfare powers than all of them. He would make the difference now that he was back. He was their assassin, their unstoppable warrior. In his last life, his last fight for them, Raspahloh had brought partial revenge. He had killed the fifth Dalai Lama, right in the Potala Palace itself. Raspahloh had slipped past the guards and done the deed on the holy child. Now, as soon as possible, Raspahloh again would be launched on the same mission— to kill the present-day Dalai Lama.

"Rise, Raspahloh," Zompahlok commanded. "Rise and begin your Bonpo E Kung training. Your present body has the girth and height enough to be melded into the lethal weapon it was long ago. But there is little time, we wish you to assassinate the present incarnation of the Dalai Lama at the beginning of the Earth Serpent year, just five months hence—for that is the auspicious time, according to the stars."

"Rest assured," Lasker said, in the perfect Tibetan of Raspahloh, for he knew all that Raspahloh had known, "I will be ready." And only a dim voice deep inside cried, *"No . . ."*

"The Dalai Lama has much power. And his retinue is full of psychics of great power. To accomplish our aim," Zompahlok instructed, "you must become totally strong, Raspahloh. Now our learned fighting instructors will take you to the maximum energy level. Your own inner skills will enable you to easily surpass them in all aspects of E Kung. Come, let us begin on the terrace. The power moon rises—as it was long ago."

"As it was long ago," Lasker said, rising from his cushion and striding purposefully forward with the head monk.

Lasker—Raspahloh—before leaving the building, was given loose green trousers and a short green robe that went to the knees. The robe had slits to his upper thigh on both sides, for freedom of movement. The training garb.

The head training monk, Phuntsok, a short and squat but powerfully muscled man, looked him over, turning him around, and frowned.

"Ah, Raspahloh," he finally said with sadness, "the musculature is there, but so undeveloped. It will take all my skill to awaken your inner power, to channel it. You must help me with your great resolve."

"I so resolve."

"Then you will focus and channel, first. In that way, before you even begin the active training, you will thus harden and change that outlander's soft body. Only then, when it is a fitting vessel, will you become what you were—the Mystic Assassin."

The bronze door was opened, and they stepped together onto the wide full-moon-lit terrace of the Hidden Realm. The horizon glimmered with moonlight on snow-capped peaks.

"We begin, you remember, with building the power centers through psycho-mantric orbit meditation," Phuntsok stated flatly, as they walked into the icy vast night.

Lasker practiced as told, exercises that taxed him utterly, every fiber in his body crying out from the strain. He drank the bull's blood and the flesh of strong

224

mountain animals; the blue goat, the rock-climbing musk deer.

As his body began to show new hardness, Lasker was assigned to the Five, a group of E Kung–trained younger monks. They never spoke, just gestured, and he caught what they meant telepathically. Lasker practiced with the *ypa*, an X-shaped hand weapon of jagged carbon steel held in the center of its axis. Thus in the moonlight, the five monks would attack with shafts of wood, and he would parry, spinning the ypa to throw their entrapped sticks. He practiced *only* on moonlit nights, barefoot in the bitter cold, out on the stone terrace. He was *re*taught the rudiments, sometimes having to stay in one E Kung defensive posture for an hour at a time—if time had any meaning. He counted the hours by the time it took for the moon to pass between different monstrous gargoyles on the temple roof.

In the worst weather, there was still training. In wind and cold so intense he felt as if he would die. In these temperatures he dressed in a lightly quilted jet black silk garment.

He practiced "chi" meditation for six hours in the daytime seated before the giant Yamantalai statue. The meditation was the esoteric art of leading psychic energy along the median lines of the body's tendons and nervous system. Bart-Raspahloh learned this procedure solely by telepathic instruction from Zompahlok, who sat silently in the flickering butter light on the cold stone floor facing him. It was the way to clarify the mind and align the body *exactly* to tap universal energy—the chi flow. It could channel awesome cosmic energy along one's muscles and tendons and bloodstream.

In a few months, Lasker-Raspahloh's organs all felt as if they were hardened like steel. He could feel and hear everything in his body, every blood cell, every nerve twinge, as if he were in an engine room of a huge ship. As if he inhabited a metal killing machine, not a human body!

He next practiced the sixteen chi meditation postures, sometimes meditating in any one of these difficult postures for hours at a time—impossible before he had learned to channel the chi force, but barely possible now. Zompahlok was pleased at his progress.

And he learned how to breathe in a new way—bone breathing. There were two stages of breathing practice. One: Inhaling and exhaling as if through the fingers and toes, not the diaphragm. Two: Bringing the breath energy up to the hands and arms, eventually to the crown of the head, then down the spinal column to the legs. He felt a numb sensation as the "sacred" breath, once he got the hang of it, was brought by willpower to each area of his body. He realized that as a modern man, Lasker's body had been slowly *dying*, for modern man knows not how to breathe.

This esoteric knowledge was easier to learn because it was transmitted without nuance, without grammar— telepathically. Progress that would take a Western or even Chinese master a year to teach was passed to him in a day—with Zomapahlok as transmitter.

Then the E Kung practice began on the terrace again. But no longer in the moonlight. Now he trained in total darkness! But he had light. Lasker-Raspahloh saw his opponents by the fiery flickering *aura* of his own body's energy field. He didn't have any need for light.

Phuntsok, the master trainer, who had watched his sparring with the five from a perch above them, came back to teach him the secret chi belt of E Kung. That was the method of connection of upper and lower body energy channels. He used the drugs and potions given to him to stimulate this, directing them with his new skill of mind-body connection, channeling the energy to his various organs. This, in the state of civilized man's rapid deterioration, was urgently needed. And he detoxified and strengthened his heart, his kidneys, all the atrophying vessels, with the chi-belt method. Lasker had been always proud that he had kept in good condition. Compared to the E Kung conditioning, Raspahloh could only laugh at Lasker's so-called "fitness." With the power of the chi-belt method, Lasker-Raspahloh now packed the detoxified organs with chi energy, like storage batteries. He filled the empty spaces in his body with chi pressure, as cushioning against blows. Layers of fat became pressurized air of immense power. There were no outward changes except his posture seemed different, he moved differently. It was not the useless dangerous Western body training—muscle building, body tension. He was as loose as a mountain cat, and much more deadly. At one point in the training Phuntsok told him to jam his finger against the rock wall of the terrace—it punctured to a depth of one inch.

He wasn't surprised.

The third cycle of the moon passed. Three months of relentless training. One night, when a brilliant crescent moon hung in the western sky, Zompahlok came to see Lasker-Raspahloh fight the five skilled training monks. They were easily defeated. And he watched him parry every attack by the steel hands of Phuntsok. And reply with blows that would have, if Phuntsok had not rolled and jumped, eliminated his trainer's life.

"Very good," Zompahlok telepathed, "you will be ready for your mission soon. But you trouble me, Raspahloh . . ."

"Please finish, old master," he said, bowing.

"Something is wrong. The reawakening has indeed occurred and you train well, but your personality is not as it was. For one thing—your eyes do not burn with the old fire. Perhaps you were too long in your present Western body."

"Perhaps so . . . but that will pass. I feel the American slipping away. A habitual person this Lasker was, his channels are ingrained in me—but they come undone with the training, you will soon see the old fire in my eyes. Even if they are Western and brown."

"I look forward to that, Raspahloh." Zompahlok turned to Phuntsok. "You do well, continue the training to the advanced level."

# Chapter 23

The advanced training began. Raspahloh, totally in control of the Lasker host body, directed its every move—while a newly continually weakening inside, the essence of that which had been Bart Lasker, complied. So the tandem entity, not yet Raspaloh, and not anymore the American, proceeded with the training. Raspahloh, possessed of all his memory of his past prowess, dating back to the time of Kublai Khan, quickly absorbed the next step: the power sphere technique—creating a power sphere of chi energy like ball lightning in his thorax, sending it up through his hand and out toward an enemy, or in this case, his monk sparring partner.

This part of the training was what Raspahloh, the assassin of Dalai Lamas, had looked forward to. All the other training had been defensive, strengthening, learning to ward off, to parry blows from lesser warriors who would attack Raspahloh. But now that he had empowered every part of the body, energized it all, made it hard as steel, wrapped in power, it was time for offensive training. The power of *killing*.

First: the smash. His hands and forearms made lethal by slamming them again and again into gravel.

He was awakened from his cold cot every morning as the orange rising sun glinted off the icy peaks. The temperature at dawn was ten below zero, now. For it was autumn. He perservered, past anything he, as Lasker, could have imagined was endurable. He walked across hot, razor-sharp ceramic fragments poured from Zompahlok's dragon bowl; he endured blows to his body with jagged "monks' sticks." The times he was enraged at a blow reaching him were the worst. Then blows would stun him from every direction. But he learned to be calm while fighting—never emotional, but careful, like a cat, like a demon cat. And then, no blow could reach him.

Raspahloh was given his sword of old, retrieved from the cobwebbed storage room. It was a sword of meteorite-honed steel, its blade as black as coal, glistening with sharpness eternal. And his opponents, too, took up swords.

He learned anew that the sword is an extension of the body energy. He became one with it, extending the chi power from his trained nervous system to the blade. The monk warriors seemed inexhaustable, and easily defeated him with their skilled sword play—at first. But whenever he received a blow to the body, even with the edge of the blade, it was held off by his chi-energy barrier like armor. He wasn't cut. He was soon skilled in making the correct sword moves against the monks. He fought in daylight, and then in the total darkness of Raspahloh's subterranean tomb, where the narrowness made it difficult to parry and thrust. But in the little beams of moonlight streaming through holes in the room's walls, he memorized. He could remember who had passed through the beam and who hadn't. Memory is as much a necessary part of fight as it is in a card game. And he moved his sword in anticipation of their next moves. The dry corpse of his past body sat watching.

The time came for him to try his skills against Zompahlok himself. Lasker had thought the head monk to be weak, but Raspaloh knew he was fierce and strong and cunning, well trained in Bonpo E Kung. The apparently dry and brittle old man's looks were deceptive, to say the least. Age can *hone* skills in fighting. A Bonpo grows in strength over the years, through mind power!

Raspahloh was lead out to the courtyard by his ancient sparring partner—Zompahlok. The old man had shucked his robe for a jet black uniform. Armed with just a fly whisk, Zompahlok took on Raspahloh, a fighter who could crush a combat marine's windpipe before the man could lift a finger. Lasker was the Mystic Assassin now—all the monks *combined* couldn't get at him, couldn't land a blow. Yet Zompahlok would challenge him with just a fly whisk.

Zompahlok circled slowly in the semidarkness then leaned forth cooing some mystical bird-sound. Raspahloh tried to drop-kick him and missed, sailed off into the inky darkness, and rolled onto his feet. His hands snapped out into the E Kung fighting stance called Migyu hand defense. Zompahlok hadn't seen anything like that for a century.

Raspahloh struck out again with a knife edge chop, and again he hit only air. Then his Blow of Death was launched—a twist of the body and back-of-the-head heel smash. His foot was caught in the fly whisk's coils and he was hurled ten feet. But he rolled and snapped to perfect, knee-bent counterposition. Just in time. Zompahlok was in the air, and his left foot grazed Raspahloh's chin. He parried with the blow called Fist Charged with Ball Lightning.

Zompahlok received the blow center-chest, but his

fly whisk had wrapped around Raspahloh's wrist and stayed most of its force.

"Good," Zompahlok said. "Enough for now."

Zompahlok took up the oaken hammer and smashed it against the gong three times, summoning all the devotees of Yamantalai to the temple. They came quickly and the greater number sat down on their cushions. The votaries lit the lamps before the statue and piled ritual offerings of goat legs high before it. Raspaloh donned the jade-encrusted robe of power offered by two attendants.

Lasker felt his body, controlled by Raspahloh, walk up the three steps to a throne constructed entirely of human skulls cemented together. Of course—it was his—it was the Throne of the Assassin.

"Let the transformation ceremony begin," said Zompahlok. The monks rose and swayed back and forth like seaweed in the wind. A sound rose from their throats, a double-toned rumbling song from their inner evil. The mantra of Yamantalai, God of Death.

Lasker-Raspahloh, the E Kung Master who now sat on the skull throne, knew all that was now to happen. And the small part of him that was *Lasker* knew it would be his extinction. He felt the cold palms of his hands cupped around the skulls that made up the arm ends of the great throne. He smelled the incense wreathing the temple, heard the chant that summoned the dark forces to the ceremony. The Raspahloh part of him was pleased, but the Lasker part was in agony. This was Lasker's last hurrah. After this ceremony was complete, there would be no more entity known as Bart Lasker.

Two guardian monks carried in the limp, drugged, naked thirteen-year-old girl they had spirited away from the nearby village the night before. They stood before Raspahloh now, waiting until the right moment in the liturgy chant. Then they set her down on the floor in the middle of the red seven-sided mandala newly embossed there. The guardian monks tied her to the iron rings in the stones, by wrists and ankles. Her mouth moved, a low moan. The monks all prostrated to Raspahloh and Zompahlok, who stood beside his throne. Then they took to their cushions.

The young virgin began to stir, her eyes flickered open. The first thing she saw, because her face had been placed toward him, was Raspahloh sitting in his magnificent green-jeweled robe on the throne of skulls.

She screamed, struggled with her bindings, in vain.

Raspahloh's voice came from lips wet with saliva. "Kill her in the correct way, that I may drink her life energy, and live forever."

"No," Lasker raged within the confines of his utter physical subjugation to Raspahloh. "No, *don't.*" But nothing came out. Lasker had no power. It was a living death, being in his body, seeing and feeling all, yet being absolutely impotent to even move a finger.

The two guardian monks rose again, and went to a low table before the great statue and pulled off the covering. Beneath the covering sheet were two three-bladed knives—ritual daggers for human sacrifice. The *phurbas*.

Holding the ritual slaughter instruments up high over their heads the guardian monks turned to Raspahloh and spoke thus: "To the great Raspahloh we dedicate the power of this sacrifice, be it also for the pleasure of our Dark Lord Yamantalai. Raspahloh by this sacrifice will again champion the cause of our Dark Lord, as our eternal Invincible Assassin."

So saying, they turned as one and walked to the naked sacrifice, who was pulling at her bindings with all her might, and screaming a high-pitched scream of ultimate fear. As all her fellow villagers, she was a Buddhist. Her people did not fear death—but death as sacrifice to the Dark One himself was to be feared. For the Dark One could take you, and hold you and keep you—as another concubine in his evil other world realm. *For all eternity.*

Raspahloh's skull throne lifted, floated off the floor of stone, and turned to the demigod. He intoned, "What say you, Great Yamantalai—do you accept this sacrifice, so that I may again champion the cause?"

The votive fires flared—a sign that the Death God took the offering of virgin flesh.

As the throne of skulls rotated back and settled in its original position, the death-delivering monks bent over the naked sacrifice, their phurbas over the bare breasts of the girl. As she screamed out one last entreaty, the triple-bladed knives plunged down.

Blood, warm and steaming, spurted up as the knives were pulled out. The killer monks brought forth the vessel of gold to collect the lifeblood running out of the virgin's split-open chest cavity.

Then they passed the bowl of blood from one monk to another, until Zompahloh handed the vessel to Raspaloh.

Lasker felt his hand lifting from the arm of the chair. And struggle as he might, he felt his hands accept the warm bowl of steaming red essence, felt his arm muscles contract to lift the bowl to his lips. The cup began to tilt, the redness touched his lips.

Far away at that moment, in northern Tibet, a beautiful young Tibetan woman prostrated before the peaceful bronze figure of the Amida Buddha—Amitabha, Buddha of Dewachen. She took her white *khatag* scarf off and placed it over the shoulder of the Buddha, took her clutched incense sticks and lit them in the butter lamp flame before the statue, then placed them in the holder. The woman was Dorjee Nima, and the purpose of her visit to the Chien-lin temple was to beg the Amitabha for her lover.

Dorjee began earnest prayers for Bart Lasker, muttering the mantra of Amida Budda: *Om Ame Dewa Hri!* One hundred and eight times, rolling each of her 108-mala bead strand in her hand at each utterance. Then she looked up at the peaceful face of the statue and said, "I know Bart Lasker is alive—save him, save him through your miracle power, great Amitabha-Amida."

Lasker felt the warm steaming blood touch his lips, *and closed his mouth! Suddenly he had power again over his own body!* Some divine energy, soft and gentle as a breeze, had come over him, lifted Lasker from the depraved hold that Raspahloh held over him. A red, benevolent glow—and in it—Dorjee's face! Raspahloh had been removed, sucked away as if by a cosmic vacuum! He would not drink the blood. But Lasker pretended to drink, and once done, took the bowl from his red lips and passed it back to Zompahlok's extended hands.

I'm alive, Lasker silently exhulted, I'm still Lasker, I'm alive! He realized he must be careful. They musn't know that the spell hadn't worked. Lasker didn't move. He had to pretend he was still Raspahloh—if he wanted to stay alive!

Zompahlok, once he had a long drink of the sacrificial blood, passed the blood bowl to the first guardian monk. That monk and then the second guardian partook of the blood. They made appreciative sounds, then licked their red-stained lips.

*Ghouls, monsters,* Lasker thought. And yet worse, he

235

knew what was to come. The girl was dead, but she did not yet belong to Demon Yamantalai.

He, having the memory as Raspahloh, knew the next ceremony words to say: "Let the desecration begin!"

He would have to endure this, in order not to give himself away. He had to avoid flinching, despite wanting to stand and rush from the hideous ceremony. Lasker could fight to escape perhaps, but all of Raspahloh's skills were now—weakened. For he was Lasker. A new strong-bodied energy filled Lasker, to be sure, but not as powerful as Raspahloh. He silently recited the protective mantra—*Om mani padme hum*—for the victim.

The guardian monks walked to the pallid corpse with the wide red gashes in her breasts. They pulled up their robes, and threw them off. Naked, they bent down, and one by one took their pleasure unnaturally in the corpse.

As the unthinkable desecration continued, Zompahlok blew on a human thigh bone horn he picked up. The signal was, Lasker knew, to summon the Yamantalai spirit to participate in the perversion with them.

The monks seated on the floor began to groan with every bloody plunge into the corpse. They enjoyed, with the necrophile monks, their unholy pleasure. It was because the monks had, through the power of their obeisance to the Dark One, linked up with the act of desecration, and were part of the blasphemy. All shared the thrill of the unnatural act of abomination together.

And Lasker was feeling it too—something like mass hysteria, like mass hypnosis. He tried to not think of the act going on before his tearing eyes, yet he, too, was dragged into the act, psychically raping the deceased girl in the most abominable way, joining as the guardian monks took their vile pleasure.

Human-skin drums, taken up by five monks, pounded, increased in volume and rapidity as the rapist monks fulfilled their pleasures. Lasker's hair fairly stood on end as the Yamantalai statue began to moan, a metallic moan that was like a wind, like the horrid sound of a thousand undead demons. The monster Yamantalai spirit was coming! Coming to partake. From the dark realm the spirit rose, and he was there, invisibly, a part of the ultimate act of depraved lust. A disembodied psychic penis slipped into the vagina of the sacrificial virgin.

The assemblage groaned and shivered as one unit, and Zompahlok and all of the seated monks, all save Lasker, ejaculated in one awesome, shuddering orgasm of demonic lust.

Lasker, trembling to his very soul, sickened beyond his imagination, sat there on the skull throne, feeling he might pass out. But he endured.

Both desecrator monks lay exhausted atop their unwilling corpse lover. The chanting started again. A song to Raspahloh, his chanting of power. Power over death, power given by the Death God. The chant said: "It-is-*oblivion!* It-is-the-*highest!* It-is-the-*emptiness!* The-emptiness-*Death-itself!* Experienced-*within-life!* Death-the-*ultimate-destiny!* We-have-called-you-forth-by-the-*ultimate-desecration!* The-death-within-life-*comes-to-each-gathered-here!* The-ultimate-state-of-*nonbeing!*"

Thus the ceremony that nearly cost Lasker his soul—were it not for the prayers of Dorjee—ended.

# Chapter 24

Lasker, after the ceremony, returned to his solitary chamber to meditate now that he had "shucked off" the last vestige of his "lesser self." He lay on the cot, his heart pounding.

They would soon know that it wasn't Lasker that had been shucked off, but rather Raspahloh. He had to escape. But he needed more than his meteorite-hewn sword to smash his way free of this abominable temple.

Lasker knew not how far it was to the little village near the avalanche site—Yarang. He would need resources, money, once he escaped, to make his way. And he believed he knew where to get that wealth.

He slipped silently out of his room through the temple, up the steps, until he stood before the shrine of Yamantalai. Lasker inched up to the pit before the statue. A guardian monk dozed there in the flickering light, leaning on a pillar. Lasker wanted to see what was in the pit. Not making a sound he leaned over it and beheld: jewels. Millions of different kinds of cut jewels. A treasure house of gems beyond anything imaginable. It was twenty feet down, however, and among the gem hoard scurried immense scorpions.

Bart needed a way down without getting stung. How?

Silently, he took several khatag scarves from a pile, tied them into a rope of twenty feet. He tied his ankle to the closest pillar to the scorpion pit and climbed down dangling by his ankle, head first. He moved a hand near the gems.

Thousands of scurrying scorpions responded, rushing over the jewels, at his hand. But they were too late to sting Lasker. He had already snatched one handful, just *one* handful—but it was perhaps worth a million dollars. To take more was tempting, but foolish. He twisted around and slid up the khatag rope and back to the temple floor, then untied his ankle. The incense streams wavered a bit as he made his way, the shadow of a warrior, past the same monk, who snored instead of tending careful guard. Bart had been anxious lest he hear the scurrying of scorpions, but that did not happen. When his lack of alertness was discovered, the lax monk would be perhaps the next sacrifice.

Lasker gained the moonlit courtyard after using all his new strength to draw back the giant beam that sealed the bronze temple door. The battlement guards were endlessly patrolling the walls, armed with their crossbows, and with alarm conches on strings at their waist. He had a plan—albeit a risky one—for descent off the mountain. He made his way toward the shadow of the low wall around the stone terrace.

"Who goes there?"

"Do not be alarmed. It is I, Raspahloh, merely taking some air."

"Forbidden." The fierce monk guard jumped down from the pedestal, sword ready, with fire in his green eyes. "Stop, or I raise the alarm."

Lasker's meteorite-steel sword flashed and the guard was beheaded.

He kept to the walls, slipped close to the second monk guard. This guard, too, was made short work of.

He had defeated the fighting monks and even matched the unearthly power of Zompahloh in his training. He was as ready to escape as he'd ever be. He silently made his deadly rounds, using everything he knew as Raspahloh to take each of the six battlement guards out, silently, one at a time.

In his times on the terrace he had discovered the means whereby the monks made their raids upon the valley below: A basket big enough for three men to ride down in was held in a crèche in the wall. Heavy rope perhaps two hundred feet long was attached to that basket, and the rope was unwound from a coil around a huge wheel. The wheel was controlled by a half-dozen sturdy monks holding six spokes, and thus the basket was lowered.

How could Bart operate the pulley ropes? How could one man lower *himself* in a basket? That was the problem. He thought for a moment and realized. Of course. It would have to be a fast descent! He cut the basket from the rope, then unwound the rope entirely. He slid the whole rope over the wall until it reached the bottom far below. He took off his soft sandals and, holding the rope, went over the side, using the soft sandals to let his hands slide rapidly down the rope. It was a thousand feet at least! He was halfway down, the sandals hot and smoking, when someone above gave a shout of alarm. The shouts of hundreds of enraged unholy monks echoed through the darkness. He increased his rate of descent, despite the friction's pain. They would try to cut the rope before he reached bottom!

Above, he saw a hundred winged figures poised on the wall. Some sort of hang glider! They started leaping off, soaring. *No!* They would soon be down on Lasker. But Lasker increased his descent, sliding so fast that the leather between his hands burned through and the abrasive rope tore his palms.

Lasker felt the tension in his rope suddenly leave. The

monks had cut it, as he had feared. Where was the bottom? Lasker fell, but he hit snow in just a second, rolled, bounced off the sharp rocks, and then rolled another forty feet. He got up and ran—the killer monks were swooping down on their stiff bat wings, dropping behind him. He clearly saw their devices. They were sailing down on kite-like black-cloth wings. A dozen, two dozen killer monks landed in the snows, shucked off their wing devices, and ran madly forward, one thought in their evil minds: *Kill! Kill Lasker!!!*

Bart made for the darkness of the boulder field farther down the mountain. He was well outlined on the white snow.

His way was lit by the orange glow of flaming arrows shot from above. The poison-tipped arrows slid by in the near darkness: he felt one brush his shoulder. Felt the numbing pain of its poison. He fell and took his sword blade and sliced at the offended flesh, started it bleeding. And then he got up, ran onward, tumbling, weaving, to avoid spears that jabbed into the ground hurled from above. The swish of a dozen thrown star knives was heard. But none made its mark. Raspahloh's instincts enabled Lasker to hurl himself aside just in time to avoid the well-aimed blades of death, hurled by swooping bat figures. As more flaming arrows poured down, Bart saw dimly ahead for an instant. He stopped in his tracks and rolled to the side, narrowly avoiding falling down an abyss. Then, he climbed down the cliff, steeled fingers clutching the slightest indentation in the rocks. He jumped the last thirty feet, rolled to take the shock off his feet, and got up running.

Soon the tumult behind him was more distant, the flaming arrows flashed by no more. The maniacal Bonpo monks were left behind.

He'd made it.

Yet Bart kept running in the thin cold air—making

241

distance between him and that awesome evil that lay behind. He ran like a track star, like Jesse Owens only twice as fast—half leaping, half running, into the distance. A wind was picking up. On it he could still sometimes hear the wild screams of the enraged Bonpo, like some horrid collective scream of a hundred wounded killer animals, crying out from another world.

When he at last looked back, a mist concealed the icy peak that held the temple. The first rays of dawn slowly dissipated the the mists so he could see the evil monastery.

The mountain was empty, except for an ancient weather-worn ruin!

The ruins were a thousand years old at least. And real bats, not killer monks, swirled around the barren peak! The evil place he had lived in for four months had been nonexistent. *Dead for a thousand years!*

He touched the pouch of emerald and rubies held on a string at his waist. They were still there. He continued walking east across the barren tracts, with nothing but his long shadow cast by the rising sun to lead him.

Lasker was dog-tired by the time the sun was high, but he kept up the pace. After walking till nearly sunset, sometimes in snow two feet deep, he found a village at last. The sign on the trail he descended onto said ENTERING TIENNAN. Lasker knew the name from somewhere—Raspahloh's memory. He pushed the thought away—whenever an idea that was not his own arose, also arising was a wave of nausea as Raspahloh's personality threatened to reassert and overwhelm.

Lasker came upon a crossroad and another sign, in unreadable Chinese characters and in Tibetan print below. RIGHT, GAMDONG, 32 LI. SHIGATSE, 123 LI, LEFT. That didn't help. Bart wanted to get to Yarang, the village the

Snow Lions rebels had been heading for when the avalanche occurred. If any of them had survived, perhaps Yarang's inhabitants would know.

Lasker wondered about his garb. He was still wearing the dark green robe covered with jade. It was torn and only two pieces of jade still clung to it. He was dusty and disheveled. His hair had grown long over the months in the Bonpo temple, and he had it tied in a topknot. He had no beard. Something had happened to his metabolism there, and he no longer grew facial hair.

Nothing could be done about his appearance, so he slapped off as much dust as possible. His face was burned from the sun and soot-dirty from the trek. Surely with his long hair and robe he would not be taken for an American! He was abysmally, madly thirsty. But he had to maintain an unhurried pace now. He could see the deisel smoke and Chinese trucks down in the town. As he rounded a bend past a half-collapsed old house, he spotted Chinese troops in twos, walking the twisted streets on the outskirts of the dilapidated town, along with the usual village folks in their work wear.

With resolve, he threw back his topknot and strode right down into the main street, winding his way past the first duo of young soldiers. *Attitude is very important—walk as if you belong.* This was one of the infiltration lessons given him by the pongo trainers. So far it worked. In the main square he bent at a running fountain and drank water, nudging away the neck of a horse partaking of the same blessed refreshment. Then Lasker looked around for someplace to go inside. A store perhaps where he might discretely trade a jewel for more acceptable garments and some *food!*

There were no stores evident, not even street stalls or carts. The town was evidently not a marketplace, but perhaps an administrative center. Yes, with all the trucks and Mao-jacketed men rushing from one place to an-

243

other. Two Chinese soldiers walked into the square casually checking credentials. They stopped a bent old man, probably a farmer, who was leading a yak down the street. The farmer dug out some rumpled papers, they glanced at them, and let him pass.

They turned toward Lasker. "You there—" said one of the soldiers, "come here." Lasker froze in his tracks.

*"Beep beep!"* Into this confrontation rushed a shiny new bus. Written on its side in red was CHINESE TRAVEL BUREAU. The windows were open and several blond-haired tourists leaned out, taking Polaroid pictures. "Look," one said, pointing at Lasker, "a *holy man*—quick, shoot his picture!"

But Lasker was already running. The bus had momentarily blocked him from the view of the soldiers. He took off down a side alley and ran behind a house by the time the bus had passed. He watched down the narrow space between two buildings as the bus slowed and screeched to a dusty halt in the square, scattering chickens and startling the tethered horses at the fountain. Out came rampaging Western tourists—photographing everything in sight. *Tibet, Disneyland of the East.* Come and see Tibet in air-conditioned buses, feed American dollars to the Chinese!

Lasker turned and went down an alley. He approached a man who was walking toward him: a beggar, sores on his arms and legs, soiled cloth instead of shoes wrapped about his feet. The man had a look of gentleness and sanity in his eyes, and returned Lasker's gaze unabashed. Lasker asked, "Is there a store where I might purchase a new outfit here? I was waylaid on the road and—"

"You are dressed most peculiarly," the man stated.

"I am a pilgrim from the far north."

"I see. . . . Well, there is no dry goods store, but there is a trader who works from his house—at the edge of town—take this path . . ." The beggar instructed Lasker

244

on the route through the back streets. "It is a house with a golden dragon painted on its wall. Could you spare some—money?"

Lasker fished into the pouch tied to his waistband, felt around, and extracted a small object. He said, "Take this," and pressed a shining green emerald into the beggar's hands. "This is for you. Tell no one where you got it. Do not spend it in this village."

The man took one look at it, and he got down on his knees and kissed Lasker's worn sandals. "Rimpoche, I bless you, who have blessed me."

Lasker cautioned the beggar again to tell no one about the gem and its source and headed toward the trader's house.

With his mouth salivating, Lasker approached the house with the golden dragon drawn on its wall. He climbed the ladder to the roof and shouted, "May I come in?" and got a mumbled, "Yes." He descended through the open hatch door—traditional Tibetan houses all have their doors on the roof. He stepped down into a home tastefully furnished with big chests and many rugs. A time-worn picture of Chairman Mao stared at him from over a fireplace, where normally a shrine would be.

"Yessss?" came the uneasy tone of the short stooped man who hurried to him through the diffuse light cast by the single oil-paper window. "What can I do for you—er—" Obviously Lasker's appearance was putting him off.

"I am a pilgrim from the north," Lasker said, "a wealthy monastery official who has been beset on the highway and thus, my clothes damaged. I wish to purchase many things, and have money to pay well."

That got a rise out of the merchant. He no longer hesitated to invite Lasker into the main room. Wringing his hands, he said, "Follow me."

In the brighter light of an electric overhead lamp, Lasker sat down on a cushion. He noticed there was a TV blaring out some sort of martial music in the side room; black-and-white images of tanks slid by on the small screen. A woman sat pulling wool and watching TV. She now leaned over, saw Lasker, and leaned back to her TV. "I am Tenzin Somam," the goateed middle-aged man said. "And you are—"

Lasker, on an inspiration said, "*Satan* Rimpoche."

"A Rimpoche? We are most honored." The man bowed his head—but there was the ring of sly disbelief and a little fear too in his voice. "I do not buy any religious goods, Rimpoche. We are not allowed to trade in cultural treasures, you know. You must go to the Chinese cultural authorities if you wish to sell anything of that nature." His eyes narrowed. "I have never seen a Rimpoche with a green robe—from what sect are you?"

"I come from a Mantrikaya monastery in Far Mongolia. I travel to Lhasa, as a pilgrim to the holy sites. As I said, my robe is torn and dirty because I was besieged on the mountain pass by bandits."

"Bandits? I will call the authorities. We must report all incidents of banditry." The trader made to stand.

"No, don't. I've already reported it," Lasker said. "I wish only to purchase some things from you now—that is why I am here."

"But if you were robbed, surely you have no money?"

"I hid my wealth, they only got some paper money." Lasker took out his pouch and drew the string, spilled out some of the emeralds and rubies on the rug.

The trader's eyes went wide, and he gasped loudly. His wife heard, put down her ball of wool, and plodded in from the other room, leaving the TV on—an ad for Bee Brand soap.

She was a stout woman, older than the trader, with much gray hair. She had many warts all about her nose. Her eyes were wide as she took in the gems.

246

"They are *real?*" the trader asked.

"Yes. Fine gems. Here—" Bart handed a small emerald to the trader. "Take this to the light and examine it. I wish to purchase supplies and a good horse and some food. Also to buy another robe."

The trader fairly caressed the gem when it was plopped into his hand and climbed the roof ladder hastily. His wife pursued him, shouting, "Wait! Be right back!"

"I do not like this man, Denpa Dolmag told her greedy husband as they stood on the roof, the husband using a small jeweler's lens to examine the emerald. "Who knows where he is from," she continued, "and no Rimpoche, no matter from how far away, wears *green!* I tell you, he might be an evil spirit sent to test us—"

"*Shut up,* old hag!" the husband shouted. "This is a genuine gem, and I can become rich from this transaction—"

"He might be wanted by the Chinese. They might have even sent him here as a test of our loyalty—"

He pushed her down the hole. "Get back down there, hag! Make this rich Rimpoche some tea. Even if he is a phoney, his gem is real enough. Now go! Be hospitable."

The man followed his wife down the ladder, sat down, and reluctantly handed the gem back to Lasker. "It appears to be a gem of moderate quality. What little do you want for it?"

"I require a horse and saddle—a fine horse. And a bag of dried meats and tsampa, plus a cake of tea, a canteen— in return for the gem."

"Ah, no." The trader smiled. "That is far too much for one small poor-quality emerald—" He explained how times were hard, how it wasn't safe to transact business without telling the Chinese village head. And if he *did* tell the Chinese, the tax would be so high. . . . But the trader

247

said he *could* make an exception to the reporting rule, only for a premium. His eyes focused greedily on the bag of gems.

The trader was difficult, but finally he took Lasker down a ladder into the stable under the TV room—most Tibetan houses are built over the stable to catch the warmth given off by the animals in the winter. Saves heating. He showed Lasker a pretty good mustang, and a worn saddle with leather stirrups that would do. Lasker nodded. "Now, what about the food, and—"

A half hour later, well nourished by small meat cakes and tsampa and buttered tea—they were like manna from heaven for Lasker, though he didn't show it—they had clinched a deal. Two emeralds and two rubies bartered for four sacks of tsampa, some butter and flour, a hundred renminbao paper money, and the canteen, horse, and saddle. Plus Lasker's robe was washed and mended by the woman. He waited in the TV room watching a man get a new tractor from a Chinese official, as the wife worked on a Chinese foot-pedal sewing machine. It took, of course, only a few minutes for the garment to dry once cleaned, due to the extreme altitude of Tibet.

Thus, wearing an acceptable garment, fully equipped, and minus four of the fifty-one Bonpo gems, the ersatz Rimpoche rode off, waving.

Bart disappeared into the gathering night almost immediately.

"How can he see where he's going?" the wife asked. "I *told* you he's an evil spirit—we shouldn't have done business with him."

"Spirit or not," said the trader, edging his wife to the bed, "these gems are real enough. Now get your clothes off, hag! In celebration, we will open a bottle of Tsing Tao beer and a tin of pork."

In the morning, when the trader pulled the small bag

of jewels out from under his pillow and spilled it out, he found four pebbles.

The wife berated him, beating him about the head with a frying pan shouting, "I *told* you he was a ghost—*I told you!*"

Lasker rode all night, using his aura as a light—a gift of his Bonpo E Kung training. No one but he could see by this light. He stopped frequently to rest the horse, which was not very young or healthy after all. He shared his water from the canteen with the steed. Bart camped at sunrise, ignited a fire with the pack of stick matches and some easy-to-come-by yak chips from the trail. He made some tsampa and butter tea. He let the horse graze on a small patch of grass and weeds by the trail.

Yarang, his destination, was still about fifty miles away, but with luck, he'd make it on this high route without having to answer any questions from the Chinese. The route directions the trader had given were simple enough, and he doubted the man would inform on "Satan Rimpoche."

There was a sudden racket—an approaching vehicle, making the grade up the dusty road. A bus. Another—or the same—tourist bus? The horse shied and Lasker had to run for it to get its reins so it wouldn't take off. This is incredible, he thought. How the world changes. A tourist bus, out here in the goddamned Tibetan outback!

He had read somewhere that before 1979, less than six hundred Westerners had *ever* been to Tibet. Now they had the fucking Chinese version of Trailways Bus Lines taking tourists around the Forbidden Kingdom!

The bus whizzed by, disappeared over the hill. Lasker, coughing in its dust, mounted up and continued on his way, heading almost directly into a beautiful golden sunrise. The clouds were of glittering streaks of maroon and amber. This beauty made him think of Dorjee, and the time they had spent together—most of all the time in the golden temple on the cliff—the *first* time.

Could Dorjee really be dead? Were all his Tibetan friends dead? He couldn't believe it. He had a gut feeling that they weren't. And he remembered that time in the Bonpo temple when he was about to drink the blood of the sacrificed girl—it was a powerful feeling that rescued him, coupled with a vision of Dorjee. Her face had floated in the red light that had saved him.

She *had* to be alive, or how could that miracle of love have happened? Or—did she reach out to save him from the *beyond*—from the Bardo?

Lasker now came to the edge of a small settlement— just a few farm houses, with some men tilling the soil beyond. Kids with the seats of their pants cut out to save diapering played with various-sized colored rocks on the side of the road. There were two boys and a girl; they turned as his horse approached. "Can I ride, mister?" the boy with two missing front teeth said.

"Shh! He's a Rimpoche," said the older one.

"Is this the way to Yarang?" Lasker asked.

"Yes, Your Eminence," the older boy said, sticking his tongue out—the proper greeting for a Rimpoche.

"Aw, cut out that 'Your Eminence' stuff," the younger kid chided. "That stuff about religion is superstition. And speak Chinese—why do you think we go to school, to keep speaking dead languages?"

"Shh! He's a Rimpoche. He can turn you into a frog."

"No, he can't," said the third child, a Raggedy-Ann-looking girl with a smudged face. Still they backed off a bit as Lasker raised his hand and started manipulating his fingers.

Lasker blessed them, and kept riding.

Bart soon recognized his surroundings—the Gayarong

Valley where the farmers were strafed by the helicopter, and above it the pass between the twin peaks. His heart pounded as he went up the rocky trail. It was cold. The ice on the mountain was solid now; there was no danger. He supposed that he was now riding over the very rocks and snow that had cascaded down on them some months ago. There were people on the high trail ahead—walking down, with packs on their backs. *Backpackers.* He rode closer, and they waved.

*Hippies*—two bearded men about twenty-five years old, with many beads and Buddhist red-and-yellow protection cords around their sweaty necks, and a young blond woman, statuesque in the Western way under her tight jeans and lumberjack shirt.

"Oh wow, it's a guru," the taller man said. The girl and the other guy dropped their packs on the gravel. Lasker stopped his horse. What the hell?

They came rushing up to him, sticking their tongues out in the greeting that one gives to a holy man. "Can you give us teachings? Make us enlightened?" the girl asked.

Lasker half smiled at the ridiculousness of the situation. Here he was, an American, and they were too, from their accents. And they wanted teachings.

He gave them a stern look and raised his hands like a boy scout leader pledging allegiance and said, "A bird is an egg, until it isn't."

"Oh wow, spacey," the girl shouted.

"Far out!" her companions added in sync.

Bart slapped his horse and galloped off.

# Chapter 25

At dusk, Lasker found himself on a pine-tree-covered knoll overlooking the small town. In the corral at the edge of Yarang were some yaks he knew by name—Dusty and Firehead. They had red protection cords on their right horns—consecrated to Buddha in return for some great *boon,* and not to be eaten. His heart rate increased. These yaks were part of the herd driven by the Snow Lions—Tsering's rebel band.

He rode down and discovered the whitewashed building that said BREW HOUSE in Tibetan. That would be Rinchen's uncle's tavern. He remembered Tsering telling him that the Tibetan Arak—the most potent liquor known to mankind—could be bought in draughts at Rinchen's uncle's place for a pittance. Lasker dismounted and he found that a door existed to the bar on ground level, a door wide open. He approached. Its inside was lit by a roaring fire, and a robust voice resounded in magnificent drunkeness, telling of spectacular achievements with women and in mortal combat. *Rinchen's voice!*

Excitedly, Bart stepped through the portal and onto the rough-hewn pine board planks. There, in the red glow of the fireplace, were several other's, including Tsering. A smile crossed his lips, the first time Bart had smiled since the avalanche.

Some of his dear friends were here, safe and sound, drinking about a large board table, listening drunkenly to Rinchen's wild boasts. They were alive; perhaps Dorjee was alive as well.

*"Tashi Delek,"* he said softly, the traditional Tibetan greeting meaning. "Auspicious meeting."

One-eyed Tsering was the first to strain his eye in the firelight to see Lasker. He clutched his wooden cup and stood up abruptly. "Lasker? Are you real or a ghost?" he muttered in amazement. The others—young Temtin, Rinchen, the big oaf Dundup—all turned their gaze upon the man outlined by the stars in the doorway, and they, too, rose.

"Who goes there?" Rinchen bellowed. "Robed fellow—are you demon or friend?"

"Friend," Lasker said.

Rinchen, wiping a line of drink from his chin, came around the table and approached Lasker. He stretched out a finger to poke Lasker's shoulder. And seemed surprised it was solid. The big lantern-jawed man frowned. "Although you *feel* like a normal object, you *must* be a spirit—a spirit of the undead—a zombie. Stay away from him, he is not Lasker. He cannot be. I saw Lasker get buried under tons of debris!" Several of those about the table, at his words, moved back.

"It *is* me. Do you have some arak for your old friend? May I sit by your fire and warm myself?"

"Is it really you?" Tsering exclaimed, coming over to put an arm over Lasker's shoulder and lead him to a chair. "We all thought you dead—"

Lasker sat down and took a short sip of the arak handed him by the rebel leader. The liquor burned pleasantly all the way down. "I'm me, and I'm not dead."

"But—what manner of clothing are you wearing? Have you joined a holy order?"

"I have not joined a lamasery. I travel this way to avoid detection." He put the cup down and, with every muscle in his body tense, asked the question that summed up all his longings and fears: "Is Dorjee Nima alive?"

"*Yes,* brother," Tsering said. "She survived the avalanche—and is with relatives in the far north of Tibet. She always believed you were not dead and she pined over you."

"Where is she? I want to go there now."

Tsering looked as if he had just sucked a lemon. "That would be a problem. None of us know exactly where Dorjee is staying. You see, she is the only eyewitness to the massacre at Tsok. Tse Ling knows this and has a price on her head. Tse Ling sent a party of soldiers back to double-check Tsok, found the stupa unsealed."

"You mean *I* shouldn't try to find her?"

"Yes. It would be best, for now."

Bart sat and put his head down on the table. Alive. Dorjee was alive—but he couldn't go to her.

At last, Bart rose and said, "I understand, Tsering. Thank you." Then there was a thumping of boots. There were more rugged men from the Snow Lion rebels entering the portal now. And Cheojey too. They stared in, wondering what stranger in green sat by the fire.

Tsering stood up and called out, "Everybody, come to the fire, do not be afraid—it is our old friend the American. He lives. He is safe, by the Buddha's blessing. *Lha Gyal Lo.*"

"*Lha Gyal Lo,*" Praise to the *Buddha,* Cheojey said, and came and shook Lasker's hand. Then staring into his eyes, he dropped the hand. "Something—about your eyes . . . Lasker, please open your shirt."

At these words by Cheojey, they all—including Tsering—froze in place.

"Your *shirt* please," Cheojey said. "Please open it."

Lasker shrugged, undid the spherical buttons. There on his chest was the talon mark of the demon that had scratched him at the Shekar Dzong, during the first ceremony.

"You have been possessed," Cheojey said. There was a wild stampede for the one door. "But you have partially recovered." The Snow Lions skidded to a halt.

"Yes," Lasker admitted.

"The Bonpo did this to you?"

"Yes."

Cheojey smiled, told him to button up. As Lasker did, Cheojey turned, "He is all right, do not fear."

Rinchen, obviously dead drunk, stepped arrogantly forward, pressed a finger hard against Lasker's chest, grunted. "So you are demon-scarred. Poss-ss-ed?" He burped. "I am bigger than any—*burp*—demon!"

Cheojey pushed Rinchen's heavy bulk away. "Lasker is all right. Leave him alone. I will ask the questions." Cheojey turned to Lasker. "How is it that you survived the avalanche?"

"I was dug out by some monks from the Bonpo monastery."

"What monastery is that?"

"I think—they called it Shekar Dzong."

A cup clattered to the rocky floor. Dropped by Tsultram the Younger. "But," stuttered the youth, "that can't be—that monastery—it has been gone for a thousand years—"

Cheojey said, "Yes, Shekar Dzong, the Hidden Realm. That is most interesting. It is supposed to exist yet, but only in another dimension. You speak such excellent Tibetan now, Lasker. Did the Bonpo teach you?"

"The Bonpo monks that rescued me were well versed in teaching. I stayed there—a long time." Lasker's eyes went to the fire. "I stayed until—"

"And what devilish things did these evil beings teach you, Lasker?" Rinchen blurted. "Did they tell you to come back here to destroy us? Friends, there are dark forces involved here. Lasker is a demon, a zombie possesses Lasker's body. We must drive him away."

"No, he stays," the little old monk insisted.

Lasker admitted, "Rinchen is close to the truth—I am two people in one. I am possessed, but not to hurt you. But—I will go if you wish. I'm sorry I returned. But take these." He spilled out the rest of the rubies and emeralds from the scorpion pit onto the table. "Perhaps you will be able to get yourselves a few draughts of *arak* with these."

"Aiii!" Rinchen exclaimed. "Where did you get these?" He picked several up, turned them over in his meaty palm, held them one at a time toward the fire so the light shone through. He bit one. "Genuine," he snorted. "*Perhaps* you may stay after—*burp*—all. We need a rich companion, possessed or not."

Cheojey said, "Lasker—could we speak in private?"

Lasker nodded. They went outside into the moonlight, and strolled. Already it was ice cold and their breath made mists in the night air. Cheojey said, "It must have been an ordeal for you."

"It was—difficult."

"They never would let anyone have their treasure— you must have stolen it?"

"Yes, I did."

"These are no ordinary jewels if they are from the Hidden Realm, Lasker. We must seek advice from a holy man as to how to dispense of them." The only sounds for a while were their feet crunching in the gravelly roadway.

"Where should we get this advice?"

"I know of a place—the Oracle Cave—right in *that* mountain," Cheojey said, pointing at the left peak above

Gayarong Pass. "It is a cave where men have seen visions and received guidance over the centuries. Go there, and meditate. Sit quietly until answers come, until the oracle spirit that inhabits that cave speaks to you. I will talk to the Snow Lions. When you return to them they will accept you—for you will be purified of any evil by the oracle within that cave."

"When should I go there?"

*"Now."*

Cheojey went to one of the houses near the tavern and gathered some blankets and a cushion. Plus food and supplies. He came back with them loaded on his horse. Lasker mounted his own horse and they slowly made their way up the slope. Cheojey gave Lasker detailed instructions as to what to do once inside the Oracle Cave. And also explained that Tinley was back with Shemer Rimpoche. "It is not Tinley's karma, it seems, to be in India."

In an hour, they were at the cave entrance. It didn't look like much to Lasker, hardly a religious shrine, just a hole in the rock face. The entrance was about six feet in height, and half that wide. "Go in—and I will close the door so that you aren't disturbed. That round boulder over there serves as a door. It is easy enough to roll in and out of place. Take the supplies and the cushion and blankets. I will be back in a month for you, if you do not return on your own."

Lasker nodded. He got down and gave his horse's reins to Cheojey and took the load of supplies. Cheojey also handed him back the pouch of gems.

"Why are you giving me these now?"

"It is best that you keep them with you. You took them from the Bonpo. Find out from the oracle what to do with them so as not to stain your karma with theft."

Lasker entered the cave with trepidation. When he heard the monk roll the rock closed behind him, shutting him in the cave, he had already lit one of the larger butter candles Cheojey had provided. Still he was all alone. At least he had his big candle—and a pack of Chinese matches. The cave was bare, perhaps twenty feet by thirty-five feet. He set down his pack of supplies, and his eyes roamed over the red-and-black wall drawings. He understood them as written in archaic Tibetan and Indian Sanskrit. Pictures of water buffalo being let to water, an elephant with two heads—some graphic pictures of females with their legs spread wide.

He smiled. These weren't profound religious drawings. This set of drawings was probably done by ancient pornographers, bored from their stay in the cave. The sayings were like graffiti: "Tenga Terpa was here, third millenium," and so on. He swept the light around. There was good air in here—a long funnel shaft twisted up and out—so no smoke would fill the cave when he cooked a meal. And there was the little fresh stream Cheojey had promised, along one wall. And a pit with some sand at the other end—for sanitary necessities.

Bart went to the middle of the floor once he had checked the circular walls. There, as Cheojey had said, was the large blue crystal—a cloudy mass of quartzite the size of a desk. It was roughly octagonal, pointed at the top. There were two cushions, all weathered and dusty, on either side of it.

Lasker figured this was it. Time to sit down and conjure this oracle. He sat down as the monk had instructed, in lotus position, and began meditation in the *Shunyata* method, letting his outflow of breath carry away any thought that arose, just staying quiescent . . . *just the breath, just the breath.* . . . His eyes closed.

Bart eventually noticed a slight increase, very gradual, in the light. Was the candle getting brighter? He half opened his eyes. The candle, on his left, was looking same. Had Cheojey rolled away the rock? He looked right. No. Then what? He turned back toward the crystal.

The *crystal* was the source of the light. It was glowing faintly, and its blue glow increased. Cheojey had said his presence would bring light.

Bart went back into his meditative trance, confident now that something would happen. It could have been hours, or a day—there were distinct rumblings of hunger in his stomach—when he felt the addition of a presence in the cave.

Someone had sat down on the other side of the three-foot-high crystal—or was it his imagination? He was still, every sense on full alert. It *must* be the oracle. There was no way for a person to enter the cave without Lasker hearing the rock door move.

Finally he heard soft breathing, and then a cough. Do oracle spirits cough?

Bart opened his eyes and saw a familiar gritty face in the low blue glow of the crystal. *"You!* he gasped.

The small skinny old man, with hair tied up in a top-knot, a scraggly beard, forehead smeared with ashes, chalk symbols drawn on his dusky face, smiled. It was a one-toothed grin. "Yes, it's me again—the hermit."

Lasker said, "How'd you get in here?"

"Through the crystal."

"Through the crystal? But—"

"You will see."

"Are you the oracle?"

"Yes and no."

"How can an answer be yes and no?"

"Yes, on the absolute plane. No, on the everyday plane of existence. Yes and no." The hermit smiled again. "You have changed a lot since I last saw you in the Cave of the Peaceful Deity—the cave with the idol with the fist-sized diamond in its forehead. You *so* coveted that big jewel, and so wished to steal it! I was quite amused."

259

"You knew what I was thinking? I didn't believe that you even noticed me back then—you were arguing so much with Tsering."

"I noticed you. You have changed a lot since then—had a little past-life experience with the Bonpo, huh? Well, that's good, very good. You *might* be intelligent enough for me to communicate with now. You had a lot of disrespect for me based on the way I looked the last time we met."

"Forgive me," Bart said. "You just looked like a derelict. That's people back—back home—in America who are drunks and—"

"Yes, I know what you mean. I *am* a derelict. But you know, looks can be deceiving. The Rimpoches respect me, they come to meditate in this cave and learn from me. They bring me gold and precious objects, because they respect me—and much good food. All because they look beyond my surface appearance. But *you,* you don't come empty-handed, do you?"

"I'm sorry . . . next time I'll bring something." Bart thought for a second. "Oh, I suppose you could have some of the Bonpo gems—"

"Yes, I suppose I could . . . we will see. I will consider how best to deal with them. But I never leave this cave. I can't spend the gems. I would rather have some—cookies?"

"Sorry."

"Well—no matter." There was an awkward moment.

Bart said, "Hermit, you have powers—I want you to teach me them. Teach me telepathy, and astral projection, and clairvoyance, and—"

"Why? Why should I?"

Lasker paused. "The Bonpo told me I am an assassin—they trained me to kill. I want to learn these other psychic powers too so that I can help Tibet." He was

260

surprised at his own statement. But it was, after all, the result of long reflection on the trail to Yarang.

"Ah—help Tibet?" The hermit laughed and stood up, favoring one leg. He limped toward a solid wall. "I suppose Khawachen could use a bit of help. Well, then . . . come."

"Come? How can we go anywhere? There's nothing but a solid rock wall."

"Just don't ask so many questions. Now come, walk behind me."

Bart got up. His legs ached and were numb from the position he had been in. He limped also. Bart hobbled along behind the hermit as the filthy shriveled man began walking clockwise around the glowing crystal. They did this sixteen times. Then the hermit turned, walked straight for the crystal. "Close your eyes and hold on to my robe," he ordered. Lasker did, holding on to his disintegrating robe.

They walked for a long time. Lasker couldn't understand it. They should have bumped into the crystal, yet they hadn't. They were now somewhere very brilliantly lit. He opened his eyes—and was very much afraid. Because they were in midair—or rather in a formless brilliant blue-white void. And they started rolling, spinning like Good Baby had done when she was going to crash.

The hermit snapped, "Close your eyes, damnit, and keep on walking—and don't let go of my robe. You are a terrible student already! Do you want us to get lost in here?"

Lasker closed his eyes and with his heart in his throat kept walking on the empty ether.

After a few more moments, the spinning stopped and the light faded. The hermit said, "You may open your eyes now."

Lasker did. He saw the Peaceful Deity statue before him! The one with the glistening diamond in its forehead!

261

How could this be? The statue was in a cave a hundred miles away, near Shemer Rimpoche's monastery.

"Is there more than one statue like this?" Lasker asked.

"No."

"Then—how did we get here?"

"Through the crystal. Actually, it's quite simple, when you know how. Now sit down and I will make some tea—take that cushion over there. Make yourself comfortable; life is short, so little can be done, but one might as well be comfortable!"

Lasker was near to swooning. The ragged hermit had defied the laws of physics and gravity and time and space. And now he was going to make tea.

The hermit came back from behind the statue. "I have a little stove back there. Always have some nice hot tea after a long journey, that's what I say." He sat down and handed Lasker one of the two cups he was holding in his filthy encrusted hands. Lasker took it and sipped. It was the hearty thick Tibetan buttered tea.

"Thank you."

"Oh, you're quite welcome. Now—what would you like to learn first?"

"How we got here—how do you do that—walking through a crystal?"

The hermit sighed. "You just have to know the principles of life, and believe them. Once I heard of a saying from the West. It is a very sad commentary on your Western civilization. It goes: 'Life is hard and then you die.' That is not so. Rather, I say, 'Life is easy and then you live again.' "

"I don't understand."

"Well, all human beings live many, many lives. You know that. You have remembered and actually absorbed much of your past-life personality—Raspahloh. Correct?"

"Correct."

"All these things are possible, because of the impermanence of all things. This is in the doctrine taught by the Buddha Sangye, as well as in the doctrine of the Peaceful Deity. Everything we experience, everything we touch, see, and so forth is the result of our karma. The Cultivators—an ancient race I will tell you more about some other time—have a saying, that you can tell what you will be in the future by what you are doing now. And you can tell what you *were* by what situation you find yourself in. It's all cause and effect. Current experience is merely a projection of our infinite mind. The particular aspect of that mind that we call our *selves,* because it acts in ways that lack understanding, accumulates *karma.* The karma leads to future misunderstanding, future rebirths in situations of its own making. The mind is like a rock thrown into smooth water. It makes ripples, and the ripples spread. So, knowing that we *create* our own reality, that it isn't hard or whatever, is the first step to traveling through space-time. You see, there *is* no space-time. And thinking that there *is* space-time makes it impossible to do what we just did. I told you to keep your eyes shut for a reason. I didn't need your disbelief to upset our journey. I had to believe that it could be done, and then do it. Your incredulity made us unstable, hence the rough ride."

"I think I have a lot to learn," Lasker said. "The Raspahloh part of me is familiar with this—but I find it hard."

"Ah yes, you would. In the West, because you rely so much on mechanical devices, you fail to know the fundamental nature of things. To be quite frank, I think it would be best to start our education into the nature of things on a more elementary level—for you—than travel through crystals."

"Yes."

"So, let's talk about moving your mind *alone,* and not your physical body. That will be easier for you, at first."

"Astral projection. Yes, I know of that. Or rather, Raspaloh—my self long ago—had known of this power."

"There you go again. *Power.* Always power in the obsessed Western mind. It is no power at all. Astral projection is the natural flow of your mind. The easiest way to begin to astral-project is to realize that every living person does it every night of his life, all his life."

"What do you mean?"

"When a person sleeps, his mind leaves his physical body and floats on its silver cord some distance away—maybe for the average person it's only a few feet away, but away nevertheless. When we dream of flying, we are aware that we have gone further out, far away from our physical body. The silver cord we 'project' on is like a fishing line, a strong fishing line that the brain reels in when it is awake. To keep the mind in the brain. But mind doesn't *have* to be in the brain. That is a misconception. Mind, when we die, and enter the forty-nine-day wandering of the *Bardo,* exists without attachment to the body, until a new body is formed by its karmic accumulation. Then the mind is reborn in another body, that of a baby. You know that, don't you?"

"Raspaloh knows about the Bardo and rebirth, Lasker finds it difficult," Lasker stated.

"Ah yes. You would. But the Bardo is another subject. To get back to astral projection—remember, we have done it already, you and I. We walked through the crystal, through space-time, to get to this cave. Accept that the mind leaves the body at night. That it travels to other realms—the dream realm—that it can soar and fly and so on. Just accept that."

"Okay."

"Good. Now, to astral-project in the simplest way, you need to lie down, or sit in meditative posture—that's even

better, for it aligns the body's chakras, or energy points—
and let yourself go. Let your mind reel out on its slender
silver cord. Just do this now, Lasker. Close your eyes and
just sit there. Imagine that you slip from your earthy coil
and unwind up through the roof of this cavern and look
down at the mountain below. Can you do that? Pretend
you are in your flying machine. Can you do that?''

''Right. I'll pretend that I'm in Good Baby.''

''So go up into the air and look down as you did from
your airplane.''

''I can *imagine* that I'm doing that. But I can't *do* that.
It's impossible.''

The hermit made an exasperated noise. ''Well, then
*imagine* it.''

Lasker spent the next half hour doing just that.

The hermit softly asked, ''What do you see?''

''It's getting light—the sun is coming up—oh, beautiful, all red—and there's a bird, a big condor, sailing
over the mountain, it just went by me.'' Lasker described
the mountain below, the valley, the rope bridge that led
across the chasm to the monastery nearby.

''What else do you see?''

''I see a caravan, ten or twelve riders, and some animals, traveling on a nearby road.''

''Keep flying.'' The hermit hummed and chanted
mantras during Lasker's wondrous ''flight.'' Then he
said, ''Now come back down into your body . . . slowly
. . . slowly. Reel your silver cord in.''

Lasker felt the warmth of the tea in his stomach. He
was back. He opened his eyes. And smiled. ''That was
wonderful. I feel—*elated.*''

''You think you imagined it?''

''I—I don't know.''

''Well, you didn't. You were there. Trust the fact that
you were there. I know, because I was at one with that
bird you saw, and I saw that caravan also, and the sun

coming up all red with the rays over the mountain. You did it, I *checked.* "

Lasker smiled. "I thought I might have. But you say you were in that bird? How—"

"I know that bird, and he let me in, because he likes me. You can find animals that like you and join them, if they let you—you can practice that some other time. Well, I don't know about you but I would like some food."

Lasker followed the hermit behind the statue and watched as he laboriously ignited a fire with tinder and flint—refusing Bart's matches—then prepared some meat cakes and brewed tea in an earthen pot. He was anxious to go back to the teachings.

"Can't you just materialize the food?"

"Lasker"—the hermit shook his finger at him—"my friend, don't you know that to do these things unnecessarily is bad karma? Life is to live. Not to perform tricks to *avoid* living. If I did that, I would be as bad as these couch people I see in your mind, the ones in your country that spend all day in front of a glass tube watching shadows—TV they call it."

"Yes, that's what they call it."

"Well, you'll just have to wait anxiously for the buns to heat. We will enjoy them all the more when they take a bit of time."

Lasker nodded.

# Chapter 26

For days, Lasker sat at the feet of the hermit, learning the age-old secrets of the ancient race called the Cultivators. He knew the passage of days only by dint of the hermit's uncanny timekeeping. The hermit, guided by some arcane instinct, would go to the statue and move one amber bead in the rosary held by the stone hand to signify the change of day.

Lasker eagerly absorbed what he heard, but always was admonished for moving too fast. "Lasker," the hermit said after thirteen beads had been moved on the amber rosary, "you have many lifetimes ahead of you for learning. In this life, concentrate on the most immediate problem—yourself. You must spend time integrating the Raspahloh and the Westerner within you. You must reconcile them. This is your karmic load in this life. It will take you a long time. I sense that your two personalities don't much like each other."

Lasker frowned. "Raspahloh thinks Westerners are barbarian ignoramuses, and I think that Raspahloh is an evil cannibal."

"Well, that's a start anyway." The hermit smiled. "At least you're communicating. Very odd karma, this path of yours."

"How do you know what you know, hermit?"

"I learned all I know from my master, who learned it from his master, and so on all the way back through history to the Cultivators themselves. Plus there are books—wonderful books in this cave too. But books are not enough. You need a teacher, direct. In the West, you mouth the words of your spiritual master, but the line of transmission of understanding is cut. The line from the Cultivators to me is unbroken."

"I see," Lasker replied. "I want to know about these Cultivators you constantly mention. Who are they?"

"They are the creators of the human race—quite by accident."

"Creators—by accident?"

"I shall explain—briefly. I can see you will not let the matter rest for another time. The Cultivators came from up in the sky in great ships—hundreds of centuries ago. Their machines were far beyond the toys of the Western world today. At the time they arrived here on this planet, there was only a semi-ape ancestor of today's human being roaming wild—but I go ahead of myself.

"The Cultivators, men and women that were much like ourselves, landed. They were devoid of the more apelike features of humanity—and devoid also of the ape rages, the emotional backwardness of humans today. It wasn't a good landing. There was much damage to their ship. They set about exploring, trying to find out if they could make this place livable for themselves. It *could* be—cultivated. These Cultivators were of both sexes, man and woman—a few hundred in all of both. But not for long. Something about being on the Earth made their women die off. Nothing could stop it, not even their advanced knowledge, nor their god—the Peaceful Deity.

"The men mourned their women's passing, and then some of them started to try to find substitute women on this Earth. They found a race of ape things that were somewhat more similar to them, but very stupid. They killed off the males and took the females back to the ship. They talked about making genetic changes in the female apes, of mating. The factions quarreled bitterly among themselves. Some wanted to do this change to the ape things, to mate with the results. Some thought it best to try to leave the Earth, despite the damage to the great ship. One faction refused to take off, they said it was too dangerous. The faction that wished to mate with the female ape things went off from the other Cultivators. The results were usually that a baby grew inside the female ape creatures that was too large—*way* too large for their wombs. Many new females died, unable to expel their child at birth. The other Cultivators came and said the matings must not continue. This faction demanded the others cease these horrible experiments, causing pain on these creatures.

"The factions fought—and with weapons that would make the current weapons of mankind seem puny. Great areas of many continents were laid waste. The "bad" people from the sky—those that wanted to continue the mating experiments—won. The ship was destroyed in the process. The matings with Earth creatures went on, causing much pain and suffering and abominations. Finally the combined species—the Cultivator race mixed with the Earth race of new apes—developed into what we call human beings today. Women today are still unable often to give birth the normal way, and many die unless the child is surgically cut out of her womb."

"Is this story true?" Lasker asked.

"Truth is relative."

"What planet did these Cultivators come from?"

"Not another planet—another dimension," the hermit replied with a snap in his voice.

"Are there any pure Cultivators left?"

269

"I don't think so, but who knows? Their techniques for longevity, for putting the body to sleep for centuries, eons, existed even then. Perhaps in some other cave, the 'Good' Cultivators sleep, awaiting the signal from another of their great ships to awaken. I do not know this. Some Tibetan Buddhists say that they have received a good deal of their more esoteric teachings from the Shambhala Realm—that is a place in the far north, underground some say, where a strange and powerful race lives.

"Now, enough history lessons. It will soon be time for you to leave me, and there are things to do before I go on teaching you anything else. I really have gone too far already without proper initiation procedures."

"What initiation?"

"Lasker, do you think that I would teach you all of this unless you are to be an initiate of mine? My spiritual child? Do you wish this to be? Will I do?"

"Yes," Lasker said solemnly, thinking of the wonders he had beheld in the cave, with the old hermit. And thinking also of his kindness, his forbearance with the Western mind of Bart Lasker. "What do I do?"

"Well," the hermit said, with his one-toothed smile beaming at Lasker, "you just snip a piece of your hair off with this knife"—he passed a knife to Lasker—"and then give it to me."

Lasker cut off an inch lock of his long hair and placed it in the hermit's outstretched hand.

The hermit said gently, "Now you prostrate to me three times, and ask for the free gift of my teachings, as much as I can give, while I feed these hairs of yours into my tea stove."

This Lasker did, because he wanted to do something in return for the old wise man. Kowtowing was the least he could do to acknowledge the many spiritual presents the hermit had bestowed. If he wanted Lasker to formally do so, so be it.

Only a small voice within was wondering what the hell Lasker was getting himself into by becoming an initiate.

"Don't worry," the hermit shouted as he rose and went to the stove and threw the hairs into the hot coals. They smoldered and shriveled. "There, that's done," he shouted. "You don't have to give up any other religions you might have—now or in the future or past, even though you have officially joined my religion." He walked back smiling profusely, and lifted Lasker with surprisingly strong hands off the floor. "See? Now that you are mine, you weigh less."

Lasker frowned. He had a most uncomfortable feeling—as if he should have considered this act of initiation much more carefully. "Er—what religion have I just joined?"

"Why, mine. The religion of the Cultivators, handed down to me from time immemorial. But never mind that—it is time to get on with your lessons, initiate, for soon you must leave. Let's see—what was next?"

"Telepathy," Lasker said, resuming his seat on the cushion. "I was using telepathy most of the time at Shekar Dzong—the Bonpo Hidden Realm. But I can't seem to reach into your mind now, though you seem to be able to read my thoughts. I've forgotten how."

"That's because you never knew how to do it. Zompahlok was doing it to you, enabling you. And Raspaloh was not a great adept at mental projection either. So now you will get—what do they call it—a crash course. Again, the problem in your mind is a case of your Western impatience. You wish to force the issue. *Force* is not telepathy. It is natural. It, too, like astral projection, flows out of understanding the nature of reality. You have nothing but misconceptions. You

271

think: This can't be done, this takes effort—all those kinds of thoughts. Now listen. All is *empty*, the Peaceful Deity taught this, and Buddha taught this also. There is, in ultimate reality, no forms, no senses, no things to be sensed—are you familiar with that sutra lesson?"

"Yes, the Heart Sutra. The monks chanted it at the first monastery I went to in Tibet. It was explained—briefly—to me."

"A most profound sutra. But Buddha didn't figure that out, he just sat still and let that understanding come to him, as the Peaceful Deity and all enlightened beings who have gone beyond suffering have done. Buddha was able to do this because he had lived many, many lives of compassion and seeking. Before the life in which he realized the ultimate truth, as once the Peaceful Deity had, long before him."

"And the ultimate truth is what?"

The hermit just stared and said nothing.

After a while Lasker said, "Let's go on about telepathy."

"Sure. So as I was saying, telepathy is easy. So easy that it is hard for a mind fettered by all sorts of bad knowledge. Just clear your mind of all effort, all thoughts of your own, get really clear, and you can send and receive thoughts. I will not teach you telepathy, I will teach you mental clarity so that your *natural* telepathic ability will come to the fore."

"You say I have natural telepathic ability. Does everyone? Even we of the Western world?"

"The Americans don't think they do—but"—the hermit smiled—"I can prove to you that Americans use it every day. You have a picture in your mind of a road—choaked with cars, all hurtling over—potholes? Yes, potholes and bumps at great speed. This road is called the FDR Drive—it is in a giant city called New York. Now—think carefully. Could anyone sur-

272

vive a ride down that road *without* having an instinctive knowledge of the minds of all those drivers around you, when they will cut in or out, when they will do something stupid like hit the brakes for no reason?''

Lasker smiled. "I suppose not."

"You suppose *right*. All the drivers are all using telepathy and can do so because they aren't *trying* to do so. So now let us begin."

"I love your examples, hermit—by the way, what is your name? What do I call you?"

"Call me hermit, that is sufficient. I know you don't like to bow and scrape, so you may call me hermit, or teacher, instead of master. Now, listen: Mental clarity is like the lotus blossom, it rises above the calm still waters, out of the mud of habitual thought into the pure blue air. Visualize that image, a lotus blossom in a lake, as you think of me, and drop all thought . . ."

And so it was that Lasker's lessons went from the time of the first crescent moon to the full moon. Then the hermit, having taught the rudiments of astral projection, telepathy, and several other subjects Lasker hadn't even known existed, took Lasker back to the Oracle Cave via the crystal. He rolled back the entrance-sealing rock with the push of a single finger.

It was time to leave. It was night, the full moon shone on them. Lasker said, "But what should I do with all I have learned?"

"Aren't you going to try to help Tibet? Or was that just a ruse to get the knowledge?" The hermit shook his finger. "Now you're *committed*, disciple. You have the mystic power, and some of the teachings of the Cultivators. You must rebel against the established order of things. Go to the source of trouble and deal with it. Do not make precise plans. Let your knowledge—and fate—guide your actions. Be the *Mystic Rebel!!*"

With those words the old man disappeared into the cave.

# Chapter 27

Lasker walked into the bright moonlit night, already unhappy to be away from the cave guru. His legs were sore from so much cross-legged sitting, and he fairly staggered down the moraine of gravel toward Yarang. He found most of the rebels at the Yarang tavern. They were just ending a trading session with the locals. Lasker came in the door, and everyone fell silent. The women left, and so did all the village people, buzzing among themselves about Lasker. Only the men of Tsering's group remained.

"How did it go?" Cheojey asked. "Did the oracle come?"

The hermit had insisted that his identity as the oracle, the wonders of what happened to Bart in the cave, were to be a secret. So, like others who had consulted the cave oracle, Lasker was vague about what had transpired. He said only that he had been meditating, and that the oracle had come to him, and told him what to do.

"And what," asked Cheojey, "does the oracle advise you to do?"

Lasker said, "I'm not sure the oracle said to do anything."

"Can you do anything about Tse Ling?" Tsering

asked. "Did the oracle tell you how to remove her, so that the people of this province will not be so ill-treated? So Dorjee can return to us?"

"Nothing—specific. Where is Tse Ling now?"

"She is in Lhasa," replied Cheojey. "Tse Ling, for security purposes, stays in the Polata Palace itself."

"It will be impossible to get to her," Rinchen said, disgust in his voice. "Lhasa is strictly controlled, access and egress," the surly man continued. He was digging out a piece of the table with his big knife as he talked. "No way to get to the Virgin Dragon and kill her—too bad!"

Tsering cleared his throat and said, "Maybe I have a way for you to get into Lhasa, if you want to—" He explained that he and his men had come across a skeleton on a high trail a few months earlier. The skeleton, judging from the clothing and papers, was that of a hiker. A British subject who had died in a rockfall. "Perhaps," the rebel leader said, "you could use his papers. The Chinese permit Western tourists great latitude in visiting the Holy City."

Lasker looked over the papers Tsering fetched from a box under Rinchen's uncle's fireplace bricks. He looked much like the photo—dark hair, brown eyes—on the hiker's international driver's license. That convinced Bart this was a stroke of fate, a way for the Mystic Rebel to move.

The hermit had told him to let fate guide his path.

Lasker turned the papers over and over in his hands, and felt the buzz of intuition that he had been taught to recognize by the hermit. "I will use these documents to get into Lhasa—to get to Tse Ling. It is time for me to become a Westerner again."

Lasker went to the ice-covered fountain outside the tavern, smashed through the glaze of ice, bathed off all the Tibetan dust, and washed out his tangled hair.

Then he re-entered the tavern and cut off his long hair with Tsering's sharp knife, until it was as short as when he first came to Tibet. He stood before a mirror and, with a brush, forced a part in it. He then put on the Western-style insulated down vest that they had removed from the skeleton, and the unfortunate Brit's hiking boots too. A bit large—but better than tight. He stuffed some cloth into the tips of the boots to make them fit. The rebels still had his belt and his shirt from the time he had fallen into their domain, and gave them back to Bart. He put on a pair of Chinese-made blue work pants—part of the traded goods, and put the metal-frame backpack on. The same pack that had broken the back of the unfortunate hiker when he had fallen on a remote trail.

He stared at himself in the mirror. "I don't *like* the way I look. I've gotten used to wearing a robe."

"You look like a tourist to me," Cheojey said. Bart sighed, asked for some supplies for his trip to Lhasa, then went to sleep in one of the tavern's "drunkard's cots."

The next morning Lasker took his horse by the reins and mounted up, started off for Lhasa. On the way out of Yarang he could not but muse at the irony of his situation. What a set of transformations—pilot to Snow Lion rebel, to Bonpo assassin, to seeker of knowledge in the cave, and then to being the Mystic Rebel who was supposed to do something for Tibet. And what's more, he called that filthy hermit his *teacher*. Surely these bizarre twists of fate proved that a man is swept along in life *not* by his own design, but by the winds of his karma, generated in many previous existences!

Lasker rode only as far as six miles from Lhasa, stopping at the small white and red painted house of a sheepherder—a clan relative of Tsering. There he left the trader's horse for safekeeping. It wouldn't do for a "tourist" to ride a horse into Lhasa. After a cup of tea in the poor sheepherder's meager house, he went to the asphalt road used by the Chinese trucks and waited. Soon a Chinese truck convoy came grinding along. Bart stuck out his hand and tried to wave down a ride. The third truck pulled over and picked him up. There were two truck drivers—young Chinese men from Annan Province. In Chinese, they asked to see his papers. When he produced his travel permit and other documents, they both smiled widely. "Britisher! Hop in, we will practice our English, please, and give you a ride."

The Chinese were nice young men who introduced themselves as Am Chow and Hoi San. Hoi was driving—they took turns. They told him that many times they had picked up Western hitchhikers near Lhasa. Once even a blond girl, Hoi said. "Imagine, she traveled alone. You Westerners are brave, though, of course, we Chinese are all good friendly people and would only help travelers," he added.

Lasker agreed. Hoi said they had been on the road six days—stopping to eat and rest at the Chinese truck stops on the way, enjoying the scenery and the chance to see more than their own province, which neither had ever been out of before their job in Tibet. They were delivering textbooks to the Nationalities Schools in Lhasa. Lasker looked over a textbook they had on the dash. It seemed to be a primary reader.

"No books in Tibetan?"

"It's a dead language," Hoi replied.

Lasker didn't want to talk too much. One of them might become aware he was speaking the American version of English. But after a while, he realized they had only a rudimentary knowledge of the English language.

They drove past more trucks heading the opposite way. The other drivers waved and shouted to them—some information about the women of Lhasa—where to find them, and how much to give them. Prostitution in the Holy City!

The ride lasted barely twenty minutes before the textbook-laden truck groaned up to the top of a long hill. Suddenly there it was—standing in the great plain before them—Lhasa, City of the Gods. He knew this place—there was instant recognition that he had been *here,* looking at this scene before. His heart pounded in the cage of his ribs. He had been here on this hill, long before the paved road ever existed. He had seen the fabulous city of Lhasa centuries ago. And at its middle—a cliff of redstone—the Mapoori—with two staircases on it, leading up into the mists that wreathed the top. Lasker knew what was up on that cliff, and as the truck descended, he saw it.

The mists parted and he beheld now, as in the ancient past, the great palace of the Dalai Lamas, called the Potala. It was a mammoth tribute to Tibetan architecture, a vast palace of ten thousand rooms built with no nails or steel or iron—towering above Lhasa. Construction had begun in 1645, under the fifth Dalai Lama, who died before it was completed. Lasker knew the place quite well—since he as Raspahloh had *killed* that Dalai Lama.

The Dalai Lama's regent had hidden the holy man's death, and said the Dalai Lama was just "meditating a lot." The regent had a monk that looked like the deceased God-King paraded out when the Dalai Lama had to be seen at festivals.

The Potala emerged from the morning mist with glistening gold points on its roof catching the sun, its many white prayer flags blowing in the wind. The Potala appeared unchanged, but the fabled city below— what had happened to it? It was three times more sprawling than Raspahloh's memory of it. Lhasa was now devoid of trees, and filled with massive tin-roofed

278

shacks of foreign slant-roof design. Diesel smoke rose from the many trucks in the streets. And the vast complexes of the Norbulinga temples, and all the lesser monasteries on the hills beyond Lhasa, with their many silver roofs, were burned-out ruins. Only the waving fields of barley before the city, and the Potala itself, were as Raspahloh remembered.

The Potala was now standing vigil above an abysmally gloomy, smoke-wreathed city of foreign squalor. You could spot some of the old low whitewashed buildings here and there as the truck descended on the hill. But now there was more of the other element in the picture—the mass of rusting tin-roof homes—thousands of them.

The truck geared down and crawled past a Chinese military complex, hundreds of parked trucks and tanks behind barbed wire. And Lasker heard a whistling noise. A plane roared overhead. Straining his eyes beyond the city, he could discern a black strip of land— an airport. An *airport* in the Forbidden City? The scar of the runway jarred his sense of place. The screaming twin-engine 727 with CHINA AIRLINES written in English on its fusilage shattered the calm of the valley as it dropped slowly toward the runway.

Lasker wanted to shout, "No, this is not the way Lhasa is! It is a holy city!"

But he held his tongue. The Chinese driver said, "Quite a view isn't it, Englishman?"

He nodded, unable to speak, dumbstruck by the tragedy of Tibet, the conquered nation. Before him was the best example of that subjugation . . . the ruination of the Holy City.

When they had entered the city proper, Lasker jumped off at a corner. He waved and thanked the drivers for the lift. Bart put his backpack on and headed through a crowd of off-duty Chinese soldiers, many of whom smiled and said, "Hello, Englishman." He smiled and said, *"Ich bin Deutsch."* That always ground conversation to a halt. Nobody studied German.

The city smelled of rancid garbage, slaughterhouses, and diesel fumes. You could get killed crossing the streets filled with trucks of every size and description. Most were military. There were more Chinese soldiers and Chinese "settlers" than there were stolid unsmiling Tibetans. Most Tibetans wore Chinese-manufactured clothing, but a few still defiantly wore the Tibetan chubas, ragged and dirty.

Lasker heard voices speaking English—he looked up, saw a Midwestern-type man in a three-piece suit standing next to a Chinese woman posted at the entrance of an ancient temple. He was asking the woman, who had a bowl haircut, "Can we take a photograph in the temple?"

"Yes, but there is a charge of ten renminbao, for the restoration fund," she replied in a high-pitched heavily accented English. Bart turned to see a tour group—a dozen men and women, some dressed the way he was, like rugged world travelers. But behind them were some more Caucasians—in suits and dresses—as if they stepped out of a taxi in New York City. They were coming around the corner led by a Chinese woman in a severe Mao jacket and pants. Her close-cropped hair and her relaxed, easy manner indicated she was a guide.

So here are "other" tourists, Lasker thought. Perhaps it would be best if I join them.

He slipped into the mass of the twenty or so foreigners making their way slowly down the Lhasa sidewalk. Bart noticed that none of the Tibetans walked on the sidewalk—they preferred to risk life and limb walking in the gutter. Why? Weren't they allowed on the sidewalks?

Then he looked down. The Chinese had created the

sidewalks out of irregular-shaped flat stones that had Tibetan writing on them. He gasped. *Mani-pile stones.* The Chinese had made it necessary to walk on the sacred prayer stones if you wanted to use the sidewalks! That's why the Tibetans walked in the gutter. His eyes narrowed in anger at the foreign oppressors who had destroyed a way of life.

The group of tourists stopped at a theater, the Happy Times Cinema. "Here are the latest films from all over the world," the woman guide said. "In the bad old days," she said loudly, "only the rich landowners and corrupt sexually perverted Buddhist monks were allowed to come here. Now every citizen of this part of China can purchase a ticket and enjoy themselves."

The crowd tittered. Lasker looked at the bill. BRUCE LEE in FISTS OF FURY, plus YANKEE DOODLE DANDY with JAMES CAGNEY. An odd match.

"When can we see the *damned* Potala?" asked a tall man in a Stetson hat—his voice had the twang of a Texan.

"The next tour of the Potala," said the guide, looking at her dainty watch, "is not until four P.M. One hour from now."

Lasker thought, how could it be 4 P.M.? The sun is barely over the eastern mountains. It must be around 10 A.M. Then he remembered—*all of Tibet was on Beijing Standard Time,* now that the Chinese ruled. Even if it meant people were in total darkness in Tibet as late as nine in the morning. The ridiculous Chinese regulations saying all of "China" had to have the same time. And Tibet *was* a part of China—now.

"I want to go back to the hotel, my feet hurt," said an American woman in ultra-high heels.

"We paid two thousand bucks for this little side trip from India, Mary Lou," said the Texan, "so you just hang your corns in there. I ain't bought this here Sony

281

Video-cam for nothing. *Boy,* are them old boys back in Austin gonna be surprised when I show them the Pot-alah when we get back.''

''We must move on now to our next stop,'' said the woman guide briskly. ''The Jo-Kan Temple.''

Lasker along with the others fished up ten renminbao to enter and gave them to the ersatz monk at the door. He put them in the box labeled in English, RESTORATION FUND. Lasker knew, from his talks with the caravaners, that all the temple reconstruction and statue restorals were done by volunteer Tibetans. They even purchased their own supplies. The money just forked over was headed straight to Beijing to buy more guns for their ''Liberation'' army.

The tourists passed into the exquisite, dimly lit ancient temple—one of the holiest places of pilgrimage in Tibet. A lot of the gilded human-sized statues were painted white plaster. Many of the gold images he remembered from his past life had been replaced with these plaster copies—the real images had been destroyed in the 1960s by Mao's psycho-boys. But some of the statues were real—like the Guru Rimpoche statue at the end of the hall. Probably it had been secreted in the mountains until the ''Liberalization.''

''Damned,'' uttered the Texan. ''Ain't enough light in here to use the damned Sony-cam!''

Louder, he said, ''I say, Miss How? Could you-all turn on the electricity a mite so's I could get me a shot of this here funny little statue?''

''There is, as yet, no electricity.''

''Damned—all the way to Tibet and I can't take no pictures.''

''Use the camera, dear—'' Mary Lou suggested.

''Can't,'' he said miserably. ''All my Kodak's gone, and they don't sell any one-ten Instamatic film in this miserable . . .''

The last part of the Texan's remark was lost when the guide started saying, "You will note the cannibal deities in abundance in this abominable relic of the past degenerate age. This temple is yet another example of the degenerate nature of the old Buddhist leaders, before the Tibetan people called upon the People's Liberation Army to free them from their corrupt domination."

Lasker thought, *Lies . . . the statues depict religious concepts—the corpse represents subjugation of the ego, the skullcap the impermanence of life. This guide knows nothing about the art treasures in here. She just spouts the party line.*

The Texan spoke up, loudly again. "When do we see the Pot-alah? Will there be electricity there?"

"Yes, the fluorescent lamps will be on. We will go soon."

But now the guide noted Bart's presence. "Sir, may I see your tour pass?"

Lasker said, "I'm afraid I just joined your tour—I couldn't purchase one in time—"

"No problem." She smiled. "That will be fifty renminbao."

"Do you take National Westminster Traveler's Checks?"

"Of course."

Bart paid with one of the dead hiker's checks. He even got change, scrawling the name of his benefactor, Bruce Arthur.

The five minutes in the sacred Jo-Kan over, the group of tourists now moved to the foot of the Mapoori, the Red Mountain.

Above them loomed the Potala Palace, where Tse Ling was posted.

# Chapter 28

The Chinese woman guide rattled off, "Construction on this palace of decadence began in 1645, under the Fifth Dalai Lama. Workers were taxed and exploited to the limit, hawling up the huge stones by hand. Many were crushed in accidents. The Fifth Dalai Lama died before the palace was completed. It is believed he was killed by other elements in the feudal government. His regent hid his death, to get the job finished."

A gray-haired woman in tennis sneakers and a pink pantsuit with red flowers on it took a Polaroid flash picture then left the tear-off scrap on the ground.

As they moved forward, Lasker picked up the film scrap and put it in his pocket.

"The palace is thirteen stories high, but the floors are not continuous, being of different heights. Through the efforts of the Chinese generosity, the palace is being restored and maintained. That is why we ask a fee of—"

Yeah sure, Lasker thought, writing up another bogus traveler's check.

They walked along the cliff wall to the base of the wide ascending steps.

Lasker said, in his British-ese, "Rather a bit of a climb."

A tired female voice replied, "Certainly is. Where's the elevator?"

"There is no elevator. Only the steps," said the guide.

A series of groans.

"For those who do not wish to make the long climb, there is a souvenir shop on the far right corner, at the cliff's base."

Many of the tourists at this point dropped out, heading for the souvenir shop.

"This whole town smells, Charlie, let's get back to Kathmandu—tonight. I hate it here—no elevators yet."

"Mah sentiments exactly, lil darlin'."

God, they're going to skip the *Potala*. Lasker couldn't get over it. Tibet was just a jaunt now, and the Potala, the most sacred spot in central Asia *skippable* because it didn't have an elevator. "Progress," he mumbled.

"Will the rest of you start the climb now?" the Chinese guide said, striding quickly ahead up the wide granite stairs.

Bart was one of twelve who chose to climb. The composition of the crowd was much less stuffy. Gone were most of the older Gucci-camerabags-and-pocketbooks set. It was now mostly a hiker-type group. Some of them had on protection cords from lamas, and others held prayer beads. Western Buddhists.

He gauged his chances, and frowned. The fewer people on the tour, the harder to slip away, to examine the wall in a certain place. He would have a difficult time of it.

The young woman with red hair and freckles was panting by the time they made it to the palace proper. She had to breath for a while from an oxygen mask

285

attached to a tank at the top of the stairs. The Chinese had such oxygen supplies all over Tibet. Even their young soldiers didn't travel in the altitudes without at least one oxygen tank available.

The woman's pulse was taken with some concern by the guide, who assured her that it was quite common to be winded. "The cool of the interior will refresh you," she said.

The tour now began. The taller Westerners had to duck to enter a plain stone slab entrance into a fluorescent-lit antechamber.

"This is the subcellar, a dark, dingy storeroom," the guide intoned. "The decadent Lamas used it as a torture chamber before the People's Liberation Army came to the rescue."

"How large is the Potala?" the freckled redhead asked.

"The Potala is a hundred and seventeen meters high at its roof. The whole structure is wood and stone, and the one thousand rooms contain ten thousand shrines and two hundred thousand statues. No nails, bolts, or metal girders were used in construction. Many of the rooms are undergoing restoration. But we still have a good long tour," said the guide. "The walls around us will vary in thickness from two to five meters. In the preceding centuries after construction began, they were filled with solid molten copper to prevent earthquake damage."

The hushed group of tourists were led through a bare-bulb-illuminated replica of a torture chamber—racks, shackles bolted into the walls. Lasker smiled. The guide had just said no nails were used in the entire palace. Yet here were metal bolts. It was obviously a phony setup. The torture chamber was peculiarly Medieval European style—didn't anybody notice?

The guide pointed out the flaying instruments, the

rods that would be heated in the iron caldron to burn prisoners horribly. There were photographs of burn victims on the wall. "You see how the Dalai Lamas' ministers tortured any political opposition, any petitioner for the people's rights."

They moved on, perhaps a few impressed that the Chinese were indeed great liberators.

Someone asked, "Where is the stuff in the brochure?"

They were assured that what they were about to see was worth the climb. "The beauty, the luxury, ahead is immense. But do not take it as an accomplishment of the degenerate Lama ruling class. It was all created at the expense of liberty, at great cost and hardship borne off the backs of the peasants. Since the wheel was not brought to Tibet until the twentieth century, all the materials to construct this monumental structure were lugged on human backs up the stairs you just ascended. Some stones weighed thirty tons."

Groans.

"We are now going up one flight into the red palace, the first constructed section of the Potala." She snapped open the theater-type rope barrier and let everyone in. Lasker could see her lips move, counting carefully. They walked into the first shrine room. There were several old monks attending the shrine and cleaning the vessels, chanting *Om Mani Padme Hum* as they worked.

"Please do not touch the exhibits, and follow me around the room," the guide said. "First we stop at these ancient prayer wheels, actually cylinders. There are eight of them, filled with prayers to the Buddha. It is the custom for visitors to turn the prayer wheels along the wall. The superstition is that turning prayer wheels brings great good luck." She turned it counterclockwise—the sacrilegious way.

Everyone had a go at the creaky brass cylinders, in-

287

cluding Lasker, who stopped each and spun them the right way, clockwise. The good luck he wanted was that the secret panel he was looking for would still be there in the palace above.

She smiled at him. "It is just a superstition, like black cats being bad luck. But we must not forget to turn the wheels, for that would upset the monks. It is said they have magic powers, and can kill by thought if we annoy them."

Giggles.

The decrepid old monks continued on their rounds. Lasker had the sense that they were real monks, leftovers from the old days. Too old to work, they had become part of this holy museum. One of them glanced casually at the tourists and his eyes fixed on Lasker's for the briefest of seconds.

Lasker wondered if he knew what this particular tourist was up to. Could he be psychic?

The group went on. There were more shrine rooms, all larger and larger, as they ascended slowly through several stories.

Flash pictures were going off right and left, despite the guide's admonition that photographic conditions were very poor in the building. "Photographic postcards are available at the checkout," she said, "for a nominal charge."

They walked on. The people hugging the line behind the guide were like ducklings following mother, unquestioning. They appeared unimpressed. Bart heard the comment, "But it's just a buncha Buddha statues."

The rooms were fluorescent-lit, and full of endless statues. The group perked up every time the guide pointed out a jewel in a forehead of a Buddha, but when the statues were not made of solid gold or silver or encrusted with jewels, they scarcely looked.

They were in the ancient jewel of Asia. The holy

288

seat of the Dalai Lamas for fourteen incarnations, ever since the fifteenth century. They were seeing exquisite art—the product of a brilliant people over many centuries. And they weren't in awe.

Maybe, Lasker thought, he wouldn't have been impressed either, if he were but a Western tourist. But he had *lived* here, in this palace many centuries ago, lived the double life of an assassin in hiding, a killer waiting to strike at the heart of all of Tibetan Buddhism—the Fifth Dalai Lama. He had killed the God-King whose salted mummy sat in endless meditation inside one of the twelve immense silver coffins contained in the palace.

"Now we must ascend another staircase," said the guide. "Please hold the bannisters."

Lasker's heart pounded. They were now entering the fifth floor of the palace he knew from ancient days, via the winding staircase of irregular-sized steps. This was it.

"These will be the last five rooms on our tour," said the guide with some relief as they reached the landing. "I think you will agree they are the most worthy to use your film on. These are the most spectacular."

They entered a large chamber, perhaps a hundred feet square. It had a hole in its high ceiling, through which a wide but tapering structure pierced.

"The structure you see in the middle of the room is a chorten. It is a twelve-meter-high tomb containing the remains of the Third Dalai Lama . . ." she droned on, ". . . three hundred kilograms of solid gold, encrusted with semiprecious and precious stones, including diamonds of up to twenty-five carats in weight adorn the chorten. This is worth, by weight alone, over fifty million pounds sterling. And, of course, it is a national treasure of the Tibetan people. Previous to the liberation, access to the rooms we have seen was forbidden under pain of death to all but high Tibetan officials . . ." People were paying attention now, intrigued by all the diamonds and rubies and so on encrusted in the vast structure behind the cloth ropes.

Lasker dropped away to a corner of the chamber behind a chorten, just out of sight of the guide. She had her back to the crowd, and would not note his absence as long as she was placing her fingers next to various stones on the silver tomb and telling their value. He had a few moments to accomplish his task.

Madly he searched for the wall painting depicting the Mahakala Protector Deity—a black cemetery demon converted to Buddhism by Padmasambhava in the twelfth century. There was a lot of crumbling wet plaster—some leak from above—and the wall was badly scarred. He could only with difficulty see any marks on the wall at all, especially in the overhead fluorescents' faint light. But the painting was there—he made out the black-and-gold outline of the left hand of Mahakala, holding the *amrita* cup, and then the face with staring eyes, scarred by what looked like bulletholes. Target practice for some zealous Red Guard youth perhaps?

Bart was looking for the necklace of the protector being. *There*—five skulls arranged on the garland of the creature. And one skull was not peeling as the others. Because, he knew, it was not painted on plaster, but was a platinum button that would open a secret panel in the wall if he pressed it. . . .

*"What are you doing there?"* Come back to the group at once! That wall is in the process of restoration and is not on the tour itinerary." The sharp words of the guide stayed his hand. He went back to the group, muttering apologies. Bart felt a rising satisfaction. If the platinum skull button in the wall painting was still there, the mechanism underneath that decaying wall most likely was still there also!

# Chapter 29

By darkness, Lasker slipped from his hiding place in the marquee of the Happy Time Cinema, where he had holed up after the tour. He stealthily made his way through the curfewed streets. He was not wearing the same clothes—instead he had donned the black climbing outfit the women of the caravan had made for him, which he had carried in his backpack. His face was swathed in a band of black cloth with just a slit in it for his eyes. He moved silently, as he had been trained. He was but a wraith, a fleeting shadow, a trick of the moonlight. None of the Chinese soldiers on patrol noticed him. In moments, he was at the Mapoori Cliff; above him loomed the darkened Potala. He took the coiled rope from his right shoulder, checked the four-pronged metal hook, then spun it a few times, and threw. The grapple caught on the beam intended, forty feet up. And Lasker pulled it tight, then started working his way up the cliff side. He climbed in the shadows of the sheer wall of stone next to the floodlight-drenched palace stairs. He swung through the open window of the "torture chamber" room, undid the grapple by jerking the rope, and rewound it. Then he put it back on his shoulder—he would probably need it again.

He now took the same stairs he had that afternoon with the guide, and froze when he heard voices. Bart peered around a corner, saw two guards. They were relaxed, feet up, watching a soccer game on a small static-filled portable TV. He waited for a goal and then, as they shouted and watched the replay, dashed past the guards, not six feet away. He plunged into the stairwell and bounded the steps three at a time, until he reached the fifth story of the Red Palace—the room with the Third Dalai Lama's giant chorten coffin. The door was locked, but it was a simple padlock. He focused his *chi* into his "steel hand" and pulled it off.

He entered the room. There was the silver chorten-coffin, glistening dully in the moonlight sifting from an airation vent in the outside wall. And there was the Mahakala, painted on the wall. He headed immediately toward the hidden control for the secret passage.

And froze in his tracks. Three ghostly figures, transparent, luminescent, dressed as monks did of old, came out from the solid wall, right out of the Mahakala frieze itself. They went in immense silence to the Buddha statues, prostrated themselves. Then the monks took up a ghostly teakettle and walked toward the Dalai Lama chorten and right through the immense coffin's metal-and-gem wall.

Lasker realized they must be the ghosts of servants of the dead Dalai Lama, still preparing his tea, from habit, still serving His Holiness, even these long centuries later.

In any case, ghosts were no danger—he had to get moving!

He went to the Mahakala painting and pushed on the platinum skull. Nothing happened.

He pushed harder. Still nothing. Bart hit it with his fist, and there was a creak, the *whoosh* of dusty air. A crack had appeared in the wall. It widened with the application of his fingernails, and then he pried open the reluctant

292

ancient door. He entered a secret stairway, and put more energy into his aura, illuminating—for him alone—his way. On both sides of him Bart could see corroded green copper walls, and above was a narrow winding staircase.

Bart pulled the secret panel shut behind him, began ascending the stairs.

He knew from Raspahloh's memories that this way led to the private quarters of the highest Lamas, and the suite of His Holiness himself, the suite the Dalai Lama XIV had abandoned in March 1959. It stood to reason that the Chinese officials, in their arrogance, would take the same quarters. Tse Ling would be sleeping up there right now—in one of the several palatial bedrooms.

Bart continued to ascend, came to a sudden split in the stairs. Was Raspahloh's memory fickle? Or had a change been made in the stairs in the intervening centuries?

He wasn't certain which way to proceed. Was it the stairs to the left? He decided yes, and was soon climbing again. It was steeper on this stair, which he took to be a good sign. Up and up, this had to be it. Finally he reached a door. It was thirteen short floors from where he entered, three "large" flights to a floor. He pulled the bar lock to the side and pushed, entered out into a room. But it was a disappointment. This was not the private quarters area; instead he was in a storage room. Where in the vast palace was he? Maybe if he poked around, he'd figure out where he was.

There were piles of ancient dusty tomes under lacquer covers—over a million pages of long Tibetan sheets on medicine. A fantastic warehouse room of old books, worthy of years of a scholar's studious attention. These texts were considered rubbish by the Chinese, someday to be cleaned out for offices. But they had cures for all current diseases, and the seven new plagues that would soon devastate mankind. He tried to remember where this chamber was in the palace. It was cold and dry here, there was a slit window—for aeration. . . .

Yes. He peered out through it—he was not low at all. Bart was *alongside* the balcony of His Holiness. This hadn't been a storeroom centuries ago, when he had lived here as Raspahloh, the assassin monk. He suddenly remembered that this had been the Treasure Room. He remembered—the young Dalai Lama, he the little boy's playmate, running through this most secret room. The Holy One, and Raspahloh, who was to grow up to betray and kill him, had played in the piles of rubies and emeralds and diamonds, in their innocence. Played with jewels, run them through their hair, piled them up, and then tired of them, useless things that they were. They went back to their quarters and their own wooden toys, which they liked much better.

What had happened to the gems and other precious gifts given to the Dalai Lama that had been stored here? *Of course*—the Chinese had looted it. Then the thieves, to cover their theft, refilled the room quickly with tumbled masses of books—to fill up the room, remove suspicion that anything was taken.

Lasker picked up a book, unfastened the wood cover, and looked at the first page: "A Medical Treatise on the Impermanence of the Vital Signs, by Rigme-Tartang-Gyatso . . ." He put it down reverently. These books were more valuable to the future of mankind than all the gold and jewels that had been stolen. A fortuitous result of immense foreign greed for them to survive.

These books were probably the last remaining in the Potala. The vast libraries in the lower levels, he knew, had been sacked during the Cultural Revolution in the 1960s, used to make fires to keep the stupid conquerors warm.

Bart re-entered the stairs now, retraced his steps, knowing where he had turned wrong. He went down three flights and to the right—through the small door hidden by dust and cobwebs.

Soon he was poised before the panel that led to the former private quarters of the God-King himself. He found the latch, wiped the cobwebbing from it, and pushed the door. He entered the Sutra Hall of the Dalai Lama, the place where His Holiness would sit and study. Above this room, on the peak of the Potala, high lamas used to blow the eleven-foot-long gold and human thigh bone horns to call the faithful to prayer, and giant dragon kites had twisted in the winds off the mountains.

This sacred place, remarkably, seemed to be undamaged. There was a Buddha shrine, a meditation couch and cushion, even a book perhaps set down by the Dalai Lama himself on March 17, 1959, when, dressed as a soldier, he had fled Tibet. Bart's eyes ran over this holy-of-holies sanctuary. Few men had ever seen this place. He went to the slit window. All of Lhasa glistened in the moonlight outside. How often His Holiness himself looked out here—and what a sight it must have been like to see electric lights and Chinese convoys and the glaring floodlights of the Chinese encampment across the Lung Po River when the invaders came.

There were some rather peculiar furnishings—a conch-sized set of carved bears—six of them—and an inverted human skull with its jaw made of silver with a matching lid—perhaps it was a skull relic of a saintly lama, kept for its psychometric powers. It had eyeballs of white coral and turquoise pupils. There was the dried caking of some liquid in it. A saffron and chang offering. Perhaps the last offering, a prayer for safe passage to India—that had been answered for the Dalai Lama.

He felt the vibrations still trembling in the room, vibrations of powers both spiritual and material reaching back like thick roots through time for centuries, and suddenly cut.

Bart also felt *her* evil presence. Tse Ling. She was near.

He found an open doorway and went through. There was a smell of perfume—expensive. He was in the bedroom of Tse Ling.

A figure lay sleeping in the wide oak bed. There were twin deer and the sacred wheel in the middle of the headboard. Tse Ling in the Dalai Lama's bed.

There were the dying coals of a small fire in the brazier by the window, so the room was warm. She lay there naked, on her side. Her saffron skin was pale in the moonlight, colorless. Tse Ling was a woman, a beautiful naked woman, not a major now.

Bart crossed the carpet. Silently he advanced to her bedside, until he leaned down and his face was so close to hers that he could feel Tse Ling's breath.

Her dark eyes popped open, instantly alert. And he stifled her scream with a cupped hand.

"You won't be hurt if you don't scream and you tell me what I need to know," Lasker said, and then suddenly realized he meant it. He *wasn't* going to kill her.

He had spoken in Tibetan, and she had understood. There was fear in those dark brown eyes, primarily fear of being raped, and anger also. Tse Ling nodded. He let up his pressure on her mouth. Her nostrils flared, she uttered in Tibetan, "What are you doing here?" He must have been terrifying, all in black, a slit for eyes. Yet, Lasker then observed a peculiar phenomenon. He suddenly saw a red glow about Tse Ling's head—the anger within her was causing a flare-up of her invisible aura. Despite her fear, she was about to claw him with her long nails. Just as she acted, he pinned her with a knee to the sheets, and held her wrists together. She was no match for him, though she almost managed to bite him on the arm. He told her, "Quit it, or I'll smother you with the damn pillow! I just want to talk!"

She quieted down, and again he removed his hand

from her lips. "You can release my wrists then," she hissed like a snake. But he didn't. Lasker whispered, "I want to know some things. First off—what is going on at Smoke Mountain?"

"It's a penal camp," she spat out. "So what?" And then he used the trick the hermit had taught him—cleared his mind, stared at her. He could read Tse Ling's fear, and her thought, which was: *Does he know about Dr. Woo?*

"Who is Woo?" Lasker asked.

Tse Ling's eyes widened, her breath again in short sharp heaves. Again he had to struggle to hold her.

When she gave up trying to overcome him, Bart could read in her mind: *Does he know about the green salt?*

"Tell me about the green salt," Bart said firmly. "Tell me, or I'll snap your neck." He began to apply pressure.

"Nuclear dump site—" she gasped. "Smoke Mountain is where we dump nuclear waste. That's all." But again he read something in her mind: *Does he know about the shipments of green salt to Dr. Woo?*

"You lied," Lasker said. "You have the green salt shipped to Woo." He didn't know yet what the hell green salt was—he tried to look deeper into her mind—but lost it. Bart relaxed again and she was open to him. He asked, "What does Woo *do* with the green salt?"

She thought: *The intruder doesn't know that the green salt is the re-refined nuclear waste. He doesn't know that Woo is making it into nuclear bombs. I won't tell him. He'll never hear it from my lips!*

Lasker was shocked. Nuclear bombs—so that's what's going on at Smoke Mountain. "Where is this Woo?"

She thought: *Hong Kong, lives on Victoria Peak.* But she said, "He's in Beijing. Woo works for my government." She was lying. Lasker could read in her mind: *My superiors in Beijing would execute me if they ever found out what I was doing at Smoke Mountain for Doctor Woo!*

The mind penetration was fading. Bart's perception of

the red aura around the woman also. Lasker was tired. He had used up a lot of his psychic energy. The hermit said that this would happen—that he could only keep it up for short periods, until he had perfected the technique.

Real fear was etched in her voice now as she asked, "Are you from—the CIA?"

He shook his head, "Guess again."

"KGB?"

"No. Not CIA or KGB. Bonpo. I'm the Mystic Rebel."

He could see her confused look in the light from the window—the dancing yellow light of a thousand butter lamps below the palace. The festival of butter statues had begun!

"What happens now? Rape? You kill me?" Her eyes narrowed in ultimate hate. "Then *do* it—I don't mind. Get it over with!"

"Not tonight," Lasker said, amazed at his own statement. But what did he expect? The Mystic Rebel couldn't kill in cold blood, because Lasker wouldn't.

He dragged her off the bed, over to some tapestries. He tore some strips of material from them and bound and gagged her.

Utterly naked, helpless, trussed on the red Tibetan rug, Tse Ling now looked pathetic. Gone was her regal bearing, her haughty speech, the arrogant eyes. She was vulnerable. Female and ultimately vulnerable.

He stood there, letting his mind empty, and picking up some of her thoughts again. Thoughts no longer hateful, or devious—but rather thoughts of a person more to be pitied. She was afraid of being killed, that was there. But more than that was her embarrassment at being naked, exposed. And above all, her fear of *man*, of being raped.

He felt compassion for her. Bart could feel empathetic to her pain, her sorrow. That empathy seemed to go back a long way—back before all that arrogance and murderous callousness Tse Ling had for human life. Way down inside, Bart could sense her humanity. But Tse Ling was raised to be a tool of the state—a brainwashed pawn. Flashes of her life—endless drilling in communism, marching in military procession, physical discipline—flashed like a set of flip cards across Lasker's vision. But beyond her brainwashing there were feelings; there was a yearning, a desire to be loved. To be loved by a *man*. That desire, buried, cut off utterly for years and years, was now rising like a tidal wave in her loins.

It rose because of the power he had shown. Tse Ling, overwhelmed by a man for the first time in her life, would let it happen now. She stared up at him, naked before him, tied. Helpless. She resigned herself. She was thinking, *He will deflower me, and then he will kill me.*

The Mystic Rebel let his mind merge with Tse Ling's. He reached deep, deeper. Her eyes fluttered. He gently told her, mentally, "Is that what you think of love? That it is just sex, power, violence?"

Her response was almost automatic. "Men want only that. To hurt, to control. Women stand for nothing." Then there was a flare-up of fear in her mind, clogging off any further transmission. Her eyes were wide, uncomprehending of the communion that had just happened—and fearful of the melding of their minds, however brief. She had never reached out *for* or been reached out *to* in her life.

Lasker couldn't kill her now—if he ever could. The evil Tse Ling was no longer a despotic oppressor, no longer the Virgin Dragon. She was just a young woman who yearned to be loved. A woman who had never known love.

He untied the slit mask that covered his face. He went to her, bent down and tenderly unknotted the cruel bindings. She could sense what was about to happen. He went into her mind to comfort her, to make her understand the expression of his compassion, his understanding.

It was like a wall of ice melting, years of hate and anger all gone in a wellspring of desire, longing for release.

When he was done untying her, Tse Ling put her arms around him. She helped him by moving her legs open. She was already moist. She gasped as he inserted his manhood, hard and throbbing, and with their minds together as their lips met, he pushed forward. Her maidenhood was unyielding; for a second her pain was great. Then it parted and he went in all the way, filling her. Her vagina encompassed him, holding him.

"Great gods," she whispered. "Great gods!"

Her lover, the Mystic Rebel, arose and he stood there naked in the flickering yellow light from outside for a moment. Then he put on his black clothes and mask, turned, and was off into the stygian darkness of the doorway, like a wraith, a being who never had been.

She lay sobbing softly, not because she had lost anything, but because Tse Ling had *felt* something, for the first time in her life.

It took Lasker twelve-and-a-half minutes to make his way down to the street level and melt into the procession of Tibetans below. In that time, Tse Ling grew chill. She pulled down and covered herself with a blanket. Then she wrapped that blanket around her naked form and stood up. She leaned against the bed, confused.

She could not stay soft and fulfilled and caring. *No.* It wasn't her. She felt something warm—the blood oozing down from her rent hymen onto her left thigh. She ran her fingers over the blood and brought it to her lips, tasted it. Salty, warm. Blood. Her maidenhood.

All her life she had her secret. She had her power. Now, there was no secret place anymore—mentally or physically. There was no secret of any kind inside her anymore. She staggered to the wall, leaned against it, nearly swooning. He—the *man*—he had taken it all. Taken away her power, her secret. Had exposed her as someone who *needs* like any other person. Needs to be *loved.*

She fell onto the disheveled sheets and lay there confused, whimpering. *I have been loved . . .* she thought. But she could not hold that thought. It was too alien. *There is no love!* She rethought it—decided: I have been . . . used. Used. *Yes!*

Anger, anger destroying all other feelings, anger rising like an ocean tide, smashing down all her other feelings like a porous coral reef, swept over her.

"Rape," she whispered. She said it again: "Rape . . ." The word got louder and louder, until her whole body was shaking. She put her hand between her thighs, so silken, so utterly private . . . before. Not now.

She put her fingers up against her vagina. Pain. It hurt there. She whispered: *"Raped."* He must be caught—he must be killed! I gave away the secret. The secret of what goes on at Smoke Mountain. The—man—used me. Used my body.

Tse Ling's dark cobra eyes became slits. She shouted out, "Come! Come quickly—an intruder—after state secrets—he must be caught. Stop him, catch him—*kill him."*

# Chapter 30

Tse Ling's Tibetan girl-servant, Tashi, burst through the door, out of breath. She looked wildly around, and her eyes fell on Tse Ling, who stood by the bed with a blanket draped over her, shaking and pale. Tashi, who was thirteen years old, spoke fluent Chinese. She asked, "What is it, what happened?"

Tse Ling just stared at her—the girl was ugly. That's the first thing one would notice about Tashi. The girl was deliberately chosen to be her maid because the girl was so ugly—the better to offset, to heighten, Tse Ling's imperious beauty. The big-boned, flat-nosed Tashi repeated, "What is it mistress . . . what happened to you?"

Tse Ling snapped, "Thanks to your dereliction of duty, there has been an attack on my person. An intruder has been here and—stolen state secrets."

Tashi picked up the phone, hammered on the receiver.

"The phone is torn from the wall," Tse Ling said.

The girl replaced the receiver, and rushed over to her mistress. She made to touch her, but Tse Ling backed away, holding the blanket more tightly about her naked body. In doing so, she accidentally hitched up the cloth a bit. Tashi's wide-open eyes dropped to Tse Ling's thigh. "There is *blood,* mistress," she gasped. "Oh—the intruder—has—has—" She let the word drop. "Oh, how horrible!"

"No," Tse Ling said. "No. I was cut—he did *not* rape me—I am intact. You did *not* see that blood. Now—come, bring me a towel from that basin—wipe off the blood."

The girl ran to the basin, filled it, and dipped in a towel. She brought the towel over to Tse Ling and started wiping her thigh as Tse Ling sat on the bed. "Oh, Tse Ling, he *did* rape—"

*"Never say that,"* Tse Ling implored. "If you know what's good for you."

"I—I won't. I promise."

"Oh go away, Tashi." Tse Ling pushed the girl away and took the towel from her. "Go call Lieutenant Tang—no, don't," she said, changing her mind as the earnest girl rose. "Stop. I will call him myself." Tse Ling watched the young girl trembling—and knew then what she had to do.

"Get me my revolver," Tse Ling ordered. "It is hanging over there, on the hook by the door." The girl raced for it and brought the holstered gun to Tse Ling. The major took it from her and said, "Now, keep dabbing the blood. Clean me off." The girl bent to minister to her.

Tse Ling snapped the gun from its holster and put it to the girl's right temple, pulled the trigger. The girl's brains splashed blood, covering Tse Ling's legs with red. The body sunk to the floor, its short fat hands twitching.

Though the screaming hadn't brought the staff, the shot certainly did. They came running now, up the stairs, and Lieutenant Tang was the first to come in, pistol ready.

"Get out of here," Tse Ling shouted, "and let me dress."

Tang backed out, wondering at what he had come upon—a near-headless body, Tse Ling holding a blue wool blanket across her apparently naked body. Her shoulders were beautiful, and her legs . . .

In a moment she called him in again. She was dressed in her uniform, her hair disheveled. "The servant girl attacked me," Tse Ling said by way of explanation. "And I killed her. There was an intruder—the servant girl let him in. I caught him stealing state secrets. We struggled, but with her assistance, he overcame me. I was tied up, knocked out. When he left, she went to get my gun and shoot me. I freed myself and took the gun from her, and shot her."

"That is very brave, Major Tse Ling. Most praiseworthy. What do you wish to have done now?"

"Find the intruder. He is a Caucasian. An American, I think. In a black outfit. He must be the CIA agent whose wrecked plane was found some months ago. Find him, and kill him. He has only been gone minutes."

"Yes, Your Excellency." Tang saluted and turned to leave, pushing back the other officers who had gathered in the doorway.

"Another thing," Tse Ling said. "Call the province where this servant girl comes from, tell them to shoot the girl's whole family—in reprisal for her despicable counterrevolutionary activities."

"But—"

Her lips started to twitch. Tse Ling was livid. "Get out of here, do it—and kill the intruder."

He saluted and left. Tse Ling frowned and picked up the receiver. She reconnected the wire to the wall and told the operator, "Connect me to Saleem Chun at Smoke Mountain Penal Colony."

Saleem Chun sat on the glassed-in veranda of the Warden's building in the center of the camp called Smoke Mountain. Smoke Mountain, to Chun, reminded him of Dante's Inferno. The sealed veranda hung over a pit in the ground: seven spiral shelves of toil, with a glowing bottom. It was a man-made canyon about two hundred yards across, filled with near-naked workers wielding picks and shovels on every level. Among the slave workers were gray-clad figures with heads covered completely with a white shield, except for their eyes, which were reflectors on the outside. They were the radiation-suited guards, who held cattle prods and whips, and were also armed with pistols, in holsters at their waists. These guards were ethnic Chinese who held no liking for the protestors, dissidents, and counterrevolutionaries of the Tibetan "subrace" that were their charges. They kept the slaves working, burying the radioactive detritus of China. For here, in this awesome pit, this scar on the earth called Smoke Mountain Prison Camp, were buried the contaminated products of China's nuclear industry: spent rods from nuclear reactors, contaminated metals from damaged reactor cores, drums of lead and stainless steel containing human body parts that had been accidentally exposed to power plant leakage. All of this was sent here to Tibet to be buried.

But some of it wasn't buried. It was saved. It was put aside—sent up a conveyor belt toward the square black shed-like building at the other end of the *pit of hell,* as they called it. There, in that building, technicians and slave workers—who actually handled the materials—worked to reprocess the best of the nuclear waste, to make it into the cakes called green salt. The green salt would be shipped out of the country on

Woo's freighters to a certain Middle Eastern nation that would make nuclear bombs from it.

This nation, devoid of the capacity to produce such weapons, paid Dr. Woo's organization *billions* of dollars for the green salt. What other munitions seller besides Woo would sell them such materials?

Now, as Chun sipped a cool martini and picked at goose pâté, scooping it onto a crisp of bread and placing it into his refined palate, he watched the hellish pit. A thousand workers, most dying slowly from radiation burns, a hundred guards, towers with .50-caliber machine guns mounted on swivels all around the pit, the whole camp surrounded by a ring of combat-ready troops, dogs, and razor wire in several layers. It *was* straight out of Dante's Inferno. And Chun never tired of watching it. It made his gourmet food taste better, knowing that the Damned out there ate only maggot-filled gruel.

The camp was best seen like this—at night, lit by arc lights, clouds of dust from blasting through the hard rock of Tibet, rising clouds of steam coming from the black building, the green glow of the yet unburied nuclear waste at the bottom of the pit.

Chun swallowed his pâté. He picked up his field glasses and watched a fallen slave on the second level being whipped. The whipped man didn't move. The guard unhitched his cattle prod and sent an electric current against the man's testicles. The body twitched, but didn't otherwise react. The guard put down the cattle prod and waved for somebody to come down from above. Two men responded, bearing a body bag. They unfolded it, the prisoner was dumped in it, and it was zipped up. They carried the bag off, toward the top of the pit to be buried in the "field." That was the only way a prisoner ever left the pit—dead.

Chun yawned and set down the martini on the white

306

tablecloth. With satisfaction he thought, *Just this last shipment,* and Woo would have enough green salt to finish the contract with that eager Middle Eastern buyer. Just this last shipment. But it was as if the Tibetan slaves knew it—it was as if they were *dying* to delay the damned shipment. The trucks that would carry the green salt stood idling, to prevent them from freezing, at the top of the pit, pointing toward the gate. Their drivers, chained to the wheels inside the cabs of their trucks, waited also.

In less than twenty-four more hours certainly, all the green salt would be tucked away and Chun could go back to his mansion in Hong Kong.

The white-tuxedoed waiter came over, holding the remote phone. "Call from the Potala, Your Excellency," he said, placing the beige phone on the table. Chun frowned and picked it up. What was it now? Tse Ling was becoming an annoyance now. She called for petty reasons, anxious for the process to be completed so she could leave Tibet and claim her reward.

"Yes?" Chun said. "What is it?"

Chun was astonished at what Tse Ling had to say. An intruder had gotten the secret of Smoke Mountain. "The American?"

"Yes. I recognized him from the photographs," Tse Ling said. "Obviously a CIA agent of the highest caliber."

"When did this happen?"

"An hour ago—my troops have combed Lhasa, without results. We believe he has escaped on the river—south. We have troops checking along the waterfront."

"Not good enough!" Chun adjusted his orange turban. "I will carry out a search too, with my special squad," Chun said, replacing the receiver.

The bungler, he thought, crushing a Carr's Water

307

Biscuit and throwing it down on the table. He stood up, shouted orders at the officers eating quietly at a table some distance away. "Get the helicopters—one fully armed troop carrier, and my personal craft. Get the twelve-man Response Team out of bed—we take off in five minutes."

They ran off to comply. Chun headed down the stairs, through a corridor. He walked to the helipad, where the jet engine of his sleek black Bell SV-311 allready whined. The Response Team poured out of their barracks into the second military craft.

He bent low under the moving rotors, his turban nearly coming off in the wind. He got in the copter and strapped into the seat next to the pilot. "To the Tsang-Po River, south of Lhasa," he said. "Work a search pattern from twenty miles south of Lhasa—small boat."

As the helicopter lifted off and tilted south into the sunrise, Chun saw not the mountains or clouds, but a superimposed face. *Lasker.* He lived. It was as Woo had feared. This Lasker was a danger beyond measure. He must be an incredible agent of the CIA to have survived all these months, to avoid detection. The report that Lasker was crushed in an avalanche was obviously a plant through some CIA agents operating within the Chinese High Command itself!

The Response Team in the black chopper behind his craft would find Lasker. They were twelve men who on Chun's order would spread out along the riverbank. There would be no hiding from these experts. The American would be caught. And Chun himself would personally conduct the special interrogation.

# Chapter 31

Lasker had managed to reach the streets below the Potala unobserved. He had found out the awesome secret of Smoke Mountain and now he had to live to tell it, and stop the green salt shipments. And that meant he had to escape the city.

The streets of Lhasa were thronged with celebrants. Millions of butter lamps and red paper lanterns held on poles were flickering in the cold night air. Tens of thousands of people marched in the religious procession.

Bart leaned against the bullet-pocked wall of a building, letting the crowd brush past him. There were young student monks, ragged pilgrims, school children, walking arm in arm. And there were mothers with babes in arms, whole families of tired-looking farmers. There were scholar monks in their high-peaked red-and-yellow hats, chanting and banging drums in a cadence. They looked like elves with giant pea pods on their heads. There were costumed figures, some with masks, for this was also customary. This allowed Bart to keep his black outfit—and mask—on. It was like a carnival, a cacaphony of whistles and cymbals, and like a gathering earthquake, the tremors of

309

the Dap Dops' tramping feet. The seven-foot guardian monks from the Drepung Monastery marched in step through the frigid streets, slamming their huge wooden staffs against the ground in unison. People stayed well away from them, for they had a reputation of using those sticks if someone crossed their path, and splitting skulls like eggshells. They were what had passed for police before the Chinese came along. Sprinkled along the walls of the buildings, watching the crowd, were stone-faced Chinese soldiers in gray uniforms, single red star on their caps. Their rifles were unslung, ready for any political act against the Chinese, even a shouted slogan of defiance.

Bart found it strange to remember a festival he had never seen: Raspahloh's memory was that this was the way Lhasa always had looked on the fifteenth day of the Tibetan New Year. They called it the Festival of the Butter Statues. From the revolt against the Chinese in 1959 until the mid-1980s, such festivals had been forbidden. But now, with new ''liberal'' leaders in Beijing, it was back—so long as the festival stayed purely religious in content.

Lasker remembered the posters he had seen that afternoon. The Pachen Lama would be among this crowd, probably at the rear of the procession that swirled down this circular road called the Barkor—Lhasa's main thoroughfare. The presence of the Pachen Lama—the highest lama of the Gelugpa sect, save for the Dalai Lama himself—was bringing the Tibetans to a fever pitch. Lasker could feel their religious fervor like a wave washing over him. Since the Chinese had moved seven million settlers into Tibet, there were naturally a great number of Chinese civilians lining the route. Lasker heard one comment to his wife, ''Why does the presence of a man in a robe always make

Tibetans so hysterical? Can't they ever drop their superstitions?''

''He's coming, He's coming, the Pachen Lama is coming now,'' the crowd shouted. Lasker knew that the high lama everyone was waiting to see had been in jail for many years, until the ''liberalization,'' because he demanded better conditions for his people. He was trying to help his people from within Tibet's puppet regime. The people worshiped him as a protector. They would beseech him for blessings. The crowd would be thickest, most unruly—and most impenetrable by Chinese soldiers—at the covered palanquin of the Pachen Lama. His procession would leave Lhasa via the west gate, and Bart was determined to be with it when it did. And thus make good his escape.

Bart heard a great outcry as the people saw a huge twenty-foot butter-statue float of Manjushri—Overcomer of Obstacles—coming their way. And behind it, the high lama's palanquin borne by six hefty monks with tassled headgear.

Lasker joined the procession behind the Manjushri statue—a statue fully dressed and with a beard on its butter face. He noted that the jeweled scabbard of a real sword was cradled in the carved arms of the deity. It certainly was cold enough not to worry about the statue melting, even in its proximity to so many candles and lanterns.

Lasker fought through the crowd, got close to the ornate box-like sedan chair. Its wooden shutter was partly drawn back, and Bart saw the robed man inside leaning forward to look at the scene. The Pachen Lama made eye contact with him, just for a second. Without a change of his impassive expression, the lama leaned back out of sight. But Lasker had felt something—a recognition. The lama knew what he was up to.

Bart stayed among the other masked figures near the

311

palanquin, figures representing ancient warriors and wizards, all symbolically guarding the Pachen Lama. He added his voice to the chanting. Perhaps the crowd considered him a Bardo demon!

An old woman, leading two young children—a boy and a girl—pushed to the palanquin. Bart could hear her beseeching the Pachen Lama, "Please, name my grandchildren—they only have Chinese names, as is the law. Give them dharma names, so that they might be Tibetan Buddhists, not Chinese."

The Lama's hand reached out, touched each child's forehead as the procession swirled onward. The high lama uttered their new names. "Tiso Dunstal, Losang Nyarang." The old woman cried out *"Lha Gyal Lo"* in happiness, fell back into the masses.

A middle-aged farmer came next to the sedan chair. Bart could hear his story: "Great Lama," he said, "I alone survive of my entire family. Tse Ling's soldiers came, found us praying. They took all our clothes— even the children's clothes—and all the bedding and blankets. It was so cold that night, yet they left us naked. We walked to the nearest house—sixty-two li away. My wife froze to death, so did my children. There is just me."

The Lama's hand reached out, gave the man something—a gau. The lama said something that made the man weep and kiss his hand. Clutching the pendant, the farmer, too, fell away.

The procession was nearing the western gate of the city. Soon—Bart thought—they would be out into the darkness. But the Pachen Lama drew back the slat— mumbled to one of the monks, who came to Lasker. The monk said, "His Eminence wishes you to take the sword from the statue—he says you will need it. Don't take the west gate—go away—south."

Bart took it for what it was—direct clairvoyant guidance—snapped the sword of Manjushri free of the statue, and plunged away from the mass of celebrants. He cut down a deserted side street. In ten minutes, he was darting out the unguarded south gate.

He made his way to the black shimmering ribbon that was the Tsangpo River. He was just at the edge of the water when he heard the Potala's alarm sirens behind. Troops poured out the city walls searching for him.

A half hour later, Lasker, having successfully eluded the frantic but unskilled troops, was about twenty miles down the river. He was in the water, holding on to a small overturned boat and drifting with the current. Just another piece of debris in the pitch black moonless night.

And he was just beginning to think he had made it.

Then came a dull thud-thud sound, rolling over the waters of the Tsangpo. Bart searched the sky and saw their lights—two choppers! They were coming fast and low over the river. He ducked his head under water and held his breath for three minutes. When he had to burst up for air, the choppers were nowhere to be seen. He listened carefully. There were no more rotor sounds.

He was freezing—had to get out of the icy water. Surely it was safe to do so now. Bart let go of the boat—which had a broken bottom and would not serve as transportation anyway—and swam to shore.

He crawled up in the dark under some junipers. Should he now move across country, back to the rebels? Or stay here tonight?

He decided to move. His eyes could discern things no ordinary man could see in the dark. He'd travel swift—and smart.

Chun had landed his men a thousand yards apart along both sides of the Tsangpo. They would find Lasker. He sat on a log watching the starlight ripple in the slow-moving river, and pulled up the antenna on his com. "Anything?" he asked. The two choppers reported nothing, and the men—all twelve—checked in one by one with the word "negative."

Chun slammed his fist into the log. It made a thud. Lasker *had* to be here somewhere. Tse Ling's troops were idiots. They had missed him. He was still in the area—Chun could *feel* it.

Lasker was just yards from the river when he caught a glance of a moving figure. One man—clad in fatigues—not Chinese outfit. He wore some sort of goggles. *What gives?*

Tushima saw Lasker too. Tushima had on night-vision glasses, and picked up the red-amber outline of Lasker's heat trace. He smiled and picked up the com. "Tushima, coordinates thirty-four twelve, Got him."

He put the com back on his belt and went toward the figure outlined in red.

Lasker crawled along under the foliage. But the pursuer was good—he kept up, kept close. Lasker got to his feet, made a run for it, hoping to outdistance the man. And then Lasker heard other noises. More pursuers—coming at him from all sides.

He had to stand and fight. But he had only the sword, and they would probably be fully armed.

He was out in a grassy field. He crouched rock-still, and watched a tightening circle of twelve men closing. Fifty yards, forty. . . . A chopper wheeled from the south, and came overhead. From above him an amplified voice shouted, "Surrender or die American." The grass bent and whipped in the rotor's windstorm.

Clutching Manjushri's sword, Bart leapt out at the closest man, the one who had initially spotted him. He expected to be cut down by automatic fire. Instead, the huge man blocked his sword thrust with a steel baton.

Lasker rolled and snapped to his feet. The man with goggles was damned good. And he had eleven friends, plus the chopper above. Lasker had seen the holster on the big man's hip. He had a gun, yet he hadn't used it. Why?

*Because they didn't want to kill him.*

That lessened the odds, for Bart sure as hell wanted to kill *them*. And escape.

He picked a weak link—one of the shorter figures in the circle, who was less agile in his gait, his baton held a bit low. Lasker ran at the man, faked a thrust, and instantly reversed the sword, swung it down from overhead, and severed the man's head lengthwise. The chopper above moved away, caught by wind.

Two other fighters ran up to join battle with him, swinging nunchaku. Bart's sword caught the first glint of red dawn on its razor edge as he raised it and swept it in a wild set of orbits, cutting down both of them.

But as soon as they fell, two other night pursuers were upon him. Or thought they were. As they swished their batons at him, he rolled away, using the sword like a scythe to cut their legs out from under them. Legless below the knees, they fell, screaming—for a short while.

Then a lone champion came forth, more cautiously. Lasker could see him clearly in the early light. This assassin was not a large man, and he was slim with long arms. He wore a dark blue *hakama,* a Japanese-style skirt, that flowed around his waist, covering his legs. At his side, its scabbard held by the red sash that crossed his narrow waist, was a samurai sword. Evidently he had decided that Lasker should be cut down, perhaps non-lethally, instead of being bludgeoned unconscious, for he pulled the sword out with a lightning draw as he continued forward. The tempered steel blade, hand-pounded by master craftsmen, glistened with slivers of light from the red sun. Lasker could see that it was as sharp as a razor blade as it turned sideways for a second and almost disappeared from view. And by the way the assassin was swinging the thing around, Lasker knew he was good.

Against the seasoned samurai, most men would have little chance. But a sound issued forth from Lasker's lips. *A sound he didn't utter.* Raspahloh, the ancient warrior, was *back.* His personality, his skill, was coming to the fore in the crisis. And the warrior's instincts knew what to do.

The samurai grinned darkly as Lasker inched up several yards and stood facing him. The samurai held his sword in front of him, firm yet relaxed, pointing at his opponent. The Japanese slowly placed one foot forward at a time, the ankle always turned to the outside for instant changes of footing or lightning fast strikes. The angle of the blade was for a debilitating, nonlethal cut.

Lasker duplicated the samurai's stance, moving the corresponding foot back as his opponent advanced, keeping exactly the same space between them. He would make the swordsman attack off balance, draw him forward, and then make his move. Lasker had to cut through the man's discipline, force him to make the slight error that would mean death.

The samurai's face grew hard as stone, his entire body seeming to freeze in place. Then he let out a roar that shook Lasker's eardrums, and he leapt forward swinging the sword around like a steel wind of death.

316

No man on earth could have avoided that Damocles blade, except the *Mystic Rebel*. The Bonpo E Kung training had taught him to anticipate, and gamble. Bart had gambled on the blade coming at that angle and spun around, body pulled low to the ground, and to the side. The sword flashed past Bart about a quarter-inch high of his right shoulder.

There wouldn't be a second chance. Lasker was now behind his opponent. He rolled to the back of the man's legs and slammed the blade of his bare hand into the nerve behind the right knee. The samurai crumbled to the torn grass, jerking as if an electric jolt had gone through his leg. His sword hand cracked against a rock, sending the sword flying. Bart took a fraction of a second to aim and lopped the man's head clean off with the singing Manjushri sword.

Bart, breathing hard, snapped up, waited for the next attack. It was not very long in coming.

"You killed my brother," a tall slender Japanese shouted. He was coming at him with another sword. He ripped the blade around in a figure eight pattern, slicing every part of Lasker's anatomy.

Only Lasker wasn't there.

Raspahloh's instincts had again saved him. He feinted to rush to the right, and then jumped left, throwing a handful of gravel and sand he had picked up as the warrior turned. And as the man was temporarily blinded, Bart leapt in for the kill, screaming a Bonpo war cry *"Ziii!"* He slammed his knee up into the man's groin, lifting him off the ground. The samurai screamed out his testicles burst apart into a sticky blood soup. As he crumpled, Lasker ripped his perfect blade into the man's throat, severing the larynx, windpipe, arteries in a flash of blood and fragmented bone.

Then Bart heard a *clank* in the again-overhead chopper. He looked up and caught a glimpse of orange turban and a falling blur. Suddenly he was imprisoned by a steel mesh net. The Mystic Rebel's honed muscles tried to tear him out of the net. But he was racked with a hundred stinging puncture wounds.

The net was hung with a thousand razor-sharp fish-hooks. *Any* movement on his part brought a paroxysm of agony.

He stood there, caught like a dangerous animal. But he had one weapon left—the power of chi breath. Bart breathed short intense breaths, sent energy up from his thorax into his muscles, making his flesh below the skin into a steel like shield. He felt the energy coursing through him, and when he next moved, the hooks could not penetrate beyond his skin. He was able to begin tearing free of the net with steel-claw power hands.

Then a tube came out of the chopper's door and there was a rapid fire series of *thucks*. Dozens of inch-long hollow chrome-steel darts hit Lasker. Many merely bounced, but some, hitting at nexus points in his energy shield—the neck, the shoulder blades—filled him with numbing poison.

And he lost consciousness.

# Chapter 32

When Lasker awoke, he was chained to a wall by manacles in some sort of cell. From his position he could see out a low, barred window. The view was of a pit—a vast canyon of horror with hundreds of near-naked toiling workers. They were digging with picks and shovels under the whips of guards dressed in radiation-proof suits. Bart guessed he was at Smoke Mountain Prison Camp. He dimly remembered now—the net, the trip by helicopter, landing behind a high iron gate topped by razor wire, the guards carrying him up to a building.

There was blood oozing from Bart's forehead into his eyes. Yes, the hooks! He remembered going down, under a weight of net—the darts in his side, his neck, numbing pain—

The cell door clanked open. A young Chinese soldier came in, saw that Bart was conscious. He went to a barrel, scooped out some water in a ladel, and gave Bart some. Bart said, "Thanks." He meant it.

More footsteps, another man entering—this one wore an orange turban. He had thin manicured hands, and wore a conservative deep-blue suit. "Feeling better? You know you have been quite a nuisance to our people, Lasker. You have been a very big nuisance. You have been asleep now for fifteen hours. Too long!''

"Who are you?"

"Chun. Saleem Chun. But you know that—you know a lot of things, *CIA man.*" Chun spoke rapidly in Chinese. The soldier left. When he did, Chun asked, "How much pain do you know how to endure?"

Bart didn't answer.

In a while the soldier came back, wheeling a metal table and on that table there was a poker heating in a brazier of hot coals.

"Crude but effective. I want to know certain things, Lasker. And fast. Perhaps you are a KGB pawn?"

"I'm not Lasker," Bart said. "I'm Bruce Arthur—it says so on my papers." Bart was referring to the dead hiker's papers he carried. He was still shaking off the blurriness and a migraine of all migraines. Bart tried his manacles. They were steel-hard tight. No leeway in the chain. He focused on this small wiry man in front of him—Chun spoke a British form of English. And he *looked* familiar . . . of course! The orange turban!

There was no mistake—this was the man who had fired the bazooka at Bart when he rode in Ahmed's cab. The man who had been watching him in New Delhi. What was he doing here in Tibet, at Smoke Mountain? Then Bart understood: Chun was Woo's man!

The turbaned man went over to the poker and lifted it up out of the coals. It hissed and smoked in the air.

"Now, I want answers," Chun leered.

"Anything I can tell you, I will," Lasker said. He put all his strength on pulling loose his manacles. And failed.

Chun said, "That was quite a display of muscles. You shook the cell! And killing so many of my men—

320

tut-tut!'' Then his taunting smile faded. ''Who sent you? CIA? KGB?''

''I'm from the Cultivators,'' Lasker said.

''I never heard of them. Who are they? What do they know of our operations?''

''The Cultivators aren't interested in you,'' Lasker said, stringing Chun along, stalling for time. The steaming rod was the only thing on his mind. ''I don't even know who you are, Chun. Who do *you* represent?''

''You know perfectly well. You got that information from Tse Ling, in the Potala. You found out what you wanted to know—but you won't live to report it. If you tell me everything, I will not torture you, merely shoot you. It's your choice, Lasker!''

He tore Bart's black shirt open and jabbed Bart's chest with the hot poker. It touched for just a second but burned horribly. ''Your choice—shall I show you what else I will use?'' Chun put the poker down and picked up a hook a dentist might use to probe a deep cavity. He turned and went to Lasker, tore it across his chest. A bolt of pain preceded a trickle of blood from his rent skin. ''Now that your skin has been cut, it can be *peeled*. Are you familiar with the death of a thousand cuts? Hanging the way you are, your skin opened carefully at the right places will split wider and wider as you weaken, as you can no longer support your legs! You yourself will tear your own body apart, inch by inch. Tell me what you know and I will let you go.''

''Like hell you will. Cowards like you get off on this.''

Chun ripped the hook device across Bart's skin again, and then as Bart writhed in pain, Chun snapped a clamp on the flesh, attached a weight like a fishing sinker to it. ''It will tear loose slowly, peeling you with it—I will leave the weight on you now. For a few hours, I will go and sit outside, and have my lunch—which

321

has been delayed greatly. When I am done, I will come back. No doubt you will then be willing to cooperate. Oh, by the way, if you scream for help, it will only make you weaker. I will come back and attach another weight—or you talk. One false statement and I will take the poker and apply it to one eye then the other."

Chun lifted long, red-hot tongs. "And *these* will be closed around your testicles. Now, I will let you contemplate your pain."

The sadist left; the cell door clanged shut. For a while there were guard's eyes in the door slit. Then they, too, went away. Lasker tried again to tense his muscles to pull the manacles free. The same with his legs. The tension on his cartilage caused the weight to slip, and tear more skin. The pain was horrible! He bit into his lips. He must not pass out!

He concentrated on the familiar mantra—*Om Mani Padme Hum*—and then the Cultivators' protector chant—*Tsa Wa Da*—*Tsa Wa Da* . . . Bart had to place his mind somewhere else, fast—or he *would* tell all he knew. Chun would kill him anyway, and Bart knew it, but in a few more moments, he would reveal all. Give his friends' names, betray Dorjee, everything.

*No!* He sent his mind reeling out the silken cord—astral-projected away. He soared upward, upward—found something—something *friendly*. Something *powerful*, swooping on high. *The King Vulture.* Turn, please turn, come lower, friend. Yes, come lower!

The King Vulture obeyed and let Bart come into its mind. Bart had been out of his body before, in the hermit's cave, but never like this, not so completely! Not so *apart* from his body. He soared with the bird. He was the giant vulture. And he circled, looked down at the Smoke Mountain Compound, at its lines of barbed wire. His-its sharp eyes found the building containing the cell by tracing the silken cord of Bart's con-

322

sciousness. There it was! Inside was his own limp body. Lasker was the vulture—he was free. He swooped exhultant, free of the pain. He could control every feather, one at a time, together. It was ecstasy. The bird part of him—it was amazed and so was Lasker. The bird knew more, much more, in the mystical-intuitive sense, than he could as a human. And it *cared*.

The bird could see spirit everywhere, all around the death camp. There were many unquiet spirits of prisoners who had died at Smoke Mountain, and who were buried beyond the fences. They were *unquiet* spirits because they had been buried, not dismembered and fed to the creatures of the sky. The spirits wandered as tortured souls near their rotting bodies, unable to leave the Earth. They yearned to be released from their bodies as was their precious belief. They were *screaming,* wailing out in their despair.

They had been the tortured, barely fed, poorly clothed slave workers. They had done the radioactive work, the digging, the refining of green salt, until they were too weak and fell. Some had still been breathing, buried alive, when too sick to work. "Vengeance! Vengeance! Free us, someone, *free us!!!*"

And it-he understood the help to *give*. And the help to *receive*. The bird reached out to the spirits and promised they would be eaten, every morsel consumed, if they but *rose up*. If their bodies rose up from their shallow graves and *came forth,* to destroy the evil men at Smoke Mountain.

●

The ground for miles around burst open and rotting decaying bodies burst forth like flowers of the undead, sprouting up. Thousands of the re-animated dead, some newly buried, some so rotted they were disintegrating as they rose, as they put one foot then the other in front of them, got up. And they headed toward Smoke Mountain.

*The undead thought as one. They would do as he said—as he, the sky thing, part bird, part man, commanded! The undead would* kill. *They would tear down the fences and kill and destroy. This was the evil camp that had killed them. These were the Chinese soldiers that had given them the unclean burial instead of sky burial. They would gladly destroy and kill all!*

*They helped each other up from their shallow graves, and then when they were all assembled, the undead turned as one and began walking. They knew no goal, they knew no thought except* kill!

*Go to Smoke Mountain and* kill, *the voice commanded. But do not kill the chained man. For he is the Mystic Rebel, the one who gives you this chance, this chance to be sky-buried and set free.*

*"Kill!" their disintegrating wormy lips muttered. "Kill!" With each step the cadence of the litany of death built up. Each torn and boney foot tramping the hard Earth set up a thunderous rhythm. Each rotted mouth spilling teeth said but one thing: Killllll!"*

Wa Lu, the commander of the Chinese soldiers on Lookout Tower Number Two, just outside the main gate to Smoke Mountain Correctional Facility, was playing cards on the bare board floor with his fellow soldiers. Wa had never expected to be so long in the Tibetan Frontier, nor had he envisioned his four year posting in the TAR—the Tibetan Autonomous Republic—to be so boring. Why, the trips into the small village of Kemmung were only twice a month. And what pleasure was that anyway? The women there were sad ex-nuns from one of the blown-up monasteries. They could make sex *dull.*

Old women—bah.

Wa threw down his hand—four kings, a jack, and a

deuce. His comrades couldn't match it. The renminbao bills crumpled on the wooden floor were pushed to his side. Wa was only slightly pleased, for he was getting back just a part of the month's salary he had lost today.

A muffled cry. Wa said, "Shhh!" He stood up, looked out past the barbed wire surrounding the camp. *There,* in the tree line—something moved! Figures . . . whoever they were, there were plenty of them. They were yelling something—garbled—in Chinese . . . *what?*

Slowly it became clear: *Kill! Kill! Kill!*

They staggered out of the woods into the open. Wa's jaw dropped. His throat constricted. A tidal wave of horrid decayed-looking people—no, not people—*corpses.*

"Look," Wa shouted, "At the far strands of barbed wire!" The three stared incredulously as the creatures were tearing out the fence posts with their bare hands!

What manner of beings were these? They looked like rotted corpses. They must be zombies, the *undead* that the Tibetans spoke of in hushed tones in the taverns. Wa had scoffed, but now—

*Never mind,* he told himself, just get going! Repel them! "Sound the alarm," he said. Tung and Li were frozen in place.

Wa went and turned the crank of the siren himself. The sound alerted the other guard towers, and their men now came running out pointing, shouting—and *shooting.*

By now Li, and the third card player, had gotten the big .50-caliber gun swung around and had opened up on the attackers. Wa picked up the binoculars, scanned the results. He saw the bullets trace across the earth, then across the horrible moving bodies—without results! Except that pieces of flesh flew off the things, and some black liquid oozed from the gaping holes left by the bullets. Some zombies were knocked off their feet by the bullets but flailed their way erect again. They kept *coming!*

In a few more minutes the animated corpses were at the base of Wa's tower—some were actually chewing on the wooden posts. The tower shook. They all were screaming now and emptying their pistols on the attackers below.

These shots didn't work either. The zombies kept coming. Wa's gun was empty. He threw it down. How could he run away? The creatures were on all sides—my god, the smell, their hollow eyes crawling with maggots. He saw one tall one look up and grimace at him, and the mouth moved, called out, "I've come for you, soldier Wa!"

He had buried that one—over a month ago—and he was back now. *"No! No!"* Wa screamed. He watched them start to climb the tower. Wa flung himself off the other side, hitting the rocks fifty feet below with a crunch.


Chun paused, put down his fork. What was going on? Was there an attack? What kind of force would dare such a thing? He went out on the building's glassed-in terrace and saw—what were they? *Bodies?*

There were hundreds of the things, some close to the pit. They were being shot, but when they fell, they just stood up again and kept walking. God, even their *pieces* were crawling toward the building. As they walked through the fields of electrified wire, sparks went flying, the wire was rending their skin, but only maggots and greenish liquid, not blood, came out. The soldiers were abandoning their posts.

The prisoners were cheering. They took up their shovels and picks, and found their overseers. Chun

326

watched one guard thrown down into the green glow of the lower pit. *What the hell was happening?*

He rushed back inside from the glass-wall terrace.

"Quick, bar the doors," he ordered.

Chun himself helped pile furniture against the barred door. It should hold—this place was fortified in case there was a prisoner uprising. He rushed to the phone and lifted the receiver. Soldiers ran about, grabbing weapons from racks.

Nothing. The wires were down. He ran to the radio room. The post was abandoned. Chun got on the radio and broadcast a frantic call for assistance to Lhasa. His reply was only static. There was a crashing on the roof—the antenna going down. And then, above, a dozen heavy footfalls.

There was bashing against the door and then the sounds of steel being bent in. Chun ran to the outside room as several soldiers fell; he jammed a full clip into his Chinese SMG. The door itself was holding—but not the wall! The cinderblock wall itself was being punctured by meaty fists. And the smell now seeped in. The smell of death. Pandemonium. Ear-bursting fire.

Chun fired the entire clip at the hands that groped through the holes. The hands shattered and smashed to pieces, leaving only waving stumps in the wall. Yet the fingers, the fingers that had been torn off by the bullets, crawled across the floor like worms, headed toward his feet.

And more fists pounded away at the walls, widening the holes. *"Chuuuunnnn, kkkiiillll Chuuuunnn."*

Laughing hysterically, Chun threw down the empty SMG and backed off toward the cell. He had one mad idea—*Lasker*. Lasker had something to do with this. There would be safety near him.

Chun took the big key from the wall rack and opened

the iron gate. He went into the dank cell and locked it from the inside.

Lasker looked dead—he hung there limply in his manacles, not a breath coming from him. Chun laughed. Lasker had nothing to do with this at all. Chun collapsed to the floor as the banging began on the cell door. A hundred fists smashed at the steel. There was a creaking, then the door bent in. He managed to take his Tokarev pistol from its holster, and when the door bent in and fell, and the giant zombie stood there, its hands opening and closing, its worm-eaten mouth uttering, *"Cccchhhhuuuunnnn . . . ,"* he fired the last full clip at it. The Zombie came at Chun and pushed him to a wall. He screamed out, "No!" but it started biting into his neck, clawing at Chun with fingernails grown long in the unquiet grave.

"No," he screamed, struggling against a titanic force, his last bit of adrenalin expending hopelessly, flaying at the thing. The zombie held him easily, forcing him down. Another smaller creature came in and bent over to also chew on Chun's body.

The big one dug at Chun's eyes, took them out on their long trailing tendrils of watery white optic nerves, and swallowed them. Chun was still struggling and gurgling out a final scream. Then as his scream died, choked by blood welling up from his cracked rib cage through his lungs, Chun's arms were torn from his shoulders. Chun convulsed and shook, then became still. A third then a fourth ghoul came in and bent to chew on him.

The zombies stopped to listen—above them—a cry— the cry of the King Vulture. They must stop. They must *do* something. What? They lifted their heads, their lips running with fresh warm blood. The zombies turned to face the shackled man—Lasker.

*Free him, free him! Do not harm him—he is the Mystic Rebel, the one that sent for you!*

They obeyed. They came to Lasker, clumsily tore at his chains, releasing his manacles from the wall. As they did this, his life force returned. Lasker convulsed and jerked spasmodically, he drew in a long deep breath, and his eyes fluttered open.

The transfer of consciousness had occurred.

The stench hit Bart's nostrils. He started to choke as he was lifted up and carried out of the cell by the big corpse who had first feasted on Chun. The walking dead man now cradled Bart in his rotted arms, walking through the corridor, and stepped over the many bodies. Bart managed, as they passed a desk, to pick up his Manjushri sword.

He took Lasker out into the fresh air. The big zombie carried him out across the fallen barbed wire and up over the hill. Bart was retching from the stench. All around them the animated bodies of the walking dead left their murderous rounds. It was all over. Their job was done. Their lips uttered happy sounds. They were now about to reap their reward—sky burial. Above, ten thousand vultures—called to the feast by the King Vulture—circled. As the zombies fell, those funeral birds dove down to feast on the carrion, fulfilling the promise.

From their hiding places, holding sticks and shovels, the prisoners of the Pit, the damned of Smoke Mountain, came out and watched. They gathered together in clutches, murmuring in disbelief. Then, en masse, the freed prisoners moved toward the gates of the camp, gates now torn asunder.

They didn't know exactly what had happened, except that they were free. They were *free*—thanks to the zombies—and whatever mystic force had summoned them!

# Chapter 33

The huge bald swollen-eyed zombie who had freed Bart now carried him away, effortlessly, like a child in his massive arms. Bart had managed the strength to unhook the weight tearing his chest. Then, owing to his semiconscious state, he was only dimly aware of what was happening. His head lolled from side to side, and Bart got a spinning, twisting version of the route the rotting corpse took with him. They went over trampled barbed wire, out along the camp's approach road, then suddenly turned and were heading up a very steep slope. Never did the big feet of his rescuer slip or slide on the loose rocks. Lasker sensed that they had reached the top of the ridge and began a descent.

Mere minutes after, a series of astounding occurrences began at Smoke Mountain.

All the meters on the vast panel controlling the processing in the Nuclear Refining Building were in the red, and moving higher. And no one was there to pull levers, close circuits, contain the emergency. The Chinese technicians manning the control room were dead. Their bodies lay strewn about, their faces frozen in stares of ultimate horror. The emergency warning buzzer was sounding. Seams swelled and burst in the pressure tubes along the wall, bringing high-pressure steam into the devastated room. The panel smoked as steam met high voltage and a shower of sparks erupted. The bodies, the furniture, everything in the room caught fire. As the fire spread, insulation around the wires in the ducts also began to flare, raising a thousand-degree heat.

In a matter of a few seconds more, even the metal sheets that made up the walls glowed, burst into white-hot flames.

A cataclysmic explosion blew the roof of the building up into the air. The shower of hot metal and flaming pieces of plastic rained down all over the abandoned prison camp. A tower of black smoke climbed into the cobalt sky. The administration building, the cellblock, the glassed-in observation terrace hanging over the pit all were inundated with flaming debris, and caught on fire.

The flames spread, ignited the group of trucks, now driverless, waiting at the pit's edge. Their gasoline tanks exploded like a series of roman candles. Molten truck tires and pieces of chassis flew about, adding to the conflagration.

Then the collapsed ruins of the reprocessing building shook with a series of titanic concussions, as superheated trapped gases ignited.

The concussions rocked the very earth itself. Large cracks opened up as plates of rock deep underground shifted and slipped. The sides of the vast death pit started crumbling down. A strange green glow—the radioactive debris superheated and beginning to become a gas—drifted over the conflagration. If it spread, if the nuclear waste itself started burning, radioactive fallout would blanket a thousand-mile stretch of Tibet.

But that was not to be. Nature reacted angrily to this new threat of the green evil. The mountains themselves trembled, then shook. Immense fissures, spouting red lava and geysers of mud and magma, erupted. The fault line on which the camp was built was brought into motion. One fissure became a dozen feet in width, and spread like a crack in a ceramic cup across the death pit.

The covered conveyor belts running up from the pits broke up and tumbled down into the sprawled bodies and green glow. The mountain slope itself changed its angle and slowly ever so slowly tilted the buildings on either side of the pit. The buildings and all their content of flaming bodies and nuclear debris slid down into the pit.

Fonts of mud and magma cascaded from the mountainside and poured a hundred thousand, a million tons of molten-rock sealant over the hellhole. Within minutes it covered all traces of the man-made evil. Smoke Mountain was no more.

Thus the earth itself, in its stupifying power, repaired the open, infected wound that outraged its body.


Bart felt the ground shake and there was a prolonged series of explosions, back in the direction of the camp.

Once the earth tremors and concussions ceased, the sky became clouded over with black smoke and ash fell everywhere. After a while, the scream of the many vultures circling in the sodden sky resumed. Lasker fell back into semiconsciousness.

The zombie walked for hours, or so it seemed. Sometimes Bart saw the starry sky looking like handfuls of thrown silver sparkles on a black velvet tapestry.

At last, outlined in the crescent moon's light, were some tangled brush—thorns and prickles, up against a rock face. The zombie walked right into the bramble, brushing through it uncaring of the rending thorns, though Bart was cut many times over. Then the zombie bore him into a narrow crevice, and they were enveloped in total darkness. The echoing steps of the undead thing carrying its human cargo went on for a while. Then there came light and warmth. The orange glow of a torch hanging on the wall. The zombie dropped Bart unceremoniously in a heap on some soft things—blankets? He didn't know or care. The undead man stood over him for a time. Then he heard the thing walking away. Bart raised his head, his blurred vision taking in where he was—a cave. The diamond forehead of the Cultivators' Peaceful Deity stared down at him!

Then he heard the shouted words of the hermit. The scrawny shape of the old wizard approached, and Bart felt small crack-nailed hands touching his face, feeling his pulse. "I—was—" he started to say. Then oblivion.

Lasker could have been out many hours, or even days. He was occasionally semi-alert, feeling the warm wet cloth wiping over his body, cleansing his wounds.

Finally, Bart sat up, feeling sore all over. He was truly in the hermit's cave. It was no phantasm of pain. He slid the blanket down and saw the damage. A huge scar, added above the scar of the Demon's talon that traced across his mid-chest. His arms, too, had wounds. His palms and the backs of his hands were torn and bleeding. His heartbeat was steady, however, and he could breathe without pain—no cracked ribs. Other than the soreness when he shifted his weight, he felt all right. Bart rapidly went over the awesome events that had put him here, on the floor of the cave. Had he really done it? "Astral projected" into the vulture? Called up the *dead* to rescue him? Or was it a dream?

Except for the fact that he was living and here, not in chains in the Smoke Mountain cell, Bart would have thought it a wild dream.

"How do you feel?" Lasker turned with a start. He hadn't heard anyone approach. He saw a robe, and then, the sandaled feet of the hermit were close to his face. He looked up. "Oh, it's you."

"Is that what you say to the teacher and physician who tended you for seven days? You really were troublesome, you know, mumbling and tossing around so I could hardly apply the special poultices that healed your awful wounds."

"Then it *was* real. The zombies, the—"

"Of course it was real. You *called* the things up from their unquiet graves to help you, didn't you? So why shouldn't it be real?"

"They—the dead—rescued me?"

"Indeed. But rather roughly, I would say. I taught you astral projection well, for you to be able to enter the King Vulture, and use him to call for help. But don't feel so smug, I was helping,"

"You—were—helping?"

"Oh yes, Don't think you pulled that cute little trick all by yourself. Calling the dead back to live, indeed. Easy to do but dangerous, very dangerous. For there are demigods of the death realm to placate when you do such things. I had to do a lot of fancy footwork so that things would turn out."

"Well, thanks."

"Thank me when you're better. We have to sit you up now, and have you drink some more broth. You had precious little to eat these past days."

The hermit gave him a terrible broth to swallow. While Lasker was gagging on the stuff, he said, "It's good for you, don't throw it up. It is made of certain mountain orchids and the fungis from the dead bodies of highly realized lamas."

Despite the statement, Lasker managed to quiet his stomach. Finally he said, "Please don't tell me the ingredients."

"Hrrumph, it's much better then the unnatural things you consume in the West."

Lasker let it drop, asking, "Could I have some clothes? It's cool."

The hermit went to a chest over along a wall, opened it, and extracted a shimmering colorless nearly transparent robe of some miracle fabric. "Wear this," the hermit said, and threw it to him. It's loose and warm. It is time to meditate anyway. You must absorb the healing rays."

"I don't understand . . ."

"Just do as I say," the hermit insisted.

In months to come, Lasker would go over and over in his mind the wondrous things that happened next. The hermit told him to prostrate himself before the strangely elongated granite figure.

Bart raised his hands above the crown of his head then in front of his heart, and then put the palms down before him on the stone floor of the cave, and placed his head down. A prostration. The hermit instructed him in the other nine preparatory things that he must do—light incense, chant several mantras that only initiates can repeat, anoint the hands of the statue with ointment, and so on.

Finally Bart sat still on the blankets, facing the statue, in the meditational state that the hermit had taught him.

He sat in the half-lotus position, just one ankle above the opposite thigh. Full-lotus made his legs numb.

The hermit lit some butter lamps. Then he extinguished the torch. The cavern was suddenly all mysterious shadows. The diamond on the Peaceful Deity's brow sparkled like white fire in the light of the butter lamps.

"Stare at the diamond in the Deity's forehead, Lasker, and begin your meditation."

Lasker did this, and drifted peacefully for a long time. Early on, the hermit slipped away. It was hours before something happened: a shift in space-time, as when he had gone through the crystal. This time, Bart didn't fear—he just let it all happen.

The whole world seemed to redden, then there was no light, only blackness in place of the glistening gemstone. Slowly, ever so slowly, a brilliant white light grew in the center of the diamond, widening like the shutter of a camera lens. It was becoming so bright Lasker wanted to shut his eyes. But faintly, as if from another plane of existence, the hermit warned, "No, you must keep your eyes on the light. It will not harm you."

The brilliant spot of diamond suddenly shot out a shaft of light to Lasker's forehead, and into his brain—at least it felt as if it had gone right into his brain. He felt as if he were going up a high-speed elevator.

The whole statue of age-dulled granite started to shine brilliant yellow-bronze. And the white point of light that was shooting forth the ray now began to oscillate, to spin. At each revolution it changed color—first red, then blue, green, yellow, then white again. The color pattern repeated, faster and faster. Lasker was getting dizzy.

Then the lights separated. Rays of the five different colors played over Bart's forehead, and went down to the scars on his body, one at a time, until all parts of his body had been touched by the rays. Bart heard hissing in the air like an electrical discharge.

A wind lifted his hair then. Bart felt as if he were plunging down into a hole in space-time itself. His ethereal robe's sleeves fluttered in it. "Now close your eyes," the hermit said, as if from afar. Lasker did, and in a while he felt himself lift off the floor. Bart wanted desperately to open his eyes to see it indeed he was levitating, but dared not.

Finally the lights faded, and the wind slowed, then ceased, and he felt his body descending slowly. Bart felt the touch of his loins on the blanket, and then pressure building underneath him. "Open your eyes."

Lasker did. Everything was as it was before all the lights and wind.

"Take off your garment and look at your wounds."

Lasker pulled the shimmering material up over his head, tossed it aside. He saw no wounds at all—save a dull red mark where the demon had scratched him. All the other wounds were absolutely gone.

"See, it works," the hermit exhulted.

Lasker felt very weak now, and he went to his blankets and fell on them, covered himself, and fell asleep.

He slept well and long. When he finally awoke, Lasker sat up and looked around. The hermit was seated beneath the torch along the far wall, scrutinizing the loose page of a strange large book. The book had an oval shape and its iridescent pages seemed to adhere to one another, unless turned. Perhaps they were magnetic. The hermit looked up. "So how is the patient?"

Lasker almost laughed. The voice was like his old doctor in Cincinnati, Dr. Schwartz.

"Better, I guess."

"Indeed. Please don't abuse this gift of health. Take it easy for a few days—no killing or plundering, no climbing into women's bedrooms and screwing them. Pull too hard on your stomach muscles or your chest and it's all over for you."

337

"The statue—the rays—what was it?"

"The power of the Cultivators. Call it faith healing, if you wish. This statue is consecrated to the healing arts. It was endowed by the Cultivators with powers that I discovered only by chance, after I spent long hours in meditation before it. That was soon after I first arrived here, many many years ago."

Lasker looked at he statue, and then back at the old man. "It's a machine?"

"Yes. And this book is its manual. In a difficult language. But it comes with a *kanu-thaa*—a translator bookmark!"

"Why did the Cultivators build the statue?"

For their own use, I suppose. Who can know such awesome beings' minds? Perhaps, in their clairvoyance, they would see that you would someday need its healing powers, hundreds of centuries after they left. They had designs for mankind, as I related to you earlier—or maybe they simply used this cave as a sort of first-aid station during their explorations of the area."

"But—shouldn't you tell anyone about this—miraculous machine?"

"I told *you*. You're the only one who ever asked. In any case, I don't think that they would like the word to spread. This cave is theirs, not mine. Someday the Cultivators might return to claim it. I merely maintain it, sweep it out, and such. If it is a machine, it might wear out if used too much. They might get *mad*. I would not like beings from another dimension to be mad at me—would you?"

"I suppose not . . ."

The hermit frowned. "Questions, always questions. Meditate more, and run around raising hell less, and you will know many things."

# Chapter 34

In a week the American could walk around quite well. He ate the cakes of Tsampa and noodles prepared by the hermit on the tiny stove; he sat and drank tea with him. The hermit never seemed to eat. Despite the admonition not to ask so many questions, Bart had to ask just one more. "Hermit, do you eat anymore? I never see you eat these foods you prepare for me."

"I eat a lot, Disciple from the Land of Ignorance. I eat all sorts of delicious colors: blues, reds, even some ultraviolets. Green is my favorite food."

"You eat—colors?"

"All colors distilled from sunlight. Nutrition is to feed the body. The purer the food one *plants* in one's stomach, the better the health one *harvests* in one's body—you people in the West ought to heed that."

"Colors *aren't* food."

"Sure they are, if you chew them right. If you chew them with psychic teeth, that is. Eating colors for energy cuts out the intermediary process of food consumption. Here—look at my teacup—see it? Haven't you noticed all this time?"

Lasker took the cracked and bent metal teacup from the hermit. It smelled as if it had never been washed, and it was chipped and bent—an old worthless teacup of some metal or another.

The hermit took it back. "It's a special cup. Each morning, I use this cup to collect sunlight—you seldom rise as early as I do. I fill my cup at the cave entrance every day at dawn, bring the cup of colors in here, and sip it often during the day. Then when it's empty, I use it for tea. You have been in Tibet for only a short while, yet you have gone through many things. At this rate, someday maybe you will drink sunlight for breakfast also." Then he said, in a different more serious tone, "We must now talk of what you will do next. The penal colony that was Smoke Mountain, where the enemies of the world were making the harmful green substance, is destroyed. But there is something you must yet do."

"What?"

The hermit went to the Peaceful Deity. He lifted his mala beads of amber from the granite hand. Beneath the coil of beads there was the jewel pouch that Lasker had left with him.

The hermit took the sack of jewels and went to the rug, spilled them out. "These gems from the Bonpo are not ordinary gems at all, Lasker."

Lasker looked them over. "Emeralds, rubies, diamonds, sapphires? Not ordinary?"

"I have been observing these gemstones for some time, and I've noticed that they change as my mood changes. They are influenced by my state of mind. Let me ask you something, Lasker. Were these gems protected by huge scorpions? Were they in a pit before the dreaded lord of the Bonpos?"

"Yes, they were."

"Ah." The hermit leaned forward. "It is as I thought. These gems you throw around, Lasker, are

340

the long-lost Wish-Fulfilling Gems depicted in all the Thanka paintings in all of Asia."

"They make wishes come true?"

"More than that. They can make thoughts, whims, even fears come true. For instance, if a person who was fearful possessed one of them, his fears could come true. A greedy man who has worried about their genuineness would see them turning to ordinary stones. To low-energy people, these are merely precious gems. To high practitioners of tantric magic, they have immense power."

"If they have power, what are we going to do with them?"

"They are not mine or yours to do anything with. They are too dangerous! Using such power would result most likely in the accumulation of bad karma. There is only one soul now on Earth that I would trust with such power, and that is His Holiness, the Dalai Lama." The hermit scooped the gems up and put them back in the pouch. He drew the string closed. He handed the pouch to Lasker. "Here, you must take these personally to His Holiness. They must be used to save Tibet. He will know how. Lasker—it has been prophesized that the entire world, until the year 2424 of the Christian Era, will gradually sink into a new Dark Age, devoid of any spiritual knowledge, sunk into war, ignorance, and totalitarianism. Only Tibet will be able to keep the flame of knowledge and spirit alive until the time of rebirth. Tibet can be the light of the world, a storage battery ready to recharge the light of learning and wisdom. These wish-fulfilling gems in the right hands are the method of saving Tibet. In the wrong hands, they make—what do you call it?—nuclear weapons—seem like a child's toy."

"Great," Lasker said with disparagement, putting the pouch down on the rug. "The fate of the world hangs in the balance and a guy from Cincinnati that couldn't tie his own shoelaces until he was five years old has to save it.''

"No, merely deliver the gems. And you're not that kid anymore! You're not even an American anymore. You're the Mystic Rebel, one who will change things— or not. It is up to you.''

"Tibet seems full of problems for me. I've been buried alive, tortured—I didn't ask to be involved—"

The hermit snapped sternly at him. "It is your karma. You must do it—must deliver the gems—if just to compensate for your past actions against His Holiness. As Raspahloh—remember?''

Lasker couldn't stand up to the man's arguments. In an hour, he was at the cave entrance, with the hermit. The hermit said he would give Lasker safe swift transportation to India. And then he bade him to wait there in the entrance, in the moonlight.

After a while, Lasker saw a shape moving in the night. It came like the wind, thundering hooves pounding the gravel slope—a riderless jet-black horse, with a red saddle and silver stirrups, raced up to the entrance and stopped. The hermit gave him a carrot.

"This is Phu-lu, the Wind Horse. He will take you to India. You will have this map,'' the hermit handed Lasker a rolled deerskin scroll, with a trail marked out. "It is a map of the Shambala Road, used by the ancient ones. It is a trail that crosses few places of human habitation, appears unpassable to all who are without the map. You will be able to traverse it easily with Phu-lu as your steed.''

The Wind Horse now reared wildly. Its flared nostrils exhaled plumes of steamy breath from the climb.

"I can't ride him—he's too wild!''

"Nonsense." The hermit soothed the horse. He said, "Pet him."

Lasker touched the horse's neck tentatively. Its hide felt hot and sweaty from the exertion. It calmed down. For a magic horse, it sure felt and looked real enough.

"It *is* a real horse, son of the hopeless Western materialists. Now go. Take your tsampa and supplies, put them over your saddle, and be on your way. Here, take the gems. Try not to lose them."

"I won't lose them," Lasker said, mounting up, taking the reins.

"Don't eat any meat along the way, Lasker. And when you get to India, take the jewels directly to His Holiness, who resides in the exile city of Dhramsala."

"That's all? Wouldn't it just be easier," Lasker protested as the mighty steed reared like in one of those cowboy serials, "to just wish myself there?"

The hermit, as a way of reply, gave the horse's rear a vicious slap that sent him running off with Lasker holding on for dear life.

"Good journey, disciple," he shouted. "I will see you again. I will pray to the Peaceful Deity that you will not screw up. Heed my words just spoken."

Lasker had trouble controlling the eager black steed, but held on and actually managed a wave back when at the top of the ridge.

The hermit, his strange teacher, his master of occult knowledge, waved back and then went into the cave.

343

# Chapter 35

The Shambhala Road certainly was like no road Bart had ever traversed. It was more a path that a mountain goat might take. If he didn't have the map to guide him, there were, even in the first half hour of his ride, a dozen places where he would not have been able to continue following that path. When dawn came, Bart was gaining altitude for the first hour, and when his head started to ache, as it always did above eighteen thousand feet, he chewed some of the small sugar-impregnated buns the hermit had provided, without stopping. The horse seemed indefatigable, racing along for hours. Finally though, it slowed. Lasker, pitying himself more than the creature, pulled the reins for it to stop. Time to make camp. He could hardly believe he had ridden all day.

Surely out in this wilderness canyon of pine trees and rolling terrain, the Chinese wouldn't spot a small campfire. He took out the flint pack and tinder and in a few minutes had a snapping fire going. He held his frozen hands and feet close to its low flame. The Wind Horse grazed on some tender young grass.

Lasker boiled some tea—you couldn't really get it more than warm at this altitude before it boiled—but it got warm. He drank it down. He thought about his bizarre life since he had dropped into Tibet. He had done more than get hurt and sick and terrorized. He had learned about karma, and reincarnation. He now had a personal memory of another life—that of Raspahloh. That fellow was so strong a personality that he had almost overtaken and submerged Lasker's identity. Almost. What had the Tulku told him of the connection between karma and reincarnation? Yes—that we are born again, and again inheriting the accumulated karma of all the lives we have lived. Either we go farther along our karmic paths, because of positive deeds, or repeat situations in order to make amends for what we have done. We always carry with us into the next life all our friends and enemies—in different guise. They change places, an endless game of tag.

As Lasker stared into the red sparks flying up from the fire, he tried to imagine what would be in that next future life for him. The Tibetans say: To understand what your future life will be, examine the direction of your present life; to understand what you *were*, examine your present life. Lasker right now was what Raspahloh had made him: a warrior, caught up in a desperate battle. But now Raspahloh-Lasker was making amends, learning the dharma, trying to undo all that Raspahloh had done. And that was plenty of bad stuff.

Bart felt so *alone*.

He wondered, as he stared into the fire, what Dorjee looked like now. What she was doing. And would she be in his next life? Would they be lovers again, as they had in past lives, in this life? He had searched Raspahloh's memories and recalled a girl that Raspahloh had abused, used, and put to death, for Raspahloh knew not of love. That girl must have been Dorjee—Lasker was sure of it. She had been reborn to give him another chance. And now there was an enemy who had all the attributes that Raspahloh once had—Tse Ling. Cruelty, obsession, hatred. *Round and round it goes* . . . Lasker smiled, stirring the fire to let the sparks fly. Would the delivery of the wish-fulfilling gems to the Dalai Lama repay his karma for killing one of the Dalai Lama's previous incarnations, when Lasker was Raspahloh? Could he then get on with his life, shuck off the karma of this evil Raspahloh, this time around? Or was there more, much more to be done before he could be free of his dreaded obligations?

Lasker was disturbed by another thing: He loved Dorjee, yet when he had made love to Tse Ling—and it was that, making *love*—there had been a connectedness, an understanding of Tse Ling. She was more like Raspahloh than Dorjee. Dorjee was kind, clear-thinking, spiritual in her nature. Tse Ling was the opposite.

Lasker suspected he would meet Tse Ling, again and again, as he would meet Dorjee, in other times, in other lives.

He camped for the night, meditating under the stars until even his combat-hardened body couldn't stand the intense cold. Then he rolled himself in the blankets, used the saddle as a pillow, and with the snarl of snow lions prowling in the distance, fell asleep. He didn't wake until the dawn's light disturbed him, and the many birds sang out that it was a new day.

This day was like the previous. He followed the map. The signposts of the Shambhala road were mostly odd rock formations. What else lasted for centuries? When he wasn't sure of which way to ride, he let the horse determine the path. Always it was right, and around the bend he would see the next milestone.

By midday, he was on a flat plateau. The high mountains in the distance were at the Nepal border—

Mt. Everest, which he had seen in the distance for some time, was a bit larger. He was making good progress.

Once, surprisingly, his path crossed a narrow paved road—even the Shambhala Road was being encroached upon by the Chinese engineers. But he soon took a turn away from the modern intrusion, hitting rockier more difficult terrain. It was all up and down, with slipping shale and many bristly plants that tore at his feet, even in their high stirrups.

Then he nearly rode off a cliff, the horse rearing up at the last second. Had he consulted his map, he would have noted the canyon ahead. He'd have to be more careful. He was tired, even if the horse wasn't. He found the trail that wound down the side of the red sandstone and slate walls of the twisting gorge, toward a roaring river. Ahead looked like a dead end, but he knew it wasn't. Lasker rode up a gulley and between two ancient pillars of stone—"eternal trees" on the old map. He found a suitable place—near a brook leading into the rapids—and made camp before dark. He had tea and some tsampa. He wondered if he could ever get used to Tibetan food. He certainly could use more red meat.

As if in response to the thought of red meat, a herd of musk deer, startled by the snarl of some mountain creature, ran madly down one of the canyon escarpments. One deer lost its footing; the small creature fell some distance, screaming in fear. Lasker went on foot to the fallen musk deer, and watched the last of its life ebb out. He spoke kind words to soothe the creature so that it would enter the next world unafraid.

He remembered the hermit's warning: "Don't eat any meat on your journey to India." But surely he meant don't *kill* anything. This deer was dead—what harm was there in taking advantage of the situation?

Bart ate some of the venison straight away. It gave

him strength. Then he skinned it and cut the best meat up into chunks and wrapped them. He lay back against the saddle a little amazed at his luck so far. And with the knowledge that it might not be so easy from here on.

At dawn, Lasker opened the map again. He had already covered one third the distance to the border. The route got more difficult now, and there were bound to be more Chinese patrols the closer he got to the border. He took out the jewels and spilled them on his bedroll. He lifted one up to the sun. It looked like an ordinary ruby. But it wasn't.

Bart rebagged the gems and got on his way again, a sack of venison hanging on the side of Phu-lu, the Wind Horse. He thought briefly about the predators—snow lions and the larger creatures like bears, and the wild yaks. They would all be attracted to a horse, and even more by the smell of blood from his sack.

But Bart wanted *meat;* he wouldn't leave the gift of the deer behind.

There was the ruin of an ancient fortress marked on the map—a set of stone buildings. He came around the spur of the mountain and found the ruin almost hidden in the valley by giant creeper vines. The vines were filled with monkeys whose wild chatter startled the horse. He had all he could do to control the animal. By shouting and gesturing, Lasker drove off the creatures, but not before the monkeys pelted him with lots of rotten fruit.

He explored the ruins. The tumbled stones bore designs and carvings that were licentiously sexual: monkey-like men with long curved lingams penetrating monkey women in a variety of unlikely positions. The carvings were more the style of Hinduism than Buddhism. Were the drawings references to the Cultivators?

Bart found a spot clear of the vines and tied the horse and rested. Soon it would be night—the third night away from the hermit's cave. He was beginning to feel an awful loneliness. Bart missed the hermit in a way that almost obscured his longing to see Dorjee. Almost.

Bart petted the Wind Horse. He found that the horse had been chewing on some of the fruit that had fallen from the vines. The fruit wasn't familiar to him. They were no larger than grapes yet shaped like pears. Lasker tasted one that didn't look so purplish. And spat it out. It tasted a lot like soap. The horse nuzzled his pockets, looking for sugar buns, no doubt. What the hell, a little can't hurt, thought Bart, reaching into his pockets.

There was cool running water in the stream running through the ruins and Lasker filled his small teapot there. He saw the golden eyes of a thousand monkeys glowing in the underbrush. They watched him silently. Their steady stares were most disturbing. Bart wondered if they did *more* than throw fruit at any intruders in their ruined temple. Maybe they were descendants of the Cultivator's genetic cross-breeding. They looked *intelligent*.

That night he found out. The neigh of Wind Horse awakened him. The gibbous moon was enough light to show the tightly packed masses of monkeys that surrounded his little clearing. Bart sat up and shouted, "Get away." It had worked that afternoon, but the monkeys didn't seem alarmed at all now that it was night. Their eyes reflecting the moonlight were steady.

He sat still, watching them as they edged forward, on forepaws and feet. They were just about two and a half feet tall, and had gray fur. Their yellow eyes now looked like searchlights, wide and glowing. The Wind Horse whinnied and trembled as one monkey lifted a hand and started untying the sack of venison attached to the saddle.

With a start, Lasker realized that they ate meat as well as soap fruit. He hoped they'd be satisfied with venison. But there were so many of them, and so little meat in the sack.

The monkey quietly untying the sack now pulled it free of the horse and backed away with it.

"Sure, take it all, guy," Lasker muttered softly, in English. "Okay! No problem. Enjoy it!"

Still other monkeys advanced on him, inch by inch.

Lasker felt for the scabbard of the Sword of Manjushri, then wrapped his hand around the hilt.

In one sweeping leap, Bart extracted the sword and raised it above him.

"Watch it!" he shouted. "Come a step closer and you're all monkey meat."

A strange thing happened. One of the bigger monkeys pointed at the sword Bart held glistening in the moonlight and sent out a chattering exclamation that was picked up by several other monkeys. The leader monkey ran about among the others chattering and gesturing at the sword.

Lasker swore he heard the word *"Mannnnnnjuujuju-jujshriiii."*

The monkey invaders, for whatever reason, turned and disappeared en masse into the dark foliage. Lasker sheathed the sword and went to the horse and calmed it.

"How about we go some other place for the rest of the night?" He received a snort in reply, which he took to mean, "You bet." He saddled up and was off into the night.

Much farther downstream Bart chose to camp on a bank of gravel for the rest of the evening. He spent the time before sleep thinking of Dorjee, forcing out of his

350

mind images of golden eyes and sharp teeth closing in on him. While he slept, Bart dreamt of making love to Dorjee in the cliff temple. He awoke with a smile on his face. To his surprise the sack of deer meat was tied back on the horse. The monkeys had returned it!

Bart rode on for the third day, again without seeing a human soul. Suddenly he rounded a bend at a trot and came upon six Chinese soldiers. They were dusty from the trail, had their rifles slung over their shoulders. They duly noted his appearance, but didn't seem at all alarmed—or aggressive. As for Lasker, his breath came in short tight spasms and the prickles stood up on the nape of his neck. But he didn't react. The soldiers didn't seem alarmed to see him.

Of course, this part of the trail was frequented by pilgrims. According to the map, there were several holy sites in these hills. And Lasker looked very much the part of a pilgrim in his tattered garment. He nodded and they nodded back. As Bart trotted past, he heard one soldier say something to the others—and the others laughed. Probably a comment upon his appearance. The hermit had given him old hand-me-downs from others who had sought wisdom in the cave.

Lasker sighed a deep sigh of relief and headed on. He passed under a waterfall and through a beautiful serene valley filled with twisted ancient trees and dotted with chortens—most were broken open. The Chinese were always desecrating the chortens in search of Tibetan "treasure." They couldn't seem to get it through their heads that what was inside the hip-high chesspiece-like chortens was precious only to Buddhists—prayers on papers scrolls, pieces of saints' bones.

He was soon off the beaten path and was now on the most treacherous part of the journey: the twisting narrow trails on the edges of a high mountain range known as Kuradrami.

Phu-lu shied as they passed under a rock overhang. Bart should have paid heed to the Wind Horse but he wanted to get to the border, ignoring the horse's instinct for danger.

Suddenly there was a rasping cat growl. A shadow leaped from above. Long sharp claws ripped into Lasker's back and the horse's neck. The Wind Horse reared and kicked. The snow lion was thrown off, taking a bit of flesh of both him and the horse with it.

Blood flowed about Lasker's hands as he desperately held on to the horse's mane, having lost the reins. The snow lion leapt up at him again, getting a hold on both sides of the Wind Horse's neck, actually *sitting* in the saddle in front of Lasker, facing away from him.

Lasker smashed his bloody fists into the creature's spine. The horse, receiving bites to its neck, stumbled sideways and fell over, pinning Lasker's left leg. Worse, the Wind Horse, with the snow lion still attached to its neck, started to roll. In a wild attempt not to get crushed, Lasker managed to extricate his leg and roll to the side. He had started to pull his Manjushri sword from his scabbard when he realized he was not standing *on* anything. He was falling. He twisted about and saw the rapids below. Bart had tumbled off the narrow trail and was heading straight down into the gorge.

*This was it,* the end of his journey. No! Maybe the water was deep. He grabbed his knees, rolling his body into a ball, and plummeted through the swirling mists spewn out by the torrent and hit white water.

# Chapter 36

Fortunately Bart hit right next to, and not on, a submerged boulder. Still, the shock of hitting the water nearly knocked him out. He plunged deep, deep down into the churning white foam. He was being carried sideways at great velocity.

Bart snapped out of his ball position and swam—or tired to swim—toward the surface.

It was sheer luck that he managed to break out of the water. He caught a glimpse of the horse plummeting through the mist with the snow leopard clinging to its neck. Then Bart was under again, moving at about a hundred feet a second downstream. It was all he could do not to swallow water instead of air. Bart twisted and tumbled, and then was pushed under as if by a giant hand and raked over sharp pellets of stone along the bottom. A submerged tree trunk slammed against him. He was blacking out from not breathing, had to get up to air. Bart used the tumbling tree trunk like a reverse diving board, pushing off it with all the strength in his legs, surfacing just in time, for he had to take a breath.

But then he was under the icy waters again. In the instant he was up, Bart saw how truly fast he was moving. The banks were a blur of motion. There was no way to fight this current. The river was not deep, maybe ten feet—less in some places—but too fast and too wide—too *everything* to resist.

He tried to reach the surface again, failed, and finally, breathed water. He was drowning. *No!* With strength, Bart couldn't imagine he possessed, he struggled to reach the surface one last time. Bart broke into the air like a jumping purpoise, gasped out the water, sucked in a bit of air, and was under again.

This bobbing up and down went on for some time as he was swept downstream. He was numb from the cold, blacking out from exertion and lack of air. The pain in his side, he realized, was from broken ribs.

It was the wildest swim any human being could endure. Survival in any way, even injured gravely, was unlikely.

*Wham.* Around a curve and down he went, having hit another submerged boulder. This time head first. His neck felt shattered. But he was beyond caring. Lasker slammed over some smooth rocks and felt himself falling over a waterfall. So fiercely did Lasker spin over and over that heaven and earth seemed inextricably mixed. The foam overhead was like clouds, the roar like a freight train. He hit bottom below the falls. Stunned, he nevertheless tried to swim. Bart was a good swimmer and made the surface, but who could reach shore in such a torrent?

He thought *Om Mani Padme Hum*, the protective mantra. It was just a reflex, for Bart had heard it uttered so often in difficult times in Tibet. It was second nature to call out to the Compassionate One.

He was rounding a bend, and there were fewer obstructions in the water. The current was slowing. Bart stayed on the surface, but every breath he took was a nightmare of pain, threatening to cause him to black out. Then his hand found a floating branch, and he wrapped his arm about it. Clinging to that gnarled javelin he was swept onward toward he knew not where.

The roaring waters gradually slowed; the white foam became ripples. Lasker saw a stretch of sand along the widening river, and despite being utterly exhausted, he pushed off the branch. Kicking like an exhausted bullfrog, he made the sandy beach at the water's edge.

He had just enough strength to pull his head and chest out of the water, and then his cheek hit the sand and he blacked out.

*Voices.* He was on some sort of knobby bed. He tried to open his eyes but they wouldn't open. Bart felt a pressure on his chest. He was breathing, but only very shallowly. What was going on? Oh yes, the rapids. He had reached a beach. It felt like sticks, knobby sticks holding up his back. He tried to move his hands but couldn't. He wanted more air but couldn't take it in. He was paralyzed. Utterly.

He couldn't see, or move, but Lasker could smell—something pleasant. Burning of sweet wood. Yes, it was juniper branches burning. Was there a religious celebration going on? Something else—he could hear. Yes, there was definitely a *voice.* A hoarse voice, like that of an old man, intoning in the stilted singsong form of Tibetan. Now one voice came closer. The voice was old, and male. He was chanting something. What was he saying? Lasker strained to listen, since he seemed unable to do anything else:

Oh nobly born son, the time hath now come for thee to seek the path. Thy breathing hath ceased, thy Teacher hath set thee face to face with the Clear Light; thou art about to experience in reality, the truth of the teachings in the Bardo—the after-death state. In the Bardo, all things are like the void, cloudless, and the bare intellect is transparent and without dimension. At this moment, know yourself, and abide in that. Oh nobly born son, know that that which is called *death* is come to you. Therefore, ye must resolve that thy mind not be distracted at this crucial moment. By taking advantage of this death, and the Bardo to follow, obtain the most perfect Buddhahood. At this time the Dharmakaya, the Clear Light, is yet to come to you. Be prepared to accept it. Oh nobly born son, keeping thyself unseparated from this resolve, try to remember whatever sacred practices of meditation and devotion to clarity thou performed under your teacher's guidance in thy brief life, now gone. Oh nobly born son, *listen*. Thou art experiencing the journey to the Clear Light. Thy present mind manifestation, that which those who know not the dharma truth call thy *earthly being,* is but a shadow. In truth, that which the ignorant call reality is voidness. It is not formed of anything, it is devoid of color or taste, not any characteristic whatever, it is naturally voidness. Oh nobly born son, *recognize* that voidness of all things, and the voidness of thine own body and temporal essence. Look upon the emptiness as being the Buddha, the all accomplished One, the One who seeks no further, having obtained all. *This is thine own consciousness, thy true consciousness, unsullied by karmic accretions. Thine own consciousness, shining, void, perfect, radiant, and inseparable from the great one hath no birth, no death, no limitations . . .*

Lasker had heard these passages—somewhere. Yes. The voice was reciting the *Bardo Thodol,* the *Tibetan*

*Book of the Dead.* It was read only at funerals, as detailed instructions to the deceased about to begin, as all those who die begin, the forty-nine-day journey through the other side, to rebirth.

Lasker, try as he might, still couldn't open his eyes. He still had that heavy feeling in his chest. But then Bart remembered his astral projection into the Great Vulture circling above Smoke Mountain Camp. *Maybe* . . . His mind searched upward, and after some time his soaring spirit found a small bird. Bart's consciousness merged surprisingly easily, as if he had no weight of his own psyche to overcome, entered its mind, and looked down. There was a clearing by a river, a gathering of figures wearing white robes, the color of mourning.

He let the bird spiral down, closer to the smoke and the group of people gathered. Lasker saw in the center of the white-clad men a pile of neatly arranged sticks— a funeral bier. A fire—the sacred juniper brush which is burned to placate the naga spirits, crackled nearby. The juniper smoke wafted up and toward the east.

The little bird didn't like the smoke, and Bart let it fly onto a tree branch close to the assembled mourners.

Lasker through the bird's sharp eyes could see the body now: a body covered with flower garlands in the customary way of the Tantric tribes that inhabit the space between Tibet and India. And on the pile of stacked wood he could now clearly see that body being instructed for its journey across the Great Divide. He could see the body that was on the funeral pyre, about to be burned. It was—his *own* body.

It was *his* funeral. The brown old man was reading the *Bardo Thodol* to Lasker. And the juniper fires contained torches, torches being heated to ignite his funeral pyre, as soon as the instructions to the deceased were completed.

A jolt of panic! Bart's silver cord jerked his consciousness back from the bird into his human form. He tried to scream, to move, to move even a single muscle. Nothing.

Could he really be dead? Had he drowned, after all, in the river?

The instruction of the old, white-robed man went on:

Oh son of noble birth, thou art in the absolute realm now, about to sever the cord to the earthly plane of existence. Give up all thy attachments, whether they be to friends, relatives, possessions, ideas thou hath cherished. Surrender to thy fate. The Bardo journey is difficult and fearsome to all but the most purified. This is why thought of death brings fear to all of us, for we have all done this difficult passage many times, neither attaining the full measure of perfection, nor plunging into hell. But we have returned to the human plane. Know that on the human plane, if all else fails, thy will find a home, and the dharma. Turn to it like a friend if thou cannot attain to the perfection of the Great Symbol. Like the sun's rays, the Great Symbol dispels the karma thou hath accumulated, if thou wilt but surrender to it. Therefore, nobly born son, now surrender all . . .

Lasker wouldn't surrender. He wouldn't. He wasn't dead—he wouldn't be dead. Yet . . . he had no power to re-animate. *But someone else, some rage within Bart, had that power. Had more determination.* It was that power, that mind, that evil intellect that had driven him to harden his body in the training at the Bonpo monastery. *Raspahloh.* And now Raspahloh, his co-being, the strength of the entity lost in time until it received host in Lasker,

358

asserted itself. And Raspahloh's power to live began to build within him. But would it be in time?

The old man continued speaking:

Oh nobly born, we fear that thy power to obtain the Light is found insufficient, as it is with most beings, save saints and arhats. Then listen to further instruction now. For thou hast failed to cleave to the great Light at time of death, if thou still hearest my voice. Know now, if thou hearest me now, that the terrifying karmic illusions have not yet dawned on thy mind, which now separates from thy body vessel. When the visions come, when the frightful terrors of the Bardo comes, meditate on the Compassionate Lord, the Buddha, which thou hast known, if not followed, in this life. For, as thou hast breached the golden path in this life, thou wilt encounter three stages in the Bardo. After the primary Clear Light—the Father—hath called you, and thou hast refused, because of thy stained understanding and practice, then the Clear light of the second Bardo—the Son—will be obtained, if thou canst but accept. Do not miss that opportunity . . .

Lasker screamed a scream of lost souls, a scream from another world! He was *not* dead, *not* dead. But the old man heard not, and continued.

For he who fails to accomplish the absorption in the Clear Light, there is then the third Bardo stage, the final dreadful stage, wherin all karmic illusion, the worst that thy mind can apprehend, will come forth. At that time, awful sounds, terrifying images, hurtful rays, and tremendous confusion and pain will encroach upon you. Without body or direction, you will be swept along as if by a terrible wind, the wind of karma. And nothing will avail you then . . .

Now the voice paused, and Lasker, still struck blind, paralyzed, could hear the man softly say, "Bring the torches forth to begin the burning of the body."

*His body!*

# Chapter 37

Lasker felt himself *changing*, becoming Raspahloh. And as that process of change continued, he felt energy coming out of a tiny spot on his heart. It was just a drop of life, a mere spark. But that spark started spreading. Slowly at first but nevertheless, spreading. Raspahloh's energy, Raspahloh's drive to be alive, was beginning to re-animate Lasker's body. He could feel the heat now, smell the dry branches underneath his body catching with flame.

And the voice began anew:

Oh nobly born son, as we remove this earthly vessel, now useless, by means of sacred fire, remember the precious trinity, the Buddha, the Dharma path, and the Sangha brotherhood. Know that whatever terrors come to thy spirit, recognize those visions, and terrors, as thine *own* mind. Recognize thine own thought forms. When thy body and mind separate, thou canst not be as before. All the samsaric world will be dissolving, therefore the appearances thou now wilt confront are radiances of the deities. The whole of the void will seem bright blue, and then from the Central

Realm shall appear Vairocana, white in color, seated upon a lion throne, bearing an eight-spoked wheel in his hand. He is embraced by the Mother of Space, and represents the aggregates of matter resolved into primordial blue light. He is glorious, dazzling in intensity. Also will shine the duller white light of the devas. Because of the influence of bad karma, the Vairocana will terrify thee and thou wilt be drawn to the duller lights, but do not follow. The dull light leads to the wandering, the chasm of fear, the fearsome apparitions that are self-projected delusion, and lead to a bad rebirth. Instead thou must embrace the brilliant light, the grace of thy Lord, the all-encompassing One. *Merge, merge with the brilliant light, in a halo of radiant rainbow fire. Go thou into the brilliant light, and abide there, forever . . . forever, forever . . .*

The voice paused, and the mouth of the speaker uttered a gasp.

For the old man beheld that Lasker's eyes were now open.

"Are you all right?"

"Yes, I suppose," Lasker muttered. They had removed his body just in time from the engulfing flames, taken him into a hut. He was on a rug now, his torn and tattered pilgrim's clothes smelling of burnt wood. Yet he didn't feel any pain—no burns apparently. They had gotten to him in time, after all.

*Raspahloh.* He had saved Lasker, and then faded into the depths of his soul once more. Bart tried to push himself up off the rug, using his hands, but he found them numb, icy cold, impossible to use. They flopped around like fish. He fell back onto the rug.

The old man in white—formerly his funeral director, now his helper—tried to help Bart sit up, but hadn't the strength. Bart saw that there was one other person in the hut—a youth. Together with the old man, the youth's hands helped Bart sit up. His chest still hurt, but he now sucked in deep breaths. He coughed out clear water for some minutes, since his lungs were still partially filled with water.

When he was done, they wiped his face with a cloth. And the dusky color of Bart's face came off. The old man uttered astonishment at his features. "He is a—a Caucasian," he said, in an amazed tone.

Lasker nodded and said, "Just a boy from Cincinnati." They were startled by his speech, and uncomprehending. Lasker had lapsed into English. He repeated in Tibetan, "I mean, I'm just a boy from Lhasa. *With nine lives like a cat, it seems.*"

He tried to stand. But his body hurt at every move. He felt around his face, found gashes across his cheeks. There were also countless cuts and nicks on his legs and arms. When he twisted about, a searing pain indicated a long wound across his back. Of course—the claws of the snow lion.

His shirt was gone and his pants little more than a loin cloth of shredded material. Bart got to his feet shakily and hobbled about, supported between two brown shoulders.

The gems. The wish-fulfilling gems. What of them? Anxiously, fearing the worst, he reached to his waist, found that he still wore the rough rope that served as his pilgrim's belt, and attached to that was the pouch. Bart unknotted the drawstring, and as the villager and the boy watched, he bent and spilled out the gems on the rug.

"The stranger has treasure," the younger one said,

363

in a matter-of-fact voice, showing no surprise or amazement.

"Yes, he does, grandson," the old one replied.

Lasker said, "You didn't take them from me? Were you going to burn me with them? Would you have retrieved them from the fire?"

"No, such things as gems are of no use or interest to us here. Though they are pretty. If you want to give them to our children to play with, that would be all right, but otherwise—"

"I'm sorry," Lasker said, scooping them up and replacing them in his bag, "I have to bring them to His Holiness, the Dalai Lama. Where am I, what is this place?"

"This is Khembalung Valley."

That didn't sound familiar. He was probably way off course. "What river was that I came from?"

"We call it the Stormy Murderer."

"A very apt name." Lasker managed a smile, and they smiled too. "Thank you for not parboiling me."

"We thought you were dead. There are many bodies in the river, and the way you were dressed, and your great height, we thought you were a Tibetan Buddhist pilgrim that had fallen in. So we read you the *Bardo Thodol* before cremating your remains. Do you want some food?"

He nodded.

Ten minutes later the boy brought in a tray of buns. They were irregularly octagonal in shape, a bit burned. They tasted wonderful. And the tea—thick like all the tea he drank in Tibet, but of a slightly licorice flavor—was heavenly.

Bart was very tired, but he wanted to ask more questions. Sleep won out over curiosity. They gave him soft pillows to rest his head on and left him.

The village in Khembalung Valley consisted of about twelve small huts, some of the circular huts having two or three wings, if the villagers had families. They were small people, nearly as small as the monkeys that had surrounded him at the ruined temple. They evidently ate fish they caught in the river, and harvested some wild grains from which they made breads and buns, and planted small vegetable gardens.

Bart recuperated for several days in the town. He watched the womenfolk, smiling gentle sylphs who never covered their breasts but wore only loincloths like the brown men. They were the fishers—they cast their nets in the water for the neon-colored fish that was the staple. They were exquisite brown miniatures, perfectly shaped, slender, with builds similar to the Indian temple statues: narrow-waisted, wide-hipped and with ample breasts.

Tearing his eyes from the sylphs—that's what he called them, he watched the little men and the children, who helped them till the fields of barley. The valley was wide and warm and pleasant. The river must have carried him some distance from the Shambhala Road. Could he ever get back to it? No way. The map was gone. Instead of backtracking, Bart decided he would push off on foot directly for the mountains. It would take weeks now. He despaired of the loss of Phu-lu, and concluded he had brought all this trouble on himself by taking the meat despite the hermit's warning.

Over a campfire supper of cooked fish and bits of tsampa, he asked the old man, who was the village chief, what religion they were. For they had said they read him the *Bardo Thodol* because they thought him a Buddhist pilgrim. What were they?

"We are followers of the doctrine of No-doctrine,"

he said. "Sects are divisive, religions are divisive, to give a name to anything is divisive. We are not divisive."

The old man would not elaborate on the matter regardless of Lasker's repeated call for some clarification.

Bart explored the valley a bit, taking along the youth who had helped the old man. He was the elder's grandson. The boy, though sixteen, came up no higher than Lasker's waist. As all the villagers, the boy spoke a softly accented dialect of old Tibetan. Very slow and clear, almost lilting.

The little riverside settlement was surrounded by rolling hills. The elder had told Lasker that perhaps he could see Chomolongma—Mt. Everest—off to the southwest once he was up on the hill. So he and the boy went to see.

Lasker climbed carefully up the small rise, favoring his sore leg, and beheld, not fifty miles away, an awesome sight. They were much nearer to the great snow-capped peak than he could have imagined.

He would have no difficulty finding his way home, he told the boy.

"You live with the God Chomolongma?" the boy asked.

"No, beyond that god," Lasker replied. He watched the "god's" snowcapped head blossom with white mist and a rainbow. Or rather a snow bow. Now all he had to do was cross through the sunflower-filled fields he saw stretched out before him.

"Why?" the village headman asked Lasker as they ate another supper by the fire. "Why leave?" The village maidens performed a slow, enchanting dance at the edge of the firelight to the tune of flutes played by the children as he spoke. "Why go on to the end of

366

our country, to the outside world you mention? Why does the Dalai Lama need these gems if he is so great? Doesn't Dalai Lama mean Ocean of Wisdom? If he is so smart, let him find his own jewels. My grandson likes wandering with you. The people like you, pilgrim. Stay here." He leaned close. "As an inducement, I will tell you some secrets—then perhaps you will see the virtues of staying here."

"What secrets?"

"For one thing," the black-eyed miniature man said, smiling, "we don't have pain here, and we live a thousand years. All of us. Then we just dry up like a leaf and blow away. How do you like that?"

"Near immortality. That's wonderful—but not enough to make me stay."

"Okay, how's this: Our women are small but energetic. And I think they find you attractive. See how they prance about shaking their ripe hips whenever you look their way? We don't have any inhibitions here to enjoying ourselves—physically speaking."

"I would destroy them if I tried to make love to them."

"No you wouldn't. They are very—adaptable."

"No dice." But Lasker was weakening.

"Then at least stay with us for a few more days, until you can walk better."

Lasker admitted that he did have a limp. He spent the next few days and nights joyfully. In the mornings he watched the neon-colored fish in the clear water, being caught up in the nets. Noon, the big meal: eating the local vegetables and fish covered with a pleasant smoky sauce. Nights were *not* bitter cold, and he watched the meteors dart across the sky. He had never seen such bright ones. And there were a billion stars, all so close you felt you could raise your hand and grab them.

He was surprised in his hut too, by the women, two of them, who while he was still groggy with sleep, tried to convince him, by dint of their beauty and their determined attempts to arouse him, to have sex with them. It would be, he supposed, sort of like having sex with fairies. An interesting prospect. But he knew that if he did make love to them, he'd stay here in this paradise. So he controlled himself. Nothing would hold him from his mission.

The time came that Lasker insisted he must leave. The old man, the grandson, and all the village sadly bid him good-bye. The women, including the two fairy-like sprites who had tried to make love to him the night before, plied him with gifts. They gave him sweets and food supplies—dried vegetables and oily fish cakes, and many octagon buns, all easy to carry for his journey. The delightful children made garlands and hung them on his neck.

The village head was not to be outdone. "Man from the Water," he said, "I have something interesting for you." He held something shiny up in the sunlight. It was a V-shaped object—golden. The headman said, "This is a sky object. We see them fall from the flashing lights in the sky every so often around this valley. It is an untarnishable thing. I know not what it is, no one does. But I have a duplicate to this object. See?"

The elder reached inside his garment at the neck and pulled out the identical V-shaped thing. "Remember me. Remember us. This sign will forever keep us together. Wear it as a pendant—it has a hole in it, which one can put a string through."

Lasker took a string from the hand of one of the little love doves and attached the sky object around his neck.

Lasker took it from the gnarled hand, turned it over and over. "This must be very precious," he said. Bart had been told about these so called sky objects. They were found in rugged parts of Tibet. The enigmatic objects were certainly odd in design and function. Most informed Tibetans believed that they did not fall from the lights in the sky but were probably blown from the ruins of ancient monasteries on the mountains.

"Thank you," he said, deeply touched.

With a lump in his throat, he set off again, the children trailing him for a while. On the top of the hill, he waved to the villagers for the last time.

Would he ever meet such people again? People that knew no evil thoughts? People who only lived and loved and asked no more of life?

He turned away.

# Chapter 38

Supplied amply with the Khembalung Villagers' food, and a large canteen of their water, he made comfortable progress in brilliantly sunny, if chill weather. But he soon came to understand that Mt. Everest only *looked* close. It was barely larger on the horizon by nightfall. And he was still in the sunflower field. How could he have underestimated the distance so much?

Bart camped in a gulley, for the wind was picking up, and the sky clouding over. When he awoke at dawn, there was a frost on the field. By the afternoon of the second day out, he was descending. The Khembalung Valley had been a valley in a high plateau, above the weather, as was most of Tibet. Bart now descended a treacherous, broken slate–covered slope for at least five thousand feet. There was snow falling the minute he pierced the white clouds below. It was another world—clouded over, devoid of life, cold, bitterly cold. He had a shawl and some warm blankets, and wore them all as he trekked onward.

Everest was much closer—but now the snow was almost a foot deep, and his feet were freezing. Surely there would be a road at its base, some civilized outpost—even if it was Chinese. He wouldn't last this way. Not more than a half hour. Yet Bart wouldn't turn back. He couldn't. He'd make even less progress heading back. If only there was a settlement.

He staggered on . . . *there*. A dark hump in the snow about six or seven feet tall, in the midst of the whiteness. Could it be a hut? He staggered toward it. Were his eyes deceiving him? Was it some sort of snow mirage?

*No.* It was a dome-like hut—made of skins and furs and some white sticks—a nomad hut?

But where were the nomad's animals? No matter! Just get to the hut. Even if no one was home—it was shelter from the wind, perhaps there was even firewood inside. He had a flint.

It seemed like a half hour but it must have been just minutes before Bart trundled through the deep snow and the howling wind and leaned up against one of the big white sticks that were the hut's superstructure. The sticks were *bones*. Perhaps wild yak bones—for they were very big. The lower supports for the hut were piled yak pelvises, the upper, a curve of giant ribs. Bizarre—but who cared? Bart staggered about and found a flap of fur, lifted it, and fell in through the doorway.

And then he saw the inhabitants. It was a couple. He had caught them at an inopportune moment—they were *screwing* on the fur-covered floor.

The male, atop the female, still humping away, turned his head and snarled. At first, Lasker thought the two were wearing enormous fur coats. Then he rubbed his eyes and looked more carefully. No. It wasn't fur coats or blankets on the couple. It was their *hides!*

Migyus! Abominable Snowmen!

A roar of nonhuman anger arose from the male, and

he pulled away from his lover on long gangly arms, his penis of huge dimensions still erect. He was *mad*. Lasker was staring right in the creature's angry red eyes. The lips parted, revealing sharp teeth. He drooled and started to approach the human intruder.

Lasker, of course, turned and ran out of the hut. In a second, one of the huge rocks that were all about the hut came sailing over his head. Bart ducked just in time to avoid it, and the next one. So that's what the rocks were for. Throwing!

Bart had not found a nomad's dwelling, but had encountered those creatures of the Tibetan Steppes that the civilized world for the most part did not believe exist. He was thunderstruck to find out they really existed, but astonishment didn't slow his mad scramble. The edge of a giant flat rock creased his scalp. Bart stumbled, saw stars, but recovered, kept running as best he could in the deep snow.

There were snarls and bellowing—two sets of slamming footfalls. That told the story. The female was after him too. And they were both gaining. It was time to stand and fight. Bart grabbed the sword out of the scabbard, turned with the blade cutting an arc in the air. That brought the seven-foot tall pursuers to a halt. But only temporarily. Lasker swished the sword again. This time the male Migyu, now devoid of his erection, actually grabbed its razor-sharp edge in his hand and yanked the sword away from Bart.

Tough skin?

The Migyu looked at the hand clutching the sword and whimpered. Its mate took the sword from him and they both stared at the blood oozing from his fingers. It had cut him—not a deep wound, but perhaps nothing had ever penetrated his thick hide before. It must have stung, though, for he continued to whimper. Lasker backed off.

He got about thirty feet and then the two turned to him once more. The female, holding the sword by its handle—she was evidently the smart one—came at him screaming her lungs out. The very earth shook with the roar. The male was sitting on his haunches in the snow, whimpering. She was obviously going to avenge her lover—for she lifted the sword over her head and started swishing it about inexpertly, but powerfully.

Oh shit. Bart ran but soon he was at the end of his endurance, frozen, exhausted, hopeless. He couldn't outrun the creature that time forgot.

Then Bart heard thundering hoofbeats and looked up to see Phu-lu, his horse, galloping toward him. The second the horse drew alongside him, Lasker grabbed its mane and threw himself on. The horse took off in the opposite direction from Lasker's sword-wielding prehistoric pursuer.

"Good ol' Phu-lu," he said between frozen breaths, holding on for dear life. "I wonder how you got here."

The frozen rider rode on, finally coming against a cliffside. There was a hole—a cave?—halfway up the cliff—about a hundred feet up. A path, big enough for a careful horse, led to it. Lasker couldn't endure much longer. He had to have shelter, start a fire. He directed Phu-lu up the path.

Bart had a fire going in a half hour, the fuel initially the kindling and cotten in his flint pack, and then dried rat turds and bat guano—smelly but who the hell cared?

Huddled there in the cave he just shook and shivered. He stared at Phu-lu, who, he now knew, was indeed some sort of magic creature, not a horse at all. The horse had no scars from his encounter with the snow lion. The steed would have carried him safely and comfortably to India if only Lasker hadn't loaded the venison onto it, attracting the snow lion. All the misadventure of the past days could have been avoided if Bart had but followed the hermit's advice and not eaten meat! But the time for regrets and speculation was over. Totally exhausted, he collapsed into a sleep.

Bart awoke startled by the horse's presence—it was a bit like a dream to have a black horse nibbling at your face when you awaken. For an instant he didn't remember how he'd gotten into this cave. He was cold; the fire was out. But it was bright and sunny outside in the opening of the cave.

There was no food—he'd lost that all in the mad scramble from the Migyu. He would have to push on in daytime, while he could, while the weather held, and reach civilization before he starved to death.

The sun outside was most welcome. He mounted the horse and rode down the path. He rode at full gallop.

By midday, the horse was flecked with foam and Bart was exhausted as well. The horse pawed at some snow and found grass. Brown as it was, he chewed on it. Bart wanted to eat the snow, but knew it would only make him thirstier. There was an especially cold spot on his chest—he felt for it—the sky object. The metal *V* was adhering to his skin. Some lucky charm. He pried it off, leaving a red mark. He put it in the gem pouch.

He rode on in a cold wind, toward the looming mountain. Where the hell was a road, people, *food,* and *water?*

Then there was a dropoff—into a verdant valley— with a river in it. Bart rode joyously down the slope. It grew warm and misty, and he headed toward the stream, jumping from his mount and drinking of the water. After a time, Bart, having drunk his fill, rolled to the side and lay on the cool moss. He continued to ride in the moss-covered valley, following the small brook. It was very overcast, and he wasn't sure of the

374

direction, but he thought he was heading south, at a right angle to the sun. He entered a dark forest of giant gnarled-barked trees, and soon he could hardly see his way. But there was some sort of path. Perhaps a musk deer trail. Below the horse's hooves were moving creatures—large centipedes and other creepy crawly things. The air grew dank and fetid.

Surely this must be near India—such conditions didn't exist in Tibet.

Mosquitoes the size of butterflies bit him. Bart scratched at the wounds, and they swelled and itched like hell. He felt some leaves falling on his back. Only when he experienced the fiery bites did he realize that they were not leaves but *leeches* dropping from the tropical vines twisting through the canopy of tree limbs.

He pulled at whatever leeches he could reach as he rode, not wanting to stop. Surely there would be an end to this infested jungle.

Snakes slithered all about the trees that encroached on his path. But he had one thing going for him—the horse didn't seem afraid of them, seemed eager to continue. Maybe Phu-lu knew something he didn't.

He was sure he had a fever. The leeches and mosquitoes were doing something to his mind with their bites. Bart was dizzy, almost falling off Phu-lu by the time he left the forest and began ascending through a mist.

In a half hour more, he came out of the jungle overgrowth and was out on a lifeless barren plain.

A giant thunderbolt rent the sky and the horse reared on its hind legs, throwing its weakened feverish rider.

Lasker landed with a sickening thud and heard his horse gallop away.

Surely this was the end. He thought, If I really am carrying wish-fulfilling gems, could they spare a *tiny* bit of help for their possessor? Was that too much to ask?

He tried to concentrate on food and men helping him. And then lost consciousness.

A heavy downpour of warm rain was pummeling Lasker's face. More to prevent himself from drowning than anything else he sat up. He heard something—an engine.

Bart wiped the mud from his eyes and tried to focus to his right, where the noise came from. Yes. A *jeep* was coming down the muddy track. He crawled as best he could over to the side, managing to get behind a rock. Whoever they were, even if they were Chinese, he had to have food. He saw they wore khaki outfits, had rifles.

Soldiers! But he wouldn't be captured. Bart would jump the two men inching the jeep along the muddy roadway. He'd take their vehicle and—

Over the roar of the engine, he heard voices. The two jeep occupants speaking to each other in some barbaric tongue. Not Chinese—what?

Just as the jeep drew alongside him, Bart laughed. *English*. They were speaking English.

Bart cried out, *"Lha Gyal Lo!"*

The engine ceased its roar and merely clattered there in the downpour. The astonished face of an Indian soldier leaned out an inch from under his canvas roof covering into the rain. "Hold it, Adnan," he said, "there's someone there—maybe another one of those mountaineers that never showed up in base camp—"

The soldier threw on a waterproof poncho and came out to Lasker, who huddled miserably on his haunches in the rain. "I say, old chap, you are English, aren't you? One of the mountaineers? You look a spot distressed. Would you perhaps like a ride back to the base?"

"Is this India?" Lasker croaked out.

"Certainly. Now, would you perhaps like some assistance?"

Bart was taken to a Red Cross Hospital, which was filled with refugees from Tibet. An old English doctor there with a penchant for awakening him at midnight to take his temperature—anally—treated him with a variety of antibiotics and sutures. Three days later, Bart signed himself out, recovered from exposure and whatever the hell else was wrong.

He didn't want to explain that he had spent nearly a year in Tibet, nor speak of any of his other activities in the Land of Precious Snows. He was visited in the hospital by an Indian and a U.S. counsel official. Bart simply said that his plane had been blown off course by a storm and he had crashed, and was lost for a week in the wilderness. That worked well enough, as crashes of small planes were frequent occurrences in the mountainous area. He managed to secure new travel papers—and a preliminary application for a new U.S. passport.

Malcolm Donnely sat drinking twelve-year-old Pinch from a gold-encrusted scotch goblet in his air-conditioned office in the Excelsior Hotel. Outside the nighttime New Delhi streets were melting under one-hundred-degree-plus heat. But here he had all the comforts of home. Donnely put his feet, ensconced in two-hundred-dollar Italian shoes, up on the mahogany desk and leaned back, thinking about Bart Lasker. Had he really survived? Unlikely, but it *could* have been his voice over the phone. If it was Bart, he'd be looking for his money. People who wanted money were why Donnely never went anywhere without his body guards, why Lasker's name had been removed from the Excelsior's "approved for admission" list.

In a few weeks, Bart would give up looking for the dough. Lasker would go on a bender. He'd need dough, and settle for half what he was owed.

Nothing to worry about.

"Hello, Donnely," came a voice from behind the swivel chair.

Donnely's breath caught. He was riveted in place. Who the hell was in the office? He pressed the secret button under the desk that would summon his bouncer, and turned around. There he was, Bart Lasker, standing by the pried-open window. Or at least someone that looked rather like Lasker, wearing a jet black outfit.

"Yes, it's me, your old pal," Lasker said between his clenched teeth. "You know me. I'm the guy that called you from the border a week ago, and asked for his money. The guy you kept hanging up on. The guy that you sent into Tibet on a flight you called 'a piece of cake.' The guy that has spent a good deal of his time in the past year being sick or wounded or buried alive or tortured as a result of that 'piece of cake' flight. I'm the guy that you owe a lot of money—one hundred and twenty thousand pounds."

"*Bart*—" Donnely smiled, disarmingly. "I thought you were dead. I thought some guy was imitating your voice. That's why I hung up. I'm glad to see you. You know—"

"Fine. Then hand over the money."

The smile faded. Donnely got up, started pacing around. Lasker kept between him and the door. "Bart, it's not that easy. I had to—cover certain expenses since then. I will—need time to gather such a sum. How much was it? Fifty thousand rupees?"

378

*"A hundred and twenty thousand English pounds,"* Lasker corrected emphatically. "And I want it now."

"Impossible, my friend, why—"

Bart moved like a flash and had Donnely hanging in the air by his shirt collar. He stared up at Donnely in a crooked way and poised his other fist in the air menacingly. *"Now!"*

"Okay. Okay." Where the hell were his bouncers?

"I cut the wire, Donnely."

"What?"

"You can stop stalling, waiting for your bodyguards. I cut the buzzer wire."

Donnely said, "How the hell did you know what—"

"It's a long story. Get the damned money. Where's your safe?"

"Now look here—"

Lasker lowered him, grabbed his arm, spun Donnely around, and inched his twisted arm up to the small of his back. "Ow, your—stop, it will break."

"The safe. Now."

Donnely went to the bar, slid back a panel behind the counter laden with crystal decanters, and revealed the safe. He twisted the combination lock, covering the numbers with one hand. He turned the metal handle, opened the round steel door.

"You know," Donnely said as he took out the stacks of bills and laid them out on the desk, "you really shouldn't be so impatient."

"Make sure you get enough, you're short . . ."

Donnely added another rubber-banded inch of bills to the pile.

"What are you going to carry it in?"

"I brought a bag," Lasker said, pulling a crumpled plastic shopping bag from his pants pocket and starting to stuff the money in it.

Donnely sat down and watched him recount and put

the money in the bag. "Bart," he said finally, "you've changed."

"Yeah."

Later, in his hotel room—in the Palace Royale, not the Dil Praneth—Lasker composed a letter to the Dalai Lama. In it he related his experiences with the Tibetan rebels, told of his meetings with the Rimpoches. He went on to summarize the other event that occurred in Tibet, ending with the statement that he had brought a precious gift out of Tibet for His Holiness, and would prefer to deliver it in person.

Bart addressed it to Dharmsala, India, the home of the Tibet government-in-exile, and posted it Air Express. Then he waited three days. A reply, sealed with red wax, came. The seal bore the symbol of two deer on either side of a wheel. The reply was from the regent, and said the Dalai Lama would be happy to grant him an audience next Thursday, at 7 P.M.

Bart banked most of the cash leased a plane—the only other Vickers P3A in all of India, the owner claimed. He flew to Dharmsala on Thursday afternoon. The plane was a beauty. He decided to buy it, if he could. He'd call it Good Baby II. In the pocket of his dark blue suit jacket was the pouch of jewels. Bart had managed to secret it in a series of temporary hiding places ever since he had reached India—loose floorboards, windowsills, and even the hollow metal venetian blind bottom at the hotel.

With a fresh haircut, shaved, showered, well-dressed, and with a stick of Doublemint Gum in his jaws, Lasker left the tiny airport in the backseat of a big blue taxi. He was only ten miles from Dharmsala, but the road was constantly going uphill the whole way. He was happy to be above the thick humid air. New Delhi's near sea-level atmosphere made him feel as if he were walking in thick soup.

Lasker saw the first chorten at the side of the road, and soon came alongside bare-headed, saffron-robed monks walking alongside the pavement.

He told the driver, "Stop!" He opened the back door. "Tashi Delek—a lift?" he asked in Tibetan.

"No thanks," one of the younger monks said. "We are not in a hurry." Bart smiled, shut the door again. Not in a hurry. That was a lot different than the rest of India. He felt relieved to be back among Tibetans who were not in a hurry after the frenetic pace of the past few days.

He saw a signpost: YOU ARE ENTERING DHARMSALA. Bart touched the pouch in his pocket. It was there. And he was *here* at long last.

# Epilogue

Lasker stood waiting before the grand entrance hall to the Dalai Lama's throne room. He had been waiting three hours—because His Holiness was meditating.

The sixteen-year-old regent, Lungpo Rimpoche, a reincarnation of an aged nervous monk that had lived in Tibet, hobbled up to Lasker and said, "His Holiness will see you now."

Clutching the pouch of wish-fulfilling gems, Lasker walked forward. Two Tibetan militiamen pulled on the huge oaken doors. Lasker saw—it seemed like a mile down the red carpet—a man with round wire-rimmed glasses sitting in a high-backed Morris chair, surrounded by retainers. The man wore a yellow-peaked hat and beneath it a large smile.

Lasker gulped and stepped onto the carpet. The regent walked alongside him to the Dalai Lama. Lasker unconsciously took the youth's forearm because the young monk seemed to be having difficulty walking.

Lungpo smiled. "You have passed His Holiness' test—just now, by taking my arm."

Lungpo stopped limping. "Please, now just act natural—after prostrating at his feet three times first of course. His Holiness is a very Western monarch, and dispenses with all formalities.''

Lasker still felt his heart pounding when they reached the chair. He prostrated, forehead to the carpet three times, and then stood there. The Dalai Lama stared at him as if bemused. His eyes flickered. He was *reading* him, Lasker realized. Reading all his lifetimes!

''Ah, now I recognize you,'' the Dalai Lama said. ''You are—you *were*—in another life, *Raspahloh.*'' He shook his finger at Lasker. ''Naughty naughty. Killing people. Especially me.'' he giggled.

''Sorry,'' Lasker said, ''I didn't know any better.''

''Yes . . . I suppose you didn't—anyway, no matter. That was a long time ago.''

Still Bart felt like a worm.

Then the Dalai Lama said, ''You have already helped Tibet greatly, Bart Lasker. Your destruction of Smoke Mountain has stopped the shipment of dangerous nuclear products to an unstable nation. And because of your information, Tse Ling is deposed. Her province has now been placed under a more liberal— at least for the Chinese—regime. And your rather— outlandish—freeing of the prisoners is most welcome. Some have already made it into India. In return for relaying details of the plot that illegally shipped nuclear by-products from the prison camp, the Chinese have agreed to deport any of the freed prisoners that are recaptured. Some of these freed prisoners are already in Dharmsala, receiving treatment at the Tibetan Medical Centre, for their radiation burns. They are most anxious to thank you in person.''

''I'm very glad . . .'' Lasker said. ''Your Holiness,'' he added at the last second.

''Call me Tenzin—that is my given name. Some tea? Please be seated. Lungpo will bring a chair if you wish. Please discuss certain matters further with me.''

"You honor me."

They had tea, and then the Dalai Lama sat quietly, his hands folded in his lap, and inquired about the weather in the north. Lasker said it was cold.

There was a pregnant silence. Young Lungpo leaned over Lasker's shoulder and said, "Perhaps we should speak of the gems?"

Lasker nearly jumped out of his skin—he had been so awestruck by this audience that he had forgotten. He pulled the pouch from his left suit pocket and handed it—with both his hands—to Lungpo.

Lungpo took them from the soiled pouch, spilled the gems onto a satin pillow, and extended the pillow to His Holiness. The Dalai Lama picked one gem and held it up. He said, "Ah, yes. These!" He put it down. "These gems have been missing a long time. Now they are back." He raised an eyebrow. "It is quite some adventure that you have been through, I thank you for your efforts in delivering these to me."

"Your Holiness, it is little enough. I would do much more for you, and for Tibet, if I could."

"So? Really?" the Dalai Lama said, and Lasker realized with a sinking feeling that he had said something he might live to regret.

His Holiness pursed his lips, then smiled warmly and said to Lasker, "Perhaps you *could* help me, if you do so wish . . . There is a problem . . . a most dangerous problem. A man such as you might confront it—if you are willing. A mission for me, and for Khawachen, the Land of Precious Snows . . ."

Lasker groaned inaudibly and nodded.